STOLEN PORTRAIT
STOLEN SOUL

ALSO BY NELLIE H. STEELE

Secret of the Ankhs

STOLEN PORTRAIT
STOLEN SOUL

A SHADOW SLAYERS STORY

NELLIE H. STEELE

A Novel Idea Publishing

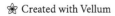 Created with Vellum

For my Family

ACKNOWLEDGMENTS

A HUGE thank you to everyone who helped get this book published! Special shout outs to: Stephanie Sovak, Paul Sovak, Michelle Cheplic, Mark D'Angelo and Lori D'Angelo.

Thanks to Kaddour Boukaabar who graciously agreed to review my French phrases and provide feedback and corrections. Thank you for making sure my French was correct and sounds like a native speaker!

Finally, a HUGE thank you to you, the reader!

CAST OF CHARACTERS

* * *

THE IMMORTALS

CELINE DEVEREAUX BUCKLEY – A two-and-a-half centuries old powerful supernatural entity who has the ability to open time portals and revive the dead. She lived as a human until she was sixteen when Duke Marcus Northcott saved her life with his blood. She then turned immortal by drawing blood from Marcus. She lived again as a human for almost twenty-five years when she was Josephine "Josie" Benson.

GRAYSON BUCKLEY – A centuries-old supernatural entity. Grayson Buckley is married to Celine Buckley, having met her after her transformation. Grayson has spent his immortal life aiding Celine in her battle with Duke Marcus Northcott, who hopes to possess her power for himself.

ALEXANDER BUCKLEY – A centuries-old supernatural entity and cousin to Grayson Buckley. Alexander Buckley transformed from human to supernatural creature in the 1700s along with Grayson. He, too, spends much of his life aiding Grayson and Celine in fighting Duke Marcus Northcott.

CELESTE VANWOODSEN – Older sister to Celine Devereaux Buckley. Celeste achieved a supernatural transformation before her sister, Celine. She hoped her sister would join her in the supernatural realm, joining forces with her good friend Duke Marcus Northcott.

THEODORE VANWOODSEN – Husband to Celeste Devereaux VanWoodsen. Theodore is a centuries-old supernatural entity who joined the ranks of Duke Marcus Northcott.

DUKE MARCUS NORTHCOTT – A centuries old powerful supernatural entity and leader of a dark coven. Marcus Northcott's full abilities are not known. He hoped to gain Celine Devereaux as an ally to his cause, saving her life with his own blood on her sixteenth birthday, however she refused to join his dark cause.

THE HUMANS

DAMIEN SHERWOOD – A computer-savvy history buff and near genius. He is Josie Benson's cousin, who followed her to Maine when she returned to her life as Celine Devereaux Buckley. He, along with friend, Michael Carlyle, traveled to 1786 to help a young Celine in her fight against Duke Marcus Northcott.

MICHAEL CARLYLE – A savvy international businessman and Josie's former boyfriend. He followed Josie to Maine with Damien Sherwood and the two traveled to 1786 to assist a sixteen-year-old Celine in stealing *The Book of the Dead* from Marcus Northcott.

DR. AMELIA "MILLIE" GRESHAM – A doctor and full-time resident at the Buckley estate. Dr. Millie Gresham monitors and assists with the physical and mental health of both the supernatural creatures and humans in the household.

CHARLOTTE BUCKLEY-STANTON – The current owner of the Buckley estate. Charlotte Buckley-Stanton is a descendent of Grayson's brother, Aiden Buckley.

AVERY HUGHES – Daughter of Charlotte Buckley-Stanton. Avery Hughes has two children, Max and Maddy.

CHAPTER 1

*C*eline sat on the swing under the gazebo, overlooking the cliffs and the ocean. It was her favorite spot on the property. She listened to the waves pounding the rocks below. Six weeks had passed since she, with the help of her family, banished her archnemesis, Duke Marcus Northcott, from walking the face of the earth any longer.

She smiled thinking of all of them, her family, both new and old, now together. Mere months ago she had been living a quiet life, sharing a home with her cousin, knowing nothing but a normal existence. She was called Josie Benson in that life. She had been raised by a normal family to live a normal life.

Then the nightmares started, growing more and more frequent until they became unbearable. After that, the visions began. She presumed she was losing her mind until Gray, her husband, found her, and guided her back to her true existence. After hitting her head, her memories as Celine re-integrated and she remembered who she was and how she had become Josie. Despite her reluctance to return to her supernatural self, to being a "witch" as most common people referred to it, she did so to save her sister after the Duke had her murdered.

Her entire family had come together to help her defeat Marcus Northcott, or as he was generally known throughout the centuries, the Duke. Josie's cousin and her ex-boyfriend, along with Gray, his cousin, Alexander, her recently resurrected sister, Celeste, and her sister's husband, Theodore, all played a part in making sure Marcus Northcott was banished from the earth after his centuries-long reign of terror.

Now, she was left to enjoy the fruits of centuries of labor. Her lips curled into a smile as she gazed out over the horizon, dark with threatening storm clouds. A cool breeze blew over the cliffs, rustling the leaves on the trees. Celine tugged her sweater tighter around her. Fall was on its way. She hoped that was all, that the crisp air only foretold of stormy weather, not stormy events.

Despite having banished the Duke, they had failed to find the painting of Wilhelmina Buckley. The painting, which had stood in the foyer of the Buckley home for centuries, went missing shortly before the terrible events of the past few months. The legend was that the house and its inhabitants were safe from harm as long as the painting graced its walls. With it missing, uneasiness hung in the air.

The common theory shared by the family was once they had vanquished the Duke they would find the painting. However, after six weeks of searching, they had not found it and therefore had not returned it to its rightful place in the house.

"Hey, don't you think you should come in? It's going to storm," a voice questioned from behind her.

"Hey, D," she said, turning to smile at her cousin, Damien Sherwood. Technically, he wasn't her cousin, he was Josie's, but then again, technically, she was Josie. "I was watching the clouds roll in, I'll be in soon."

He joined her on the swing. "Reflecting?"

"Yeah, reflecting," she answered.

"Want to share, Jos, eh, Celine? I'm sorry that really will take some getting used to. I've been calling you Josie for twenty-five years!"

She laughed. "It's okay, D," she said, patting his hand. "Just random thoughts. Our move is mostly under control, but there's still a great deal to do. By the way, thanks for handling the house listing. And I still haven't figured out what to tell Josie's... well, my mom."

Damien gave her a tight-lipped smile. "No problem, Celine. I've been trying to keep everything on the down-low from Aunt Monica. I don't envy you figuring out how to handle that. Is there any way I can help?"

Celine shook her head. "No, I'll figure it out. Thanks, though." She placed her hand on his, patting it.

"Is there something else?"

Celine didn't respond for a moment. "You're worried, aren't you? That something is going to happen?" Damien continued.

"Perhaps it's an old habit. But yeah, I'm worried."

"But that Duke guy is gone, right? I mean, that whole ceremony thing worked the way you wanted it to, right?"

"Yes, it did and yes, he's gone, but I can't shake this feeling."

"Perhaps it's that painting thing. We'll find it! I know we're close."

"It is strange that it hasn't turned up."

They sat for a few moments in silence, each contemplating their own thoughts on the matter. "Perhaps..." Damien began after a while, "perhaps you're just tired from everything. Worn out. Maybe you just need some rest. It's been a big change, learning the truth and then us moving up here. It's a lot to process."

"I'm a supernatural entity, D, I don't get tired," she chuckled.

"Well, you can still get overwhelmed, right?"

Celine stared out over the vast ocean, silent for a moment. "Yes, I can still get overwhelmed. Perhaps that's it," she said, smiling at him.

He returned her smile, rubbing her hand. She hadn't told him the entire truth, but she didn't want to get into it all with him. Even if he wasn't her blood, she still viewed him as family, and she wanted to protect him at all costs. If anyone was overwhelmed, it would be Damien. He had lived through an unbelievable set of events, learning that his cousin, Josie, was a two-and-a-half-centuries-old supernatural entity with a vast array of paranormal powers named Celine Devereaux Buckley. He traveled through time to meet Celine when she had been a normal human to retrieve a book that could banish her arch-nemesis, Duke Marcus Northcott, back to the depths from which he came. On top of that, he was in the midst of moving from New York to Maine, to stay close to Celine.

Gray's approach interrupted their conversation. "Hey, it's going to storm, don't you two suppose you should come in?"

Celine smiled at him. "Just enjoying the last few peaceful minutes," she answered.

Silence filled the air for a moment before Damien stood. "I'm going to head in, I don't want to be caught in the storm, I'm only human, after all," he joked with a wink.

"We'll be in soon," she said, realizing that Damien had been making an excuse to leave the couple alone to talk.

Gray sat on the swing next to Celine, taking her hand in his. She smiled up at him again before resting her head on his shoulder. He wrapped his arm around her, pulling her close.

"It must be nice for you to have Damien here after living for so long without any family," he conjectured.

"It is," she answered.

"But?" he asked.

"But what?" she evaded.

"You don't sound very enthused. But I don't imagine it's Damien that's the problem, or Michael for that matter." Gray was referring to Michael Carlyle, Josie's ex-boyfriend, who was also entangled in the mess with the Duke. He had been instrumental in helping them defeat him and also decided, after the incredible events he had experienced, to move to Bucksville. It wasn't surprising given the enormity of the experience that he shared with Celine and Damien. And, despite the tricky circumstances of their relationship, Celine was glad to have another strong ally close by.

Celine shook her head. "I'm happy they're here, but I worry about them. Wrapping their minds around all this new information must be difficult. I just want them to have an easy transition."

Gray snickered. "I know you better than that, Celine. Those worry lines on your forehead are not about Michael and Damien having an easy transition. Although, I'm sure your concern for them is adding to it."

"Are you saying I have wrinkles?"

"Stop avoiding, Celine. What's bothering you?"

"The continued attacks in town. There was another last night."

"Oh," he said, turning his gaze to the water and away from Celine, "you heard about that. I didn't realize you had."

Celine's eyes narrowed. "It's been in the town's newspaper. So, you knew, and you didn't tell me."

"I didn't want to upset you," he said.

"Upset me or not, it has to be dealt with."

"You've just gotten five minutes to breathe, Celine,

without being chased by that madman. I wanted you to enjoy it."

"I had twenty-five years to breathe, Gray." Gray was silent. Celine continued, "I won't break. I won't leave again."

"I didn't say you would," he said with a sigh.

"No, but you're keeping things from me because you are afraid I might, you don't want to overwhelm me. I appreciate that, Gray, but it will not happen again. This is on me, I did this. I couldn't face that it was my fault before, but now I can."

"Stop putting it all on yourself. You did the best you could. Now it's up to us, all of us, to work together to fix things. With the Duke gone, it should be a breeze."

The surf of the ocean thundered against the rocks below. The storm was approaching, its arrival announced by the crashing waves. "It's hard to believe he is finally gone."

"Well, believe it," Gray said, smiling at her. "Because he is. Now, let's get out of this weather before we're caught in the storm."

"Okay, but, in all actuality, I don't mind being caught in a storm with you," she grinned, winking at him.

"You're becoming as big a flirt as your sister," he said, pulling her off the swing.

Celine rolled her eyes. "That's taking things a bit far," she said, allowing herself to be pulled under his arm as they made their way back to the house. She took one last glance back toward the sea as black clouds pushed up the coast. No matter what the future held, it was good to be home.

* * *

The deluge of rain began soon after they walked through the front door of the house. "Made it just in time," Gray said. "Did you plan it that way?"

"Sorry, I don't control the weather. At least not all the time," Celine answered, laughing.

Gray gave her a kiss on the cheek. "I need to talk to Millie before dinner," he said, referring to Dr. Amelia Gresham, a family friend and permanent resident at the Buckley estate.

"Okay, I'll be in the sitting room," she replied, giving his hand a squeeze.

Celine crossed the foyer to the sitting room. She found Michael inside, nursing a scotch as he stared out one of the large windows overlooking the property.

"Back from the house search already?" Celine asked, pouring herself a drink.

"Yep," he responded with a sigh.

Celine raised her eyebrows. "That doesn't sound good."

"Gave me a lot to consider, I guess," he responded.

The evasiveness of the answer did not escape Celine. Something was troubling him, but she wasn't sure what it was. "You realize there's no rush, you're welcome here as long as you like," Celine said, sipping her brandy.

Michael studied his drink as though it held the answers to life. "Yeah, yeah, I know."

"So, if you haven't found anything you like yet, there's no real rush. Wait until something comes on the market and move then," Celine said.

Michael didn't respond. "Unless there's some reason you want to move right away?" she prodded.

"I imagine it might be best for me to live elsewhere."

"Are you regretting your decision to stay?"

"No, it's not that. I…" He paused. "After what we experienced, I can't imagine going back home and living a normal life."

"Then what is it? Something is obviously bothering you, Michael."

7

He shook his head, turning toward her. "It's just not as easy for me as it is for Damien."

"How do you mean?"

"We came back, he threw himself into his work. He doesn't have any emotions to process. His relationship with you hasn't changed. He's still your cousin, more or less, you still treat him like family. And that's great, but it's different between us. I wasn't over you before we came here, you realize that. But before we came here, you weren't married to someone else. I supposed we could still end up together, now we can't. It's a lot to process."

Celine understood what he meant. Her life had changed altogether, although the processing on her end was far easier given that she possessed all the information from both her own life and Josie's. Still, she often found it hard to reconcile all the information into one life. Josie had been her own person, a separate entity from Celine. She had a family, friends, a job, but she no longer existed. At least not the way she was.

"Michael…" Celine began.

"No, don't," he said, waving his hand to stop her. "I'm not… I'm fine. I get it, I'm not making a play for you and I'm not trying to be a crybaby. I just figured it might be easier to process things living away from you and Gray."

"I don't have a good answer for you, I'm sorry. I understand the adjustment will be hard, perhaps the hardest for you. Damien, I don't think, has entirely processed it yet. But he's got the ability to pretend things haven't changed much, because for him, they haven't."

"Yeah, I know, and it's fine. I told you, I'm not whining or trying to get you to feel sorry for me, I am just explaining."

Celine nodded. "Well, in the meantime, you're very welcome here. And I'll do my best to make the adjustment as easy as possible on you."

"Thanks, Celine. I appreciate that," he said, finally looking at her and giving her a slight smile. Celine returned his smile, hoping that whatever she said offered him some consolation. He opened his mouth to say something else, but before he could, Gray and Millie entered the room. Closing his mouth, he greeted them, then excused himself from the room.

"What's the matter with him?" Gray asked as he left.

"The housing market in Bucksville isn't great at the moment, I gather," Celine answered.

Michael pulled the zipper on his hoodie further up. The air was growing cool as the sun set. It painted the post-storm sky with deep reds, purples and oranges as it slipped below the horizon. Michael stood on the cliffs overlooking the ocean. His conversation with Celine did little to settle him. It was impossible at times for him to watch her with Gray. He had to constantly remind himself that she wasn't his Josie. She wasn't the woman he had fallen in love with, the woman whom he had not yet gotten over. He had considered leaving a dozen times, but he had been telling the truth earlier. After what they had been through, he couldn't return to his normal life. A life of studying marketing campaigns and reading expense reports could never be enough for him. Not now that he realized the true depths of the battle between good and evil. Not when he knew he could help. So he stayed. In time, the sting of losing Josie would lessen. Until then, he would make it work.

He was so caught up in his thoughts he didn't hear the leaves rustling as someone approached him. "And what is so interesting on that horizon?" Celeste said, crossing her arms against the chill of the evening air.

"Oh, I didn't even hear you," he said, startled. "Lost in thought, I guess."

"Let me guess," she said, staring out at the darkened sky. "A woman?"

Michael also turned back to search the night sky. "A lot of things." His evasive answer was calculated. He wasn't a fan of Celeste. She was party to the misery that Celine endured on her sixteenth birthday and for centuries afterward. Michael did not like Celeste, nor did he trust her.

"Oh, no," Celeste uttered, sliding her eyes sideways to glance at him. "That particular expression on a man's face only comes from one source: a woman." Michael did not answer. "In fact, I'd bet my life you're out here all alone staring into the night sky because of my sister, Celine."

Michael closed his eyes for a moment, trying to shut Celeste out. "What do you want, Celeste?" he asked, opening them again.

"Only to help," she said, coming nearer to him.

He sniggered. "I'm being serious," she said, batting her eyelashes at him.

"How could you possibly help?"

"I think I can. I understand how lonely you must feel thinking of Celine with Gray, recognizing the history they share."

"I thought you said you wanted to help, not remind me of all the painful facts that I already know."

"Perhaps we can find some solace with each other," she suggested.

"Ha!" Michael said, "You're a little old for me."

"Very funny," she answered, rolling her eyes. "I am being sincere."

"Seriously? You're coming on to me?" he asked. "Aren't you married to the devil's right-hand man?"

"I wasn't suggesting anything untoward, only perhaps

some companionship?" she said, tracing her finger down his sleeve.

He glanced toward her, her big blue eyes were fixed on him. They were so like Celine's eyes. He remembered when Celine's eyes had stared at him like this. There was something fixating about those eyes. He found himself unable to look away. She embraced him as he turned toward her, unable to stop himself.

"That's right, Michael," Celeste said, wrapping him in her arms, "let me hold you. I will make you forget all about Celine."

CHAPTER 2

"Is Michael still house hunting?" Damien asked. Celine, Gray, Millie and he spent the evening in the sitting room following dinner.

"No," Celine answered, "did you want a nightcap, D?" She poured a drink for Gray before turning toward Damien for his response.

"No, thanks," he answered, a perplexed expression on his face. "So, where was he during dinner?"

"Ah." Celine hedged, reflecting on her earlier conversation with Michael. "I'm not sure. I imagine he might be avoiding me a little."

"Why's that?" Millie asked, as she sat back on the couch.

"He's having some trouble adjusting. It was a lot to accept."

"Is there anything I can do to help?" Millie responded.

"Or me? I realize a lot happened, but I'm okay," Damien chimed in.

"The situation is a little different for you, D," Celine said, dancing around some of the social aspects of the issue.

"How?" Damien asked, understanding escaping him.

"She means you didn't have to accept that she's married and not as available as you assumed," Gray said, exposing the root of the problem without sugarcoating it.

"Ohhhh," Damien said, realization crossing his face. "Right, I guess that would be… awkward, yeah."

Celine gave him a half-smile. "Yes, so I imagine he's avoiding Gray and me as much as he can."

"Perhaps he should go back to where he came from," Gray said, making his position clear.

Celine rolled her eyes. "You're not helping. And he considered that. But after everything that happened, I don't imagine going back to a normal life is an option for him. He'll come around. He just needs some time."

Damien put his hand on Celine's as she sat next to him on the couch. "I'll talk to him," he said, giving her a slight smile. "He has plenty of friends here to help him get through it. So, what else can you tell me about this missing painting?" Damien asked.

"Ah, well," Celine began, "let's see. Benjamin Abbott painted it in 1791. He was not only a talented artist, but he was a recommendation from a friend. His paintings had the ability to capture a piece of their subject's soul."

"She means that literally," Gray chimed in. "That wasn't just a figure of speech. The Duke himself enchanted him a few years into his painting career. Ironic that his own creation would end up providing us with protection against him."

"Yes," Celine continued, "with a piece of my soul captured in the painting, a piece of me would always remain here. A constant guardian over the house and the family, regardless of what happened."

"So, I commissioned him to paint Celine, well, Wilhelmina. That was Celine's alias then," Gray explained, "and we hung the finished painting in the foyer."

"And the legend of the protectress painting was born," Damien concluded.

Celine smiled at him. "You got it!"

Damien was silent for a moment, processing the information. "Hey, on another note, how did you two meet?"

"Yes, I've often wondered that myself," Millie chimed in.

"A story for another time," Celine said. "Now I think it may be time to hit the hay."

Damien yawned. "Yeah, I agree."

Celine looped her arm through Gray's, also reaching out to grab Damien's hand as they made their way to the foyer. Millie trailed behind them, announcing that she planned to visit the library before retiring.

The group said their goodnights and were about to cross the foyer to the stairs when the front door opened. Michael, bundled in his hoodie, trudged through the door. The hood was pulled tight around his head.

"Hey, Michael! We missed you at dinner…" Damien said, his voice trailing off toward the end as Michael stalked past as if they were invisible.

"Good night!" Damien called after him as he climbed the stairs.

"He's being a little melodramatic, isn't he?" Gray asked.

Celine shrugged. "I guess he needs to work through some things. He'll come around when he's ready."

Gray and Celine left Damien at his room and continued to their suite. "You know," Celine said in the privacy of their room, "you could be a tad more supportive. They've been through a lot."

"What can I say? I don't like the guy," Gray admitted.

"He's been through a lot."

"We all have, you don't see me sulking about it."

"We are not human, Gray. We have a vast advantage in dealing with things."

Gray sighed, turning away from her. "I'm sorry, I can't bring myself to feel sorry for him."

Celine placed her hand on Gray's arm. "He's not a threat, Gray. I realize that might not sound like much but it's true."

Gray turned back to face her. "I believe you, Celine. And I trust you, but I lost you for nearly twenty-five years."

"And a year ago, I was with Michael. Yes, I understand why you don't like him. But that will not happen again."

"I won't let it," Gray promised.

"Neither will I," Celine answered, taking his hand in hers.

Gray smiled at her. "I'll try to be nicer to Michael. I understand that he's no threat. I'm not sure he understands that, but I do."

"You are the only man for me, Grayson Buckley."

"And you are the only woman for me, Celine Devereaux."

"Good morning, everyone!" Damien said, entering the dining room and heaping a serving of eggs, bacon, and toast on his plate.

"Good morning, D," Celine answered first, followed by the others in the room: Gray, Millie, Avery and Charlotte. Missing from the house's adult occupants was Michael. "You seem chipper today, did you sleep well?"

"I did, thanks! No Michael, huh?"

Celine shook her head while Charlotte answered, "Oh goodness, I hope he isn't ill. Perhaps someone should check on him?"

"Yes, he missed dinner last night," Avery added.

"I'll check on him after breakfast," Damien offered.

"If he is ill, please come get me," Millie chimed in.

"Yes, that might be a good idea if you checked on him, Millie," Charlotte agreed. "Perhaps even if he isn't ill yet, he's coming down with something. I dare say he caught it off the children."

"I'm sure he's fine, perhaps he's just sleeping in," Gray suggested.

"Either way, it won't hurt to check," Damien said. "I'll let you know, Millie, if I need your medical expertise."

Damien devoured the meal in record time, something he often did when he was nervous about something. Celine didn't miss this familiar mannerism, concluding he must be upset about Michael.

"Okay, I'm going to try to find out what's going on with Michael," he said, wiping his mouth before standing to leave.

"I'll walk you to the foyer," Celine said, also standing.

Once they were out of the room and alone, Damien asked, "Hey, do you think Gray's cousin, Alexander, would mind if I visited him and asked him a few questions?"

"No," Celine answered, "I don't imagine he'd mind. Why?"

"I had some questions about the painting and some other stuff."

"Other stuff?"

"Yeah, other stuff," he said, avoiding her question.

Celine raised an eyebrow at him. "You know you can't get away with side-stepping the question, D. Not with me."

Damien scrunched up his face. "Just stuff, like about that Duke guy and stuff. Nothing major, just some background."

"You know you can ask me anything."

"Yeah, I do. I didn't want to bother you with it. I'm sure you'd like to forget about him. I don't want to be the person plaguing you with questions about something you'd rather forget."

Celine smiled at him. He was a sweet person and a wonderful friend. She was proud to call him family. Damien was the silver lining that had stemmed from her decision to become Josie. They reached the foyer and Celine squeezed his arm, saying, "He won't mind, D. And thanks for checking on Michael. You're a good friend."

Damien returned her smile. "I hope I can help. I wish it was as easy for him as it was for me. I'm just happy that I still get to be your family, even if I'm not your family."

"You'll always be my family," Celine said, throwing her arms around him in a hug.

"Thanks, Jos...ah... Celine, sorry. I really need to get used to your real name. Oh, hey, before I go up, I know Michael's searching for a place. Do I need to? Are you sure it's okay that I stay here? I realize you live here because Gray is Charlotte's cousin, well, sort of, but it's her house. I'm grateful for Charlotte's hospitality, I don't want to wear out my welcome though."

"I'm sure Charlotte is thrilled to have you with us. And Max and Maddy love you! They'd miss you if you left," Celine said, calling attention to the obvious affection from Avery's children, Charlotte's grandchildren. "In fact, I think Avery would be quite upset if you left, she thinks you're having a positive effect on those kids."

Damien grinned. "I'm glad to know I'm having a positive effect on someone and I will not get kicked out. Well, I guess I'll head up and see what's up with him. Are you heading out?"

"Yes, I'm going for a walk. I'll be on my swing if you want to report back," she said, winking at him.

"Aye, aye, captain," he said, giving her a salute before heading up the stairs.

Celine watched him climb the stairs before heading out in the bright sunlight of the fall morning. The air was crisp and cool, smelling of salt from the ocean. Lost in her thoughts, Celine wandered the property. Celine tried to enjoy the scenery, noting the subtle changes already occurring in the leaves' colors. She listened to the rustle of the trees overhead. Despite the beauty that surrounded her, a nagging sensation still plagued Celine. She assuaged her fears by convincing herself that she needed time to adjust to her new situation. A situation that did not include the constant threat of Duke Marcus Northcott. Convincing herself this was the case, she made her way to the swing overlooking the ocean, her favorite spot. She settled on the swing, kicking the ground to begin the familiar and comforting swaying motion.

* * *

Damien knocked on Michael's door a second time. He had received no response on his first try. This time he pounded louder. He waited a moment, then pressed his ear to the door. No sounds came from inside. Was he still asleep, he wondered?

He tried a third time, also calling through the door, "Hey, Michael? You in there, buddy?" Again, he received no response. Perhaps he had left the house already this morning before anyone else was awake.

There was one way to find out. Michael's bedroom and his shared a bathroom. If the bathroom door was unlocked, he could slip into Michael's room and see if he was gone.

He made his way to his bedroom and through the connecting bathroom. Trying the door, he found it unlocked. He cracked it open a smidge, peering into the room. It was almost black, the drapes drawn across the window. He blinked a few times, trying to make out details in the blackness. He assumed Michael was still in the room, deciding he wouldn't have left his curtains drawn if he had left. He was also sure he could make out a lump lying in the bed.

Had Michael slept in like Gray suggested? If he had, it was unlike Michael. An early riser, Michael liked to be up and moving before the sun on most days. Was the stress of their new situation taking this much of a toll on him?

Damien stepped into the room. "Michael? Hey, Michael?" he whispered. He received no response. He tried again, this time louder. "Michael? You awake, buddy?"

A groan emanated from the bed. So, Michael was here. "Mike? Buddy? You okay?" Damien approached the bed.

"Huh? What?" Michael answered, turning over to face the direction of his voice.

"You okay? You missed breakfast and dinner last night. We were worried. Are you sick or something?"

"What? Sick? No." Annoyance filled his voice.

"Oh, ok. Well, I just wanted to be sure. I knocked a few times, but you didn't answer. So, I figured I'd try the door and check on you."

"Go away, Damien," Michael said, turning away from him.

"Oh, sure. Sleeping in, I take it? Did you want me to save you some breakfast or anything?"

"Nope," he mumbled.

"Okay. Well, I'll head out then. Oh, hey," he said, approaching a few steps closer, "I recognize you're kind of under a lot of stress with everything that happened. If you want to talk about anything, I'm cool with that. Sometimes I can't process it myself. It would be nice to have someone to talk to about it. I mean, the whole time-travel thing was enough, but then that on top of Josie not being Josie and…" he babbled.

Michael grunted, annoyed, leaping out of bed. He tossed on a hoodie and pulled on a pair of jeans.

"Oh," Damien said, surprised he was up, "yeah so anyway, it's getting to me too, so I bet it's getting to you. So, if you need to talk…"

"You really can't take a hint, can you?" Michael barked, pushing past him to retrieve his shoes.

"Sorry, bro," Damien said, holding his hands up as if surrendering. "I didn't mean to bother you. I just, look, we all are worried, that's all."

Michael scoffed. "Did Celine send you?"

"No, I sent me! I mean, Celine is worried, but no one understands how hard this is to comprehend better than me." Damien walked to the nightstand, flicking on the light.

"Whoa, turn it off," Michael said, holding a hand up to block the sudden burst of light.

"The light? Sorry," Damien said, without turning it off, "it was really dark."

Michael uncovered his eyes, finishing tying his shoe. He stood. "Look, sorry if I was short with you. And yeah, it's a lot to deal with, but I'm dealing."

"Oh, okay. That's good. That's great," Damien said, considering his next move. "But given the circumstances I'd like to talk about it. I'm putting up a good front, for Celine's sake, but I could use a friend."

"Perhaps you should talk to Millie," Michael said, putting his watch on, not making any eye contact.

Damien nodded. "Maybe. Although it would be nice to talk to someone who went through it, too."

"Maybe later."

"Okay, yeah, sure. Later is great."

"Great," Michael mumbled, turning to leave.

"Do you have a time later on? Before dinner or after or…" Damien began.

"Just later, Damien, not now," Michael cut him off.

"Yeah, sure, right."

Michael sighed, sagging his shoulders, his back turned toward Damien as he approached the door. "Look, why don't we grab dinner in town tonight. We can talk then."

"That's awesome, yeah. Meet you at the café in the hotel around 5:30?"

"Sure," Michael said, opening the door. "Oh, Damien?" he said, turning to face him for the first time.

"Yeah?"

"Next time, stay out of my room." He slammed the door before heading down the hall.

CHAPTER 3

*D*amien made his way down the path, walking toward Celine's favorite spot on the property. The coolness in the air surprised him. He wasn't used to fall coming so early. The price he paid for moving north, he speculated. He paid it willingly. He wanted to stay close to Celine. The prospect of being separated from her concerned him, particularly after what they had experienced.

Perhaps that explained why he had an easier time adjusting to his new surroundings and truths. Where he had been grateful, Michael, it seemed, had become filled with bitterness. It may not be enough for Michael to only stay connected to Celine. Perhaps he just needed time. At least that was what Damien hoped.

Damien turned the corner, spotting a familiar sight on the edge of the cliff. Celine sat on her swing, covered by the gazebo. The swing glided back and forth in a lazy motion. Even when she was Josie, she had enjoyed the swing on their front porch. Despite it being a small thing, he appreciated seeing familiar aspects of Josie still existing in Celine.

He trudged up the hill, wishing he had better news to give her.

"How did your conversation with Michael go?" Celine asked as he plopped onto the swing next to her.

"Eh, not great, but not terrible either," he answered. He recapped the conversation. "I don't know, he was just weird, but maybe he'll be better at dinner tonight. At least he agreed to that. Perhaps he just feels weird opening up to one of us. We are all strangers to him, at least you and I are family. Well, kind of family, you know what I mean."

"We're family, D," she answered, putting her hand on his shoulder. "And thank you for trying. You're a good friend."

"Well, I assume the conversation with Michael didn't go as planned?" Gray joined the conversation as he approached the pair of them.

"Not totally, but he agreed to dinner, so we made some progress!" Damien said.

"Well, I guess that's something," Gray answered.

"I think I'll head to Alexander's. I hope he's in a more talkative mood than Michael was."

"Okay, D. Thanks," Celine said, squeezing his hand as he stood. "Have fun!"

Damien grinned at her. "Thanks!"

Gray took his spot on the swing. "Why's he going to Alexander's?"

"He wants to ask him lots of questions he doesn't want to ask us," Celine said, staring off into the horizon.

"What?" Gray inquired, wrinkling his brow.

"It's his way of dealing with things. He wants answers to a myriad of questions, but he doesn't want to 'bother us' by asking."

"Uh, that's… well, I'm not sure what to say."

"Plus, I think he still sort of views you as the enemy."

"Me? What did I ever do to him?"

"Nothing, but you are the man who blew apart our lives. Well, Josie's life. I think he still views you with some suspicion."

Gray rolled his eyes. "I'm ready to retract my statements about having your family here."

Celine smirked. "You'll get used to it. Anyway," she said, putting her hand on his knee, "we need to talk."

Gray sighed. "There were no attacks last night. Everything is calm for the moment. There's nothing to talk about except how you want to spend your days relaxing." He leaned back, putting his arm around her.

"I wish that were true. It's not about the attacks. It's about us."

Gray leaned forward again. "There's nothing to talk about. Let's just be happy, Celine."

"Gray," she answered, "we need to talk about what happened. I was gone for twenty-five years. By my choice. We need to discuss that."

"No, we don't," he argued. "It's done and over with. You're back now. Let's leave it."

"Gray," she admonished, "we need to have this out. We can't avoid it."

"We can try."

Celine sighed. "I need to say some things."

"It wasn't your fault, Celine. It was his."

"As much as I'd like to blame Marcus Northcott for this, this rests entirely on my shoulders. I made this choice; I understood what I was doing. I left you for twenty-five years. It could have turned into a lifetime. I'm sorry, Gray. I need you to realize that."

"I do realize that, Celine. And as for your decision, I didn't like it, but I understand it. You needed a break from that maniac. He tortured you for centuries. So, you can try to take the blame on yourself, but it rests entirely on him, not you. Besides, this had to happen."

"He tortured all of us for centuries. And it had to happen? How do you figure that?"

"He tortured you the most. We were just collateral damage. Without you becoming Josie, you'd never have met Michael and Damien. We'd never have gotten hold of that book and never been able to get rid of that bastard."

Celine smiled at him. "I appreciate your understanding, Gray. And as long as you realize it will never happen again, we can consider the subject closed."

He smiled at her, wrapping her in his arms. "Consider it closed, Celine. Let's focus on being happy." He kissed the top of her head. "And let's discuss more important things."

"Such as?"

"Such as what the hell your cousin is asking Alexander."

Celine laughed. "Oh, I'm sure the list is long and varied."

* * *

Damien sauntered through the woods leading to Alexander's house. His musings turned from Michael's changed demeanor to the task ahead of him. He was aware of some details, but many others were unclear to him. He hoped to find answers from his inquiry with Gray's cousin. The questions he intended to ask weren't odd or offensive, but he still felt uncomfortable asking Celine. He didn't imagine asking Celine would have upset or angered her. But he didn't want to bother her. From what he ascertained, the Duke had tormented her for centuries. She had finally found peace. He didn't want to force her to relive a past she had desperately tried to leave behind.

Alexander's house appeared in front of him as he rounded the corner. His pace slowed as it came into view. In an instant, his project seemed less appealing. Perhaps his questions could wait. Perhaps he should make an appointment with him rather than show up out-of-the-blue on his doorstep. It was almost lunch time; it was rude to turn up unannounced. His mind created a dozen reasons to retreat.

He turned around, intending to return to the main house. He wavered for a moment, vacillating about his decision. At last, he opted to follow through with his plans. He would regret it if he didn't. If Alexander couldn't or wouldn't answer his questions, he was free to decline or reschedule.

He marched forward down the path with a determined step. He approached the door, and, setting his jaw, he reached for the lion doorknocker. Before he could grasp the ring, the door popped open.

"Damien!" Alexander greeted him.

"Whoa, whew," he said, letting air escape his mouth, "you startled me."

"Forgive me, it wasn't my intention. I saw you coming down the path. Please, come in!"

"Oh, right, sorry, still letting my heart slow down." He bent over at the waist, his hands on his knees as he recovered before following Alexander into the house.

"Did you forget something?"

"Huh?"

"Did you forget something? I saw you turn back before heading to the house."

"Oh, no, ah, nope. I…" He stammered. "Ah, I thought I heard something in the woods. Was just the wind." He chuckled nervously.

"Ah I see," Alexander said, motioning toward the living room, "I was just about to have lunch, won't you join me?"

"Oh, gee, thanks. I'm famished. Although, I didn't mean to interrupt."

"Nonsense, Damien! You're family! Please, come in! It'll be nice to have some conversation over my meal."

Damien smiled at him, following him into the living room where he had lunch already set out. He plopped on the couch, helping himself to a sandwich while Alexander poured him a glass of iced tea. "Mmm, this is good!"

"I'm glad you are enjoying it," Alexander said, pouring his own glass of tea and taking a seat opposite of Damien in an armchair.

"So, speaking of conversation, I was hoping you wouldn't mind having a candid conversation with me about a few things."

"Yes, I've been expecting you."

"You have?"

"Of course. I'm psychic, you know. That's how I knew you had arrived."

"Oh! Are you?" Damien fidgeted in his seat.

"Yes. Right now," Alexander said, narrowing his eyes, "you're wondering if I can read your mind at this very moment."

Damien gave a nervous chuckle.

"And now," Alexander continued, "you're wondering how often I've read your mind."

"Uh," Damien began, swallowing hard. A loud laugh from Alexander cut him off.

"Oh, I'm just fooling you, Damien. I'm sorry to take advantage. I'm not psychic."

"You're not?"

"No, not even a little."

"Then how…" Damien began.

Alexander cut him off as he struggled to get his question out. "Celine told me you'd be stopping by. She also told me I was free to answer all your questions, so fire away when you're ready."

"Oh." He chuckled. "Okay, thanks!" He took another bite of his sandwich and then a gulp of tea.

"Since you're still preparing, might I ask you a question first?"

"Sure!" Damien volunteered.

"Why not ask these questions to Celine?"

"Oh, well," he said, setting his glass down. "This is the first time in, well… centuries she's experienced any peace. I didn't want to be the guy asking her to drudge up her horrific past just to get some answers."

"How kind of you, Damien. You are a loyal friend to Celine. And if needs repeating, I'm happy to help in any way I can."

"Thanks. Well, she's more than just a friend to me, she's family. I mean, even though she's not actually my family, she's like my family. You know what I mean. Anyway, you and Celine, you've been friends for a long time, too, right?"

"Yes, she is one of my oldest and dearest friends."

"Did you know her before she…" He danced around the question. "Before she was, you know, what she is now."

"No. We met after that fateful night."

"How did you meet?"

"Grayson and I were already well into the fight against people like Marcus Northcott. We heard about the girl who had defied him. Word gets around fast in our circles. We set out to find her. What better ally to have than someone with such powerful convictions, not to mention her talent?"

"Speaking of 'the Duke,' how did he become what he was?"

"That, my dear Damien, is the stuff of legends. Some say he drank a special concoction in Africa, others say he walked through Hell and bargained with the Devil himself, still others say it was a trick of his genetics. I'm afraid no one knows the true story."

"Hmm," Damien answered, considering the information, "so...." He stammered before finding the words for his next question. "Alexander... would you mind if I asked how you and Gray became... the way you are?"

"Not at all. It's not much of a story, I'm afraid. It's rather a case of foolishness with the wrong sort. Before we realized it, we were in this position. Rather a stroke of luck for the good guys, I'd like to think, anyway," he said, smiling.

"Oh, right. I'm still getting used to the whole... thing. Sometimes it still doesn't seem real."

"Yes, I'm sure both you and Michael are still adjusting to the new situation."

"So, what can you tell me about the painting that's gone missing?"

"Ah, yes, the painting. Celine mentioned that you have undertaken finding it as your personal mission."

"Yes, well, I'm trying to help. I think it's playing on Celine's mind."

"Well," Alexander said, shrugging, "Gray commissioned that painting of Celine in the late 1700s. Benjamin Abbott painted it. I assume Celine has already told you about his unique ability to capture his subjects?"

Damien nodded as he ate his sandwich. Alexander continued, "Well, the painting is a guard, a watch dog, for the house and the family. Celine, who was calling herself Mina at the time to protect her identity, for all the good it did, felt it was in the best interest of the family."

"For all the good it did?" Damien questioned.

"Yes, no matter what name she used, where she tried to hide, that dreadful man found her."

"He really tortured her, didn't he?"

"Yes, she never experienced a moment's peace."

Damien frowned at the thought. "Speaking of Celine,

how did she become Josie? I mean, if she's like you and Gray and the Duke, how did I grow up with her?"

"Twenty-five years ago, Celine was at her breaking point. She made a bargain. She desired a life away from the Duke, a normal existence. Our adjudicator granted her twenty-five years to relive her life. If in that time she remained normal, she could have a normal life, die a normal death. If not, well, you know the ending."

"Yes, I do. If not, she returned to her life as Celine. Well, at least she had somewhat of a normal life."

"And she picked up some fantastic family. She is very grateful for you, Damien."

Damien beamed with pride. "That's why I want to solve this painting mystery. To give her some peace, so she can enjoy her life now! So, anything else relevant? You were here when it was painted, I guess? Anything else you remember from back then?"

"Nothing much," Alexander said, raising his eyebrows. "I was here, on and off, I was also traveling. There was nothing significant that I deem has any relevance to the painting going missing. The Duke had made an appearance, Celine and Gray left not long after and the painting remained, guarding the house."

"Okay. So, tell me the details surrounding Celine's missing painting."

"Well, I suppose in hindsight, there were some red flags, but we didn't see them. It was too late when we picked up on the signals. Events were already unfolding, the Duke was back and the painting went missing. I don't think anyone would question the fact that Marcus Northcott is to blame for its disappearance. However, we still could not track it down even realizing who did it."

"Do you think he destroyed it?"

"No, I would very much doubt that."

Damien raised his eyebrows. "Really? I'm not sure I understand that logic. Wouldn't he want it destroyed?"

"He's far too arrogant to destroy it. He's also far too possessive. To him, since it held a piece of Celine's soul, he, too, held a piece of Celine's soul. He'd want to keep it."

"I understand, so he'd have kept it to keep a piece of her. And he'd have wanted to keep it close if your logic is correct. I assume you checked wherever he was staying when he was here?"

"Oh, yes, despite it being dangerous, we had a good look around, both Gray and I."

"Hmm," Damien pondered, "Not much to go on, is it? Well, thanks for letting me pick your brain. I won't keep you any further."

"It's no trouble at all. I hope it will help. It would be nice to have the painting back, it has hung there for so many years, it's as though it's part of the house itself!"

"I'm determined to find it!" Damien said, standing. "It was nice to have lunch with you and thanks for the information. If I have more questions…"

"Stop by any time and ask," Alexander finished for him.

Damien smiled at him, sticking his hand out to shake Alexander's. "I can let myself out. Thanks again." Damien shook his hand and exited the house.

He made his way along the path toward the main house. The air seemed to be chillier than it was earlier. He shrugged his hoodie tighter around him. He considered making his way past the swing to see if Celine was still there. The nip in the air coupled with the later than expected hour changed his mind. He wanted to make some notes and check a few things before he met Michael in town for dinner.

CHAPTER 4

$\mathcal{D}$amien made his way to town, finding a parking space near the inn where he was meeting Michael. It was a straightforward task, since town was never crowded. It was also an acute change from his former residence where the closest city would be packed, and parking spaces would be limited.

Damien walked toward the inn, pulling his hood over his head. He was glad he didn't have far to walk. The weather in his new home was also far chillier than his old one. He hadn't yet adjusted to the new climate.

Stepping into the inn, he glanced into the café. Michael was already there, a surprise. Damien wasn't late, but he had assumed Michael may try to avoid the conversation by begging out at the last minute. Unzipping his hoodie, Damien made his way to the table, greeting Michael when he arrived. He hung his hoodie on the chair before taking a seat.

"Back where we first started," Damien said after sitting down.

Michael gave a weak laugh. "Yep."

"I still remember that first night here. Wow, so much has happened since then, huh?"

Michael smirked. "That's putting it mildly."

Damien laughed. "It really is. Anyway, it's nice to be back here. I've been dying for those fries I had the first night." The waitress arrived and took their order. Damien ordered the same thing he had on his first trip to the café.

After the waitress relieved them of their menus and left them alone, Damien said, "So, nice to get out of the house, huh?"

"Yeah," Michael said, noncommittal.

Damien persisted in trying to get him to talk. "I mean, I want to stay there even if the house is creepy, but it can be overwhelming sometimes. On that note, how's your house hunt going?"

"I've kind of put that on hold," Michael answered.

"Oh, really? That's great!"

"Great?"

"Yeah. I'll admit, I will be the first one who isn't looking forward to seeing you go once you find a place."

"Why?"

"Like I said, we've been through a lot. That house, those people, it's just all overwhelming. Isn't that the reason you're rushing to move out? Well one of them, I'd guess the other part is the situation with Celine?" Damien pushed for answers on what was bothering Michael.

"Yeah, it's a lot to process, but I'm okay. It's hard seeing her with Gray, but we weren't meant to be, I guess."

Michael was being very laid back about the entire situation from Damien's perspective. It was a perplexing turn of events given this morning's conversation. Damien struggled to come up with an answer, to dig deeper. "That's a good way of viewing the situation, I guess. I mean, yes, she's married, but she still cares about you as a close friend. I know it's not the same and not the outcome you wanted, but she cares."

Michael gave a weak smile. "Yeah, I realize that."

"Is that why you postponed your search?"

"Eh, part of the reason. There is nothing I liked on the market either. I'm not going to buy a place I'm not happy with. Besides the situation with Celine, things aren't that bad at the house. I'll make it work."

"That's a good attitude. Plus, I'm happy that you decided to stay for now. It's nice to have someone normal at the house."

"Not all of them are like Celine."

"Yeah, but they've all been dealing with this way longer than we have. It's like second nature to them. They don't bat an eyelash. The whole idea still freaks me out a little when I consider it. It's nice to have someone else around who's new to the circumstances."

Michael flashed a smile at him. "Nice to know my newbie status makes me valuable to you."

Damien laughed. For the first time in days he thought he saw a genuine emotion from Michael. "You know," Michael suggested, "you could always move with me."

"Bachelor pad?"

"Of sorts, yeah."

Damien pondered the idea a moment. "As weird as it is…" he began.

"You don't want to leave Celine."

"Right."

"I can understand that. Like I said, in retrospect, I'm not ready to leave yet either."

The news gladdened Damien, although it surprised him. Michael's mood seemed to have changed a great deal from this morning, as did his decision. Still, Damien counted this in the win column. The waitress delivered their food, and he spent the rest of the meal trying to make some light conversation.

Several times through the meal, Michael glanced at his watch. "Got another place to be?" Damien asked.

"No," Michael said, shaking his head, "just trying to see when the sun sets here. Seems a lot earlier than at home, doesn't it?"

"Yeah, yeah, I bet it's already dark out by now," Damien said. The answer seemed to upset Michael for a reason unknown to Damien. Damien let it slide, determined to continue enjoying their meal.

As they finished, Damien offered to drive Michael back to the house.

"I've got my car," Michael answered, "and a few stops to make. I'll see you back at the house later."

"Okay, sounds good!" Damien said, standing and pulling on his hoodie. "See you back at the house then!" The two exited the café and went their separate ways. Damien returned straight to the house, intent on sharing the good news with Celine that Michael seemed to be back to his old self.

* * *

Michael unlocked his car door, waving as Damien passed him on his way back to the house. As soon as the lights from the car were out of sight, Michael slammed his car door, re-locking it. He had a very important errand to run, but he didn't need his car. He retraced his steps past the café, turning down the street where the town's bar was located. Bypassing the bar, he turned the corner into the alleyway behind it. He spotted a figure at the opposite end of the alley. Her back toward him, but he recognized her.

He approached her. "Fancy meeting you here," he joked.

The woman turned to face him. "There you are, I was beginning to think you weren't coming."

"I wouldn't miss it. Damien roped me into dinner. I barely got away," Michael complained, rolling his eyes.

In response, she held her arms out to him. Michael moved toward her, embracing her. He held her close, relaxing in her arms. He sighed, saying, "I have missed you all day, Celeste."

"And I have missed you, darling."

Celine and Damien stood outside his room. "Like I said," Damien said with a shrug of his shoulders, "he seemed completely different, like his old self. I mean, obviously he's still dealing with processing everything, but he seemed a lot better than he did earlier."

"Hmm, perhaps the extra sleep did him well," Celine said, although she did not accept the idea. "He didn't come back with you?"

"No, he said he had errands to run." Celine pursed her lips. "You don't believe me, huh?"

"No, I believe you, I just don't understand it. Michael was never moody. He hated not getting his way, but the flip-flopping and mood swings aren't like him."

"Maybe he was just having a rough morning?" Damien offered.

"Perhaps," Celine conceded.

Damien put his hand on Celine's shoulder. "I'll still keep my eye on him, don't worry. But perhaps he turned the corner!"

Celine nodded to him as Michael appeared at the end of the hallway. "There he is!" Damien shouted.

Michael made his way toward them without a word. He

walked straight to his room, steps away from them without speaking. "Everything okay, buddy?" Damien asked him.

"Just great," Michael responded. "See you tomorrow." He disappeared into his room, closing and locking the door behind him.

Celine glanced up to Damien. "Looks like his mood just swung back around that corner, D."

Damien stared into her eyes, seriousness setting in. "I think it's you," Damien joked, bursting into laughter.

Celine shook her head at him. "Very funny, D."

He grinned at her. "I'm going to turn in. Don't worry, I'll keep my eye on him."

She smiled at him, giving him a kiss on the cheek and a tight hug. "Thanks, D. Good night, sleep well." Celine left him to head to her own bedroom, hoping she could sleep. Something weighed on her mind, but she couldn't identify what it was. Something was off, and that worried her.

CHAPTER 5

*D*amien awoke early the next morning, opting to make himself toast before breakfast was set out. He grabbed the first cup of coffee from the pot the housekeeper set out. Laptop and snacks in hand, he planned to spend his day in the library. He was intent on tracking down the painting. Worry clouded Celine's face. He understood her concern about Michael; he had tried to solve that problem once. His efforts were rewarded with the briefest of turn arounds only to be met with a setback last night. But there was something else, something more. Michael's reaction to the new circumstances of their lives was not the only cause of those worry lines. Something else was weighing on her. Damien's guess was that it concerned the missing painting. She must be worried about the family's safety. Despite the Duke's defeat, she wouldn't feel settled until they found the painting and life had returned to normal. At least normal for Celine.

While he continued to monitor the situation with Michael, he needed to make some progress on this mystery. He needed to help Celine; he wanted to solve at least one problem for her. He was determined to find something. Arriving at the library, Damien cleared a space on the desk. He set up the two laptops he carried with him. He opened a word document, an excel spreadsheet, internet browser with several tabs for various searches, and, as always when he worked, his music player.

Music filled the room from one of the laptop's speakers as he clicked to play his favorite song. Damien strode to the cabinet against the back wall. The first weekend he and Michael stayed here Charlotte directed them to this cabinet when searching for photo albums. That had been before they had discovered that his cousin was not his cousin.

It was also when they had first glimpsed the painting, an identical representation of Celine when she had first come from Martinique. Damien pulled all the photo albums from the cabinet, spreading them out all over the floor. He grabbed personal books with family histories from the shelves, hunted down books on art from the collection, history books, anything that he deemed could help him.

He poured over each one, searching for any evidence of the painting. Damien made notes, flagged items, entered dates in his spreadsheet and typed observations in the document file. He used his web browser to follow up on a few items, searching for additional clues.

Exhausted, Damien dove into a bag of cheese puffs, examining the mess that lay around him. He didn't have a theory… yet. He checked the time. It was almost 6 p.m. He had worked on the project for close to twelve hours. He was no closer to a solution by his estimation.

Disappointment filled him. He would give up for the day. Dinner was in an hour, perhaps he needed real food. And a break. He'd resume his search tomorrow. Damien left all the materials spread where they were. He'd tell Mrs. Paxton, the housekeeper, not to disturb his things. A fresh start in the morning would be just what he needed to solve this.

He freshened up before dinner, then did his best to enjoy the evening with his new adopted family. His mind was distracted, and he excused himself soon after dinner. Questions swirled in his brain and he realized sleep would be impossible even if he tried. Instead, he opted for a stroll in the crisp evening air. He hoped the fresh air would clear his mind, unjumble his thoughts and soothe his frayed nerves.

He sauntered down the main path from the house, taking the branch that led to the cliffs overlooking the sea. The waves thundered against the rocks below. They sounded angry tonight, a close match to the chaos filling his brain. He imagined the water crashing against the rocks, spray flying high into the air.

Damien tried to push his investigation to the back of his mind as he approached the cliffs. He was careful not to approach the edge. In the place of his queries, a new thread entered his mind. His research into the past in this area had unearthed several people who had perished on or near these very cliffs. Widows distraught when their husbands or children never returned home. Disturbed souls who had thrown themselves onto the rocks below when life proved too much for their natures. Tragic accidents when individuals had ventured too close and slipped over the edge, meeting with the rocks then being dragged into a watery grave.

It only added to his view of the house and property: spooky. No wonder Michael wanted to move, he mused. He kicked the gravel on the path under his feet, staring out at the dark ocean in front of him. The evening air did little to clear his mind. He continued down the path. As he approached another fork in the path, he saw a figure moving in the darkness. The small amount of moonlight Damien used to navigate was not enough to provide details.

Damien kept to the shadows, not sure who he may encounter on the darkened path. Silent, he strained his eyes to distinguish the person. Creeping closer as the individual turned onto the path he was on, he made out Michael's form. Relief washed over him.

"Hey, Michael!" he called.

It did not appear Michael heard him. He opened his mouth to call out again but decided against it. Michael was hurrying down the path. He seemed intent on getting somewhere and getting there fast.

Without realizing, Damien followed him to the edge of the property. He kept a significant distance from him. He couldn't pinpoint a reason, but it seemed like an appropriate thing to do. Michael approached an old house. Climbing the front stairs, he pushed through the front door, disappearing inside.

Damien waited a few moments before approaching the house. He crept up the front stairs, peering in the windows. Michael was nowhere to be found. The house was in disarray, appearing as though it had been abandoned for at least half a century. Reluctant to enter the house, Damien trekked around the outside, peeking in any window he could reach. He saw nothing. Leaning back, he glanced toward the second-floor windows. No light shown from any of them.

Where was Michael? The moonlight wouldn't be enough to light the rooms inside, he would need some kind of light. No lights were showing through any windows. Damien checked the front windows again. No sign of anyone. He considered entering the house. Given the exchanges with Michael of late, he decided against it. He preferred to spare himself another argument.

Damien descended the front stairs, giving one final glance to the house. He shook his head as he found the path back to the main house. Another mystery. Another mystery he couldn't solve. What was Michael doing in some abandoned house? And where was he in the house? Was he considering buying the property and renovating? He hadn't found any places in town. It was a possibility. A remote possibility, Damien surmised. The house was in terrible shape. He could build a new house for much cheaper. This left him back at square one. With no solid reason for Michael to be in an abandoned house on the estate.

Damien sighed as he glanced at the main house standing in front of him. His entire walk back had solved nothing. He returned with more questions than he departed with. Dejected, he pushed through the entryway into the foyer.

Celine and Gray were making their way across the foyer as he entered.

"Hey, D," Celine said, "everything okay?"

Typical, he mused, Celine could read him like a book. "Yeah," he lied, his voice an octave higher than normal as it typically was when he lied.

Celine gave him a stare. "I'll be right up, Gray," Celine said. After he left, ascending the stairs toward their rooms, Celine said, "Want to tell me what's going on?"

"I'm fine!" Damien lied again, his high-pitch voice a dead giveaway. Celine crossed her arms, a smirk on her face. "What?" Damien asked, shrugging.

"Your expression says it all."

"It's nothing." Celine remained quiet. "Honestly, I'm fine. I just took a walk to meditate. I've just been trying to process a few ideas and I'm tired. I didn't eat enough today. Well, I ate a lot of junk food, that might be it. I probably have indigestion. I…" Damien babbled.

"D," Celine interrupted him.

"Yeah?"

"What are you trying to process? What's got you taking night walks around the property?"

He shook his head, shrugging his shoulders. "Nothing major. Just trying to research some stuff on the painting. Not coming up with much." Damien left his strange encounter with Michael out, not wanting to add more to Celine's plate.

"Aww, D." Celine smiled at him, threading her arm through his as they made their way up the stairs. "Thank you for trying. But don't stress about it. We'll figure it out."

"I know it's bothering you though. I don't want it to bother you. You just got your life back and you finally have a minute to breathe. I hate seeing you upset."

"I know, D. But I don't want you stressing out and working to the point of exhaustion. Take a breather, get some sleep. And please stop wandering around the property all hours of the night."

Damien nodded as they reached his bedroom door. "Yeah, I'm going to turn in now and try to get some sleep." He took a step into his room. "I'm okay, I'm not working too hard." Turning back, he said, "And don't worry, I didn't get too close to the cliffs. I was careful!"

Celine laughed. "Good night, D. Love you."

"Good night, Celine. Love you, too."

Celine continued down the hall toward her suite. "What was wrong with him?" Gray asked as she entered.

"Working too hard. When Damien works on a project, he throws himself into it entirely. I just worry about him taking on too much."

"I'm sure he's fine."

"I don't like him wandering around outside at night."

"I understand, but he is a grown man."

"Grown or not, he'll always be my family and I'll always want to protect him."

Gray smiled at her. "You are a wonderful woman, Celine Devereaux."

"You exaggerate," she said, giving him a kiss, "but I don't mind."

"Don't worry, I'll keep my eye on him, too."

"Thank you, Gray."

"Don't worry, Celine. I always have your back."

* * *

Damien tossed and turned in his bed, unable to sleep. Questions still battered his brain, bouncing around, leading him down avenue after avenue in search of a solution. None came to him, nothing added up. It reminded him of his first experience in this house weeks ago. Nothing had added up then either. The most unbelievable solution ended up being correct. It left him with only one emotion: frustration.

Annoyed, he rose from his bed, pacing the floor in the dark. Back and forth he wandered across the wooden floorboards, working through theory after theory. His bare feet padded across the floor in rhythm, trying to soothe his mind. An idea struck him, and he decided to check his notes in the library.

He crept down the hallway, careful not to disturb any other household members. He slinked down the stairs and hurried to the library. After an hour of tracking down information in his notes, he nixed the idea from his head. He tossed his laptop back onto the desk in frustration, sighing. Sleep, perhaps that was what he needed to make sense of this puzzle. Perhaps now he could relax, having tested another theory his brain had created.

He exited the library, plodding down the hall to the foyer. As he approached the large room, a door slammed. A figure moved in the darkened room toward the staircase. He recognized Michael. Damien recalled last witnessing him enter the abandoned house. Where had he been all this time? In that wreck of a house?

Damien, from his dark corner, spied him lumbering up the staircase. He must be returning for the night. Damien waited until he had a good head start before proceeding to his own room. Damien wasn't in the mood for a confrontation with Michael. He wanted to go to sleep without becoming unsettled by another mystery. He would need all his energy to tackle his work tomorrow.

CHAPTER 6

$\mathcal{C}$eline strolled down the path from the main house to Alexander's home on the estate. The morning air still had the night's chill. Snow would fall soon, much earlier than it had in the last place she lived. The holidays would soon be upon them after that. Celine was still unsure how she would handle Josie's parents. She had explained little to them thus far. Only noting that a job opportunity had taken her to Maine and while visiting, she and Damien had chosen to make the move permanent. Her mother suspected this had something to do with her birth family, but Celine had provided her no confirmation. Withholding information was not her style, but she was unsure how she would inform them of the events of the last few months. Perhaps this was what gave her the unsettled sensation she had been experiencing of late.

The trees whispered overhead, blowing in the fall breeze. Leaves drifted from their perches high above to the ground below, floating down in a lazy waltz. She spotted Alexander's house ahead. Shrugging her sweater tighter around her, she hurried toward the house.

She knocked at the door and waited. Alexander, also an early riser, opened the door within minutes. "Good morning, Celine," he said. "Come in! To what do I owe this pleasure?"

"Good morning," she answered, stepping out of the chilly air and into the house. "Sorry for the early morning call, do you have a few minutes?"

"For you, Celine, always. Although, you appear troubled. Let's go into the sitting room. Would you like some tea?"

Celine sighed, sinking into the loveseat. "Tea would be nice, thank you." Alexander disappeared for a moment, retrieving another teacup and saucer to share his morning brew with Celine.

"Now, what concern rousted you from your bed this early, Celine?"

"Just a visit, I missed you."

"Hmm, while I appreciate the sentiment, I sense something more."

Celine frowned at him. "You know me too well."

"Well, we have been friends for centuries." He chuckled.

"It's nothing major, just a feeling I can't shake. Perhaps it's because I haven't decided what to do about Josie's parents."

Alexander considered the statement. "That does present a rather tricky situation."

"Yes, it does. I don't want to lie, but I don't want to tell the truth."

"When the time is right, I'm sure you'll find the right words, Celine." Celine offered him a slight smile in response. "As difficult of a situation as that is, I still don't expect that's what's troubling you."

Celine stared into her tea for a moment before speaking. "Have you sensed anything… off?"

"Off?" Alexander questioned.

"Yes. My intuition tells me something isn't right."

Alexander pondered for a moment. "Besides the recent

attacks, which seem to have lessened, no. I haven't sensed anything off."

"Hmm," Celine said, pursing her lips.

Alexander studied her for a moment. "Is it Celeste that worries you?"

She shook her head. "No, no, it's something else."

"Such as?"

"I'm not sure. I can't put my finger on it. There is nothing concrete. Just a gut reaction that something is… warning me. I can't shake this sense of foreboding."

"Have you spoken with Gray about this? Does he sense anything?"

"I haven't mentioned anything in particular. You know Gray, he's so focused on forgetting the past, he doesn't want to dwell on anything unpleasant. I am loath to bring this up to him, I'm sure he'll think I'm overreacting. And perhaps I am."

"Perhaps."

"This is the part where you tell me I am overreacting and it's nothing. Only a reaction to centuries of being tortured by a madman."

Alexander laughed. "Oh, my apologies, I forgot my lines." He winked at her.

She glanced to him in anticipation. "Well?" she prodded.

He sighed, turning serious. "Unfortunately I can't tell you what you want to hear, Celine. I've learned over the centuries to trust your instincts. Something very well may be wrong."

Celine sunk her head into her hands. "Ugh, wrong answer."

"Again, my apologies, but I'm not sure there is a correct answer."

A moment of silence hung in the air between them. Alexander broke the silence. "Is there anything specific you can pinpoint about this feeling? Anything specific?"

Celine contemplated his question. "No, just that uneasy sense of foreboding."

"You've sensed this before?"

"Yes. It usually had to do with Marcus. I'd grown so accustomed to associating this sensation with him I'm not sure if I can't separate the two or if it has something to do with him."

Alexander rose, approaching Celine. He put his arms around her shoulders as he sat down. "I don't doubt your senses and I'm not discounting them either, but, Celine, he is gone. You must trust that."

Celine patted his hand on her shoulder, nodding her head. "I do. But I can't rid myself of this sensation, nor ignore it."

"It is unwise if you ignore something like this, I agree. But perhaps the perception stems from something else?" he questioned.

"Yes, it must. You're right. It's likely that when I've experienced this before it's so often been related to Marcus Northcott that I cannot distinguish the true source."

"I'm happy to help if you come across any clues."

"Thanks, Alex." She sat for another moment with him before saying, "Well, I'm going to head back to the house. I'm sure Gray is wondering where I've disappeared to."

She rose from the couch, Alexander stood with her. "Feeling more settled?"

"Yes," she assured him, despite being unsure herself. She offered a smile to further convince him.

"If you need anything, Celine, it goes without saying I'm always here for you. I'll walk you to the door."

"Thanks," Celine said, threading her arm through his as they walked toward the foyer. "By the way, how did your meeting with Damien go?"

"Quite well. Oh, I hope the prank I played on him didn't upset him too much."

"Prank?" Celine asked. "Really?"

"Yes, he didn't mention it? I told him I was psychic, could read minds."

Celine laughed. "Oh, poor Damien. I bet he believed you."

"He did! I felt terrible afterward. I'm glad the prank didn't upset him."

"Me, too. He's a good sport though. How is he handling things? Does he seem okay based on the conversation you had?"

"He seems to be doing reasonably well. He was very curious, although he dances around his principal objectives quite a bit. Perhaps because he is still acclimating to the situation."

"He does that when he's nervous. He also throws himself into his work. He spent the day locked in the library yesterday. He's intent on solving the case of the missing painting, along with anything else he perceives is a problem."

"Are there others?"

"No, not really. Michael is having a more difficult time adjusting to the new circumstances of his life. Damien's taken it upon himself to make Michael's adjustment easier. He's a good friend. But I worry about Damien and his adjustment."

"That may be contributing to your sense of apprehension."

"Yes, it may be."

"Perhaps I can venture to the house for a second conversation with him. I rather like Damien, I hope we can become friends. Perhaps that will also ease his transition."

Celine smiled at him, squeezing his hand. "Thank you. I'd appreciate it if you did that. Damien needs a friend other than me. He and Gray haven't warmed up to each other yet."

"It is my pleasure. He's not fond of Gray?"

"No. Damien's intimidated by Gray. Too much residual tension from everything that occurred. He still views Gray as the antagonist of the story."

"I understand. Well, I shall visit him soon."

"Great, thank you, again." Celine kissed him on the cheek before departing. She took the long route home, despite the chilly weather. When she arrived, Gray informed her Damien had already locked himself in the library for another day of work. "He's like a mad scientist in there," he quipped. "Where have you been?"

"Visiting Alexander."

"Oh?"

"Yes, just checking in."

"Everything all right?" Gray questioned, sensing there was more to the story.

"I had a favor to ask him."

"Do tell."

"I wanted him to stop by and speak with Damien. I'm concerned about him and how he is dealing with everything. It would be nice if he had another friend here, someone he can talk to about everything."

"Poor Alexander. I could have talked to him."

Celine raised her eyebrows at him. "That is a disaster waiting to happen. He's still not your biggest fan."

"Is that why he stares daggers at me from across the breakfast table?" Gray joked.

"Funny. He'll come around, but you're not his favorite person. Perhaps I should go check on him."

"I wouldn't. He told everyone he'd be working and didn't want anyone disturbing him."

"Hmm, typical. Okay, I'll leave him to it then. I'll be in the office doing some work. See you later?"

"Okay, I also have some work in town at the shipyard. See you later, darling."

* * *

Damien's headphones blasted music. The little sleep he had received last night recharged him enough to continue his work. He spent the morning tracking down more information on his latest theory. He made excellent progress. This needed to be solved soon. Celine missed breakfast this morning. He could sense her upset. It must be due to the missing painting. Once they settled that issue, she could enjoy life. No more crazy dreams. No more double life. No more being chased by this evil creature. Just happiness.

He smiled to himself. If his theory was correct, they'd soon have this wrapped up. There were only a few more angles to check before he presented his hypothesis to everyone else. He dug back into his research after downing the rest of his soda and a few more nacho cheese tortilla chips.

After a few more hours he was satisfied with his theory. His conjecture was solid. All signs pointed to this being a valid supposition given all the information. He would present his theory to everyone before dinner. He slid his headphones off as thunder sounded overhead. The sound made him gulp. He hated this house during a storm, and this area had plenty of them. Tempted to pull the headphones back on, he nixed the idea in favor of seeking out Celine and the others.

Exiting the library, he hurried down the hall as thunder crashed overhead again and lightening lit the space. As he entered the foyer, he caught sight of Celine descending the stairs. Gray entered from the sitting room.

"Hey, I was just coming to find you two. Wow, I still think

this house is creepy in a storm," Damien said, making his way across the foyer.

Michael joined them, shaking off his umbrella as he came through the door. "It's pouring out there!" he exclaimed, removing his windbreaker and hanging it on the coat tree near the door.

"Perfect timing, buddy," Damien said, as he saw him.

Michael gave him a strange look. "No, I don't suppose so, perfect timing would have meant I missed the downpour."

"Oh, I meant I wanted to talk to everyone and everyone just happened to be here at the same time."

"What's up?" Celine asked.

"I wanted to discuss a theory I've been working on about the painting! Let's go to the library." He headed across the foyer and down the hall.

Celine glanced to Gray, a slight smile on her lips. He was watching Damien cross the foyer and giving him a bizarre stare. Damien's enthusiasm when he threw himself into a project could be overwhelming, Gray hadn't gotten used to that yet. Michael followed behind them as they trailed Damien.

They entered the library. It was apparent Damien had been working hard on the mystery. Books and papers littered the desk and floor. Two laptops sat open on the desk; various applications scattered across their screens. Discarded soda cans and bags of snacks lay scattered about.

"Looks like a hurricane hit in here," Gray said.

Celine smirked at him. "So, what's your theory, D?" she asked.

"Well," he began, "I had a few theories I've been research-ing. I mean, first, and most obvious, someone walked in here and just took the painting off the wall right before you noticed it was missing. Right? So who would do that? The Duke, right? Or one of his goons…"

"Goons?" Gray questioned. Celine gave him a light tap on his chest and shook her head. "What? Who calls them that?" he whispered to her.

"But no one found the painting anywhere. And you'd think someone would have been able to find this painting because there's only so many places he could have put it. The painting's huge, right? You can't stick it in a drawer or something. But no one found it. I mean, I get that he's got some powers and stuff, but outside of the possibility that he diverted it to another dimension or something, it should be around…" Damien babbled.

"What are you prattling on about?" Gray interrupted.

Celine issued Gray a stern look.

"Yeah, man, get to the point," Michael added.

"Oh, sorry," Damien said.

"Will you two let him talk?" Celine defended him.

Damien smiled at her. "Thanks!" She nodded to him, encouraging him to continue. "Okay, long story short. I don't think the Duke took the painting when everyone assumes it went missing."

"Oh, that makes perfect sense," Gray answered. "Yes, he most likely took it before it went missing. Or did you suppose after?"

"Ah, what?" Damien asked, his train of thought broken by the interjected comment.

"Nothing, continue, D," Celine said.

"Right. I started speculating, the painting disappeared, but that doesn't mean it disappeared just before everyone noticed it was missing. What if the painting disappeared before that? Long before that?"

"What are you suggesting?" Celine asked.

"What if the painting disappeared right after it was painted?"

"But it didn't, that painting hung in this house for

centuries," Gray answered.

"Did it? Everyone ASSUMES it did. But suppose the Duke traveled back in time and stole it a long time ago?"

"That's impossible," Gray concluded.

"Why? We traveled through time."

"Gray's right," Celine confirmed. "You traveled through time, but I opened the portal. It wouldn't be possible for me to open the portal and enter it."

"Perhaps he had someone else open the time portal so he could enter it?" Damien conjectured.

"How would that even work?" Gray questioned. "He existed then. Were there two of him?"

"Perhaps?" Damien answered. "Or perhaps he melds into his own body back then?"

"This is a rather far-fetched theory if you ask me," Gray concluded.

"Seriously? You and your wife have both lived for centuries and have strange powers and you find THIS far-fetched?" Damien asked.

"What makes you sure this is what happened, D?" Celine prompted him back to the subject at hand.

"I researched everything I could about the Duke, the painter, the painting, the house, art, everything. There is no reference to that painting anywhere after its completion. It's like it never saw the light of day. No one mentions the portrait, it's not listed as an official work of Benjamin Abbott, and when I checked pictures of the foyer in any family albums or histories, the painting's never there."

"Wait, wait, wait, it was there in the pictures. We saw it," Michael said. "When we first got here, we saw that painting, we remarked about how it looked just like Josie, eh Celine, her," he said, pointing at Celine.

"Yes, I know. That's the first place I searched when I started my research. But look at the album now." Damien grabbed a photo album from the midst of the books and plopped it in front of them. "This is the picture in its place. And the caption now says *Painting of Ships in the Harbor.*"

"This makes no sense, that painting isn't there now. The wall is empty. And how did you find a picture of Celine's portrait when you first came?" Gray pressed.

"I'm not sure. Were we seeing what the Duke wanted us to see? Now that he's gone maybe he can't cover his tracks anymore."

"Why would he want you to see the painting of Celine when she was Mina?" Gray questioned.

"So, no one realized WHEN the painting went missing. Everyone here assumed it was stolen and hidden in this time period. That notion stopped everyone from realizing when the painting actually went missing and searching for it when and where it could be found."

"How does this help us find the painting, D?" Celine asked.

"Well, we now realize when your portrait went missing..."

"In theory," Gray added.

"We can go back and retrieve it before he steals it," Damien finished.

"This is the most ridiculous theory and plan I have ever heard," Gray said, crossing his arms. "We have no confirmation this happened, he's guessing. And there are some fairly sizable gaps in his theory. Is it possible for the Duke to send himself back in time? And even if he stole her portrait then, wouldn't the painting be around somewhere, wherever he put it? How does everyone remember the painting despite it being stolen immediately after it was created?"

"Just because we don't know the answers doesn't mean he's wrong," Celine said.

"I'm with Gray on this one," Michael chimed in. "And I'm not going to travel back in time for some half-baked theory."

"Come on, Michael," Damien argued, "even if I'm wrong, the painting existed back then, we can 'steal' it before it's stolen. It's not like we're getting anywhere pursuing any other avenues."

"No way, I'm out," Michael answered.

"Okay, I'll go myself," Damien said.

"No." Celine shook her head. "I'm not sending you alone. It's too dangerous."

"What about Gray? Or Alexander?"

"They both existed in that time. We do not understand what ramifications, if any, there are to sending someone to a time they existed in already. We can't risk it," Celine explained

"The Duke did."

"According to you," Gray retorted.

"Even if you are correct, Marcus has no regard for consequences. I wouldn't follow his example on anything," Celine responded.

Frustrated, Damien appealed to Michael once more. "Come on, buddy. Just one quick trip."

"I told you," Michael said, annoyance plain in his voice, "I'm out. No way."

"Why? Are you having luck finding the painting with your investigation in abandoned houses?" Damien countered.

"What? I don't know what you're talking about."

"Oh, really? You don't? I saw you. Last night at the..."

"Look, man." Michael cut him off. "I don't know what you imagine you saw but I'm not doing anything in any abandoned houses. Come talk to me when you have a real theory." Michael turned on his heel and exited the room.

"I'd agree with Michael. Come back with solid evidence," Gray added, following Michael out of the room.

Celine and Damien were left alone. Celine eyed Damien, filled with concern for his feelings. Damien stared at the floor, his theory shredded by both Michael and Gray. "Sorry, D," Celine said, grabbing his hand. "I don't assume you're wrong. I'm not dismissing your theory out of hand, but we need more proof before we do anything as dangerous as sending you back in time." Damien didn't respond. "Listen, tomorrow, we'll start fresh. I'll help, we'll go over everything. Determine if we can find more proof of your theory or another hypothesis. If we can prove you're right, then we'll talk about sending you back to find it. Okay?"

Damien sighed, squeezing her hand. "Okay, yeah. Thanks, Celine."

"I appreciate all your work on this. We'll find the painting, D. Now, how about some dinner?"

"I'm going to turn in for the night. I'm exhausted, and I ate a ton of junk food already. I'm not hungry."

"You sure?"

"Yeah, I'm sure. I'm okay, Celine," he assured her. "I'm just tired."

She smiled at him. "Okay, D. Get some rest, see you in the morning." She embraced him in a tight hug before he slogged out of the room. She sighed as she watched him leave. He tried so hard and all his attempt earned him was grief from both Gray and Michael. While she wasn't on board with sending Damien and Michael to the past again, especially if it was a wild goose chase, Michael and Gray had overreacted. His theory wasn't that far-fetched. And she knew Damien well. He didn't float rough theories. He had researched this, he had vetted this theory through his mind, considering it from various angles, playing devil's advocate to himself, he wasn't proposing an ill-conceived postulate. Perhaps with her help, they could iron this out and either find the painting or obtain real proof of when it disappeared.

Celine strode to the door, entering the hallway. A gust of icy air rushed past her. Celine froze as the icy sensation seemed to penetrate through her and race through her veins. She shuddered as the sense of foreboding settled over her again.

CHAPTER 7

*D*amien turned toward the foyer as he exited the library. He didn't intend on going to bed, he wouldn't be able to sleep. His mind churned, the last conversation playing on a continual loop in his head. How could they dismiss his theory so easily? What other theory made sense? Why did Michael refuse to help him? And why did he lie about his whereabouts last night? Not even Celine seemed to believe him. She said she did, but she didn't defend him. Why?

He pushed through the front door into the cool night air. The air remained damp even though the storm had passed. The trees still dripped with rain. Damien shoved his hands into his pockets and strode down the path with no destination in mind. He roamed around the property without aim, lost in contemplation.

As he approached the overlook near the cliffs, he spotted Michael standing near the edge. Damien had no inclination to speak with him. He was about to veer off to another path to avoid meeting Michael when he discerned movement ahead. He paused as he strained his eyes to identify the person approaching. His eyes widened as he recognized the individual. "Celeste?" he whispered.

Celeste, her blond hair pulled into a high bun, approached the cliffs where Michael stood. Was she meeting Michael, he wondered? That was unlikely. There was no love lost between Michael and Celeste and that was putting it mildly. She closed the gap between her and Michael. Damien slinked behind a tree, surveying the two as Michael turned to greet her.

The two exchanged a brief greeting. Damien couldn't make out the conversation. But he witnessed the two embrace before engaging in a passionate kiss. Shock coursed through Damien. What was he witnessing? Michael and Celeste? Were they engaged in an affair? The proof seemed irrefutable.

Damien fled the scene, not wanting to witness any more. Confusion and dismay flowed through him as he raced to the house. He entered the house, proceeding straight up the stairs to his room. He locked the door behind him. He would never sleep tonight. Disappointment from his theory presentation and astonishment at the scene he witnessed on the cliffs would keep him tossing and turning.

Celine sat across from an empty chair the following morning at breakfast. Damien had been a no-show, along with Michael. Celine picked at the food on her plate. Things were falling apart here faster than she expected. Damien had thrown himself into the search for the missing painting and, having had his idea rejected by Gray and Michael, became dejected. When Damien perceived rejection, he climbed back into his shell, alienating himself from the world. Michael had been moody for the past week, snapping at anyone who offered concern.

Gray, who joined Celine for breakfast, noted their absence also. "Looks like your two buddies are having a rough morning," he commented.

"No wonder," Celine answered. "You could have been a tad nicer last evening."

Gray rolled his eyes. "His theory is ridiculous, and it's a terrible idea for them to travel back in time, again. Especially when it may not be necessary."

"I realize that, and I agree. I don't want to send either of them back to 1791, but his theory wasn't that ridiculous."

"It's a stretch."

"It's not, Gray. Most of the issues you and Michael brought up he had an answer for. It's no less plausible than any other hypothesis. And he makes an excellent point, we have had no luck here locating the painting."

Gray sighed, pondering a moment before answering. "Okay, okay. It's not a terrible theory in retrospect. But I still think we shouldn't do anything rash until we learn more."

"I agree."

"Besides, there is no rush."

"I suspect Damien just wants to solve the problem, so in his estimation he's contributing something."

"I understand, but we don't need the painting. We already have the real thing." Gray stood from the table and kissed her on the top of her head. "I'll be in the study, reading the morning paper."

She smiled at him. "Okay, I'll check in with you later after I finish some work."

"I'm still trying to get accustomed to you as a business woman," Gray replied.

"Yes, I found I quite liked running my own business when I was Josie. Who knew?" she joked. Gray smiled at her then strolled toward the door. "Oh, Gray?" He turned to face her. "If you see Damien…"

"I'll try to be a little nicer," he finished for her.

She smiled at him, offering a wink. "Thanks."

That addressed one concern. Damien's theory wasn't terrible, and it was the only thing that made sense given all the information. At least if Gray ran into Damien, he might be more encouraging this time.

She stared at the other empty chair. One other problem remained, one that she couldn't solve by asking Gray to be nicer. In fact, she wasn't sure she could solve it at all. Michael may need to come around on his own, she surmised. She hoped Damien was still on board with helping Michael despite their minor argument last night.

Celine spent the morning taking a long walk, unable to concentrate on work much. She wandered through the wooded areas of the property, hidden by the trees for much of her walk. As she emerged from the forest to approach the rocky cliffs, she experienced a strange sensation. She stood on the cliff's edge, staring at the sea when the hairs on her neck raised. Discomfort washed through her and she developed goosebumps. She experienced the distinct sensation that someone was watching her. She whipped around to face the trees behind her, scanning the area for any sign of a person. "Hello?" she called into the darkened area.

Movement caught her eye to the left. She swiveled her head toward it. A deer sprung from the camouflage of the trees, staring at her for a moment before racing past her. Celine breathed a sigh of relief. The deer must have been the source of her ominous feeling of being watched. Paranoia from centuries of being chased and tormented was getting the better of her. She gave one last glance at the woods. Not spotting anything else, she left her cliff side perch, traveling back to the house.

As she approached the grandiose structure, she spotted Alexander making his way toward the house on another path. "Hello, Celine," he called from across the yard. They met in front of the house before entering together.

"Hi, Alex," she answered. "Enjoying a walk before lunch?"

"I'm on a mission. I hoped to speak with Damien."

Celine smiled, realizing he was following up on their discussion yesterday. "I haven't seen him yet this morning, he missed breakfast. However, I've been out most of the morning, so he may be here. Will you join us for lunch first? Perhaps we'll see him there."

"I'd love to, thank you."

They left their coats in the entryway and navigated to the dining room. Gray, Damien, Charlotte and Avery joined them. Celine was pleased to see Damien in attendance, relieved that he wasn't avoiding the family.

Celine chose a seat next to him, putting her arm around him in a half hug. "We missed you this morning," she said.

"Yeah, yeah, sorry, I slept in. I was beat after those two research days, more tired than I realized," he responded. The explanation didn't sit well with Celine. She always had a way of telling when he wasn't being totally truthful. This, she judged, was one of those times. Something was still bothering Damien. Perhaps it was only residual disappointment from the critical reception his hypothesis received.

"Too tired for more research this afternoon?" Celine pushed.

"Umm…" Damien hedged.

"Oh, I hope you don't mind, Celine," Alexander interrupted, overhearing their conversation, "but I was hoping for a conversation with Damien after lunch."

"Of course," Celine answered, "first access granted. We can talk afterwards, D."

"Ah, what about tomorrow?" Damien answered. "Perhaps

everyone is right. Maybe we should let it cool off. Revisit it and determine what we come up with."

"Oh, sure. Tomorrow's great, we'll attack it tomorrow. Together," Celine acquiesced, giving his knee a squeeze. Yes, she reflected, this was classic Damien Sherwood avoidance. She wouldn't push it, instead hoping his conversation with Alexander helped the situation.

* * *

After lunch, Alexander and Damien disappeared to the library. "I'm glad we have a moment to chat, Damien," Alexander said.

"Anytime," Damien answered, "is there something I can help with?" Damien drummed his fingers on his leg, a nervous habit. Alexander's sudden appearance and interest in a private conversation made him edgy. Did he, too, want to discount any conjectures about the missing painting?

"I was hoping there may be something I can help with," Alexander countered.

"What do you mean?" Damien inquired, still jittery.

"Well, since our conversation, I was curious to know if any of the information helped you. I'm interested to know if you've made any progress."

Damien made a face. "Oh," he said, staring at the floor as he scuffed his shoe against it, assuming Alexander was here to further devalue his theory.

"It appears the answer is 'no.' Am I correct?"

"You mean you haven't heard?"

"Heard? Heard what?"

"No one told you about my incredibly stupid theory?"

"No?" Alexander said, phrasing it as a question.

"Well, long story short. I've made no progress except one spectacular fail at a hypothesis that everyone laughed at."

"I cannot believe Celine laughed."

"Well, no, she didn't. She agreed it was possible, perhaps even probable."

"What was the theory?"

"Forget it. Thanks for checking in though," Damien said, nodding to him.

"I'd rather not forget it. I'd like to hear your theory myself, if you don't mind."

"Umm…" Damien hesitated.

"I promise not to laugh. I'm sure it's not, as you say, 'a fail.' If Celine didn't deduce it was, I'm betting it has merit. Perhaps a fresh mind can help you tweak any minor issues that may exist with it."

Damien shrugged his shoulders. "My idea was that the Duke didn't steal the painting in this time, that he went back to when it was painted and stole it then."

"And what makes you suppose this to be the case?"

"Well," Damien said, warming up to the conversation, "I researched everywhere possible. I examined every photo album here, scrutinized the painter's life and listed works, dissected every resource I could to find even a trace of this painting and never found one."

"But there are photographs of it," Alexander contended.

"There WERE photographs of it," Damien refuted. "Here, take a peek in the album where the picture of the painting used to be." Damien handed him the open photo album he had used as evidence the night before.

Alexander furrowed his brow in confusion. "*Ships in the Harbor?*" he read from the caption below the photo.

"Yep. That's not what Michael and I saw in this book when we arrived weeks ago. We saw a painting of a woman, identical to Celine, with a caption that read 'Portrait of Wilhelmina something-or-other Buckley.'"

"Laurent," Alexander added. "Wilhelmina Laurent Buckley."

"Yes, that's it!" Damien exclaimed.

"But the painting was already missing then. Why has the photograph changed only now?"

"My guess is the photograph changed after the Duke was banished. Was he masking it somehow, so no one discussed where, or when, to search for it?"

"Hmm."

"Anyway, that was the theory," Damien finished, unable to read Alexander's reaction.

"I quite agree with you and Celine. It seems probable."

"Really?" Damien asked, encouraged.

"Yes. What were Michael and Gray's objections?"

"That it was impossible for the Duke to both open the time portal and enter it. And what would happen if he did, since he already existed there. And it really fell apart when I suggested we go back and retrieve the painting from that time period."

Alexander reflected on the misgivings voiced by Gray and Michael. "I'm not convinced he didn't find a technique to travel to the past. We haven't any insight on what occurs when someone returns to a time they exist in, but that doesn't mean it's not possible to achieve."

"That's what Celine said. But she agreed with everyone else about not rushing into time travel."

"I understand her hesitancy. I imagine it has more to do with her desire to protect you than any misgivings she has with your theory."

"I guess. I just want to help. This may be our only chance to find that painting."

"You may be correct. I support you in the endeavor and I will tell Celine as much."

Damien's eyes brightened. "Thanks! Now if you could

only convince Michael. He refused to even consider the idea. He's not been himself lately." Damien shook his head, recalling the scene he witnessed last night.

"Having trouble with the adjustment?" Alexander asked.

"To say the least."

"Is there cause to be concerned?" Damien shrugged, unable to vocalize anything. "Damien?" Alexander pressed, meeting his gaze.

"Uh… I just… he's… there was…"

"Has something happened with Michael that's disturbed you?"

"That's putting it mildly."

"I realize we're not close friends, although I do hope we become better friends, but in the meantime, is there anything you'd like to share?"

"I think… I think Michael is having an affair with Celeste," Damien blurted out, glad to have it off his chest.

"What?" Alexander seemed shocked at the admission. "What makes you suppose so?"

"I spotted them meeting last night. He's been so sketchy the past week, disappearing and stuff. Anyway, last night, I just… right place, right time. Or maybe wrong place, wrong time. Anyway, I was walking off some frustration and came across them on the cliffs."

"Perhaps it was a chance meeting."

"Uh… people don't cuddle like that at a chance meeting."

"Oh my," Alexander responded. "I understand the reason for your concern, yes."

"Whew, I'm relieved to have that out. I didn't know what to do. But I had to tell someone. It's been on my mind since it happened, and I just didn't want to tell Celine. I've been avoiding her. She can read me like a book. She'll know something is wrong and then I'll blurt it out to her. And then I'll be the person who tells her that her ex and her sister, her very married sister, are having some torrid affair. Then she'll have something else to be upset about and worry over," Damien babbled.

Alexander held his hand up, trying to soothe Damien's nervous jabbering. "Leave it with me, Damien. I shall handle it."

"Oh…" Damien paused, confused as to what he meant. "What are you going to do? Don't tell Celine, she'll be so upset. She just made up with Celeste, I don't want to ruin it for her. She just got her sister back."

"I will not discuss this with Celine without speaking to you first. But I will handle broaching the subject with her if the need arises."

"Do you think we should tell her? I can tell her. I'm not… afraid, I just don't want to see the disappointment on her face."

"Not just yet. I agree the timing isn't appropriate. Let's not disappoint her unless we have to."

"What should we do?"

"I'll speak with Celeste. We're not the best of friends, but I am better acquainted with her than you."

"Eh, okay. I will not fight you on that. I don't really know Celeste and she's kind of scary."

Alexander chuckled. "Put it out of your mind, Damien. I'll take it from here."

After a few more moments of conversation, the two parted ways, leaving Damien in the library with a renewed interest in his research project. Celine snuck in moments later, tapping Damien on the shoulder and startling him.

"Geez, you scared me!" he exclaimed.

"Sorry," Celine answered, "I didn't mean to. I wanted to check in with you. Doing some work on the painting search?"

"Yeah, I am." Celine smiled to herself. It seemed his

69

conversation with Alexander had improved his mood. "I don't presume I'm wrong, Celine."

"I'm not sure you're wrong either. I would prefer to be more certain before we do anything bold, that's all. Time travel is uncertain and unpredictable. I don't want to risk your life."

"I realize that. Alexander said the same thing. But you don't have to protect me."

"I'll always protect you, Damien, whether or not you want me to." Damien smiled at her. "So, you discussed this with Alexander? What did he conclude?"

"He deemed it a probable solution given the evidence and despite the holes in the theory Gray mentioned."

"Gray can be a little quick to judge," Celine admitted. "Plus, he's a fan of being more cautious. He doesn't want to risk your life for nothing either."

Damien made a face. "I'm not sure he's that interested in protecting my life."

"He is. He realizes how important you are to me. Which makes you important to him. But even if you are correct, the prospect of returning to the past doesn't please Michael."

Damien bristled at the mention of Michael's name, afraid of giving away some detail about what he had witnessed. "Yeah," he stated, not willing to say anything more.

They were silent for a moment. Then Celine said, "Okay, so show me what evidence prompted you to conclude this theory is correct. If we go through your thought process together maybe we can sew up those holes and convince everyone or come up with another solution."

"Okay, Celine, that sounds like a plan." Damien and Celine spent the next several hours wading through every piece of research and evidence he amassed in his two-day quest. They stopped just before dinner. After reviewing everything, Celine was convinced the theory was solid and probable. While they hadn't nailed down the exact details on how the Duke had achieved his own time travel, she was sure he had the ability to achieve something on this scale. She agreed to present the evidence again to Gray and determine if he was more receptive to the theory after giving it some consideration. They would also need to approach Michael again if Michael and Damien were going to travel back to retrieve the painting. While Gray assumed they did not need the painting with Celine back, she would have felt more comfortable with the painting returned to its rightful place. They had commissioned it for a reason.

Dinner conversation was kept light with Charlotte, Avery and Millie attending. Michael was absent, a growing trend for him. They spent some time after dinner chatting with the entire group. Despite wanting some closure on the painting mystery and the next course of action, Damien enjoyed the distraction. It allowed him to escape any awkward conversations with Celine in which he may spill the beans about Michael and Celeste. He retired for the evening exhausted and proud of himself for not admitting the tawdry details to Celine.

CHAPTER 8

*A*lexander waited in the darkness outside the abandoned house. In a few moments, he expected to see Celeste emerge. He had witnessed Michael enter the structure earlier. He had spent a few hours inside before emerging, traipsing down the path toward the main house without detecting Alexander's presence.

So, Damien was correct in his assessment. Michael and Celeste were involved. Celine would not be pleased. Her nerves were already on edge, something disturbed her. Perhaps it was this very thing. But there was no reason to upset her if the situation could be resolved without her involvement.

Movement caught Alexander's eye. Celeste emerged from the front door, descending the stairs from the porch onto the pathway below. As she approached his hiding spot, Alexander stepped onto the path, blocking her passage.

"Celeste, might I have a word with you?" he said.

She rolled her eyes. "Just one? Could I be so lucky?"

"Do you imagine your latest course of action wise?" he asked, launching into his demand unbuffered.

"I don't know what you're talking about, but I'm sure whatever it is it's none of your business. If you'll excuse me." She stepped to her left to move around him.

He side-stepped to block her. "Oh, Celeste, I'm sure you do. I saw Michael leave just before you did. Michael, Celeste, really? You could find no one else?"

"What is your point, Alexander?"

"My point is the pain you will cause to your sister when she inevitably finds out the truth. Do you assume she'll forgive you again? She has only just forgiven you for your involvement in what happened to her centuries ago."

"The pain I will cause my sister? Have you no concern for the pain my sister has caused me?"

"Any pain she may have caused you was unintentional."

She rolled her eyes again. "Always so quick to defend her. What will happen when Saint Celine slips from the pedestal you all set her on?"

"Keep to the point, Celeste. You must end your involvement with Michael now!"

"Why? He is nothing to her. Unlike Damien. And I didn't touch her precious Damien."

"He is her friend. She will not tolerate this, I assure you."

"Really?" Celeste said, eyeing him, "Perhaps you should run along and tattle to my sweet baby sister. Let her deal with me herself."

"I am giving you a chance, Celeste. A chance to stop before you ruin your relationship with Celine, again."

"Stay out of my business, Alexander," Celeste warned before pushing past him down the path.

* * *

Celine wandered through the woods. She rose before dawn and completed some of the work for her business before she exited the house, needing fresh air to clear her troubled mind. Something was off. Something weighed on her mind. She loved the way the trees hid her from the rest of the world. It made her feel safe as she meandered without direction.

She stepped off the path into a thicket of trees, allowing them to envelope her in complete privacy. She breathed deeply, filling her lungs with the odor of decaying leaves and pine scent. Overhead, birds chirped from their high perches. She closed her eyes, breathing deep again and listening to their songs.

After a moment, she noted another scent on the wind. Thick and musky, it filled her nostrils. She snapped her eyes open. Pain shot across her forehead from temple to temple. Her mind jumbled, random memories shot across her brain. She doubled over, suffering from a sudden wave of nausea.

Within moments, the sensation passed. She sniffed several times, but no longer detected the musky odor. The pain in her head passed and her queasiness ceased. She tried to recall the memories that had filled her head in that moment. They were so fleeting, she had trouble bringing them back to the forefront of her brain.

She concentrated hard, trying to induce her brain to revive them. She closed her eyes, focusing her energy on retrieving them. After a moment, she unlocked them in her mind: her confrontation with Celeste and Marcus on the beach that fateful night where she became what she was, Celeste's dead body on the foyer table, Celeste arriving to the beach ceremony where they banished the Duke.

Why had these memories flooded her mind? And why had pain accompanied them? She had experienced something similar before, when she had been Josie, when she had been human. While her memories as Celine tried to push their way into Josie's human mind, Josie had experienced pain, confusion, nausea. Why was she continuing to experience these symptoms? These memories were not new. Her mind was not integrating the memories of two lives.

She had no explanation for the incident. As she opened her eyes and glanced around, trying to solve the mystery, she realized she was close to Alexander's house. She wondered how the conversation with Damien had gone from his perspective. She needed the diversion from her own strange experience. She pushed ahead through the trees, intent on thrusting her painful memories from her mind and replacing it with a conversation with Alexander.

Celine knocked at the door, blowing air into her clasped hands to warm them as she waited. "Good morning, Celine," Alexander greeted her after opening the door.

"Good morning, I hope you don't mind another visit. I wanted to see how your conversation with Damien went yesterday."

"Not at all, come in." He showed her to the sitting room. She sank onto the couch next to him.

"So, how did it go? He seemed to perk up after you left, so I'm assuming it went well."

"Quite well, I judge. I expect we shall be good friends."

Celine smiled. That was encouraging news. "Good. He needs another friend, someone to talk to. Did he tell you his theory about the painting?"

"He did. I found it plausible, although, I do understand your reservations about sending him back to 1791 to recover the painting."

"I don't want to send him at all. However, it may be the easiest and fastest solution. But I worry."

"I understand your worry. Speaking of, how are you feeling? Any more ominous impressions?"

Celine reflected a moment before answering. "No," she lied, "well, yes, general things, like the worry about the painting and Damien's reaction to Gray's rejection of his theory."

Alexander opened his mouth to answer but a knock at the door interrupted him. "Oh, excuse me a moment." He disappeared to the front door. Celine overheard voices. It sounded like Damien's voice. She rose and walked to the foyer. Damien was walking into the house.

"Hey, did you get a chance to…" He stopped dead upon seeing Celine. Clearing his throat, he followed up with, "Oh, hey, Celine, fancy meeting you here."

"Hey, D," she said.

Damien glanced wide-eyed to Alexander. Celine did not miss the exchange. "I'm glad you're here," Alexander told Damien, "I wanted to follow up with you about our conversation yesterday. Shall we go into the sitting room?"

"Uh, o-o-okay," Damien stammered.

Celine wondered why he was so nervous. Perhaps he was nervous around Alexander. Yet, he had sought Alexander out to have a conversation. Something was bothering him. That much was obvious. Alexander led them back to the sitting room.

"I was just speaking with Celine about our conversation yesterday, in fact," Alexander continued as they sat down.

"You were?" Damien asked, gulping.

"Yes. We were attempting to determine another, safer way to reclaim the missing painting. Yet, I'll admit neither of us had any ideas."

"Oh, right, yeah, the painting," Damien said, nodding. "Yeah, good, I mean not good, I mean… well, you know what I mean."

What else could he have thought Alexander was referring to, Celine pondered. And why was he so nervous? "I haven't had a chance to speak to Gray. Perhaps we can run through everything with him again tonight or tomorrow night. Give him some time to come around."

"Yeah, okay," Damien said. "Maybe tomorrow. Give him some time to adjust to the idea."

"Okay…" Celine began.

"In fact, yeah, tomorrow is better. I might not return for dinner. I have some stuff to do. Alexander and I were going to work on some stuff and whatever…" Damien babbled.

"Oh, I assumed you'd stay here for dinner," Alexander chimed in, picking up on Damien's nervous energy.

"Oh, haha, yeah, that's right. Sorry, I didn't remember if we settled that."

Celine studied the two men as the strange situation unfolded. Something peculiar was going on between them. While she wanted to learn what it was, she also appreciated their budding friendship and wanted to encourage it. She would respect their privacy. "Well, it sounds as though you two have your work cut out for you. I will leave you to it!"

"Oh, great. I mean… it's not great that you're leaving, but great that we can keep working. Not that we can't work with you here because there's nothing that, you know… It's just…" Damien rambled, stumbling over his words.

"Let me walk you to the door, Celine," Alexander said, cutting him off. Celine and Alexander stood. Celine said her goodbyes to Damien and followed Alexander to the door.

"Good luck with your work. And thanks, Alex, I'm glad Damien has someone he can come to with his ideas."

"It is my pleasure, Celine. I hope we can come up with something between us. I don't want you worrying about this."

"With you two on the case, I won't be!" Celine said her final goodbyes, giving Alexander a hug and kiss on the cheek before departing. She stared back at the house for a moment before strolling along the path back to the main house.

* * *

"Whew," Damien began as Alexander entered the room again. "Wow, thanks for the save. That was close. I stopped by to talk about Michael and Celeste and then Celine was here and that threw me off and I couldn't stop thinking about it and I didn't want Celine to suspect anything…"

"No problem, Damien. I don't expect Celine suspects a thing about what you witnessed."

"Okay, good, yeah. So, did you talk to Celeste?"

"I did. I'm afraid I didn't get very far. Celeste is extremely obstinate."

"Reminds me of someone I know," Damien said, alluding to Celine's stubborn streak. "Did you call her on it? Tell her we know they are having an affair and we don't want Celine finding out?"

"Yes. While I did not tell her the source of my knowledge, I did tell her I had no doubt about what was occurring."

"And she didn't care?"

"It appears not. Although, I did not expect her to comply with my request."

"So, we've made no progress on that front either." Damien sighed, throwing his head back on his chair. "I don't know how I'll face Celine with this hanging over me. I don't know what I expected. I didn't actually expect Celeste was just going to agree to stop seeing Michael because we asked. Although it would have been nice if she had."

"I agree, however, I did not expect Celeste to concede she was wrong. We are not friends, she and I, so I went in at a disadvantage."

"Hmm. Do you suppose it would help if I asked her?"

"No. Don't do that. I would not recommend it. Stay away from Celeste for the moment. You will achieve nothing and may even worsen the situation."

"Oh boy, that's the last thing we need. Okay, agreed, I'll stay away from her."

"Good. Now, what shall we plan for the rest of the evening? I assume you'd still prefer to stay to avoid another conversation with Celine?"

"If you don't mind. Sorry to be a bother, but I'm afraid I'll blurt it out. I just don't want to hurt her."

"I don't mind in the least. Do you play chess?"

"I do!"

"It's been so long since I've had a good game," Alexander said. "Gray and I play but not as often as I'd like."

"Awesome, let's do that!"

Damien spent the afternoon and evening engaged in a few games of chess with Alexander, avoiding the main house. He left Alexander's late in the night. He hiked back to the house through the chilly night air. Before going to the house, he took a detour, bringing him to the cliff's edge. Living near the ocean was still new to him and he loved hearing the waves crash against the rocks and the smell of the salty air.

He stood for a few moments on the rocky outcropping, listening and staring out over the vast ocean in front of him. He turned back toward the house, starting back up the path. A noise ahead of him on the path startled him. He ducked behind a tree, waiting for the source of the noise to reveal itself. Within moments, two figures came down the path. As they approached, Damien made out the forms of Michael and Celeste. He cursed under his breath.

They walked past him, unaware of his location. "Don't worry, my darling, Alexander hasn't scared me off. Stay away from him, don't make trouble where it isn't needed," he overhead Celeste telling Michael.

Damien shook his head, disappointed in the situation. They had failed, Celeste and Michael had disregarded their request. They had no intention on complying. Poor Celine, he reflected. She would be heartbroken when she learned the truth.

The games of chess had helped relax his mind, but the latest twist of events had him tied in knots again. He stood for a few moments pondering what to do. Should he return to Alexander's? He concluded disturbing Alexander now wouldn't help the situation. He would go home, try to sleep and see Alexander in the morning.

CHAPTER 9

*D*amien was surprised to find Celine missing from breakfast the following morning. Although it allowed him to avoid an awkward, nervous discussion with her. He was growing more and more tense as the situation continued to unfold. He wasn't sure how long he could hide the truth from Celine. He didn't like being dishonest. Still, he wasn't sure how she would react. Perhaps letting Alexander tell her was best. Or perhaps it was a cop out. Either way, he was glad he was not faced with the decision yet.

Following breakfast, Damien went straight to Alexander's house. He banged on the door, glancing around, his nerves on edge. Alexander greeted him. Damien pushed through the door into the foyer before Alexander had the words out of his mouth.

"Sorry for coming so early," Damien said. "I didn't know what to do."

"What's happened?"

He shook his head. "Michael and Celeste were together last night. I spotted them coming down the path. I darted behind a tree so they didn't spot me. But I overheard them.

Celeste was assuring him she wasn't put off despite anything you said."

"I am not surprised in the least. Please come in," Alexander said, motioning to the sitting room.

"Thanks. The guilt is weighting on me from keeping this from Celine. Do you think it would help to talk to them again? Perhaps I should talk to Michael? Or I could try Celeste?"

Alexander sighed as he sunk into a chair. "Neither will do any good."

Damien closed his eyes and shook his head. "Ugh, you're right, but I feel like we have to try. For Celine's sake."

"You're a good friend to her, Damien. But I urge you not to speak with either. I will approach Celeste again. I do not want to see you embroiled in this mess and making enemies for no reason."

"But if we can prevent Celine from being upset..."

"That is my point. I doubt we will achieve that. Is it worth the confrontation only to arrive at the same result?"

"Perhaps? At least we'll know we tried."

"Celine would not hold it against you if you said nothing."

"Yeah, I realize that, but that doesn't mean I should let her down on purpose."

"You aren't planning on leaving this go, are you?" Alexander inquired.

"No, I won't," Damien replied, insistent.

"You are a true friend. She is lucky to have you. Perhaps the best approach is to work together. Confront Celeste and Michael together in a last-ditch effort."

Damien reflected for a moment. "Okay," he agreed, nodding his head, "yeah, that might work. Perhaps if we both talk to them, double-team it, they'll listen."

"Don't get your hopes too high, Damien. I doubt this will effect any change, but as you said, at least we tried."

Damien pulled his cell phone from his pocket. "I can text Michael now and see if he can stop by…"

"I'll work to make arrangements with Celeste. Perhaps we can reconvene this evening."

"Okay, yeah, I'll tell him that. Is six good?"

"Half past seven may work better."

"Seven thirty it is! I'll text you once I have a confirmation from Michael."

"I shall do the same regarding Celeste. Perhaps you should come earlier, we can discuss a strategy."

"Yes, excellent. I'd like to avoid dinner. The longer this goes on, the more I'm likely to spill the proverbial beans."

"Perhaps you'd prefer to dine here for the evening."

"I appreciate that. Thanks!"

"Excellent! See you around six then."

"Okay, see you then. I'll see myself out!" Damien rose from the chair, putting the final touches on a text to Michael. He sent it, then made his way to the foyer and let himself out the front door. He kept a continual eye on his phone as he walked from Alexander's house to the main house. He planned to retrieve his laptop and hole up in his room for the day, doing some work and avoiding as many people as he could manage. It would also give him a chance to plan out his conversation for the evening. While the conversation would never go the way he envisioned, he'd still spend hours practicing his points.

When he arrived at the house, his phone chimed. Damien swiped it open to find a message from Michael: *Busy tonight, sorry.*

Damien texted back: *Make time... it's about the missing painting... we have to help Celine find it... it's why we stayed!!!*

Damien retrieved one of his laptops from the library, receiving another text before he left for his room. *It's why you stayed.*

Damien responded: *No... it's why WE stayed... WE found out some incredible things... WE time traveled!!! WE helped Celine before and wanted to keep doing that... keep fighting the darkness. Come on, man!*

He pocketed his phone and traveled the halls to his room, locking himself inside. He sunk into the armchair by the window, opening it a crack despite the chilly air. The rhythm of the ocean soothed his mind as he attempted to do some work. He opened his laptop, but before he could begin anything, his phone chimed again.

A new text from Michael awaited him: *Okay, fine... when and where?*

Damien texted back the time and location and after receiving a confirmation from Michael, he texted Alexander to confirm Michael's attendance. He focused on writing some computer code for his latest work project, spending the rest of the morning and afternoon engrossed in his work.

After finishing, he hurried from the house to Alexander's, arriving fifteen minutes early. As they dined, Damien outlined his talking points and practiced speech for Michael and Celeste.

"Well, it's a wonderful speech, Damien. I am convinced," Alexander said as they entered the sitting room following dinner.

"Fifteen minutes to go," Damien said, his leg bouncing up and down from nerves.

"Would you like a drink?" Alexander offered.

"No, yes, maybe." Damien ping-ponged on his answer. Alexander prepared him a drink, Damien sipped it nervously.

Within ten minutes, there was a knock on the door. Alexander appeared with Michael in tow. Damien greeted him as he sat on the couch. "Thanks for coming, buddy."

"Let's get this over with. Please don't tell me you want to convince me to go back in time with you."

"Ah, no, that's not it," Damien hedged.

Another knock sounded at the door. "Excuse me for a moment," Alexander said, departing to answer the door. He returned with Celeste.

Michael hung his head. "Oh, you've got to be kidding me," he said, annoyance plain in his voice. He stood. "I'm not doing this."

"Michael, wait, just listen," Damien said, also standing.

"No, no way. This is out of line. You tricked me into coming here in the name of helping Celine to stage... what, an intervention? It's not bad enough your buddy here attacked Celeste over this last night and now this?"

"I'd scarcely call what happened an attack," Alexander chimed in.

"It wasn't a trick." Damien continued, "It is to help Celine. She'll be devastated if she finds out about this."

"Oh, really? Devastated that two consenting adults are spending time together?" Michael questioned.

"One of those consenting adults is her married sister," Damien countered.

"What's your point?" Michael asked.

"My point is how can you do this when it'll hurt your friend? And you," he said, motioning to Celeste, "when it will hurt your sister?"

"I don't see how this is any of my sister's affair," Celeste contended.

"Oh, Celeste, you're fooling yourself if you assume Celine would not care what you are doing with her friend," Alexander warned.

"Perhaps my sister should remind herself that she is part of the reason this occurred," Celeste answered.

"How can you blame this on Celine?" Damien cried, throwing his arms in the air.

"I will not stand here and listen to you insult me or Celeste. We're together, get over it. Let's go, Celeste," Michael said, turning to leave.

"Wait," Damien said, "before you go, I want you both to reflect long and hard on how Celine will feel when she finds out about this... thing between you two. Consider how disappointed she'll be, how much she cares about both of you and you're both throwing it away for what? Will this even last?"

Michael shook his head at Damien. "Don't lecture me, Damien, I don't want to hear it." Turning to Celeste, he said, "Let's go."

"Celeste," Alexander chimed in, "I'd consider thoroughly how this revelation will affect your sister."

Michael spun around to face Alexander, seething. "Leave it, Michael," Celeste warned him. "You made your case last night, Alexander. Stop wasting my time. Come, Michael." She grasped his hand in hers, pulling him toward the door.

The couple disappeared, the door slamming behind them as they made their way out. Damien let out a sigh. "You were right," he said, shaking his head and throwing his hands in the air. "They didn't even care."

"I'm afraid they didn't, but we did our level best."

Damien sunk onto the couch, head in his hands. "How are we going to tell Celine?"

"I'll tell her," Alexander offered.

"I appreciate that, but no, I don't want you to have to do it yourself. It'll be better if we're both there. And maybe Gray, too. You know break it gently to her with plenty of people to support her."

"That's very thoughtful, Damien. Yes, I agree. Perhaps tomorrow morning is the best time."

"Should we put it off?"

"Yes. It's best to break it to her after a good night's sleep, when she's had plenty of rest."

"Ooooooh," Damien said, "good idea. I'll never sleep tonight but, yeah, perhaps that's the best time to do it. When she's clear and fresh in the morning, not when she's got to go through the whole night upset, not sleeping."

"We'll meet tomorrow morning following breakfast," Alexander assured him.

"Sounds like a plan."

"Fancy a game of chess before you go? Perhaps it will help you sleep."

"I doubt anything will help me sleep tonight, but I'd enjoy a game, yes."

After the game's conclusion, Damien wandered back to the house, taking his time despite the chilly night air. Moonlight cast an eerie glow across the property, adding to Damien's assessment that the property was spooky. Damien's mind rambled from one thought to another as he meandered the path. He tried to avoid dwelling on the conversation that he'd have with Celine the following morning. He dreaded it. Yet, it must be done. They would give her one more peaceful night before breaking the news to her.

The house loomed large on the horizon. Damien took a deep breath as he studied the dark structure's silhouette. Lights still glowed from the inside; someone was still up. With any luck, he could avoid them and go straight to his room without any interaction.

He approached the house and entered the foyer. Celine and Gray were making their way across the room. Just my luck, he mused. "Hey, D!" Celine greeted him.

"Hi!" he called, meeting them in the middle of the room.

"Late night researching with Alexander?" she asked.

He smiled at her, wide-eyed. "Yes, er, no. I mean, that's

not what we were doing. I mean, we were, but then we were playing chess. He's excellent at chess. I mean, not like I'm getting my butt kicked every time, but it's challenging, so that's fun," Damien babbled.

Gray stared at him, crinkling his brow in confusion at his rambling. "Heading to bed?" Celine asked.

"Yep, yes." He feigned a yawn. "Gosh, I am so tired. I'm going to go right to bed and go to sleep."

"Is everything okay, D?" Celine asked, realizing his nervous babbling signaled he was anxious about something.

"Yep. It's all good. I'm all good. Just tired."

"Well, you better get to bed then! We're heading up too, we'll walk with you."

The trio started across the foyer, on their way to retire for the evening. As they approached the stairs, the door opened, Michael came through.

"Hi, Michael, good to see you," Celine said, stopping to greet him.

"Hey, buddy!" Damien called to him from across the room. "Late one, huh?"

Michael didn't respond. He appeared frozen in place, unable to move. Even from across the room, Celine noted that he appeared unwell. "Are you okay?" she asked, as she approached him.

There was no response. Michael took one stumbling step further into the room before collapsing.

CHAPTER 10

"*M*ichael!" Celine shouted, rushing toward him. Gray and Damien followed her lead, gathering around the limp form on the floor. "Help me turn him over."

Celine pulled him onto his back with Gray's assistance. Damien hovered over them, unsure how to help. As they turned him over, the source of his illness became apparent. Celine gasped, glancing to Gray.

"Oh my God!" Damien exclaimed in shock. "Something attacked him! Bit him it looks like!"

A dark look settled on Celine's face as she studied the bite marks, two puncture wounds on his neck. Blood still oozed from them both. "Get Millie," she directed Gray, who raced toward the sitting room where Millie was spending the evening reading.

"What could have done that?" Damien asked, kneeling down next to Michael.

Millie rushed into the foyer moments later, kneeling next to Celine to assess her newest patient. Celine stood, fury raging through her. She stalked to the front door, pulling on her coat in a forceful manner.

"Celine," Gray said, approaching her, "where are you going?" Damien turned his attention from Michael to the conversation unfolding between Celine and Gray.

"You know exactly where I'm going," she replied, ice in her voice.

"Don't," he said. "We need you here."

"Millie knows what to do. You're here. Keep him safe. I have to deal with the source. We have to make sure it doesn't happen again." Celine turned on a heel and exited the house. Gray stood for a moment at the door as she disappeared down the path before directing his attention back to Michael.

The exchange puzzled Damien. He had, however, witnessed that exact look on Celine's face once before when she left the house and almost killed the man who had killed her sister. He opened his mouth to ask Gray about it, but Millie interrupted him.

"We must stop this bleeding. He may need blood. I need my bag and we need to move him to his room."

"Damien," Gray said, "help me carry him while Millie fetches her bag."

Damien nodded, stunned into silence. He lifted Michael with Gray, carrying him up the stairs and down the hall to his bedroom. When they reached the room and had Michael on the bed, he found his voice. "Sh-Shouldn't we call an ambulance or something? Take him to a hospital?"

"No, not for what he has. Millie can treat him, and we can keep him safe."

"Keep him safe? From what?" Damien questioned as Millie entered the room, doctor's bag in hand. "And where did Celine go? I can't believe she left!"

"Don't worry, I texted Alexander, he'll keep an eye on her.

I'll be right back. I need to get something." Gray hurried from the room, leaving Damien alone with Millie and an ailing Michael.

"But…" Damien began.

Millie interrupted, "Damien, I need your help."

"Okay," he answered, approaching the bed.

"Here, keep pressure on his wounds with this while I prepare a bandage," she instructed, handing him gauze.

"Umm…" Damien hesitated, never good in a crisis.

Millie guided his hands over the wound with the gauze. "Just like that, steady pressure."

Damien nodded, turning to face his task at hand. Michael was pale and lifeless. "Don't worry, buddy, you'll be okay," Damien whispered, trying to reassure him.

"I'm going to put this salve on the wound then dress it. Be ready to hand me the tape when I need it, okay?"

"Okay," Damien agreed, allowing Millie to remove the gauze and place the salve on his wounds. Michael winced and moaned in pain as she smeared it onto the puncture holes. Damien winced with him. The wounds appeared deep. Purple bruises edged them.

Millie placed a bandage over top, requesting the first piece of tape from Damien. He handed it to her, his eyes never leaving Michael.

Gray returned, carrying an object in his hand. He placed it on Michael's chest. "Will he need blood, Millie?"

Damien's face wrinkled in confusion. "That's what you went to get?" Gray and Millie ignored him, continuing their conversation.

"I'm not sure. If the bleeding continues, yes. But, for now, it's under control so I'm hoping he doesn't."

"Good. He can't be left alone."

"No, if this happens again, even once, it will likely kill him."

"Damn it!" Gray barked. "What the hell was she thinking?"

"She wasn't. Probably judged him an easy mark."

"Well, it might be her last."

"Yes, I can't imagine Celine will be very forgiving."

"She? Celine? Would someone explain to me what the hell is happening? My friend is really sick, close to dying by the sounds of it, and no one even mentions a hospital. Celine runs off and other than Millie bandaging his wound, the treatment you race off to retrieve is... is... a cross?!?!" Damien shouted.

"Calm down," Gray said. "We're doing what is best for him."

"Best for him? You stuck a cross on his chest and a band-aid on his neck. Then you're like 'oh, he was an easy mark but if this happens again he'll die but oh well, good enough!'"

Gray rolled his eyes. "Trust me. That cross will make sure it doesn't happen again. But he can't be left alone. Not even for a second. He's in just as much danger from himself as he is from another attack."

"Attack from what? How is he a danger to himself? How does a cross protect him? What kind of animal is afraid of a cross?"

Gray turned to face him. "A vampire," he replied.

* * *

Celine stormed down the path, one destination in mind: the abandoned house near the edge of the property. The wounds on Michael's neck penetrated her brain. Her mind burned with only one instinct: anger.

She reached the house, blowing the doors open in front of her. She stepped inside, scanning the room. It was empty. She would wait. It wouldn't matter, time would not cool the fire of rage burning inside her. Her prey would soon be subject to that rage. She would pay for what she had done.

Celine waited in the darkness, hidden in the corner of the room. She did not wait long before she spied movement on the porch. A figure approached the door, entering it. With no warning, Celine fired a shot from her hands, a fireball designed to stun but not harm her intended victim.

The intended recipient leaned to the side, avoiding it. "Watch it, Celine, those things hurt," he chided.

"Alexander," she groaned, "what are you doing here?"

"Checking on you. Gray texted me about what happened. Celine, now isn't the time to confront your sister. Michael needs you."

Celine crossed her arms, her face set, determined not to be undermined. "You should go. This is between me and my sister."

"Celine…"

"I don't want to hear it, Alexander. I am furious with her."

"I understand but now isn't the time to act rashly. You should focus on Michael."

"I am focused on Michael. I'm focused on ensuring that he won't be attacked again."

"She's your sister, Celine. Please, let's go, cool off, deal with her when you're rational."

"When I'm rational? Careful, Alexander, or you'll be next on my list," Celine warned.

"Celine…" Alexander began. Celine silenced him, holding one finger in the air, cocking her head to listen.

"Too late," she whispered as Celeste approached the house. She entered the doorway as Celine tossed a fireball her way. Alexander tipped her arm as she launched it, throwing her aim off, allowing Celeste to escape the attack. Celine growled in protest, launching another, this time hitting her mark. Celeste, however, was prepared, firing one back at her sister, knocking her back a step.

"I still have my powers, too, Celine, despite what you turned me into."

Celine held her hand in front of her, initiating a continual attack. Her sister returned fire. The room lit up in a dazzling light show as the two women continued their respective assaults.

"Ladies, please!" Alexander shouted. "This is getting us nowhere."

"What did you expect her to do when you told her?" Celeste asked, breaking off her attack along with Celine.

Celine's eyebrows raised. "When you told me?" Celine questioned. "You knew?"

"Oh my," Celeste said, cackling, "you didn't tell her? Tsk, tsk, Alexander, you'll now be on my sister's naughty list, too."

Celine tossed a quick fireball at Celeste, knocking her onto her backside. "Be quiet, Celeste, no one is speaking to you." She turned her gaze back to Alexander. "How long have you known?"

"Yes, Celine, I was aware. I've known for a few days. I attempted to reason with Celeste first, hoping she would realize the error of her ways and this could be avoided. When that didn't work, I planned to tell you. We planned to tell you tomorrow morning," Alexander explained.

"We?" Celine questioned.

"Oh, yes, your precious Damien knows, too," Celeste said, standing and brushing herself off.

"I said shut up, Celeste," Celine snapped, knocking her down again.

"You know, Celine," she said, standing again, "that is really getting tiresome."

"Damien spotted Celeste and Michael together," Alexander explained. "He innocently assumed they were having an affair. He was devastated and very concerned about the effect it would have on you, Celine. He came to me. I realized the true extent of what was happening and attempted to curb it before it continued. We had no luck. Don't be angry with him, Celine, he didn't want to hurt you."

"How touching," Celeste said. "He's nearly as saintly as you are, Celine."

Celine let out a cry as she lunged through the air at Celeste. She pounced on her like a cat on a mouse, pinning her down. "Get off of me!" Celeste shouted, trying to free herself but failing. The foundations of the house rumbled as Celine's anger penetrated every surface of the structure.

"You were asked to stop and refused?!" she shrieked. "You realized I'd find out! You didn't care! This wasn't an accident, you continued it even after you were warned to stop!"

"Celine, please!" Alexander put a hand on her arm, trying to pull her away. Celine squealed, shaking his arm off and blowing him against the far wall while maintaining her grip on Celeste.

"Remember, sister dear, you made me what I am," Celeste said through clenched teeth, doing her best to hold her own against Celine.

A tear rolled down Celine's cheek. She held her sister down a moment longer before unhanding her and standing with a sigh. Alexander, now recovered, placed his hand on her shoulder. "Let's go, Celine."

"Wait," Celeste said. "When it started, Celine, it was a chance meeting. He was at the wrong place at the wrong time, nothing more. I didn't pick him, it wasn't deliberate. Yes, I continued. It was easy."

Celine wiped the tear from her cheek. "You almost killed him, Celeste."

"I'm sorry for that. I didn't mean for it to happen. In fact, I don't know how it happened. I was careful."

Celine remained silent for a moment. She turned and approached Celeste. "Never harm a member of my family or one of my friends again, Celeste. I will not tolerate it. Do not push me on this," she warned. She turned on a heel and exited the house into the cool night air. Alexander followed her.

They walked in silence for a moment. "I'm sorry, Celine," Alexander admitted, breaking the silence.

Celine stopped walking. "It's not your fault, Alexander. I'm sorry about what happened. My anger got the better of me."

"No harm done. Although your powers seem stronger than ever," Alexander said, chuckling. "That last one stung!"

"Sorry." Celine shook her head. "I was so angry, but Celeste is correct. This is my fault."

"It's not, Celine."

"I made her this way."

"You saved her from death. You revived her. She is alive because of you."

"But I made her what she is. Her actions are my responsibility."

"Her actions are her responsibility, not yours. You did nothing more than save your sister."

"I need to find a solution. Figure out how to restore her to what she was, she can't continue like this."

"Correction, WE need to find a solution, Celine."

Celine gave him a half-smile. "Thanks," she said, hugging him and wiping another tear that had escaped her eye. "I should get back."

"I'll come with you. We will need to be on constant watch, guarding Michael. I can help."

"Thanks," Celine answered. Together, they started down the path. As they turned on to the path leading to the main house, Celine stopped dead in her tracks.

"Is something wrong?" Alexander asked.

Celine did not answer. She stared straight ahead, her forehead crinkling and a pained look crossing her face. She gasped, grabbing her head.

"Celine?" he inquired again. "Are you all right?"

The sensation passed and Celine recovered. "Yes," she answered. "Sorry, just a strange feeling."

"Strange feeling?"

"Yes. It's the second time it's happened. Within an instant, a memory will pop into my mind. When it happens, a pain shoots across my head. It's odd, I've never experienced this before. Well, not as me. Josie experienced painful memories when my memories were integrating with hers."

"Painful memories? You said this is the second time?"

"Yes."

"What were the memories?"

"The last time, it was Celeste dead, the confrontation on the beach just after I turned into what I am and Celeste the night we banished Marcus."

"And this time?"

"Celeste introducing me to Marcus for the first time."

"Hmm." Alexander reflected. "Perhaps your worry for Celeste is becoming physical."

"Yes, perhaps. I can't figure out what else it would be. I've never experienced this before, but that makes sense. Anyway," Celine said, waving concern away, "it's passed now, I'm fine. Let's get back to the house."

"If you're sure you are all right, we'll continue."

"I'm sure, thanks."

CHAPTER 11

"*A* what?!" Damien exclaimed. "Are you serious? Is he serious?" he asked, turning to Millie.

"Yes, I'm serious. Why do you always ask that? Have I ever not been serious?" Gray asked.

"I'm just... I can't... I don't..." Damien stuttered.

Gray rolled his eyes again, guiding Damien to the armchair in the room. "Sit down before you pass out. Millie, perhaps we should give him something for his nerves."

"All right," Millie agreed, reaching into her bag.

"Hey, wait a minute, no way! You're not drugging me!" Damien shouted, leaping from the chair.

Gray sighed. "Fine, I'll wait for Celine to do it."

"Celine..." Damien mused aloud. "Where did she go? Why isn't she here?" Michael's breath increased, becoming ragged. "Is he okay?"

Millie checked Michael's pulse, listened to his heart. She touched his forehead and cheeks. "He's feverish," she reported.

"Is that normal? Is he getting worse?" Damien queried.

"Quite normal," Millie informed him. "It's good news. It

means he's fighting. The next twenty-four to forty-eight hours are critical. We must keep him resting and quiet."

"I'll stay with him," Gray assured Millie.

"Good. I'll check in every few hours. Alert me if there are any changes."

"Keep him resting? I doubt he'll be able to move with the state he's in!" Damien cried.

"Victims of vampires often exhibit surprising energy at the most unexpected moment. He'll be compelled to seek..." Gray began.

"I can't believe this," Damien blurted out, "I just can't believe he's been bitten by a vampire." He shook his head. "Wow. His affair with Celeste seems so trivial now. I wonder if she knows... oh, I wonder if she was with him when it happened? I wonder if she's hurt! What if they were together?"

"His affair with Celeste?" Gray asked, incredulous.

"Yes." Damien hung his head. "I caught them meeting a few nights ago. I didn't say anything. Well, I told Alexander, but no one else. I didn't want to hurt Celine. But now, oh." He groaned. "Her sister could be hurt because I said nothing. Oh, this is all my fault!" Damien panicked.

"Damien, Damien," Gray said, grabbing him by the shoulders, "calm down. You don't understand..."

"No, you don't understand. I understand. That's the point. A vampire is on the loose and attacked Michael! He's been meeting with Celeste. Every night, in fact! She could have been with him."

"Celeste was with him," Gray answered.

"We have to go search for her! She may be hurt, dying, or worse!" Damien tried to wriggle from Gray's grasp.

"Damien," Gray said, tightening his grip. "Celeste isn't hurt."

"What? How are you sure?" Damien asked, confused.

"Because Celeste is the vampire."

Damien's eyes grew wide. "No," he disputed, "no, she's... she's... like Celine, isn't she?" He wandered away from Gray, contemplating the latest shock.

Gray opened his mouth to explain but Celine's return interrupted him.

"How is he?" she inquired as she burst through the door. Alexander followed her.

"Holding his own," Millie answered. "Feverish, but he didn't need a blood transfusion, and we were able to stop the bleeding from the wounds."

"Thank God," Celine answered. She eyed Damien, who stood frozen across the room. "Is he all right?" she asked Gray.

"More or less," Gray answered. "He's just learned there are vampires and discovered Celeste is one."

Celine closed the distance between them, drawing him into an embrace. "Are you okay?" she asked Damien.

"I... I guess so." He shrugged. "I don't understand anything but I'm okay. You don't need to put me under your magic sleep or anything."

Celine grinned at him. "We'll talk, I'll try to explain everything. Just let me sit with Michael for a bit, okay?"

"Sure," Damien agreed, returning her smile. He glanced to Michael.

"He'll be okay, D," Celine assured him. "We'll make sure he's okay." Damien nodded to her. "Meet you in your room in a bit?"

"I'll sit with him for a little while, too. I'll keep you company," Damien suggested.

"Okay," Celine said.

"Want me to stay?" Gray asked.

"No, I'll be all right. I'll take first watch, although I doubt Celeste will bother him now. Hopefully, he'll be able to rest.

Can you wait with him for a moment while I grab a cardigan though?"

"Sure."

"Thanks, Gray," Celine answered. "D will stay with me for now." Celine approached Alexander. "Thanks for walking me back."

"You're welcome, Celine," Alexander answered. "I'll stay here tonight. You'll need the extra help to ensure Michael recovers."

"Thank you," she said, hugging him.

Celine left the room, leaving the men alone with Millie and Michael. Gray glanced to Alexander. "What happened?"

"She didn't kill her, she came close, but she didn't," he answered.

Gray shook his head. "Why would Celeste be so stupid?"

Alexander shrugged. "It seems it began with convenience rather than being intentional."

"What changed Celine's mind, she was furious when she left here."

"You know Celeste, she knows how to manipulate Celine. Celeste blamed Celine, told her it was Celine that made her this way."

Gray shut his eyes, shaking his head. "That's not true, but I'm sure it struck at Celine's heart."

"It had the intended effect, yes," Alexander admitted. "Celine is carrying a tremendous amount of guilt about what Celeste has become."

"She's been searching for a solution since it happened, we haven't found one yet," Gray said.

"Was I the only one unaware of what was happening?" Damien inquired.

Alexander smiled at him. "I'm sorry, Damien. I didn't keep it from you on purpose, but I didn't want to be the one to tell you."

"Wow, I must have looked like a complete idiot when we made our appeal to Michael and Celeste."

"No, not at all. Everything you said still fit the situation, despite it not being an affair," Alexander answered him.

"You confronted them?" Gray asked.

"Yes, I spoke with Celeste. When that didn't work, Damien insisted we speak with both of them, one last ditch effort before we told Celine."

Gray nodded to Damien. "Wow. I'm very impressed."

"Anything for Celine," Damien answered. "I didn't want her to be hurt."

"Celine is lucky to have you," Gray answered.

"Thanks. Well, I'm lucky to have her, too."

Celine entered the room, pulling on her cardigan. "Okay, I'll take the first watch with D."

"I'll check back in a few hours, switch with you," Gray said.

"Thanks," Celine answered. "How is he, Millie?"

"Holding his own," she answered. "I'll be in my room, wake me at once if anything changes."

"Will do," Celine answered.

Gray, Alexander and Millie left the room, leaving Damien and Celine alone to stay with Michael. Celine wandered to the bed, perching on the edge, taking Michael's hand in hers. She gazed at him. "I'm sorry," she whispered.

Damien placed his hands on her shoulders, giving them a rub. "It's not your fault," he said.

"It is," Celine answered, glancing at Damien. "I made her the way she is."

Damien cocked his head, not understanding what she meant. "Wasn't she like you before you were... you know, like you?"

"Yes, she was. But when she... the night I brought her back, she became what she is now. It was my mistake, I was sloppy. I've been trying to find a solution, but I haven't found one yet."

"To turn her normal again? I mean, not normal, like you. Not that you're not normal, but…" Damien babbled.

Celine held up a hand to stop him. "Yes, normal, for us." She turned back to face Michael. "I never expected she would do this to Michael or anyone in this house, though."

"So, this explains the attacks in town?" Damien inquired.

"Yes. That was problematic enough. I was searching for a solution, but at least those were contained incidents. She never attacked the same person twice."

"Why?"

"She's smart, at least I assumed she was. If she kills someone with one of her attacks, intentionally or not, we'll have another vampire on our hands."

"Oh, wow, really?"

"Yes, which is why it's vital we keep Michael alive."

"Poor Michael, yeah. I understand." They sat for a few moments in silence, Damien sinking to sit on the other side of the bed. "Do you suspect Celeste will come back for him?"

"It's hard to say. I'd like to say no, but if she becomes desperate enough, she may. The larger danger lies in his need for her."

"What do you mean?" Damien questioned.

"It's difficult to explain, but Michael will feel drawn to her, even if she isn't calling to him. As much as she needs blood from him, he longs to be with her, too. As much as you try to, preventing them from seeking out their host can be tricky."

"But seeing her again could be deadly!"

"Yes, reasoning with him will be impossible. That's why we need someone to be with him 24/7. We must make sure he stays here."

Damien nodded. "I'll help." He reached across to hold Celine's hand. "We're a team, remember?"

Celine smiled at him. "Thanks, D."

The pair stayed with Michael until two in the morning. Gray and Alexander took over, allowing Celine and Damien, in particular, to rest. Celine promised to stay with Damien so he could get some sleep. He was concerned he wouldn't be able to fall asleep given all the excitement. With Celine in the room, he was asleep in minutes.

When he awoke, a note lay on his night table from Celine explaining she was checking on Michael. Damien leapt from bed, changing his clothes and racing to Michael's room.

He tapped on the door before poking his head inside. Gray and Celine were waiting inside, Celine leaned over Michael, pressing a cloth against his head. "Hey," Damien whispered, "how is he?"

"Hey, D," Celine said, "come in. He's okay. He's been a little restless, but he hasn't woken up yet. He's still a little feverish."

"Is that normal?"

"That he hasn't woken? Yes," Gray answered, "and perhaps for the best. He isn't as much of a danger to himself if he's asleep."

Damien nodded.

"How did you sleep?" Celine asked.

"Like the dead, I mean..." Shock crossed his face. "I slept well is what I mean."

"Did you eat?"

"No. I came to check on Michael first. I can stay with him for a while," Damien offered.

"Get something to eat first, D."

"I'm okay," Damien answered. Celine raised an eyebrow at him. He held up his hands. "Okay, okay. I'll grab some breakfast then come back up!"

Celine nodded to him, smiling. "Why don't you go with him?" Gray suggested. "The sun's almost up, he should rest comfortably now."

Celine paused a moment before answering. Millie joined them in the room. "How's the patient?" she asked.

"He had a good night," Celine answered. "He was restless about half an hour ago, but he's settled now."

Millie checked his vital signs. "Still feverish, although I'm not surprised. All things considered, his progress is good."

"Good," Celine answered.

"On that note, you two should go for breakfast," Gray suggested to Celine and Damien.

"Oh, yes, please go, I'll stay with Gray and Michael for a bit," Millie assured them. "I'd like to do a more comprehensive exam."

"Okay," Celine agreed. Alexander joined them before they left for their morning meal. Everyone greeted each other, discussing Michael's condition for a moment longer before Celine and Damien departed.

"Millie, you should get some breakfast, too. Alex and I can hold down the fort."

"All right, if you don't mind."

"Not at all," Gray assured her.

"I'll return after breakfast to check on him," Millie said, excusing herself from the room.

"He hasn't awoken yet?" Alexander inquired when Millie left.

"No, other than some restless moaning just before daybreak, he's been quiet."

"I hope the trend continues."

"So do I. Celine doesn't need his health or lack thereof on her conscience."

"Yes, she has enough on her mind."

"I quite agree. I wonder if the magnitude of what's weighing on her is causing these painful memories."

"Painful memories?" Gray asked.

"Yes, she may not have had the chance to tell you with everything that's happened. The only reason I am aware is because I was with her last night when one occurred."

"Tell me more about it."

"She said it was the second she had. Both involved traumatic moments with Celeste and the Duke. She said pain shoots across her head when she experiences them, but it passes within moments. She told me she experienced something similar as Josie when her memories were integrating, but never as Celine."

"No, I don't recall her ever experiencing anything like that, but I recall her describing something similar when she was Josie. She's taking everything onto herself, as usual. It's taking a toll."

"I'm sure this incident adds to it."

"No doubt. I will speak with her about it. I don't want her suffering alone again like she did years ago."

"Please remind her I am here for her, as well," Alexander requested.

"I will. It helps to have her family here. Damien helps, despite her feeling responsible for him and his safety."

"He cares for her, too. He was so very concerned about her learning about Celeste and Michael. We planned to tell her this morning. I was hoping she would find out when Celeste was 'resting.' We were trying to avoid what happened last night."

"Good plan, too bad it didn't work out," Gray answered.

"Yes, it is unfortunate. But perhaps now we'll be able to stop the situation."

"Let's hope so. For all of our sakes. Have you found

anything that could be helpful in restoring Celeste to her rightful state?"

"I have found little. A few vague references, nothing concrete."

"Damn. Celine and I both researched it and haven't found a solution yet either."

"We'll keep searching. This is only temporary."

"Even temporary, it is causing enough problems."

"Yes, I agree. Especially for poor Michael."

CHAPTER 12

*G*ray and Alexander stayed with Michael for most of the morning. Celine and Damien checked in multiple times, but Celine insisted Damien get a little more rest. In the afternoon, Avery along with Charlotte and Alexander continued to monitor Michael's progress. For most of the day, he remained quiet and resting. Still feverish, he experienced a few bouts of restlessness and pain. Millie checked in often, administering pain medication and changing bandages as needed.

As evening approached, Celine and Damien relieved Avery, Charlotte and Alexander. Gray promised to join them later. Both of them opted to eat a light dinner in Michael's room. Damien's concern grew since Michael had not yet awoken. In the middle of their dinner, Michael groaned, opening his eyes. Each of them dropped their sandwiches to rush to Michael.

"Michael?" Celine asked, taking his hand in hers.

"Hey, buddy," Damien said, "how are you feeling?"

Michael moaned in pain. "It's okay," Celine said. "D, can you get Millie?"

"Sure," Damien said, hurrying to leave the room.

"Michael, can you hear me?" Celine asked again as Damien began to exit the room. He didn't respond for a moment, glancing between Celine and Damien. "It's okay. You're in your room. You collapsed last night. Millie was able to stop the bleeding from your neck. You're going to be okay." She placed her palm on his forehead. He was still warm. Beads of perspiration were forming, so she hoped his fever was breaking.

Millie entered the room with Damien. "I see the patient is awake," she said, grabbing her stethoscope and blood pressure cuff.

"He hasn't spoken yet, but I explained to him what's happened," Celine reported. She stood, stepping back to allow Millie full access to Michael. Damien put his arm on her shoulder. Both of them waited in anticipation to hear Millie's findings.

"All right, Michael. How are you feeling?" Millie asked, listening to his heart before taking his blood pressure. She shined a light in his eyes and took his temperature. She also checked his bandage and wounds.

"I feel…" Michael began.

"Yes?" Millie asked.

"Tired, weak," he muttered just above a whisper.

"That's to be expected. You lost a lot of blood and we almost lost you. But you're recovering well. You still have a slight fever. Your wounds appear to be healing. Your blood pressure is slightly low but nothing to worry about. Your heart rate is good. Given the circumstances, you're doing well."

Celine squeezed Damien's hand. The news was good. Millie said the first forty-eight hours were the most critical. They were almost through twenty-four with signs of improvement. Michael was still pale and weak, but he was recovering. They needed to remain vigilant to ensure there were no setbacks.

"You should try to rest more, Michael," Millie instructed. "You're not out of the woods yet."

Michael's forehead crinkled. "Are you in pain?" Millie asked.

"No. What time is it?" Michael inquired.

"It's close to seven thirty in the evening," Millie responded.

"Is it dark?" Michael asked, his voice rising to a higher pitch.

"Michael," Celine said, circling the bed to sit down on the opposite side and side-stepping the question, "you need to rest. Don't worry about that now."

"Is it?" he insisted, becoming perturbed.

"Yeah, it's already dark," Damien answered.

Michael groaned, pushing himself to sit up. "Whoa, whoa," Celine said, holding his shoulders, trying to ease him back into bed. "You need to rest."

"No, no, I need to go."

"Michael, you cannot go. You are far too weak," Millie told him.

"Get off of me!" Michael said, trying to shake Celine's hands from his shoulders, a haunted look in his eyes. "I need to go to her."

"No, you don't," Celine insisted. "Michael, she doesn't want to see you. She isn't calling to you."

"No, that's not true!" Michael exclaimed, anger in his voice. "You're lying. I need to go to her."

"Hey, buddy," Damien said, approaching the bed. "You're way too sick to go anywhere. Just rest."

Michael grunted, pushing Celine away. He threw the covers off, crawling from the bed, unsteady on his feet. "Michael, stop!" Celine yelled. To Damien she said, "Get

STOLEN PORTRAIT STOLEN SOUL

Gray."

Damien nodded, racing from the room. Celine grabbed Michael around the shoulders. He shoved her aside, taking a few tentative steps to the door. Celine grasped his shirt, pulling him back. "No!" he shouted. They struggled for a moment before he managed to escape her grip, knocking her onto her backside. Millie, who had filled a syringe with a sedative, approached him. He batted at her, trying to evade her. She was unable to stick him with the needle. "Leave me alone!" he shouted as he made a run for the door.

Still on the floor, Celine flung her hand in Michael's direction, hurling a small fireball his way. It struck him square in the back, knocking him forward into the closed door. Celine sprung to her feet, ready to blast him again, if needed. Gray and Damien sprinted into the room. Celine pointed to Michael. "He's there, get him back in bed."

Gray grabbed hold of Michael, struggling to get him upright. Damien assisted and together they returned him to his bed. Michael struggled but could not free himself from the two men's grasps.

"Hold him down, I'll give him a sedative," Millie directed. She stuck the needle into his arm, pressing the plunger down to deliver the narcotic. The fast-acting formula accomplished its goal, putting Michael to sleep within moments. His struggling ceased, his eyes closing, his body going limp.

Everyone breathed a sigh of relief as Michael slipped back to sleep. "How could he make it that far?" Damien inquired once the emergency was over.

"Vampire victims can exhibit surprising surges of energy and strength when they sense the need to get to their hosts," Gray answered.

Celine nodded. "We couldn't give him the sedative before he made a run for the door."

"I'm surprised you managed to stop him," Gray said.

"I had to use a rather extreme tactic," Celine admitted.

Gray raised an eyebrow, a smirk crossing his face. "You didn't..." he said.

Celine, a wry expression on her face, nodded. "Yes, I'm afraid I had to blast him. Just once, just a small one."

"Blast him?" Damien asked.

Celine approached the window, opening it, and tossed a fireball out. "Ohhhh," Damien said, realization dawning on him. "Really? Does that hurt?"

"Oh, yeah, they hurt!" Gray said. "Especially for a human."

"I didn't want to do it!" Celine exclaimed. "He left me no choice!"

"I don't blame you. It would take that much to stop someone intent on getting to their host."

"Remind me never to tick you off, Celine," Damien said. "Why didn't you use your magic sleeping trick?"

"I couldn't get a good enough hold on him to try. He was intent on getting to Celeste."

Millie checked Michael's pulse. "He seems to be asleep for now," Millie said.

"Good," Celine said. "Why don't you finish your dinner, Millie. We should be fine now."

"If you're sure," Millie said. "I'll check back after I've finished."

"We're sure. I'll stay, too, Millie, just in case," Gray said.

"Great. I'll check back after dinner. Alert me if there are any changes." Millie departed on her way back to the dining room.

"Whew, I can't believe you blasted him," Gray chuckled.

"I can't believe he needed it," Damien said. "I didn't realize how much of a danger to himself he'd be."

Celine shook her head, not as amused. "We have to do something. This will not stop."

"There's not much we can do, Celine," Gray said. "We've

found nothing. I spoke with Alexander, he found nothing new either. The best we can do now is keep an eye on him. Make sure he makes a full recovery and doesn't find his way back to Celeste. Although she may think twice before she uses him again." Celine stood in silence, arms crossed, staring at Michael. "Celine, you must let this go. We're doing all we can. We'll keep looking for a solution, but you can't let this eat you up."

"I'm not. Just because I want to find a solution sooner rather than later doesn't mean it's eating me up."

"You are. Alexander told me about the painful visions you've been having. You can't keep doing this to yourself."

"Painful visions?" Damien questioned.

Celine rolled her eyes. "Yes, she's been having physical symptoms and visions, memories," Gray said.

"I was planning to tell you, but it only happened once. It didn't seem that important. Then it happened again last night while Alexander and I were together."

"What's causing it?" Damien asked.

"I'm not sure. I've never experienced this before. At least not as me. I suffered something similar when I was Josie. As my memories started to return and integrate with Josie's, they would come in snippets and they'd often be painful. But I haven't experienced this with my own memories."

"What are the memories?" Damien inquired.

"The first time it was of my argument with Celeste and Marcus on the beach that dreadful night, Celeste dead and Celeste leading Marcus to the beach ceremony when we banished him. The second was only one memory. It was Celeste introducing me to Marcus."

"This is what I mean," Gray insisted, "you're twisting yourself in knots over Celeste."

"I'm fine, Gray."

"Are you sure? This doesn't seem normal," Damien contended.

Gray raised his eyebrows at her. "See, even the human doesn't think it's normal."

Celine shook her head at them. "I'm fine. We need to be more worried about protecting Michael as he recovers." She wandered to the bed, perching on the edge and taking Michael's hand. "And finding a solution for Celeste."

* * *

Celine, Damien and Gray spent the first part of the night with Michael. He was quiet, able to rest under sedation. They turned in around midnight for a few hours of sleep, relieved by Millie and Alexander. Celine was up early, as was Damien. After breakfast, they went for a stroll together. Avery and Charlotte were with Michael since the least amount of danger existed during the daylight hours.

They paused at the gazebo, deciding to spend some time enjoying the view. They sat in silence for half an hour, appreciating the other's company with no need for conversation.

After a while, Celine took hold of Damien's hand. "How are you holding up?" she questioned.

"I'm okay. Better than you, it seems."

"I'm fine, I told you that."

"Can I help in any way?"

"You're already doing it. For me and for Michael," she said, smiling at him.

"Speaking of, we should probably go back to the house. Make sure everything is okay."

"Yeah," Celine agreed. "Let's take the scenic route, though, through the woods. Avery and Charlotte should be okay for another hour."

"Sounds good to me!"

They departed the gazebo, leaving the peaceful coastal view behind, trekking into the wooded area of the property. The trees closed in around them, enveloping them in a pocket of deciduous and fir trees. They sauntered along, letting the fresh air ease their minds.

Celine froze. "What is it?" Damien asked.

She shook her head. Damien glanced around. "What?" he asked again.

Celine doubled over, crying out in pain, grabbing her head. "Celine!" Damien shouted. She panted with pain, groaning. After a moment, she swallowed hard, taking several deep breaths.

"I'm okay," she said. She grabbed his hand, steadying herself as she stood. "I'm all right."

"What happened?"

"Another of those painful memories."

"Of Celeste again?"

"She was involved, yes. It was a memory of an argument between myself, Teddy, Celeste and Marcus. It occurred soon after the night in the caves. THE night."

"You mean 'that night?'" he said.

"Yes."

"What do you suppose is causing them?"

Celine shook her head. "I'm not sure. Just before this one occurred; I had a strange sensation. Like someone was watching us."

Damien glanced around again. "I didn't see or hear anyone."

"Neither did I," Celine admitted. "Let's get back to the house."

"Sure," Damien agreed. They increased their pace, taking as direct a path as they could to the house. "Perhaps you should lie down," Damien suggested as they entered the house.

"I'm fine. I'm going to check on Michael." Celine climbed the stairs, leaving Damien behind, shaking his head.

"Everything okay?" Gray asked, entering the foyer.

Damien stared after Celine's disappearing form. "She had another one of those painful vision things while we were walking."

"Another one?"

"Yeah, she said she felt like someone was watching her then had the painful memory. She insists she's okay, but what's causing this?"

"I don't know. She's never experienced anything like this as Celine. No matter how vexing the circumstances, no matter how upsetting, nothing like this has ever happened."

"Perhaps because she feels responsible this time?"

"She's always felt responsible. The Duke chased her around the globe. Any danger that any of us were in she deemed was her fault. This isn't much different."

Damien sighed. "Another mystery. The painting, the painful visions, fixing Celeste. How do you deal with this continual bombardment of turmoil?"

Gray chuckled, heading upstairs to check on Celine. "You get used to it. And it is easier when you're not human."

CHAPTER 13

"*H*ello, Aunt Celine!" Avery said as Celine entered Michael's room. "Look who's awake!"

Several pillows propped Michael up in bed. A tray balanced on his lap, almost empty now. His coloring had improved, he was no longer deathly pale.

"Hey!" Celine said, smiling at him. "It's good to see you awake."

"And eating!" Charlotte chimed in. "He's had two eggs, toast, bacon and some orange juice. Quite a hearty breakfast! Very good for his recovery."

"Sounds like it!" Celine answered. "How are you feeling?"

"A little better," Michael answered.

"Has Millie examined him yet?" she asked Charlotte and Avery.

"Yes, she's very pleased with his progress," Charlotte answered, beaming.

"Are you finished?" Avery asked Michael. He nodded in return. "I'll take the tray down. I'll be back later, we'll play that card game I promised you."

"Thanks," he said, smiling at her. Avery gathered his tray

to return to the kitchen. Gray and Damien entered just as she was ready to leave.

"I think I'll excuse myself, too, if you will be here for a bit," Charlotte said. "There are several things that require my attention. I can relieve you later this afternoon."

"Of course, Char," Gray answered, "we can stay for a while."

Charlotte excused herself from the room, leaving Michael alone with Celine, Gray and Damien. Damien was thrilled to see Michael awake, eating and appearing to improve.

"Hey, buddy!" he said, plopping on the bed. "It's good to see you awake. Your situation was touch and go for the past few days."

"Yeah, it's good to be awake. And sorry about last night," Michael said, shaking his head.

"Don't worry about it, you weren't yourself," Celine said, perching on the bed.

The four spent the rest of the morning and most of the afternoon enjoying each other's company. Celine seemed to be fine, experiencing no more painful visions. Michael talked and laughed like his old self. Damien, relieved at the upturn in Michael's health, relaxed, crossing his fingers that one issue may resolve itself. Avery joined them in the mid-afternoon, bringing cards for a card game she had promised Michael to pass the time. The afternoon acted as a much-needed stress-reliever for everyone.

As evening approached, Celine and Gray remained vigilant for any signs of change in Michael's demeanor. All seemed well as the sun lowered in the sky. Avery excused herself for dinner, leaving the rest of the group to dine with Michael. None of them were ready to leave his side yet.

As evening rolled to night, Damien was encouraged, confident Michael was on the upswing in his recovery. They played another hand of their card game. Halfway through the round, Michael began shifting around, seeming uncomfortable. Damien asked him if he was becoming tired or in any pain. He didn't respond. In another instant, his demeanor changed. He became restless, agitated and distressed.

"Michael, are you okay?" Damien asked.

Michael pushed back the covers. "I have to go," he mumbled.

"No, no, you can't do that," Damien said, standing and grabbing him by the arm. Gray assisted, grasping his other arm.

"No!" he shouted, struggling against them. "She needs me, I have to go."

Celine attempted to soothe him to sleep, however his violent thrashing wouldn't allow her to.

"Get Millie," Gray said. Celine was already at the door. As she opened it to exit, she found Alexander outside.

"Celine, Celeste is in the sitting room insisting on seeing you. I asked her to leave, but she was resolute in staying until you spoke with her. I'll stay with Michael."

Celine shook her head. "He's agitated, she's too close. Get Millie, he needs a sedative."

"Don't worry, I'll handle it," Alexander assured her.

"Thanks," Celine said, nodding at him. "I'll try to get rid of Celeste. That should help, too."

They went in opposite directions, each on their own mission. Celine descended the main staircase and crossed the foyer. She pushed open the doors into the sitting room. Celeste sat on the loveseat.

"Really, Celeste? Are you trying to kill him?" Celine asked, closing the doors behind her.

"You'd never come if I sent for you, so I had to come here."

"Are you trying to make this worse for Michael?"

"No. I realize my presence is disturbing Michael. How is he?"

"Alive, no thanks to you."

"I'm sorry. I didn't intend to kill him."

"What you intended and what occurred are two different things, Celeste."

Celeste dropped her eyes to the floor. "Well, I won't keep you, I only came to ensure he was all right." She walked to the door. Turning back, she said, "I truly didn't mean to harm him. I quite like him. I'm sorry, Celine."

Celine sighed. "It's not your fault, Celeste, it's mine. And other than a compelling urge to get to you, he's doing okay. He's awake, alert. He's recovering."

Celeste offered a slight smile. "I'm glad. I don't blame you, Celine. You saved me. I'd be dead without you, and likely not in a very nice place. I should have been more responsible. I can't help my cravings, but I should have avoided Michael."

Celine moved to her sister, wrapping her in an embrace. "I'm searching for a solution. We all are. We haven't found it yet. But we will."

"Yes, I realize how hard you're working, and I appreciate it. Don't worry, sister dear, I'll be all right." Celeste pushed a lock of Celine's hair behind her ear. "I'll be more responsible."

Celine offered her another hug. "I'll check in with you in the next day or so. This time I'll visit you." Celine winked.

"Deal," Celeste agreed.

Celine threaded her arm through Celeste's. "I'll walk you out." They walked to the entryway. "Be safe, Celeste," Celine said.

Gray approached Celine as Celeste disappeared through the door. "He's asleep," he reported to her. "What did she want?"

"To check on Michael. Believe it or not, I think she is fond of him and concerned."

"Really?" he questioned.

"Yes," she responded, glancing up at him. "She apologized. So did I. We agreed not to assign blame. We need to find a solution, though. She shouldn't be forced to survive like this."

"I agree. We need a solution and I'm glad to hear you're not blaming each other. I hope you are now willing to stop blaming yourself. Perhaps now these painful visions will stop."

"I hope so. Should we relieve Damien?" Gray nodded, and they made their way to Michael's room. Alexander and Damien were keeping vigil over a now sleeping Michael. After spending a few moments with Michael, Celine and Damien withdrew to his room for the night.

"What did Celeste want?" Damien asked once they were alone.

"To make sure Michael was recovering."

"Really? Guilty much? She almost killed him!"

"Yes, I realize that. And, yes, she is guilty. But I created her in her current form. It's everyone's fault and no one's. It's just a bad situation. We need a plan to resolve it."

"And you haven't found anything yet?"

"No, not yet."

"I can help, just tell me what I'm trying to find. I'll comb every resource I can, investigate everywhere."

"Thanks, D. Thank you for offering to help. I'm not sure you'll have much luck, but if there's anything I need you to explore, I'll tell you right away. For now, you should get some rest. It's been a long day."

Damien yawned. "Yeah, I am tired. I can't believe you don't get tired. That's awesome."

"We get tired, just not the same way and it takes longer."

"Still, that's pretty cool," Damien said, crawling under the covers. "You should sleep, too. Although it makes me feel better you're here."

"It reminds me of when you used to sleep in my room before I remembered who I was. When Gray dropped off that music box. It's nice to return the favor."

Damien smiled at her, yawning again. "Good night, Celine."

"Good night, D."

* * *

Celeste wandered the path across the estate. A powerful urge for blood coursed through her. She detested what she was, but it did nothing to lessen the craving. She had seen her sister earlier. No longer shocked or angry, they had shared a tender moment together. She had vowed to be more responsible. Michael was no longer an option. Still, she needed a victim, willing or unwilling.

She paused, gazing at the horizon. Faint traces of pink were creasing the darkened sky. Her time to satisfy her hunger would end with the impending dawn. She lacked time to search for a victim. Instead, she hurried along the path back to her haven. Her coffin, which kept her safe during the day, was hidden in an abandoned house. A secret room behind a bookcase was a perfect hiding spot. With luck, she would meet someone along the way to relieve her appetite.

As she approached the abandoned house, she spotted a faint glow emanating from inside. "Perfect," she murmured to herself, a smirk crossing her face. "Perhaps my victim has found me."

She rushed toward the house, entering it. The man's shadow loomed in the corner. Any resistance she met with should be no match for her hypnotic powers. She approached the figure. As she closed the gap between them, he stepped forward, revealing not only his identity but an object held in his hands.

The silver cross gleamed in the dim light. It burned her eyes, a searing pain flared through them. Even as she shrunk away, shielding her eyes, she could still envision its imprint in her retinas. A wave of nausea passed through her body and a shudder overtook her whole being.

Celeste sensed the man moving toward her. Her skin crawled as the cross inched closer to her. She smelled the musk of his cologne mixed with the brandy that still lingered on his breath. Hatred burned through her for the man controlling her with the holy object.

She risked a glimpse at the window across the room. Pink streaks were brightening in the sky. Dawn inched closer. If she didn't return to the safety of her coffin soon, the intense pain she experienced now would seem minimal. She attempted to flee but found herself unable to move, as if stuck in quicksand.

Her breathing became labored as she focused her energy on surviving. Her world closed in as her vision narrowed to a pinpoint. "TAKE IT AWAY!" she screamed.

"Oh, Celeste," Duke Marcus Northcott replied, "it's lovely to see you again. But I cannot remove this. Not if I intend to persuade you to my cause."

"Your cause? I would never work for you again." Celeste spat out the words.

"Well then, my dear, I suggest you enjoy this sunrise, because it will be the last one you will ever witness."

Celeste glanced toward the window again. The sky was brightening, pink streaks turning to red and orange as the sun threatened to rise over the horizon. If she wasn't entombed in the safety of her coffin soon, she would die the moment the sunlight touched her skin.

"What is it you want?" she asked through clenched teeth.

"Nothing yet, my dear, nothing yet. But soon." He approached Celeste, reaching to caress her cheek. "Soon, I'll want something from you. Something… special. Something only you can provide."

She shrunk away from his touch. "And if I refuse?"

"If you refuse now, or later, you shall find no way to return to your coffin. In essence, my dear, you shall sentence yourself to death."

"And if I accept? What is it you'll demand from me?"

"Let's not trouble ourselves with the details now, my dear," he said, motioning toward the window, "you have little time. I recommend you hide yourself away."

Celeste considered the proposal. She hated to be beholden to the Duke, but he was correct. To refuse sentenced her to death. She had no choice. For the moment, she must give in. "Fine," she conceded, "you have your favor, now stand aside."

"Of course, Celeste!" He pocketed the cross, striding to the door. He turned back before departing. "Oh, Celeste, don't tell Celine I'm back. I'd hate to ruin the surprise for her." He turned on his heel and strode out of the house.

CHAPTER 14

*C*eline startled awake, gasping for breath. She glanced around the room, getting her bearings. She was in Damien's room; she had fallen asleep in the chair near the window. Damien was still asleep in his bed. Celine let her heart settle back to normal speed. Her breathing became normal, her pulse slowed.

She shook her head, recalling the dream. The same dream that plagued her as Josie when her memories were returning. The same dream that plagued her for her entire life. It was the night she became what she was. The night the Duke stole away her innocence. She ran through the caves, book in hand, dress covered in blood, panicked, frightened. The damp walls closed in on her. Marcus followed close behind her. She raced as fast as she could to deliver the book. She woke before she reached the end of the cave, however, she knew this story well. She lived it and despite it being centuries ago; she recalled it like it was yesterday.

She assumed once the Duke was gone these nightmares would cease. They had not. Although, after centuries of torment, dealing with only the nightmares was a vast improvement over dealing with the man. She smiled at Damien asleep. She considered checking on Michael, but she didn't want Damien to wake up alone again. Instead, she waited until he was awake, viewing the morning sunrise through the window of Damien's ocean-facing room. The calm water sparkled as the yellow rays reflected on its surface.

When the yellow glow coursed through the windows, Damien awoke, stretching and yawning. "Good morning," he said to Celine.

"Good morning," she responded. "Did you sleep well?"

"I did, how about you? Did you get any sleep?"

"Yes, I did," she answered.

"But?" he asked, sensing there was more.

"But nothing, I was just watching the sunrise," she fibbed.

"Hmm," he answered. Before he continued, a knock sounded at the door. "Come in!" he yelled.

Gray poked his head in. "Good morning! Did I wake you?"

"No, we were up," Celine answered. "How's Michael?"

"He's okay. Millie's with him now. He's been restless since Celeste was here. She's been continuing the sedatives to keep him quiet."

Celine was already out of her chair. "Really? Why didn't you wake me?"

"I figured I'd let you two rest. Alexander and I had it under control."

Damien also bounded out of bed, changing into his clothes. "He's still restless even after sunrise?"

"Yes. He's can't seem to relax. Keeps rambling on about Celeste needing him."

"Let me change clothes and I'll meet you there," Celine said, heading down the hallway to their room.

Within a few minutes, she returned to Michael's room,

joining Millie, Gray and Damien. Michael flailed his arms at her. "Finally! Perhaps you will listen to me!"

Celine hurried to his bedside, perching on the edge. "Of course, I'll listen. What is it, Michael?"

"I have to go. Celeste needs me. She's in trouble, she needs my help."

"She was here last night. She is okay, I spoke with her. She was worried about you and how your recovery was going. She wanted to ensure you were okay. You need to rest."

"No," Michael insisted, "no, she needs my help!"

"You can't see her now anyway," Celine countered. "The sun has already risen."

"I need to go watch over her, protect her," Michael continued.

Celine shot a glance to Millie, who prepared a needle.

"Tell you what," Celine said, patting Michael's hand, "I'll check on her myself now. And I'll go back tonight and talk to her and make sure she's okay. I'll report back as soon as I can."

Michael shook his head again before spotting Millie's actions. "No!" he shouted, "no more of that. I need to go to Celeste." He struggled, trying to leap from the bed. Alexander caught him, holding him down along with Gray. Damien squeezed between Celine and the night table, also assisting. Celine shimmied back, allowing Millie access to Michael. Within minutes of her administering the latest round of sedative, Michael dozed off.

"He's getting worse, not better," Gray remarked.

"Yes," Celine answered, standing and walking a few steps away, lost in thought. "It's strange."

"Strange?" Damien questioned.

"Yes," Alexander chimed in. "In most cases, vampire victims improve at least a little after being away from them. It's natural he was disturbed when she was near last evening.

But the fact that he's remained so, even after sunrise when she can no longer call to him, is abnormal."

"She can call to him? Like mentally?"

"Yes, she can," Gray answered.

Celine remained pensive. "I will check on Celeste," she said after a moment.

"I'll come with you," Gray offered.

"Okay, thanks. I just want to make sure Michael's not correct. Are you two okay to stay here?" she asked Damien and Alexander.

"Sure! We'll hold down the fort!" Damien said.

"Thanks!" she replied, offering him a hug before leaving the room with Gray.

* * *

Celine sped down the path, Gray followed behind her. "Celine, wait," he called to her.

"I just want to get there," Celine shouted, turning to face him.

"I'm sure she's fine," Gray said, attempting to comfort her.

"Something's wrong, Gray. He's anxious when he shouldn't be."

Gray caught up to her. "It didn't help that she showed up last night. It might be a residual effect."

"Let's hope so, but in the meantime, let's not delay this any longer. Come on." They continued down the path to the abandoned house. As the house came into view, Celine raced toward it. She took the front steps by two, pushing through the front door. She glanced around the room, finding the control for the mechanism to display the secret room. Her sister's daylight haven lay inside. Celine dashed to it as Gray joined her. "Close the door," she instructed to keep the sunlight at bay. Gray closed the opening, toggling on his flashlight. Celine cracked the lid of the casket. Gray shined his light inside. Celeste lay inside, appearing as though she was asleep.

Celine let the lid close, breathing a sigh of relief. Her sister, it appeared, was fine, unharmed and resting during the daylight hours. "I told you she'd be fine. Your sister's like a cat, she's got nine lives," Gray said.

Celine shot him a glance. "Yes, she's fine. Which doesn't explain Michael's continued reaction."

"Check with her tonight, but for now it seems like you can relax for the moment."

Celine nodded. Any more information would have to wait until Celeste was awake after the sun set. She ran her hand across the smooth wood, taking a deep breath. "Stay safe, sister," she murmured. They left the hidden room, careful to close the passage behind them before leaving the house.

"Shall we take a walk before we return to the house?" Celine inquired.

"Sure," Gray agreed. "It's a nice, sunny day. Let's enjoy it a little."

Celine smiled at him; he summarized her opinion perfectly. It had been a while since they had enjoyed a quiet moment together. Celine reached for his hand, he grasped hers, squeezing it. They started off on the path that wound toward the cliffs overlooking the sea. It was a calm, cloudless day. The ocean lapped against the rocks in a gentle motion, the thunderous waves absent today.

They paused at the edge. Gray wrapped Celine in his arms, kissing the top of her head as they enjoyed the view. "It's nice to enjoy this with you," he said.

Celine agreed. Despite all the problems surrounding them, the beauty here had a calming effect. She was content for the moment to leave her problems behind her and indulge in this comforting scenery. "As much as I hate to say this, we should get back," Celine suggested, tilting her head to gaze at Gray.

"Yes, you're right. Although, Michael should still be sleeping."

"Hopefully, but I don't like to leave Damien for too long either."

"You still love him like family. It's nice to see you so happy with your family around."

"This is a first for me. I guess I'm a little overprotective."

Gray grinned at her. "It's a good look on you. Come on, let's get back." He put his arm around her shoulders, and they left the seaside scenery behind.

"Overprotective or not, let's opt for the scenic path through the woods." Celine winked at him.

"Sounds like a plan," Gray answered as they veered onto the path leading deeper into the woods.

The trees closed in around them. Celine took a deep breath of the forest air. Something seemed strange as she breathed in. She slowed to a stop. The hairs on the back of her neck prickled. Her nostrils flared, trying to detect what was different about the smell. Her mind whirled with the sensation of being watched.

"Celine? What is it?" Gray asked.

She doubled over as pain shot across her forehead. Memories flashed across her brain in a blinding mix. Nausea overcame her. She dropped to her knees.

"Celine!" Gray shouted, kneeling beside her. Celine moaned in pain before the sensation began to pass. She gulped air as tears spilled down her cheeks. She grabbed Gray's hand, squeezing it.

"I'm okay," she choked out. "I just need a minute." She took a few more deep breaths as Gray rubbed her back. She wiped the tears from her cheeks as the nausea passed, and the pain subsided. She exhaled, long and hard. "It passed. I'm okay." She breathed another shaky breath.

"What was it, another painful memory?"

"Yes," she answered. "That was the worst of them."

"You okay?"

"Yeah, yeah, I'm okay. It seemed much more intense this time. But as soon as it passes, it's like nothing happened."

"What was the memory?"

"Umm," Celine creased her forehead, remembering. "There were a few, but they were all jumbled. The one that stuck out was an argument we all had soon after I became what I am. Celeste, Teddy, Marcus and I."

"Each memory has been about Celeste, right? You're upset about her. It's manifesting itself physically."

"This has never happened before," Celine answered, climbing to her feet and shaking her head.

"You've never been this worried about your sister before," Gray said, also standing.

Celine nibbled on her lower lip a moment before answering. She shook her head again. "It's far-fetched. I can't imagine it would manifest like this."

"Like I said, you've never worried about her this much."

Celine shot him a glance. "I've been worried before about plenty of people. This has never happened."

"None of them were blood relations."

"It doesn't add up, even with that explanation. Something's wrong."

"Nothing is wrong," Gray said, putting his hands on her shoulders. "Celine, look at me. Nothing is wrong, other than the minor trouble with Celeste, which is eating you alive with guilt. We'll fix it, it's temporary. But nothing is wrong. The Duke is gone, we have nothing to fear."

She sighed. "I just can't shake this feeling."

"Residual effects from the centuries of being pursued and

tormented. You don't remember how to just live with no threats or danger."

"You may be correct," she agreed, relenting to his explanations whether or not she believed them.

"I am. Now, do you feel strong enough to walk?"

She nodded. "I do, I'm fine. Like I said, as soon as it's over it's like nothing happened."

"Then let's get back. We will check on Damien and then you will get some rest. Proper rest, not sleeping in Damien's chair."

"I've been resting."

"Sure you have, and yes, I realize we don't get tired in the traditional sense but we do get run down. You need to rest."

She rolled her eyes at him. "Okay, Dad, I will rest."

"Very funny, Celine."

"I promise I will, just after I check on Damien. Let's go."

* * *

When Celine and Gray returned to the house, they found Michael sleeping with Damien watching over him. Millie's sedative kept him resting. Still, Damien appeared worried, the crease in his forehead deepening by the hour despite Michael's lack of responsiveness.

At Gray's insistence, Celine retired to their suite for a nap in the early afternoon. She laid in bed, staring at the wall. Worry consumed her. Worry for Damien, worry for Michael, worry for Celeste. The anxiety robbed her of any sleep. She rolled onto her back, staring at the ceiling for a fresh perspective.

After another hour, restlessness overcame her, and she rose from her bed. Wandering down the hall, she let herself into Michael's room. Damien still sat at his bedside. Celine slipped her arms around his shoulders in a hug. Damien clasped her arm. They spent the next few minutes in silence.

"How are you holding up?" Celine asked, sitting on the edge of the bed across from Damien.

"Okay, he's been quiet."

Celine offered a half-smile. "That's good, but how are YOU?" she inquired, emphasizing the last word.

He paused a moment before responding. "Okay," he said, his voice rising an octave higher than normal. Celine raised her eyebrows at him without answering. "I'm fine!" Celine tilted her head, continuing to make eye contact. "Doing good. Plagued with worry but good, overall!"

She nodded her head. "Plagued with worry. That sounds about right."

"I'm trying to be okay with this, but…" He paused. "it seems so complicated and like he's getting worse."

Celine grabbed Damien's hand. "It is. It's strange, too. He's improving, physically anyway, but the other symptoms: his restlessness, apprehension, need to be with Celeste, all of that seems to be worse."

"Why?"

"I'm not sure." Celine glanced at Michael, shaking her head. "What a mess I've made."

"Is it the same for Celeste? Would she experience the same thing?"

"No. It's not the same for her. I'll check with her tonight again but she seemed fine. I'm not sure why he thinks she's unsafe and was so concerned earlier."

"Wow, that's not fair, just Michael gets stuck with the bad side effects."

"To be honest, Celeste's got a bad case of side effects, too," she said, grinning at him.

"Good point."

"Any progress on getting her back to normal?"

"No."

"Too bad you can't just wave a magic wand and turn her back. Or a magic finger or whatever you use."

"Sorry, it's not that easy," Celine admitted. "Although…" She paused, thinking.

"Although what?"

"I have an idea. It's not a great idea and it probably won't work, but it's worth a shot."

"What is it?"

Celine glanced at him. "Promise me you'll keep it to yourself."

"Okay?" he said, unsure.

"I mean it, you can't tell anyone."

"Not even Alexander or Gray?"

"No one. It won't be a very popular idea with either of them, especially Gray."

"Okay, sure. I won't tell anyone."

"Promise?"

"Scouts' honor!" he replied, holding up three fingers.

"Good. I'm going to summon the adjudicator. Best-case scenario, they restore Celeste to her rightful self. Worst case, they don't. Although even if they don't, perhaps they'll have a suggestion about dealing with the situation."

"Do you think this adjudicator person will fix her?"

"It's a long shot. They prefer not to get involved in these matters. But I persuaded them once, perhaps I can persuade them again to procure a second life for Celeste."

"So… okay, this might sound stupid but how do you contact this adjudicator? Is there a hotline you call? Like one-eight hundred-help me?"

Celine laughed. "No. It's more complex than that. I'll do it tomorrow, after I speak with Celeste tonight. If Michael is correct and there is a problem, that'll give me more leverage."

"Okay. Good point. So, how's noon tomorrow? While everyone is at lunch, we could sneak out and…"

"No," Celine interrupted him.

"Huh?"

"No, there is no 'we.' I must do this alone."

"What? No way! I mean, okay, you don't want me telling Gray or Alexander, which, by the way, is sketchy to begin with, but now you want me to let you do it alone?"

"It's fine. I'll be fine."

"Why can't I come with you?"

"It's complicated. It's not dangerous for me, but it's tricky. It's something a human shouldn't be involved in."

"Why don't you want to tell anyone else?"

"Adjudicators aren't the easiest beings to work with. What they determine is fair may not be in line with what anyone involved thinks is fair. Plus, the last time I spoke with an adjudicator, well, it didn't end so well for Gray."

"Right. I am in no way okay with this but, okay, I won't say anything. Just let me know when you're going so I can worry the entire time you're gone."

Celine smirked at him. "I will do that, D. You don't have to worry though, I'll be fine."

"Yeah, remind me of that when you disappear for twenty-five years."

"Funny, D."

"Well, I hope it works!"

"Me too and you promise NOT to tell no matter how worried you are, right?"

"My lips are sealed, I won't tell."

"Won't tell what?" Gray asked, entering the room.

Celine turned to face him. "Uh-oh, we're caught. I was swearing Damien to secrecy. The truth is I didn't get much rest earlier."

"Oh?"

135

"Yeah. Yeah, that's it, no rest. Didn't sleep a wink. There it is," Damien rambled. "You know me, I can't keep a secret so I'm glad this one is out. Whew!" Damien raked the back of his hand across his forehead. "Glad that's over."

Celine squeezed his hand, signaling him to be quiet. He cleared his throat as Gray made his way across the room. "No rest, huh? Well, I'm glad I know the secret. Now I can insist you rest more this afternoon." He squeezed her shoulders.

Celine made a face, rolling her eyes. "I will try to rest before I visit Celeste. Make sure he stays sedated, please!" She stood. "You should rest, too, D."

"I hate to leave…" he hesitated.

Celine tugged his arm. "Come on, you can sit with him this evening while I go check on Celeste."

"Go ahead, I'll be here. Millie will be checking in soon," Gray insisted. "You both need some rest."

Celine and Damien agreed, leaving the room and heading to Damien's room. "How about you take the bed and I take the chair this time," he offered.

She smiled at him. "You sure?"

Damien plopped down on the chair, stretching out. "I'm sure!" He grinned. "See, perfect for me for a tiny nap."

She returned his smile. "If you're sure, I'm not arguing." Celine stretched out on the bed. With her plan settled, she could relax. Sleep came easily and she drifted off within minutes. Damien settled into the chair, drifting off soon after Celine.

* * *

Damien awoke an hour later. He peered at the bed. Celine lay on her back, appearing to be in a deep sleep. He smiled, glad she was getting some rest. Outside the window, the autumn sky was a crisp blue. Damien crept to the window, easing it open. The waves crashed on the rocks below. Damien settled back into the chair, listening to the sounds of the ocean and smelling the saltwater in the air.

His musings turned to his move to the area. The location couldn't be more beautiful and serene. It was a complete contrast to the upheaval he'd experienced in every other aspect of his life. He stared at Celine, her chest rising and falling in a steady rhythm as she slept. She was dealing with so much. On top of the situation with her sister and Michael, she also had to tackle the relocation, explaining it to her, or rather Josie's parents. The only thing that differed between their situations was she was returning to a life she was accustomed to, whereas it was a new frontier for Damien.

He focused his attention again on Celine, pulling his mind back to their present situation. Celine's breathing increased, her chest rising and falling rapidly. Within moments, she shot up to sitting, gasping for breath.

"Celine!" he shouted, rushing to her side.

Celine gulped air, grasping his hand. She swallowed hard. "I'm okay, just a bad dream."

"Like before?"

"Yes, same dream. Even though I understand the dream's meaning, it still produces the same effect." She breathed hard, concentrating on calming her breathing. Damien rubbed her back. Her breathing calmed. She nodded at Damien. "I'm good."

"You were sleeping so well!"

"I was. And I did manage to get some sleep before the nightmare, so I can report I've rested!"

"Gray will be happy!"

"Yes, he will be! What time is it?"

"Umm, it's almost four-thirty."

"Not long before the sunset at least. Then we can determine if there is anything wrong from Celeste's perspective. Find out if Michael's outburst has any validity to it."

"I'll go with you."

"No, you stay here with Michael. I'll take Gray with me."

"Okay. Should we check in on him now, speaking of?"

"Yes, let's check on him before dinner."

The pair went to Michael's room, meeting Alexander and Gray. They had just missed Millie, who had reviewed Michael's condition and administered another round of sedative for the evening hours. She recommended keeping him sedated until the following morning and determining then if he could maintain a calmer composure.

Celine assured Gray she had slept and felt rested and ready to check on Celeste as soon as the sun set. They waited with Michael, eating a light dinner as the sun dipped below the horizon.

As the sun lowered on the horizon and the skies darkened, Celine and Gray set off for the abandoned property. The moon rose above them, at times obscured by clouds. An owl hooted in the distance and a dog howled from deep in the woods as they made their way down the path.

Celine shrugged her sweater tighter around her as the autumn chill frosted the air surrounding them. Worry for her sister drove her forward at a rapid pace. They arrived at the abandoned house as darkness saturated the sky. As they pushed through the door, Celeste emerged from her hiding spot.

Celine sighed with relief. "Oh, Celeste, you're okay."

"Of course, sister dear, whatever would be wrong?"

"I don't know. Michael has been extremely agitated, insisting you needed him and were in some danger."

Celeste widened her eyes, crinkling her brow with confusion. "I can't imagine why. I am fine, present condition excluded, of course."

"Are you sure?"

"Yes, I'm sure. Celine, are you quite all right?"

"Yes."

"She hasn't been sleeping well," Gray admitted to Celeste.

"I have been worried about both you and Michael. He seems to be worsening in some respects. And his outburst this morning after sunrise regarding your wellbeing disconcerted me."

"I'm fine. I'm in no danger. I am in need of some… sustenance," she said, choosing her words carefully. "Other than that, I'm fine." She approached Celine, grabbing her hands. "I'm the older sister, I'm supposed to be fretting over you, not the other way around."

Celine smiled at her. "Still, I'm relieved to see for myself you're okay. I hope Michael will be relieved as well."

"Perhaps now you can relax," Gray said.

"Relax? Have you been that distraught?" Celeste asked.

Celine shook her head to disagree. Gray began, "She's been having painful visions of you."

"Painful visions? What does that mean?"

"I've been experiencing some…" Celine paused, searching for the words, "memories that unexpectedly shoot through my mind. They're accompanied by nausea, head pain, things like that."

"What? Celine!" Celeste stared at her sister.

"I'm fine. I don't understand what is causing these, but they aren't that bad. I'm fine!"

"How many have you experienced?"

"Three, only three."

"All memories involving me? And you've been sick? Celine, why didn't you tell me? You must take care of yourself."

"Yes and yes. It's nothing to worry about. I'm taking care

of myself. Once we've got you back to yourself, I'm sure they'll subside. This will pass."

"We'll sort it out. Until then, you must relax! Celine, you must stop taking these things all on yourself."

"I've said the same, she doesn't listen. Stubborn, like she's always been," Gray chimed in, throwing his arms in the air.

"You always have been that, yes," Celeste agreed. "But you must listen this time, Celine."

Celine held back from rolling her eyes. "I'm fine," she said, glancing between both of them. "I will not fall apart. Nor leave," she said in a preemptive strike, glancing at Gray.

"No one's accusing you of anything, darling," Celeste said, stroking her hair. "We're just concerned for you. You mustn't worry about me. I'm sorry Michael isn't improving. I'm uncertain why that might be. I am not calling him at all."

"No, I realize that. I'm not accusing you of inciting him. But something is off. I'm not sure why he seems to be so concerned you are in danger."

"Is he still?"

"I'm not sure, we have kept him sedated since this morning when he tried to race off to protect you. Millie recommends keeping him sedated until morning when the danger is lessened for him."

"I see. Please keep me updated."

"I will. And please, Celeste, be safe. Teddy is watching you, isn't he? Does he need any help?"

"He is. And I will be, sister dear. There is no need to worry. Now, I want you to go home, rest and relax."

Celine nodded. "Don't worry, Celeste," Gray said, "I'll make sure she rests. Are you satisfied, darling?" he asked, turning to Celine. "Can we go now?"

Celine nodded her head again. "Yes. I am. We can go." She turned to Celeste, embracing her. "I love you."

"I love you, too, sister dear."

Celine and Gray left the house. As Celine stepped from the porch to the pathway, she doubled over in pain. Her mind exploded with a flood of memories as pain swept across her forehead. She dropped to her knees as she yelped in pain. Within moments, the fog in her mind cleared. She reached out for Gray.

"Celine, another? Are you all right?"

"Another. But I'm okay." She stood on shaky legs, gulping for air.

"Celine, something is wrong. I think you'd better talk to Millie when we get back."

"I agree. You may be right."

"Are you okay to walk?"

"Yes. Yes, I am. Let's go."

CHAPTER 15

"*B*ravo, my dear Celeste," Marcus said, stepping from the sanctuary of the hidden room. "Well played. I don't expect Celine suspected anything. She looked well, didn't she? Her beauty is timeless."

Celeste's face was set in stone. She responded with silence.

"Oh, don't be so sour, Celeste! You've done well! I am complimenting you."

Celeste shook her head, her mouth still set in a grim display. Marcus passed behind her, whispering, "Take the hint, my dear, smile."

"Must you constantly harass me?"

"Harass you? Celeste! Surely you jest!"

"I do not. Your presence sickens me. As does lying to my sister, misleading her, blindsiding her with whatever disgusting plan you have concocted."

"Do not trouble yourself with the particulars, my dear. The only detail you need concern yourself with is that no harm will befall you."

"But what harm will come to Celine?"

"None! I have never harmed Celine in the past, I do not plan to ever harm her."

"Haven't you?" Celeste cocked her head to the side. "She would beg to differ."

"Celine and I don't always see eye-to-eye, it's true. Again, that is none of your concern."

"No? The well-being of my sister falls under my purview in my estimation."

"What about your own well-being, Celeste?"

"What about it?"

"I should take care, if I were you. We wouldn't want anything to happen to you."

"Would it ruin your precious little plan?"

"Hmm." Marcus hesitated, placing a finger on his chin in a dramatic display. "No, but thank you for your concern. What it would ruin, however, is any chance you have at recovering to your true self."

"Recovering my true self?"

"Yes, my dear. I can end your existence or restore you to your true self. No more fearing the sunrise or those pesky holy objects."

Celeste grimaced, blinking her frustration away. He was correct. She was a hostage to her condition. And by extension, a hostage to him. One slip, one fall from his good graces could cost her life itself. There may be no reviving her this time. Whether or not she liked it, Celeste could not afford to anger the Duke.

"If you're considering betraying me, I'd rethink that course of action. You've done that once before and consider how it turned out. Celine cannot help you, Celeste. You must realize that. Oh, I realize she is 'working hard' to find a solution, but she won't. She lacks the formal training and knowledge to correct this situation. Had she not run off and married that fool, Buckley, she may have learned from me, but alas, she did not and here we are. She cannot help you, but I can."

"And I'm expected to trust you?"

"Have I ever let you down before, Celeste?" Celeste stared at him, tilting her head. "You'd be wise not to answer," he warned her. "Do as you are told, Celeste."

"Don't worry, Marcus, I will not ruin your plan."

"Wonderful, enjoy your evening, Celeste! Until we meet again, au revoir!"

* * *

Gray and Celine entered the foyer. Gray climbed the stairs on a search for Millie. Celine withdrew to the sitting room, pouring a brandy for herself as she waited. She sipped at it, making her way to the fireplace. The bench in front provided a warm seat for her after the chilly evening air. The flames danced as she gazed into the fireplace. Her mind wandered through the past several days, over the incidents she experienced.

Was worry overcoming her? It had never happened in the past. Even before her audience with the adjudicator, she experienced nothing like this. What was happening to her? Why couldn't she shake this sense of foreboding?

Gray returned with Millie in tow, interrupting her musings. "Hello, Celine," Millie greeted her. "Gray tells me you're experiencing some distressing symptoms."

Celine nodded. "Yes, I am." Celine recounted her recent experiences with the painful memories. Millie listened, interjecting questions every so often. When Celine finished, Gray asked if Millie had any idea or suggestion for exploring or treating the issue.

"I'm not sure of the cause, but I have some ideas to

explore the situation further," Millie said. "Do you mind if I check your vitals now?"

"Not at all," Celine agreed, swallowing the last of her brandy.

Millie excused herself to retrieve her medical bag, returning within a few moments from upstairs. She checked Celine's vital signs, pupil dilation, response to stimuli, reflexes and a myriad of other physical aspects. "Everything appears normal for you, Celine. I'm not ruling out exploring physical causes further, but that would require an MRI or CT scan. I'm not sure either is necessary now. I would, however, like to explore mental causes further. Would you mind trying hypnosis now?"

Celine was quiet for a moment. "Celine? Are you opposed to that?" Gray asked.

"No, not at all," she said. "I was just remembering the last time Millie hypnotized me."

"When you were Josie?" Gray asked.

"Yes."

"Afraid Josie will pop out?" Millie joked.

Celine offered a small laugh. "No," she admitted, "but it is strange. I'm experiencing the same symptoms I did as Josie and we're pursuing the same treatment course. The parallels are somewhat alarming."

Gray chuckled, pouring a brandy for himself. "Let's determine if we can get to the source of these symptoms," Millie said, removing a shiny pendant from her pocket. "You know the drill, Celine. Sit back, relax, concentrate on the pendant and my voice."

Celine adjusted herself into an armchair near the couch, leaning back and staring at the pendant as Millie let it sway back and forth. She listened to Millie's voice, prompting her to relax her limbs and her mind. Her mind relaxed, and she slipped away as Millie's countdown neared one. When Millie finished counting backward, Celine was completely relaxed and under hypnosis.

Millie pocketed the pendant. "Celine, are you relaxed?"

"Yes," Celine murmured.

"Celine, you have been experiencing some curious incidents of late. Memories that cause pain and sickness. Can you recall each of these incidents?"

"I can," Celine responded.

"Celine, is there anything troubling you that would cause incidents like these?"

"Danger."

"Danger?" Millie pressed. "Can you elaborate?"

"Danger," she said, her breathing becoming elevated, her brow pinching together.

"Celine, relax, you are safe, there is no danger here." Celine's breathing stabilized. "Now, Celine, I asked if there was anything troubling you that would cause the painful memories you've been experiencing. Is there something rooted in your subconscious that concerns you?"

"Many things concern me, but before each incident I sense danger."

"Danger from what?"

"I'm not sure."

"Does it concern you that the painting is missing?" Gray chimed in.

"Gray, please!" Millie warned him in a whisper.

"Yes, but that is not the danger."

"Ask her about Celeste," Gray whispered to Millie.

Millie gave him a wide-eyed glance but complied. "Does Celeste's condition concern you? Is this the danger you are sensing?"

"Celeste's condition is concerning, and it is my fault. But this is not the danger."

146

"What is the danger then, Celine? You know what it's not, why can't you identify what it is?"

"It's clouded. I cannot identify it. The sensation is so strong it affects me physically."

"So, the danger is the direct cause of the physical symptoms you are experiencing? And the memories... are they related to the danger?"

"I'm not sure. But the sense of danger is so overwhelming it makes me ill."

"Is there anything else you can relay to us about the memories or the sense of danger?"

Celine was silent for a moment. Her brows pinched together as she processed her thoughts. Her breathing quickened, and she gripped the arms of the chair, digging her fingers into the fabric. She moaned, screwing her face up, pinching her eyes tighter.

"Celine, what is it? What's wrong?" Millie asked.

"Non, non," Celine began in French, "il vient. Je dois partir."

"Celine, speak English, you are safe, relax and describe what's happening," Millie instructed.

Sweat beaded on her forehead, her body became rigid, her breathing frantic. "Cave, blood." She groaned in pain. "I cannot move, I'm dying, he stabbed me."

"It's the night she became what she is, she's reliving it," Gray noted.

Millie nodded, recognizing the event from Celine's previous descriptions.

Tears streamed down Celine's face as she continued, hysteria entering her voice. "Marcus," she cried, moaning in pain.

Millie glanced to Gray. "Pull her out of it," he said.

Millie nodded. "Celine, Celine," she shouted over Celine's moaning, "it's just a dream. You're safe, relax. I'm going to bring you out of the hypnosis. Celine, listen to me, when I reach one, you will wake up." Millie counted backward to one and Celine awoke. Millie collapsed onto the couch, breathing a sigh of relief.

"Well, those faces do not look good," Celine noted, staring at Millie and Gray.

"You had a bit of an episode," Millie explained.

"You relived that night in the caves," Gray elaborated.

"That's not surprising, that night has haunted me since it happened. Nothing about the painful memories?"

"Not much. You just kept saying danger, danger," Gray explained.

"Danger, danger? Like the robot on *Lost in Space?*" Celine joked.

"What?" Gray inquired, screwing up his face.

"Never mind. What else did I say?" Celine asked.

"You told us it wasn't Celeste or the painting that made you feel this way. Just some foreboding sense that affected you physically."

Celine leaned forward, furrowing her brow. "What is it then?"

"No idea, we don't seem any closer to the truth, although according to your subconscious we've ruled out a few things," Gray responded.

The door swung open and Damien poked his head in. "Everything okay with Michael?" Millie asked, jumping to her feet.

"Yeah, he's asleep. Alexander is with him. Everything okay in here? I was getting a drink and heard some shouting." he said.

"Yes, everything is okay. Millie hypnotized me in an attempt to discover what is causing these painful memories I've been experiencing."

"And?" he asked, stepping into the room.

"Nothing. I just kept saying danger, danger."

"Like the robot on *Lost in Space?*" Damien joked.

"Same thing I said," Celine replied with a giggle. Gray glanced between them, confusion on his face. "Anyway," Celine continued, "I babbled on about danger but failed to identify what was causing it."

"And the non-identification caused that much turmoil?" Damien persisted.

"No." Celine shook her head. "My nightmare cropped up again. That was the source of the commotion."

"Ah. That's the same nightmare that woke you the other day from your nap."

"Yeah. It pops up from time to time," Celine informed him.

"Hmm. Well, perhaps you should relax for the night, try to get some rest?" Damien suggested.

"Best suggestion I've heard all day, Damien," Gray agreed.

"I'd concur with that," Millie said. "We will try again in a day or so. Or sooner if you have another painful memory."

"Sounds good," Celine said. "I'll be in Michael's room."

"No, no," Gray argued. "You'll go to bed. Alexander and I will stay with Michael."

"I concur," Damien said, chuckling.

"As do I," Millie said. "I'll check on Michael now, update you on his condition then retire for the evening." She gathered her medical bag, leaving the room.

"I'm fine to sit with Michael, but I will yield to everyone's opinion and try to rest," Celine said, holding her hands in front of her to admit defeat.

"Good, let's meet Millie and get her update so you can relax for the night," Gray said.

They waited outside Michael's room for Millie. After a brief exam, Millie reported to the group that Michael seemed stable and was resting under the effects of the sedative. After receiving the news, Gray insisted Celine rest. He entered Michael's room, joining Alexander for the night watch.

Damien and Celine remained outside. "Want some company?" Celine asked Damien.

"I'd love some, but you're supposed to be resting."

"I will be resting. If I go back to my room, I will toss and turn. I will never sleep."

"Come on, we'll bunk together then," Damien suggested.

"One more thing. I'll meet you in your room in a minute," Celine said, rushing off down the hall.

Within a few moments, she joined him in his bedroom, a pint of chocolate ice cream and two spoons in her hand. "NOW we can relax." She giggled, climbing onto the bed next to him.

They dug into the pint, enjoying the cold treat. "So, what's up with this whole sense of foreboding and danger thing?" Damien questioned between spoonfuls.

"No idea. We ruled out a few things, but I guess I couldn't pinpoint what was causing it."

"What did you rule out?"

"The missing painting and Celeste's condition. Millie inquired about both. I said it wasn't either. Only that I sensed danger each time I experienced the phenomenon."

"Is there any pattern to it? Does it happen at a specific time?"

"No," Celine answered. "It's happened at various times of the day and night."

"How about in the same location?"

"Nope, that's been random, too."

Damien's wheels were turning as he tried to piece the puzzle together. "No identical times or locations... memories are always different, too, right?"

"Yes, each time it's been a different memory."

"But each one has been of Celeste?"

"Yes. Every one has included Celeste."

"It all points to worry over Celeste, I'm surprised your subconscious self doesn't think it is."

"I'm not. I'm worried about Celeste, but it's nothing that would cause something this extreme. I've never experienced anything like this before, not even during the events leading up to my request to leave my life as Celine and become Josie. And at that time, I was so distraught I couldn't eat or sleep. But never anything like this."

"Do you think it's because you were human again? Like a residual side effect from your days as Josie?"

"A new inability to deal with the perception of danger?"

"Something like that?"

"That sounds… improbable. I'm back to normal. I haven't lost any of my abilities. I'm not even rusty. I've slipped back into the fold without even skipping a beat."

"But we can't know for sure. I mean, it's not like there's a big history of this for us to reference, right? How many people have been human and then turned into… well, flip-flopped between human and… people like you and Gray and Alexander for us to compare to?"

Celine chuckled as Damien stumbled through his point. "No, I doubt that has happened often in the past. But it just doesn't seem to fit. And it's okay, you can call us supernatural creatures, D. You don't have to worry about offending me."

"No!" Damien exclaimed. "I hate that! I'm not calling you a creature! You're my cousin, you're a sister to me, not some B-Movie beast."

"You mean you never saw *Creature from the Martinique Lagoon*?" Celine teased.

"Not funny, Celine," Damien said, "and for that, I get the last scoop of ice cream." They tossed their spoons into the empty container and Celine set it aside on the night table.

"Okay, we better try to get some sleep. If Gray finds out

we spent the night eating ice cream and trying to solve this mystery instead of resting, I'll be in trouble!"

Damien yawned. "And I'll be tired. I hope you sleep," he said, climbing under the covers. "Can you turn the light out when you're ready?"

Celine watched him nestle in the covers. She smiled down at him. She was lucky to have him as her family. She was also glad he would not spend the night obsessing over her new memory crisis. With the light shut off, she collapsed into the pillows next to him.

Damien drifted off to sleep within moments of the lights being out. Celine listened to the rhythmic sounds of his breath as he slept next to her. Turning toward him, she reached for his hand, clasping it in hers. She closed her eyes, trying to shut the world out. Unease plagued her about the information from her hypnosis session. As she suspected, the two major stressors in her life were not the source of her difficulty. What was the cause? What danger was so pervasive that it would affect her physically?

She pushed the thoughts from her mind, concentrating on the warmth of Damien's hand. She focused on his presence, knowing she wasn't alone. She squeezed his hand in hers, closing her eyes and taking several deep breaths. His hand played the role of a lifeline, tethering her to the real world, bringing a sense of normalcy and relief. With the close connection, she relaxed and drifted off to sleep, still clutching Damien's hand.

When she awoke, Damien was gone. She glanced around the room, finding herself alone. The digital clock's face was blank. She tried the light; it was not working either. The power must be out, she determined. She'd have to find a flashlight and search for Damien after checking on Michael.

Thunder sounded overhead as she climbed out of bed. Lightning illuminated the room as she navigated to the door.

She stepped into the hallway, finding it was deserted. Her bare feet padded down the hall toward Michael's door. His door was ajar to his darkened bedroom. She pushed it open, glancing into the room as lightening tore through the sky.

The room was empty, the bedsheets rumpled. Celine stepped inside, scanning the room. While the power outage was concerning, she didn't understand the need to move Michael. Had something happened? If so, why wasn't she told. She made her way to the bed. Lightning lit the room again, revealing an additional detail. She hadn't noticed earlier, but the sheets were blood-stained.

She gasped, grasping the sheets to examine them closer in the dim light. Something must have happened to Michael. Had his wounds reopened? They were almost healed. Was he attacked again? Why hadn't they woken her?

She tossed the sheets down, exiting the room. She called into the darkness, searching for anyone still in the house. There was no response. The stillness of the house disconcerted her. She called out again, her voice echoing off the walls.

A noise drew her attention down the hall. She followed the hallway past Damien's door, continuing guardedly in the darkness. Thunder crashed and lightning lit the next hallway. A figure loomed at the end. "Hello?" she called out. "Gray? Alexander?"

She received no response. She continued down the hall toward the figure. "What happened to Michael?" she asked, still not receiving a response.

Halfway down the hall, the hairs on the back of her neck stood on end. An overwhelming apprehension filled her. She gazed at the figure in front of her, suddenly alarmed. "Who are you?" she queried.

Thunder boomed, drowning out any potential response. As the lightning brightened the hallway, she stared at the figure. Shadows obscured any details. She swallowed hard, backing away from the figure. She inched backward as the figure approached her. Without warning, she bumped into something behind her. Glancing backward, she was surprised to find a wall at her back. A wall sealed the hallway which was once open to another wing.

Celine turned, pushing against the wall. The figure advanced toward her. Celine whipped around, placing her back against the wall, ready to fight. She reached out to cast a preemptive warning strike with a fireball, nothing happened. She jiggled her hand again, but to no avail. The figure closed in on her along with the walls. A scream escaped her mouth as lightning flickered across the figure.

CHAPTER 16

eline shot up to sitting, gasping for breath. She clutched at her blanket, realizing she had been asleep, dreaming. The commotion awoke Damien. Confused, he sat up next to her. "Celine?" he asked, groggy from sleep. "What's wrong?"

"Bad dream," she answered.

"The nightmare again? Do you want me to get Millie?"

Celine shook her head. "No, no, not that nightmare, it was a different one. I'm fine, just startled."

"You sure? You seem pretty rattled."

Celine took a deep breath, "Yeah, yeah, I'm good. Let's go back to sleep. Sorry for waking you."

"Sounds good," Damien said, yawning. He collapsed backwards into the pillows behind him, falling asleep in an instant.

Celine eased back into the pillow. She watched him sleep, unable to fall asleep herself. The nightmare still disturbed her. It seemed like a warning. Who was the figure? Why was she trapped? Why could she not use her powers?

Perhaps it wasn't a warning. Perhaps it was a normal

nightmare, like normal humans experienced. Damien may have a point. Maybe there were side effects from her second transition from human to supernatural creature. She chuckled to herself. She was not opposed to stating what she was even if Damien found it offensive to call her a creature.

Her mind returned to the dream. Just what she needed, another nightmare to plague her, she mused. At least this time, exhaustion wouldn't become an issue for her. She'd discuss the dream with Millie in the morning. Something was off, the painful memories, the foreboding ambiance that accompanied them, the nightmares. It all pointed to something, but she couldn't figure out what.

She sighed, trying to relax into sleep. One concern plagued her. She rose from the bed, approaching the window. She eased it open, breathing in the salty air. Extending her hand out the window, she tossed a fireball down toward the cliff below. She lobbed a second one just to be sure. Satisfied that her powers were intact, she closed the window and returned to the bed. She eased down the bed, covering herself with her blanket and nestled into the pillow. Sleep came to her without trouble after she flexed her supernatural muscles.

* * *

Bright sun streamed through the windows into Damien's room. Celine yawned, opening her eyes. She squinted against the bright light, checking the clock. It was almost 8 a.m. Damien was still asleep. Celine dropped back onto the pillow. It had been a long time since she slept this late in the morning.

Her mind turned to her recent experiences. She reminded herself to speak with Millie about her dream, concerned it had something to do with her painful memories. Damien stirred.

"Good morning," she said as he opened his eyes.

"Hey, good morning!" he answered, yawning. "What time is it?"

"Almost eight."

A knock sounded at the door. Gray poked his head in. "Good morning, did I wake you?"

"No, we were up," Celine answered, sitting up. "Everything okay?"

"Yes, but we have some developments with Michael." Celine was already hopping off the bed. "We have it under control, Celine, no need to rush."

Damien climbed out of bed, too. "We didn't mean to sleep so late."

"I'm glad you slept. Assuming you slept?" Gray questioned.

"I did," Celine assured him. "What's going on with Michael?" she asked as she slipped her slippers onto her feet and pulled her hair into a loose ponytail. She pulled on her robe, tying the belt around her waist.

"Millie recommended letting the sedative wear off after daybreak, when the danger was lessened. She gave him his last dose around 2 a.m."

"And?" Celine prompted, realizing if the news was positive Gray wouldn't have disturbed them.

"As soon as he awoke, he went right back to insisting he had to go to Celeste."

Celine sighed, crossing the room to meet Gray. "Have you sedated him again?"

"Not yet. That's why I came to get you. I wanted you to see him first."

Celine nodded her head, waiting as Damien pulled his

second shoe onto his foot. Together, they made their way to Michael's room. Alexander and Millie waited with Michael.

"Oh great!" Michael grumbled, rolling his eyes. "A bigger audience to watch the show. Come on in! Enjoy!"

Celine glanced to Gray; her brows knit in confusion.

"Whoa!" Damien exclaimed. "You had to handcuff him to the bed?"

"Oh, they did, they did. Because I was acting 'insane,'" Michael muttered. "This is ridiculous! I don't have time for this. I need to get to Celeste."

"Michael…" Celine began.

"No, no, nope. I do not want to hear the gentle 'Michael, you need to relax, calm down, Celeste is fine' bull."

"I saw Celeste last night, Michael," Celine continued. "She's fine. I spoke with her. She's not in any danger."

"You wouldn't tell me if she was," Michael said, pulling at the restraint.

"I wouldn't lie," Celine said. "Gray and I were both there. He can tell you the same."

"And I have," Gray chimed in. "He doesn't listen."

"Something is wrong," Michael insisted.

"She's fine, Michael," Celine asserted. "Teddy is watching her. She's safe."

Michael pulled against the restraint again. "Won't hurt for me to make sure then, will it?"

"We can't take that chance," Celine said. "You're still recovering."

"I'm fine. I'm almost healed, look!" he exclaimed, pulling his bandage aside to show the almost healed wounds. "I can't keep laying in this bed day after day."

"Can you all give us a minute alone?" Celine requested of everyone in the room.

"Celine?" Gray questioned.

She nodded at him. "Please, Gray, just a moment."

"Whatever you say," Gray agreed. "We'll be right outside."

"I'm not sure I recommend that," Millie began.

"Just for a moment, Millie, please," Celine assured her.

Gray, Alexander and Millie proceeded to the door. Damien stood, arms crossed, at the foot of the bed. Celine raised her eyebrows at him. "What?" he asked.

Celine motioned to the door. "I think she means you, too," Gray informed him.

Damien glanced around, surprise on his face. "Oh! Oh I... but... I mean... okay," Damien said, rushing to the door to join the others. "Figured I could stay since we're like the threesome but yeah that's cool," he said, as they withdrew from the room, closing the door behind them.

Michael sighed as the door closed. "There's nothing you can say that will change my mind, Celine."

"I don't plan to try," Celine admitted.

Michael expressed shock followed by confusion on his face. "What?"

"I can assure you Celeste is okay. I checked on her. I talked to her last night, she told me everything is fine. But you're right. Something is wrong. I can't put my finger on it, but something is amiss."

Michael sat straighter, tugging against the restraint again. "Even more reason to let me go! Celine! You can't keep me drugged and asleep through this! Let me help!"

It was Celine's turn to sigh. "Michael, I need you to stay safe. I can't let you go to Celeste. I realize you have this desire you can't overcome, it's a common side effect from what you've been through. That's why it's too dangerous to let you go."

"Stop sidelining me! I'm not fragile. I can take care of myself!"

"I don't disagree with you, but this isn't about your

inability to care for yourself. I need your help, I do, but not with this."

"Then what? I'm sorry, I'm confused. Something is wrong, but I can't help."

"Listen, I'm working on something; I just need a few hours. If my plan works, the danger might be gone."

"And if not?"

"If not, I'll need your help to retrieve that missing painting."

"The painting? What about Celeste?"

"I'll handle Celeste."

"No! No way! And what is this plan you have?"

"I can't get into that, sorry. I need you to stay here, stay calm and wait for me to attempt to sort some of this out."

Michael closed his eyes, sighing. "So, I should sit tight and do nothing while you run around doing who knows what by yourself."

"Myself? That's not true."

"It is. You cleared the room before talking to me. You're planning to do something no one knows about. I will not let you. Either tell me or I'll tell them."

Celine set her jaw, unimpressed by Michael's threats. "Oh, Michael," she said, gazing at him with disappointment, "I can't let you do that." She caressed his cheek, sending him straight to sleep. He slumped in the bed, his chin falling to his chest.

Celine stood, giving him a final glance before pacing to the door. She opened it, meeting everyone grouped outside.

"Well?" Gray asked.

"He's asleep. There was no talking to him."

"What did you expect? He's stubborn! You shouldn't have wasted your time, Celine," Gray chided.

Celine shot him a glance, rolling her eyes. "He should sleep for a few hours at least without requiring a sedative. At least he was calm enough for me to put him to sleep without needing drugs."

"I'll keep one close just in case," Millie said. "Gray, will you join me to sit with him?"

"Sure. Celine, you coming?" Gray asked.

"Uh, would you mind staying with him? I wanted to clear my head with a walk."

"Everything okay?" Gray asked.

"Yes. Just wanted some fresh air while he's asleep."

"I'll walk with you, Celine, I'm returning to my house for a little while to rest," Alexander offered.

Not wanting to create suspicion, Celine agreed. The two started down the hall.

"Guys, I'll just be in my room doing research!" Damien shouted as the group disbanded. "So, if anyone needs me, that's where I'll be... in my room."

Celine winked at Damien before following Alexander down the hall. After donning jackets, they made their way out of the house, taking the path to Alexander's house. They chatted on their way, making light conversation. Celine thanked Alexander for his help with Michael thus far. As they approached his home, he told her he planned to return in the evening. Celine embraced him, thanking him again and telling him she'd see him in a few hours.

She circled back, pretending to be returning to the main house. After the woods closed in around her and his home was no longer visible, she veered off, heading toward the cave that led to the beach.

Celine stood for a few moments at the water's edge. The ocean breeze blew her blonde curls away from her face as she pondered the task ahead of her. Adjudicators were difficult creatures to summon and speak to. Was she desperate enough to try this? Her mind wandered back to the last time she summoned one of these preternatural beings. Indeed, she had been desperate enough then, at her wit's end, unable to eat, sleep or rest. It was a terrible, trying time. She pushed it from her mind. Difficult or not, she had to try. She took one last glance at the sea spreading in front of her before she turned to the cove to begin her task.

* * *

After Damien announced his plan to "research" he made a show of stalking to his room. He slammed the door shut in a loud display, standing on the other side of it with his ear pressed to the door. The hallway was quiet. He inched the door open a crack, peeking out. It was deserted. He snuck out, peering around to make sure he was alone. Satisfied that he was, he eased the door shut behind him without a sound.

He crept down the hall past Michael's room, hurried down the stairs and out the front door after pulling on his jacket. Celine and Alexander were still visible, walking down the path toward Alexander's house. He followed them at a safe distance, keeping to the edges of the path so as not to be noticed.

If he was correct, Celine's need for "air" was a diversion for her to get out of the house and summon the adjudicator. She had told him it was too dangerous for him to go with her and she had insisted he keep it from her fellow supernatural friends. But Damien was not about to let her do this alone. Even if he had to hide in the shadows and watch from afar, he would. Anything to make sure she was safe.

Damien hung at the edge of the forest as Celine and Alexander chatted outside his home. Within a few moments, Celine wrapped Alexander in a hug before turning away from the home. She started toward the woods, toward Damien's hiding spot. He backtracked further in, hiding himself behind a large pine tree.

Celine passed by him on the path to the house before veering off toward the cliffs. Damien emerged from his hiding spot, following her at a safe distance. As she approached the cliffs, she disappeared into a cave.

Damien followed her with some reluctance, afraid to become lost navigating inside. It also reminded him of his last experience in a cave on the fateful night when Celine almost lost her life. The walls closed in on him, the daylight waning away as he entered.

It didn't take long to descend to the beach. Damien peeked out from the cave opening, noting Celine standing a few feet away, staring at the ocean. He snuck out of the cave, hiding himself behind a large rocky outcropping.

After a brief moment, Celine navigated up the beach to the cove. She took a deep breath before holding her hands in front of her, palms up. She closed her eyes, murmuring a few words. Damien couldn't overhear what she was saying. The wind began picking up, swirling the sand around her. She spoke more words into the air before her body went rigid. Her eyes shot open, her arms reached, appearing as if they were being ripped from their sockets.

Her body went slack, and she collapsed to the beach. Damien almost ran to her, fearing for her wellbeing. Before he emerged from his hiding spot, a black cloud began forming a few feet from Celine. It swirled and spun, churning inches above the sand. The sand beneath it splayed out, driven away by the whirling of the cloud. Lightning flashed from inside the cloud.

CHAPTER 17

$\mathcal{D}$amien stared at the cloud as it changed shape, forming into a humanlike figure. The creature morphed, shedding the black cloud like a snake sheds its skin. Damien was speechless by what he witnessed. A pale figure hovered over Celine's limp form. Black hair poked from its head, black eyes stared down at Celine, black nails protruded from its hands. Large gray wings poked from its back.

"Rise," the creature said in a voice that reverberated, making it impossible to determine gender.

Celine climbed to her feet, tiny compared to the creature in front of her.

"Celine Devereaux Buckley, why have you summoned me in the presence of a human?" the creature boomed.

"Human?" Celine questioned. "I am not human."

"Not you, another."

"There is no human here," Celine countered.

The creature sniffed in the air. "You are mistaken. Show yourself human."

An expression of shock and dismay crossed Celine's face

as a realization struck her. "Damien?" she called. "Damien, it's okay, come out."

Damien stood, revealing himself from behind the rocky outcropping. "Hey, hello!" Damien waved, climbing from behind the rocks. "Nice to meet you. Sorry, I didn't mean to intrude. It's a pleasure to make your acquaintance, sir, ma'am, oh winged one," Damien stumbled, clearing his throat.

"Damien, stop," Celine said with a shake of her head.

"Stand before me and be judged, human," the adjudicator decreed.

"No!" Celine yelled, stepping between the creature and Damien.

Damien swallowed hard. The creature's black eyes glowered at Celine. "You protect this human, Celine Devereaux Buckley?"

"I do. He is off-limits to you. He shall not be judged."

The creature approached them, its gaze flickered between Damien and Celine. This close to it, Damien noticed its eyelids closed side-to-side rather than up and down. Celine stood her ground, refusing to budge as the creature's fiery breath wafted across them.

"I said no!" she snapped, moving to shield Damien further.

The creature slid back. "You are fortunate, human, to be protected by such a powerful being."

"Yeah," Damien croaked out, clutching Celine's hand as she reached behind her toward him. "I know."

"Let's get down to business," Celine insisted.

"Why have you summoned me again, Celine Devereaux Buckley?"

"I have an issue. I require your assistance."

"State your case."

"My sister, Celeste Devereaux VanWoodsen, has morphed

into a creature of the night. I need your help to return her to her original state."

"How did this come to pass?"

Celine hesitated, weighing her words. "She was in a lifeless state. Her lifelessness forced me to act quickly to revive her. The procedure I used was… impure. It resulted in her altered state."

"What brought her to her lifeless state?" the creature questioned.

"Marcus Northcott orchestrated her demise to punish me for refusing to join his coven."

"And you attempted to reverse his punishment?"

"Yes."

"Are there any other details relevant?"

"She is my sister; I did not want to lose her. I had only just regained her."

"After your requested absence."

"Yes," Celine answered.

"You did not remain human, Celine Devereaux Buckley."

"I did not. I could not."

"You chose your fate, Celine Devereaux Buckley. There is always a choice."

"Can you help me?" Celine pressed.

"No," the creature stated.

"Please, Celeste does not deserve to pay the price for my folly," she persisted.

"Celeste made her choices centuries ago. I will not undo what is done." Celine set her jaw in frustration, contemplating her next move. "Our business is ended, Celine Devereaux Buckley. Goodbye."

"If I could just interject…" Damien began. Celine spun to face him, wide-eyed, covering his mouth with her hands.

Fire shown in the creature's eyes, turning them from black to red. Its wings opened wide, flapping in agitation.

"SILENCE, HUMAN," it bellowed. Panic flashed through Damien's eyes, wide with fear. "You dare to defy me?" it roared.

"No, he does not," Celine answered.

"I shall speak only to the contemptuous human who dares to challenge me."

Celine whipped around to face the adjudicator. "You have made your ruling. No one is questioning you. Return to the realm from whence you came. Leave this human alone."

"Step aside, Celine Devereaux Buckley, this is not your affair."

"It is my affair," Celine argued, fire entering her voice, "he is my family, blood or not. If you cross him, you cross me. Make no mistake, I will use every power at my disposal to defend and protect him."

The creature glanced between Celine and Damien. "You realize the consequences of this choice?"

"I do," Celine assured the adjudicator.

"And you would still defend him knowing this?"

"To the death," Celine said, setting her jaw and flashing a fiery stare at the creature.

The fire died in the creature's eyes and they returned to black. It furled its wings against its back. "So be it, Celine Devereaux Buckley, I shall leave the human alone. Recognize, human, how fortunate you are to have such a strong ally pledge their allegiance to you," the creature stated. Damien nodded his head in silent confirmation of the creature's statement. "Goodbye and good luck in finding a solution to your problem, Celine Devereaux Buckley. Perhaps you should seek the counsel of Marcus Northcott. He is well-versed in dealing with such situations." With that, the creature opened its wings and shot skyward, disappearing somewhere above the clouds. The sky darkened and thunder boomed overhead. Within moments, the clouds cleared, returning to a bright, sunny day with no signs of the adjudicator.

Celine turned around, wrapping Damien in a tight embrace. "Are you okay?" she asked, stepping back to study him.

"I... I... I think so," Damien stuttered. "I'm sorry, Celine, I didn't mean to..."

Celine cut him off with a wave of her hand. "It's okay," she said, "but never do that again, D, never."

"I thought the adjudicator would be this fair, benevolent thing that just wanted to help," Damien explained.

"Just, yes. Benevolent, no. Adjudicators can be harsh in their judgements. They exhibit no emotion. Damien he could have... I don't even want to say it. Never do this again, it's far too dangerous!"

Damien nodded, realizing his folly. "I only wanted to help," he said just above a whisper, his eyes sinking to the ground.

"I understand," Celine said, softening. "There is so much you don't comprehend about this world yet, D. Please trust me going forward."

"Okay, I promise I will," Damien agreed.

They stood in silence for a few moments, recovering from the experience. "Well, that was a bust," Celine finally replied. "We should head back to the house. I think our only option is to go with your plan."

"My plan?"

"Yes. It looks like you'll get your wish to time travel and get that painting after all," Celine said.

"Really? I thought you said it was too dangerous?"

"It's more dangerous here for Michael." Celine grabbed Damien's hand, pulling him toward the cave. They navigated through the cave path up to the top of the cliff, heading for the path leading to the house.

"So, in the interest of understanding," Damien queried as they walked, "why did that thing want to judge me?"

"You're not a supernatural creature yet you've seen it. Once you showed yourself to it, it wanted to judge your soul and assign a fate to you."

"A fate? Like where I go when I die?"

"Something like that. Then it would send you there immediately."

"Immediately?" Damien gasped. "Like I'd be dead?"

"More or less," Celine answered.

"And then at the end? It seemed really mad."

"It was."

"What would it have done to me?" Damien questioned.

Celine stopped walking, shooting him a glance. "You don't want to know. It wasn't anything pleasant." She resumed walking.

Damien gulped, standing for an extra moment as he recovered. After a moment, he rushed to catch up with Celine. "I don't mean to be a pest, but why did it back down and leave me alone? I mean, you threatened it, but why did it give up?"

"That was a battle the adjudicator would never have won," Celine explained. "It tested me when it asked if I recognized the consequences and would still defend you. When I answered yes, it realized I was serious, and the battle was lost."

Damien pondered the information as they took the shortcut through the woods. They wound around through the forest. As they passed a clump of pine trees, Celine shrieked, dropping to her knees. She clutched her head. Damien knelt next to her, grabbing hold of her, trying to determine if she was okay.

Within a few moments, Celine lifted her head. Tears streaked her face. "I'm okay," she assured him.

"Another painful memory?" Damien inquired.

"Yes. That was the worst of them."

"Perhaps because the adjudicator didn't come through to help with Celeste. Perhaps that is the reason you're suffering from these, no matter what your subconscious says."

Celine shook her head, furrowing her brow. "I need to discuss it with Millie. Perhaps we can learn more from another hypnotherapy session."

Damien nodded in agreement. "Let's get you home," he said, helping her to her feet. Damien kept a firm hold on her as they finished their walk to the house.

They entered the foyer, Damien still guiding Celine, despite her insistence that she was fine. Gray was descending the stairs. "Where have you been?" he demanded.

"Out, why? Is something wrong?" Celine asked, detecting a hint of trouble in Gray's voice.

"She had another one of those attacks," Damien interjected.

"Are you all right?" Gray asked, meeting them.

"I'm fine, what's wrong?" Celine pressed.

"It's Michael. Nothing's working. He awoke from the sleep you put him in not long after you left. Millie tried a sedative, it did nothing."

"Wow," Celine mustered.

"Yes, it's been quite the fiasco," Gray informed her. "You'd better come upstairs."

"She can't handle this right now! She needs to rest and talk to Millie. This last attack she suffered made her collapse!" Damien exclaimed.

Gray stopped in his tracks, glancing at Celine. "I'm fine," she insisted. "We'll discuss it later after I've dealt with Michael."

"Are you sure?" Gray asked.

"Celine!" Damien entreated.

"I'm sure, I'm fine. We must deal with Michael."

"I'm not sure how you plan to deal with this, he's uncontrollable," Gray informed her.

"I can't figure out why. Celeste seemed fine. But his behavior will not stop until she is no longer a vampire, or he is away from her."

"We can't achieve the first one at the moment," Gray said.

"I realize that. We've not found a solution and nothing I've tried has panned out. That only leaves us with the option of keeping him away from her."

"Is there anywhere far enough away to stop his hysteria?" Gray asked.

"How about 1791?"

"What?" Gray questioned.

"We're going back to 1791 to find the painting!" Damien announced.

"Is the painting that important right now? Is this the best option? It's rather dangerous," Gray commented.

"No more dangerous than him staying here near Celeste," Celine retorted.

"We can find a solution," Gray said.

"Isn't Celeste around in 1791?" Damien questioned.

"She is, but she's normal. She'd have no effect on him and he will have no desire to be with her," Celine answered Damien first, then continued, "the painting is an issue even if it isn't the danger making me sick, this kills two birds with one stone. We don't have a solution in sight for Celeste. We're running out of options. My last idea failed. Miserably, I might add. I have no ideas, I see no other options. It would be safest for him to be away from this situation until we solve it. Then we can concentrate on solving Celeste's issue and not babysitting Michael."

"Your last idea? Which was what?" Gray questioned.

Celine was quiet for a moment, biting her lower lip. "Well?" Gray prompted.

"I went to the adjudicator," Celine admitted.

Gray's eyes grew wide and his eyebrows raised. "You did what? Celine, what the hell were you thinking?"

"We had no other solutions! I tried it as a last-ditch effort!"

Gray was incredulous. "Alone? You went alone to do this; you didn't even bother to tell me?!"

"Well, I was there," Damien interjected.

Celine sighed, closing her eyes. "Not great timing, D," she mumbled under her breath.

Gray threw his hands in the air. "You took HIM?" he shouted. "A human?"

"Hey!" Damien objected.

"No, I didn't take him. He followed me; I wasn't aware."

"I hope the adjudicator was none the wiser," Gray commented.

"Well…" Celine began.

"Oh, please don't tell me, Celine," Gray chided.

"It sensed him," Celine said.

Gray covered his face with his hands before speaking. "Do you realize how irresponsible you both were? You," he said, pointing to Damien, "are lucky to be alive."

"Yeah, I gathered that. This is all on me, though. It was my fault," Damien said. "She didn't know I followed her, and she saved my life."

"You're lucky, Celine, that the creature didn't press the issue with your cousin. For not being blood relatives, you two are alike. Headstrong, the both of you."

A new voice entered the conversation. "What is going on down here? What are you shouting about? Is something wrong?" Alexander asked, descending the stairs.

"Nothing," Celine began.

"Well, unless you count the fact that Celine considers sending Damien and Michael to 1791 to find Mina's painting to be the best solution to the current situation since her meeting with the adjudicator failed," Gray explained.

"Celine," Alexander said, shock plain on his face, "you called on the adjudicator?"

"Yes, she did. And no, she didn't tell me," Gray shouted. "Oh, but she told the human," he said, pointing to Damien. "who also went to meet the adjudicator." Gray threw his hands in the air, turning away from them in frustration.

"You're lucky to be alive!" Alexander said to Damien. "Celine, what were you thinking?"

Celine sighed. "I didn't take him, he followed me. He realizes now what a terrible idea following me was after encountering the adjudicator. But we had no options! I had to try!"

"Well, I gather this idea did not pan out," Alexander said.

"That's putting it mildly," Gray said, rejoining the conversation.

"My point is, perhaps we should make a decision on the situation with Michael. Charlotte, Millie and Avery are with him, but I am not keen on leaving them alone for long with him," Alexander answered.

"Yes, thank you," Celine said. "Let's please deal with something that we can control."

"Fine," Gray acquiesced, "but we're not finished with this conversation, Celine."

CHAPTER 18

*T*he group ascended the stairs, traversing the halls to Michael's room. They reached his room, hurrying inside as raised voices wafted into the hall. They walked into an argument between Michael, Avery and Charlotte.

"… just asking you to check on where they are," Michael argued.

"You want us to leave, that's all. And I told you, they'll be here when they're here," Avery answered.

"Oh, thank heavens!" Charlotte exclaimed. "Here they are. Now you can relax." She patted Michael's arm, smiling at him.

"It's about time," Michael responded, aggravation clear in his voice.

Celine approached Michael, perching on the edge of the bed.

"Don't touch me," Michael warned. "You will not put me into your special sleep, Celine."

"We'll let you talk," Charlotte said, steering Avery from the room.

"You need to settle down, this is nonsense," Gray said, wagging his finger at Michael.

"You need to let me loose and let me help Celeste," Michael retorted, pulling at the restraint tethering him to the bed.

"Enough, both of you!" Celine shouted.

"It's not enough…" Michael began.

"Stop this!" Alexander shouted. "Nothing is being settled with this bickering. We must discuss this matter in a sensible way."

"Yeah, besides, there's a new plan in place. And it means you'll be out of those handcuffs in no time!" Damien promised.

"Finally!" Michael declared. "Tell me quick so we can get moving. Celeste needs me!"

"Wait, wait, before we discuss this, are you sure, Celine?" Gray asked.

"I'm sure," Celine said, nodding. "This is the best option we have."

"All right, I trust you. Let's do it," Gray agreed.

"I need…" Celine began.

"She needs us to go back to the past and get the painting back!" Damien blurted out, grinning from ear to ear.

"What? I can't do that. I've got to be here to help Celeste!" Michael argued.

"You cannot help Celeste. She insists nothing is wrong and you cannot be too near to her, it's too much of a temptation. Michael, if she bites you again, you could die. You could become what she is," Celine explained.

"I don't care!" Michael began.

"No one cares if you care," Gray said, exasperation in his voice. "You'll do what she tells you and that's it."

Celine stood from the bed, pacing around the room.

"Come on, buddy!" Damien pleaded. "It'll be fun! The two of us back in action. Time traveling!"

"How about the two of us back in action right here where we're needed!" Michael countered.

"What if you hear it straight from Celeste that she is fine? Would you go then?" Celine asked.

"Celine, are you crazy?" Gray questioned. "You can't put the two of them together."

Celine ignored him, focusing on Michael, awaiting his response. He considered the question. "I suppose if she insisted that she didn't need me, I could go," he answered after a moment.

"Fine. I'll see that she's here as soon as the sun sets. Then you can hear it for yourself. After that, I'll send the two of you back to 1791."

"Deal," Michael agreed.

"Celine, I will ask again… are you crazy? You can't put them together. It's a disaster waiting to happen," Gray contended.

"I trust Celeste, she won't harm him."

"Well that's a first," Gray answered.

Celine checked her watch. "Only a few more hours to wait. We need to prepare a few items before they travel back. Let's work on that," she said, ignoring Gray's last comment.

"I'll help!" Damien offered, excitement in his voice.

"Great! Then I can fill you in on some details before you travel back. Would you mind waiting with Michael until Celeste is here?" Celine asked Gray and Alexander.

Gray glanced to Celine. "Before you leave, I'd like to have a word with you first, Celine."

"I'll stay," Alexander offered. "If Millie will stay with me, we should be fine."

"Of course," Millie accepted.

Celine sighed. "Okay," she said, shrugging her shoulders.

Damien, Celine and Gray exited the room into the hall-way. Gray guided Celine toward their suite. Damien followed them, glancing between the two of them. When they reached the double doors leading to their suite, Gray said, "Did you need something, Damien?"

"Oh," Damien said, realization dawning on him, "you meant you wanted to talk alone."

"If you wouldn't mind, yes," Gray answered.

"Can you give us a few minutes, D?" Celine asked. "I'll meet you in your room as soon as I'm ready."

"Sure. I want to review all my notes anyway," Damien agreed, wandering back down the hall to disappear into his room.

Celine and Gray entered the confines of their room. "I have a lot to do…" Celine began before being cut off by Gray.

"Yes, it seems so. Would you mind including me on all those plans? Perhaps you could try it before you decide to do something and then just do it."

"You're angry," Celine answered.

Gray sighed. "I'm frustrated, Celine. You're making some questionable choices and I do not understand why. I don't even have any idea you're making them until they're already executed."

"I don't think Celeste seeing Michael will be a problem. I have every faith she won't be that stupid this time around."

"To reiterate, faith in your sister is a novel concept for you. That is beside the point. While I don't trust Celeste as much as you seem to, her visit with Michael can be managed."

"So, what's the issue?" Celine asked.

"Celine, you went to the adjudicator. You said nothing, you took it upon yourself to do that. That doesn't sit well with me."

Celine did not answer for a moment. "What do you want me to say, Gray?" she finally managed.

"Why, Celine?"

"We didn't have any viable options, and it seemed worth a try."

"I mean why didn't you tell me?" Gray clarified.

"Because I knew you wouldn't agree."

Gray shut his eyes for a moment, sighing. "So, you deliberately did something you knew I wouldn't agree with and instead of being honest about it, you did it behind my back."

"I did it because you wouldn't have agreed for a unfair reason, not because you wouldn't consider it a viable option."

"Unfair reason?"

"We haven't had a pleasant experience with adjudicators. The very mention of the word would have set you off, and I realized that. It wasn't worth discussing and arguing about when I knew how you'd react."

"Why? Because the last time you visited the adjudicator without my knowledge I lost you for almost twenty-five years?"

"Exactly," Celine agreed. Gray sighed again. "There's no danger of that happening again, Gray. But I didn't want to venture to convince you of that."

Gray eyed her. "All right, it's over. I'm not happy about it, but it's over. Please let's discuss things together from this point forward. Celine, I don't want to lose you again and I'm not accusing you of anything but..." He paused. "Anything could have happened."

Celine considered his words for a moment. "I'm sorry," she admitted. "I won't do it again. I'll come to you first."

"Good," he said, pulling her into an embrace.

"Then at least you'll know what I'm doing when I ignore your warnings," she said, giggling.

He shook his head at her. "Oh, Celine, you're too bull-headed for your own good."

She grinned at him. "Now, what are your real thoughts about sending them back for the painting?"

"It's not the worst idea," Gray admitted. "Michael needs to be away from Celeste. Far away. And 1791 is pretty far. Albeit, the Duke is there, so it's an unsafe time. But I guess we're also there to protect them. So, I guess I'm on board with sending Frick and Frack back for the painting."

Celine rolled her eyes at his last statement. "There's no good solution. Michael is in grave danger here. Sending them back places them in danger too, but they can be discreet. Maybe they won't even run into Marcus. Come on, we have a lot to do," she urged, starting to leave.

"Wait, wait, wait," he said, pulling her back. "We still have to discuss that you had another attack. The worst of them from what I understand. You collapsed?"

"I'm fine, we can deal with it later," she said, attempting to sweep it under the rug.

"We'll deal with it now, Celine," Gray insisted.

"Yes, I had another attack. Yes, it was the worst of them. It was intense. I plan to talk to Millie about it again. This is happening for a reason, I just don't understand what it could be. Damien suggested perhaps a residual effect from being human a second time. I don't know." She shrugged.

"Glad you got his expert opinion," Gray joked. "Why don't I get Millie now. Let's discuss this before we do anything else."

"All right," Celine agreed.

"Good," Gray said, rubbing her cheek.

"See, I'm not impossible," Celine joked. "Ask Damien to sit with Michael. I'll wait here."

"Okay, I'll be right back," Gray said, excusing himself from the room.

Celine sunk into an armchair. Countless things crowded into her mind, however she was glad to be facing this one. The last episode she experienced was by far the worst. Something was amiss. She hoped it turned out to be something as simple as what Damien suggested, but concern grew within her it was not that simple.

Within minutes, the door opened and Gray ushered Millie into the room.

"We're keeping you busy of late," Celine said.

Millie laughed. "It keeps me out of trouble," she said, opening her medical bag. "I will perform another physical exam and then we'll proceed as usual. Another hypnosis session."

"Do you suspect there is a physical cause?" Celine asked.

"No, I don't, but I'd like to check once again to determine if there are any physical changes." Millie ran the standard battery of physical checks. "Nothing different, nothing of any concern. All right, Celine, let's try the hypnosis again. Relax into the chair, get comfortable. And Gray, this time, no interjecting, please."

Gray rolled his eyes at Millie but agreed. Millie began her pendulum swaying, instructing Celine to concentrate on only the movement of the object and Millie's voice. Within moments, Celine was under the effect of Millie's hypnosis.

"All right, Celine. Now that you are fully relaxed, I'd like to learn more about the incident you experienced earlier today in the woods with Damien. Okay?" Celine nodded. "Good. Can you describe the events leading up to your episode?"

"We were returning from the beach. We took the path through the woods. As we entered a clump of pine trees a sense of danger overcame me. A memory passed through my mind, but it brought pain. I could not stand; I was so overwhelmed by the sensation."

"What was the memory, Celine?" Millie inquired.

Celine's brows pinched together. "That night in the caves."

"The night you became what you are?"

"Yes. I remember calling out to Celeste, but she did not respond."

"Celine, is there anything else that you can tell me about this incident in particular?" Celine shook her head. Her brow crinkled and she pinched her forehead. Her breath increased. She gripped the chair, digging her feet into the floor. "Celine, what is it?" Celine moaned, wincing. "Celine, tell us what is happening," Millie insisted.

Celine's nostrils flared. "That scent... something about it..." Celine's breath became more ragged. "Someone is watching..."

"Who is watching, Celine?"

Celine shook her head, moaning. "My head... my heart..." she muttered, breathless.

"What's wrong with her?" Gray asked. "Is she okay? Physically? Why is she complaining about her heart?"

Millie continued, ignoring Gray. "Celine, what's wrong with your heart."

"My heart... my heart... someone is watching," Celine continued.

"Who, Celine? And why does it affect your heart?"

Celine moaned again, louder. Her eyes pinched tighter. Perspiration formed as she thrashed in the chair. "I can't... I can't..."

"Celine, calm down, you're safe. Tell us what is happening, what you feel."

"Blood... darkness... cold... who is there? Who are you?" Celine grimaced. "Get away... get away..."

"Something's wrong," Gray said, "bring her out of it."

Millie nodded, agreeing as the session spiraled out of

control for Celine. "Celine, I will bring you back now. I will count backward from ten and when I reach one, you will awaken." Millie counted backward until she reached one and awoke Celine.

Celine's eyes opened. She peered around as she took a deep breath. "Well?" she asked.

Gray rushed to her. "Celine, thank God. Are you all right?"

Confused, Celine responded, "Yes, I'm fine, why?"

Millie approached, stethoscope in hand. "You were complaining about your head and your heart. I'd like to listen to your heart again if you don't mind." She placed the diaphragm of her stethoscope against Celine's chest, listening for a few moments. Celine squeezed Gray's hand. After a moment, Millie pulled it away, hanging it around her neck.

"Well?" Gray demanded, impatiently.

"Everything seems fine. Her heart rate isn't even elevated at this moment. No irregular rhythms, murmurs, nothing out of the ordinary. Celine, do you recall why you mentioned your heart?"

"My heart? No, I have no idea. I feel fine. I don't even recall feeling anything strange regarding my heart during these episodes."

"Physically, I find nothing wrong with you. But I'm afraid after this session, we have more questions than answers."

"So, we learned nothing?" Celine asked.

"Not very much," Gray admitted.

"No," Millie added. "You told us a sense of danger overwhelmed you just like before. Then you became perturbed. You rambled, but in disjointed sentences. You mentioned a smell and that someone was watching you. Then you complained about your head and heart, several times. Finally, you said the words 'blood,' 'darkness' and 'cold' before you asked who else was there and told them to get away."

"What?" Celine asked, screwing up her face. "What was I talking about?"

"I'd like to know the answer to that question, too," Gray stated.

"That makes three of us. Regrettably, these sessions aren't getting us anywhere at the moment," Millie concurred.

Celine sighed. "No, it doesn't seem to be providing us with any information. Something is disturbing me, though. Once we get Michael and Damien back to some semblance of safety, maybe we can explore some different avenues."

"Yes, let's do that," Millie said.

Celine nodded her head. "Now, I've got to speak with Damien, prepare them for their trip before I collect Celeste."

"You're sure you're all right, Celine?" Gray questioned.

"I'm sure. Gray, I'm fine," Celine said, taking his hands in hers. "You need not worry, I'm just fine. I can't fathom what's causing these painful memories, but it's a minor problem. I'm healthy, physically and mentally." She gave him a peck on the lips and a smile before standing to collect Damien.

Celine spent the rest of the afternoon discussing details of the upcoming trip with Damien, arranging clothing, money and letters of introduction to allow them to be received by the Buckleys of 1791. As evening approached, Celine, along with Gray, set out to retrieve Celeste as she awoke from her daytime slumber. Celine spent much of the walk reassuring Gray that she was fine.

They fell silent as they approached the abandoned house. Celine and Gray climbed the stairs and entered the ramshackle house. Celeste was closing the secret room. "Celine! This is a surprise," she said.

"I need your help, Celeste."

"Anything. Is everything all right, Celine?" Celeste asked, approaching her.

"Michael is still agitated. He needs to be away from you. I know a place where he will be safe, but he won't go, at least not voluntarily, until he's heard from you that you are not in trouble."

"From me?" Celeste questioned.

"Yes. I realize this is an odd request, but could you talk to him? Tell him you're okay?"

"Of course," Celeste agreed.

"Celeste…" Celine paused, searching for the right words.

Celeste rolled her eyes, sighing. "I won't harm him if that's what you're about to address."

Celine shrugged. "Sorry, I had to ask."

"I understand, sister dear. I promise to behave myself. Now, shall we?" Celeste motioned toward the door. The trio hurried across the estate to the main house. They proceeded straight to Michael's room. Damien, Alexander and Millie waited with Michael, still restrained for his own safety.

As they entered the room, Michael strained against the handcuffs. "Celeste!"

"Hello, Michael," Celeste said, keeping her distance.

Michael reached for her, but she remained steadfast, not moving past the foot of his bed. Michael glared around the room. "Would you mind giving us a moment alone?"

"We would. Whatever Celeste plans to say, she can say in front of all of us or not say it at all," Gray retorted.

"Oh, I get it, you want to make sure she says whatever you're forcing her to say," Michael contended.

Gray opened his mouth to respond, but Celine beat him to it. "Let's give them a moment."

"Are you sure that's wise, Celine?" Alexander asked.

"He will not believe anything she says while we're here.

You have two minutes," Celine said, eyeing Michael, "not one second longer. Make it quick, Celeste."

Celeste nodded as everyone filed out of the room. They stood in silence outside Michael's room waiting, apprehension thick in the air. The two minutes seemed like an eternity. At the stroke of the one-hundred and twenty second mark, Celine pushed through the door. "Finished?" she asked without pause.

"Not really," Michael said.

"Yes," Celeste answered. "We are."

"Celeste..." Michael began.

"Michael, please. Do what I've asked, what Celine asks. When you return, we'll see each other again."

Michael sighed but nodded in acquiescence. "I'll walk you out," Alexander offered.

"Thank you," Celeste answered. She approached Celine, giving her sister an embrace. She squeezed Celine's hands. "I love you, Celine. Good luck to you both," she conveyed to Michael and Damien before disappearing from the room with Alexander.

"Well, seems like that's settled," Gray said. "When do you plan to send them back, Celine?"

"No time like the present," Celine answered. "Let's get you two dressed and ready to go!" Damien, period clothing in hand, tossed a set at Michael and the two disappeared into the bathroom to change.

"I wonder what Celeste said to him?" Gray asked as they waited.

"No idea, but she must have been convincing since he agreed."

"Are you positive this is a good idea?" Gray questioned again.

"It's not worse than leaving him here. Even with Celeste's assurances, the temptation may be too strong. Besides, we need to find that painting. Everyone in the house will sleep a lot more soundly if it's back. Damien's explanation may leave something to be desired, but it does make decent sense. Although…" She paused.

"Although what?" Gray prompted.

"It does seem rather backward to be sending them from a time without Marcus to a time with him."

"It doesn't sit well with me either. We're finally rid of that bastard and here we are dealing with him again."

"I agree, but I don't see a way around it."

"Me either. You're right, this is the best plan," Gray agreed.

Damien and Michael emerged from the bathroom. "Here we are! How do we look?" Damien asked, excitement brimming in his voice.

"You are way too excited for this," Michael said, pulling at his collar.

"You look great," Celine assured him. "Remember what I told you and stay safe. Avoid Marcus at all costs. Here are your letters of introduction, although if you run into me first, I'm sure I'll recognize you."

Damien pocketed the letters. "Thanks, and we will. We'll be back soon, Celine. I promise." He squeezed her hand, then embraced her.

"Be careful, D," Celine warned again. "I love you."

"I love you, too," Damien answered.

"Okay, ready?" she asked.

"As we'll ever be," Michael answered.

"Here we go!" Celine said. She stretched her arms in front of her, closing her eyes and knitting her brows in concentration. Within seconds, a rogue wind gust blew through the room. The windstorm steadily increased, and a twinkling began on the wall in front of Celine. It grew from a pinpoint to a large oval, obscuring most of the wall behind it as the winds continued to whip through the room.

"Portal's open," Gray shouted above the din.

"And away we go," Damien said as he and Michael stepped into the blackness.

Once they disappeared into the portal, Gray rested his arm on Celine's shoulder. She collapsed from effort and the force of the closing portal. "They're gone," Gray informed her.

She sighed. "Now we wait." She climbed to her feet with Gray's help. "I'd like to lay down. Would you mind?"

"Not at all, I hope you get some rest. I will speak with Alexander, perhaps walk him back to his house. I doubt he'll be staying since we no longer need to keep vigil over Michael."

Celine nodded. "See you later," she said, kissing his cheek.

CHAPTER 19

*R*eturning to her room, Celine reached into her pocket, pulling out a slip of paper. She unfolded the note. Celeste had slipped it into her hands before departing after visiting Michael. It was obvious Celeste had wanted the missive to remain a secret, so Celine had discreetly pocketed it to read later.

Her brow furrowed as she read:

Celine – There is something I must speak with you about. I'd prefer to do so privately, but I understand if you disagree. Meet me at the old mill at ten. Yours, Celeste.

Celine regarded the note. Was there a problem with Celeste? Something was amiss or Celeste would not have summoned her to meet. She purposefully set the meeting at a different location than her hideaway. Who was she trying to avoid? Questions filled Celine's mind. She checked the time; it was almost 9:30 p.m. She should leave now to meet with Celeste.

Celine shoved Celeste's note into her pocket. She

scrawled a note to Gray saying she had gone to see Celeste, deliberately leaving the location of the meeting out. Celeste had preferred to meet in private for reasons unknown to Celine. Celine intended to respect her wishes, assuming it was a delicate or familial matter she wanted to discuss.

Checking the time again, she hurried from her room to the foyer, donned her jacket and hastened out the door, heading toward the old mill.

When she reached the property, the mill was dark. She wondered if she had missed Celeste. Pushing through the wooden doors, she called out to her sister.

"Down here!" a distant voice called from the building's basement. Celine followed the voice, detecting a sliver of light from the lower floor. Celine followed the light beam down the wooden stairs. The basement opened around her. She squinted into the dim light, searching for Celeste. "Celeste?" she called again.

"Here, Celine," Celeste answered from a corner of the room. She stood inside a small chamber once used for storing mill products. Celine made her way toward the room. "What's with all the secrecy, Celeste? And why here?"

Celine entered the storage chamber. "I'm sorry, Celine," Celeste said.

"It's fine, Celeste, but what…" Celine began before Celeste tossed a fireball her way. Unprepared, it knocked Celine onto her backside. Celeste fled from the room, slamming the door behind her. A key turned in the lock. "Ouch!" Celine shouted as she stood up, dusting herself off. "What the hell, Celeste?"

Moments after she stood, pain shot across her head. A wave of nausea passed over her and she doubled over as the sensation took hold. It passed within moments and she regained her posture. A figure loomed outside the door. "This is not funny, Celeste," Celine said, approaching the door. "Let me out." She jiggled the handle, then blasted it with a fireball. The door and its lock stood fast.

Grasping the bars of the door's small window, she peered out. As she searched the darkness, the figure came closer. Realization dawned on Celine and, on instinct, she stumbled back a step, gasping.

"Hello, Celine. I cannot tell you how thrilling it is to see you again," the figure said. Celine recognized the voice of Duke Marcus Northcott. A tear rolled from her eye and she fought to steady her chattering jaw and weak knees. "Once again, I've left you speechless, Celine."

Celeste pushed in front of Duke Northcott. Tears streamed down her face. "I'm sorry, Celine," she choked out. "I had no choice."

"How touching," Marcus said. "Although she is telling the truth, Celine. She had very little choice, given her new limitations. Oh, you were clumsy in saving her, weren't you? If only you would have remained under my tutelage, you could have saved your sister without reducing her to the foul creature she has become."

Anger replaced panic inside of Celine. She set her jaw, firing another fireball at the door. She unleashed two more before trying a continual assault against the lock. It was to no avail. She dropped her arm, breathless from the effort.

"Tsk, tsk," Marcus chided. "That won't work here, Celine. I've enchanted that lock. I doubt you'll figure a way out of it. I learned some new tricks while I was away."

"How have you come back?" Celine questioned.

"Oh, I made a compelling case to Bazios. I can be quite persuasive. Turns out, after a bit of clarification on some points you exaggerated to him, he saw things my way. So, here I am!"

"What do you want, Marcus?"

"What do you expect I want, Celine?"

"We've been down this road before, Marcus. It doesn't end well for us."

"This time, my dear, it will be different. We're starting fresh, Celine. And this time, you will join me."

"I wouldn't hold your breath," Celine argued.

"Don't be stubborn, Celine. We were preordained to be together. Your heart and mind call out to me whenever I am near."

Celine pondered the statement. "My heart..." she murmured. Realization set into her mind and her gaze lifted to his eyes. "You... you are the danger I sensed. The painful memories, the physical reactions... it was all because you were near. The memories weren't centered on Celeste, they were centered on you!"

He smiled. "Yes, my darling Celine. Oh, how I enjoyed watching you in those moments. So delicate and beautiful, yet so fierce and passionate. Your encounter with the adjudicator was magnifique! How you defended that vulnerable, defenseless human you consider family. A waste of your talents, but still, such passion! How is dear Damien, by the way?"

"Do not even speak his name."

"There's no need to be so dramatic, my dear. I will not harm him. I suspect he isn't here to be harmed anyway. You opened a time portal earlier this evening, didn't you, my dear?" Celine did not answer. "Where are the intrepid time-travelers off to this time?"

Celine remained silent. "Nothing to say, my darling?" Celine turned her back to him, crossing her arms. She stalked to the small opening that offered a view of the night sky. She stared up at the cloudless sky. The full moon bathed the landscape in white light. "A Hunter's Moon," Marcus continued.

"How appropriate," Celine commented. She stalked back

toward the door. "Enjoy your moment, Marcus. It will not last. Gray will search for me, they all will."

"You give that imbecile far too much credit, Celine. They won't find you. I'll make sure of that. In the meantime, you'll have plenty of quiet time to reflect on your circumstances and my offer."

"Your offer?" Celine laughed. "I want nothing you offer!"

"Oh, Celine, stop being stubborn and consider the possibilities!" He paused for a moment. "Now, I shall leave you, Celine, to contemplate your future. Will you live it trapped in this basement or will you join me? The choice is yours. I bid you adieu, mon chérie. Until we meet again!"

Celeste followed Duke Marcus Northcott up the stairs and out of the abandoned mill building. "Well, I hope you are happy," Celeste spat out.

"Oh, I am delighted, Celeste! Our plan was perfect."

"YOUR plan," Celeste corrected. "I had no hand in this. You disgust me."

"You had your hands as deep as mine in this, my dear. You lured her here. She wouldn't be here without you."

"You forced me, I had no choice!"

"Forced or otherwise, you did it."

"Yes, I did," Celeste agreed. "And if I'm not mistaken, you owe me something for that."

"Mmm, you are not mistaken. However, you have not yet completed your task. Only then do I owe you."

"I lured my sister here, allowed you to lock her in that basement! I've done what you asked!"

"My dear Celeste, do not entertain the idea that you allowed me to do anything. You merely simplified my task. And I shall reward you for your part in this when Celine has agreed to join me. Until then you shall remain as you are." Celeste grimaced, crossing her arms as she glowered at the ground. "Oh, Celeste, surely you understand that I cannot allow you to return to your former glory yet when there is still so much work ahead of us. No, you shall remain as you are until Celine has complied to my request." Marcus began walking away. He turned back, raising his voice to say, "Consider it motivation to convince your sister to see things my way. Au revoir, Celeste!"

* * *

The footsteps faded away as Celeste and Marcus climbed the stairs. Silence fell over the structure. Celine wandered to the opening, glancing up at the moon again. How appropriate Marcus should capture her on the night of the Hunter's Moon. She had been his prey for so many centuries. How could she assume they were rid of him, that one simple ceremony would rid them of his presence?

It all made sense now. The painful memories had all included Marcus in some way. Everyone, including her, had been blinded over their concern for Celeste. They assumed the memories were focused on Celeste. The musky odor, a mix of cologne and brandy, a scent Celine always associated with Marcus, the feeling of being watched, it all fit. He was the danger she sensed, that she mentioned to Millie in her hypnotic state. She hadn't been referring to a physical problem with her heart during her last session. She had been trying to imply her heart recognized his presence. His blood had saved her life centuries ago. Since then they had been bonded. Their hearts beat as one, able to sense one another's presence in some form. Marcus' ability to sense Celine was stronger than Celine's capacity to sense him. It explained her physical symptoms and her dream in which she saw him but couldn't identify him.

She glanced around her new home. The room was small, dark, damp, cold. It reminded her of the caves that fateful night when she had turned into the creature she was. She tested a few areas on the door, the walls and the opening to the outside with her powers. Nothing budged. Marcus' enchantment surrounded her, rendering her powers ineffective. She assumed this was why he was certain she wouldn't be found. Presumably the magic keeping her inside would prohibit anyone searching for her from realizing she was here.

She slid down one wall to a seated position. Her thoughts turned to her sister. Celeste had a hand in her current predicament. For once, it was not her sister's fault. Celine understood that. She harbored no anger or resentment toward Celeste. She sighed, her eyes returning to the moon in the sky.

She wrapped her arms around her knees as she drew them into her chest. Her head sunk to her forearms. A tear fell from her eye. She wiped it away. She would not give in to panic. She would remain strong; she would survive this. She resolved that she would escape this place and see her family again.

CHAPTER 20

1791, Bucksville

*D*amien and Michael stepped out of the time portal's blackness. This time they arrived in darkness. Celine had sent them to a clearing of trees on the estate, far enough from the house that they would likely find it deserted. Their eyes adjusted to their surroundings. It was a familiar setting. Their previous trip through time had sent them to the island of Martinique in 1786. On this trip, they not only had the familiarity of their surroundings on their side, but also experience.

"We made it!" Damien exclaimed after a moment.

"Looks like it. At least, I think we did. Hard to tell this time, huh?" Michael answered.

"Yeah. Well, one way to find out! I guess we head to the house, introduce ourselves."

"Sounds like a plan," Michael agreed.

They took the path leading to the main house. A few

minutes into their walk, Damien stopped. "I'd say we're in the right place... or time," he said, motioning in the opposite direction of the main house.

"Wow!" Michael exclaimed. The two men gazed to their right. "Is that..."

"Alexander's house. It's just being built!"

"It will be kind of weird to see the main house new," Michael said as they continued toward the house.

"Yeah, it will be!" Damien agreed.

The pair continued until the house was visible. They paused for a moment before continuing their journey. A nervous energy filled them both as they approached the house. Michael fidgeted with his collar while Damien babbled a few details he had received from Celine before departing.

They reached the door. Michael cleared his throat, then knocked.

"Here we go," he said.

"Yep. Oh, don't forget, she's going by Mina in this time, don't call her Celine."

"Geez, I hope I can keep all these names straight," Michael said, wiping a bead of sweat that had formed on his brow. They waited another moment. "Hey, man..." Michael started as the door opened.

"Yes?" a man wearing a black uniform queried.

"Michael and Damien Carlyle to see the master of the house," Michael said. "We are distant cousins of Mina Laurent."

"Please come in," the man stated, standing aside. "Please wait in the drawing room." He motioned to the room. Michael and Damien filed into the room while the presumed butler closed the doors behind them.

"Wow, so weird," Damien said. "It's so different yet the same."

"Yeah," Michael nodded. "It is weird. Hey, there's something I wanted to say to you," Michael began again.

Again, they were interrupted. The doors opened and another man entered the sitting room. This one was no servant. "Good evening," he greeted them. "I am Amos Buckley. Welcome to my home. My man tells me you are relatives of Mina, my newest daughter-in-law."

"Yes," Michael answered him. "Distant cousins. We are traveling on business and hoped to visit with Mina. I have a letter of introduction here, sir."

Amos took the letter, holding up a pair of spectacles to read it. "Ah, Lord Blackburn is an acquaintance. Well, you realize this country doesn't hold to titles anymore, but still his character is above reproach. Well, I'm sure you'd like to visit with your cousin. I'm afraid she might be abed at this late hour though. Shall I have her awakened?"

"No, no, sir, that won't be necessary, and we apologize for disturbing your home at this hour, but we wanted to introduce ourselves as soon as we arrived."

"Not at all, sir! The long journey has surely tired you. I imagine you hoped we might offer you a room and a warm bed! Perhaps I might offer you a brandy while your rooms are prepared."

"Please don't trouble yourself, sir. We can stay at the inn."

"Nonsense! I'm sure Mina will be pleased to have relatives as she settles in to her new home. I have already ordered rooms to be made up. If it's acceptable, we'll send for your trunks in the morning."

"Most acceptable and we are grateful for your hospitality, sir."

"You are most welcome. Now, about that brandy," he said, pouring three glasses and passing them out. "Tell me, do you quite enjoy Boston?"

"We do, sir, although, your town seems charming, a pleasant change from city life."

"It will grow on you, sir. I, myself, found Boston polluted with people, most irritating." Damien held back a chuckle, as did Michael. Michael began to answer when a man entered the room, heading for the drink cart. "Oh, gentleman, I'd like you to make the acquaintance of my son, Mina's husband, Grayson Buckley. Grayson, please meet Michael and Damien Carlyle, distant cousins of Mina's."

Michael and Damien smiled at him. Even having been through this experience once before, it was still unnerving meeting someone you already know from the future. "A pleasure. Mina will be so pleased to have family visiting." Gray smiled, extending his hand to each of them.

"The pleasure is ours. We are eager to see Mina again, it's been so long," Michael lied.

The butler entered the room again, announcing himself with a light knock at the door. "Yes, Ramsey?" Amos asked.

"I have had the rooms prepared as requested."

"Excellent, Ramsey, excellent."

"If you gentlemen aren't too tired, perhaps you'd join me in a second brandy. It would give us a chance to learn more about each other. I'll show them to their rooms afterwards, father, assuming they are agreeable," Gray offered.

"We'd be happy to," Michael agreed.

"I have put them in your wing, Mr. Buckley, down the hall from your suite."

"Thank you, Ramsey," Gray said.

"Well, I'll leave you gentleman to your brandy," Amos said, finishing his and setting his glass down. "Good night."

"Good night, father," Gray said.

"Good night, sir," Michael said, with Damien echoing the sentiment.

Gray walked his father to the door, closing it behind him.

Damien almost choked on his sip of brandy as Gray turned around. He held a small gun in his hands. It was trained on Michael.

"Whoa!" Damien coughed, raising his arms in the air.

"Now, you will tell me exactly who you are or I will shoot you," Gray threatened.

"We told you," Michael stated again, "we are distant cousins of Mina."

"That's a lie," Gray countered.

"It's not," Michael disputed.

"Are you with him? Do you work for the Duke?"

"No!" Damien exclaimed with Michael following suit. "No way! We do not work for him!"

Gray offered a quizzical glance to Damien. "So, you know of him? How would you know him?"

"Okay, okay, it's true," Michael explained, "we're not cousins of Mina's. Because Mina isn't a real person, is she? That's not her real name. We're friends... not of Mina's but of Celine's."

Gray pushed the gun forward, inching closer to them. "I don't believe you," he said through clenched teeth.

"This entire thing could be cleared up very easily by Celine," Damien said, jumping into the conversation. "She will vouch for us."

Gray's eyes narrowed as he considered the prospect. "And she'd recognize your names?"

"Yes," Damien said, hoping she remembered. "She'd recognize our names."

Gray considered the prospect a moment longer. "Fine. Stay here, I'll check with my wife and we'll determine if she does, indeed, know you."

"We'll be right here," Michael assured him.

Gray exited the room, locking the door behind him. "Wow, it didn't take us long to get in trouble," Michael said to

Damien.

"Yeah, Gray's even less kind now than he is in the future. Boy, I hope Celine remembers our names."

"Me too. Do you think she does?"

"No idea, but I sure hope so. It's been, what? Five years?"

"About that, yeah. Maybe we shouldn't take the chance? Perhaps we should try to get out of here, leave a note instead?"

"That's an idea," Damien said, pondering it.

Before they could discuss it any further, the doors burst open. They both turned toward the doorway, hoping it wasn't Gray returning with his gun raised. Instead, they spotted Celine. In a dressing gown, curls falling down around her shoulders, she rushed into the room. Spotting them, she raced to them both, pulling them both into an embrace. "Michael! Damien!" she shouted. "I never imagined I'd meet you again!" Her thick, French accent was already beginning to wane, Damien noted.

"Celine!" Damien said. "We're so glad to see you. I'm so glad you are all right!"

"Me too," Michael said.

"Do you have the book?" she asked, releasing them from her embrace.

"No," Michael said. "No, we don't have the book. We…"

Damien cleared his throat. "No, we took the book to where we were instructed."

"Which was?" Celine questioned.

"Sorry, Celine. We can't say," Michael stated.

Gray, who had watched the scene unfold from just inside the doorway, joined the conversation. "So, they are the ones who helped you, Celine?"

"Yes, Gray. It was these men who helped me that fateful night." She turned back to Michael and Damien. "You should know, I'm going by Mina now. Not that it's done me a lot of good. Duke Northcott has tracked me here. He arrived last week in Boston. Alexander, Gray's cousin has sent word that Marcus is preparing to make the journey to Bucksville. You must leave before he arrives. It is too dangerous for you here."

"We can't, Celine, eh, Mina," Damien said.

"He's right. We need something first," Michael said.

"What?" Celine asked.

"Your portrait, Mina. We need your portrait."

"My portrait?"

"Yes, the one being painted by Benjamin Abbott. We need it," Damien answered.

"Out of the question," Gray said, joining the conversation.

"But…" Damien began.

"I said no," Gray reiterated. "I commissioned that painting for a reason, it is to remain in this house."

"That's just it, Gray. It will not remain in this house," Michael said.

"Yeah, the Duke… he takes it," Damien explained further.

"And how are you aware of this?" Gray questioned.

"They are not of this time, Gray," Celine informed him.

Gray raised his eyebrows. "Really? That's convenient."

"What's that supposed to mean?" Michael asked.

"It means I don't trust you. At all. And you'll take that painting over my dead body," Gray said, then stormed out of the room.

"My apologies," Celine said. "Gray can be overzealous when protecting me. The beginning of our marriage has not been easy. The Duke has seen to that."

"I can't imagine how difficult the last few years have been for you," Damien lamented. "It's okay. But we do need that painting."

Celine shook her head. "Gray is right," she said. "He

commissioned that painting for a reason. It cannot leave this house, ever."

"That's what we're trying to tell you," Damien said. "The Duke takes it, it doesn't stay in this house, it doesn't protect this family as you intended."

Celine cocked her head to the side. "You are aware of the mystical properties of the painting?"

"Yes, we are," Damien informed her.

Celine considered the information for a moment. Then she shook her head. "Then you realize the reason it has been commissioned and the reason it cannot leave this house."

"But..." Damien began.

"Yes, I understand what you've said, but now we are aware. We can take steps to prevent it."

"What if you can't prevent it?" Damien asked.

Celine stared up at him. "We must try our best. You must have some details you can make us aware of to help us."

"We don't have many," Damien said.

"Then how do you know the Duke steals it?" Celine questioned.

"It's a long story, most of which we can't share, and we're only going on a hunch," Damien said.

"Hmm." Celine paced the room as she pondered the conversation. Turning to face them, she said, "It's late. We should discuss this at another time. Let me show you to your rooms. If I know Ramsey, he's put you in our wing."

Damien and Michael nodded in agreement. "Yes, I think he has," Michael added.

Celine smiled at them, motioning to them to follow her to their rooms. "Despite the news you bring, it is good to see you both."

"It's good to see you too, Celine," Damien said. "I worried about you the night we left you on the beach. I hated to leave you."

"I've survived," Celine assured them. "And you should be careful, I'm using the name Wilhelmina now. Mina for short."

"Yes, we know," Michael assured her. "Hopefully we won't slip up and call you Celine."

"Thank you. Well, here we are," Celine said, stopping outside a pair of rooms, side-by-side. "Sleep well. I shall see you in the morning." She left them outside of the doors, making her way further down the hall to the double doors that led to her suite of rooms.

"Well, this is weird," Damien said as they entered Michael's room. "They put us in the same rooms we're in during our time."

"Yeah," Michael agreed. "Wait." He paused. "Something is different. Is this room bigger or something?"

"There's no door to the bathroom," Damien said, pointing to the empty wall that contained the bathroom door in their time period.

Michael grimaced as realization dawned on him. "You're right. Because there is no bathroom."

"No, there isn't. We're before the time of indoor plumbing. Indoor plumbing doesn't become popular with the wealthy until the 1840s," Damien rambled, as was his tendency.

"Thanks for the history lesson. I still cannot understand how you enjoy this so much. There are so many inconveniences! The missing bathroom at the top of the list!" Michael exclaimed.

"It's fascinating," Damien argued. "I mean, we get to immerse ourselves in another culture! Experience how life was lived in a bygone era, a simpler time."

"A time without bathrooms."

"A time where people stood on principle and ceremony," Damien countered.

"A time where people died of typhoid," Michael

responded. Damien rolled his eyes. "What? They did! People died of the common cold when they were thirty!"

"I'm just saying if you take it in the right spirit, this is kind of like a gift. We truly get to experience something."

"I'll be happy when we've experienced it, past tense," Michael said. "So far, we're not getting very far. Gray distrusts us more than he does in the future. Celine seems unsure of trusting us and the infamous Duke that we worked so hard to be rid of in our time is on his way here." He sunk onto the bed, resting his head in his hands.

"Yeah, it didn't go as well as I'd hoped," Damien admitted. "We've got to convince her somehow."

"But how?" Michael asked. "We can't give her many details, not that we have many to share to begin with. And besides, she has a point."

"What's that?"

"If we take the painting now, it doesn't protect anyone as it was intended. What's the difference if we take it or Marcus Northcott takes it?"

Damien paced the room. "At least we'd have it back in our time, I guess. I don't know, we'll figure something out. Perhaps a good night's sleep will help."

Michael nodded, hoping Damien was correct. "Well, I'll leave you to it then," Damien said.

"Hey," Michael said, stopping him, "before you go…"

"Yeah?" Damien asked.

Michael stood. "I wanted to apologize for my behavior the last few weeks. I… " He paused, searching for the words. "I wasn't myself."

Damien offered him a smile. "I understand. And it's not your fault."

"I didn't realize what an ass I've been until we came here. I guess being away from Celeste has cleared my mind of the fog it was under. It's like…" He paused again. "Night and day."

"She no longer has any draw on you."

"I didn't realize how much of a draw she had. And how do you know?"

"Celine explained it to me, about how vampires interact with their victims."

"Vampires," Michael shuddered. "What kind of world have we gotten ourselves into?"

"I was pretty blown away, too. But I'm glad you're okay and back to your normal self. Apology accepted."

"Me too! And I'm glad you accept my apology. Now I need to apologize to Celine. We had quite the argument. I knocked her down again." Michael rolled his eyes. "That's becoming quite a habit of mine."

"I'm sure Celine, of all people, understands. Besides, she's like indestructible. You couldn't hurt her this time!"

"Yeah, true. And she did even the score this time," he admitted.

"Yeah, I heard that she blasted you!"

"She did, not that I blame her."

"Did it hurt?"

"Hell yeah it hurt! It was like being electrocuted, stabbed and shot all at the same time."

"Wow, that's some ability!"

Michael chuckled. "Don't remind me."

Damien laughed, too. "It's great to see you back to your old self."

"It's good to be back. Now, let's get some sleep, form a plan to retrieve this painting and get the hell back to civilization."

"Deal. See you in the morning!" Damien said, retiring to his own room.

* * *

Celine closed the doors to her suite behind her. "So that is the legendary Michael and Damien?" Gray uttered as she entered the room.

"Yes," Celine answered. "They helped me that night. It's wonderful to see them again. I didn't think I ever would."

"That may have been for the best," Gray stated.

"Why?" Celine asked.

"Do you trust them, Celine? Completely?"

"Yes," she answered. "Yes, I do. Do you not?"

"I do not."

"Why, Gray? What has given you cause to distrust them?"

"The lack of information they're willing to share." Celine tilted her head, signaling for Gray to continue. "Consider the chain of events, Celine. They show up five years ago with a mysterious, unsigned note instructing you to trust no one but them, give them the book and send them on their way. Then they arrive here, just prior to the Duke's imminent arrival. They don't have the book but claim they delivered it to the appropriate person. And this time around, they desire the Abbott portrait. The portrait with the piece of your soul being painted into it. It's a little too convenient."

"What are you suggesting?"

"What if the appropriate person, the person they are doing all this for is the Duke himself?"

Celine walked away, crossing her arms, considering the theory. "Marcus? They took the book from him only to give it back?"

"Perhaps."

"And now they seek to gain the painting."

"I'm not suggesting this is the truth, only one potential scenario. And I'm cautioning you about giving them your full trust."

Celine pondered it a moment more. "I understand your concern, Gray."

"I apologize, Celine. I realize how much you want to trust that they are friends. But I advise you to keep your head."

"I will," Celine promised. "But I ask a favor of you in return."

"Anything, Celine."

"Give them a chance. Perhaps they aren't lying. Let's not create enemies we may not have. We face a large enough adversary in Marcus."

Gray smiled, taking her in his arms. "For you, my darling, I will try."

CHAPTER 21

*D*espite the excitement, Damien slept well, falling asleep within minutes and staying asleep until morning dawned. He stretched, yawning as the sun crept through the window into his room. For a full moment, he forgot where he was, or rather, when he was. In a strange twist of fate, the butler of the house had placed him in the same room he lived in during his present time. The memory of where he was flooded back as he spied his period clothing draped over the chair.

A variety of feelings and thoughts inundated his mind. Relief washed over him first as he recalled his last conversation with Michael. Michael's mood had flipped like a light switch when turned on or off. The reversal was amazing. He harbored none of the agitation or moodiness Damien had witnessed in the past few weeks. With Celeste's influence no longer a factor, his best friend was back in fighting form.

And none too soon, Damien reflected, as his thoughts turned to the situation at hand. He needed Michael to be clear-headed in order to solve this mystery. He hadn't convinced Celine to send them back to 1791 for them to come up with nothing. They must return with the painting. There was no room for error. He couldn't let Celine down. He wouldn't. While he realized this may not solve all the issues, he hoped the small contribution helped.

As he laid in bed pondering their next steps, a light knock sounded at the door. He leapt from his bed, pulling his clothes on and hurrying to the door. He assumed it was Michael, ready to start the day. He pulled the door open, still trying to tuck his shirt in. "Hey, come in. OH!" he exclaimed, startled. "Celine! I didn't realize it was you, I assumed it was Michael. Just a sec." He closed the door and finished dressing before opening it again and letting Celine in. "Sorry, come in," he said, retrieving his jacket from the chair and pulling it on.

"Good morning," Celine said, making her way into the room. "I brought you both some things I figured you could use." She set a stack of clothing on his rumpled bed.

"Oh, thank you," he answered. "I worried we would have to feign lost luggage again."

Celine giggled at the joke, remembering their arrival to her father's home five years ago. They had claimed their luggage had been lost in an unexplained accident and were forced to borrow her brother-in-law's clothing for dinners. "If anyone asks," Celine said, "Gray retrieved your trunks early this morning."

"Understood," Damien said as another knock sounded at the door. Damien opened the door to find Michael.

"Good morning, ready for life in the olden days?" he joked before noticing Celine. "Oh, Celine, ah, Mina, good morning."

"Good morning, Michael. I dropped some clothes off for you."

"Thanks."

"It's incredible," Damien said, "your accent is fading!"

Celine smiled at him. "Do I sound American now?"

Damien laughed. "You've got a long way to go, but you sound more… well, yes, American."

"My English has improved likewise. Although, Gray was quite impressed when we met that I already knew the word 'prank.'"

The three shared a laugh, recalling Celine's discovery of that word. "Will you both be coming to breakfast?" she asked.

"Yes, I'm famished," Damien said.

"Same here," Michael said. "Lead the way, Mina."

On the way to breakfast, Damien and Michael used the opportunity to inquire about the household. They learned more about who lived in the house and on the estate and more general information. Within the household, besides Gray and Celine, now calling herself Mina, were Gray's father and mother, Amos and Elizabeth. Gray's older brother, Aiden, and his wife, Leigh, also lived in the house, although they were traveling at the moment. Gray's cousin, Alexander, lived in the household as well while he awaited the completion of the new home he was building on the estate.

Following breakfast, Celine offered to show them around the estate. It was interesting to both Michael and Damien to see Alexander's house in the process of being built. Having been in the house several times, Damien was stunned to see some of the components when they were brand new. His enthusiasm seemed to mask any familiarity he had with the estate, ensuring they gave little to nothing away about what the future held.

As they made their way around the property, Celine branched off on a path neither Damien nor Michael recalled being on before. When they inquired about where the path led, she informed them it led to a small cottage. The estate manager had lived there while the main house was being built before moving into the main house's servant's quarters. It was now being occupied by Benjamin Abbott. He used the cottage as his temporary residence and painting studio.

They approached the cottage. Celine knocked, but received no answer. She found the door unlocked and, opening it, she called in. She received no answer.

"Benjamin must not be home," Celine said.

"Do you suppose he'd mind if we let ourselves in to take a peek at the painting?" Damien asked.

"I'd expect he would. Artists are notoriously sensitive about people viewing their unfinished works."

"How far along is he with the painting?" Michael inquired.

"Just over halfway according to his last progress report."

"Hmm, is there any estimate on when he'll finish?" Damien asked.

Celine paused a moment before answering. "I'm not aware of any estimate," she answered. "Shall we return to the house? It must be close to the lunch hour."

"Yes," Michael agreed.

The trio traveled up the path leading to the house, making light conversation as they went. They enjoyed lunch with the family, doing their best to make conversation while subtly trying to gain information about the family.

After lunch, Michael and Damien excused themselves, stating they wanted to retire to their rooms for the afternoon, feigning exhaustion after their travel. Within minutes, Michael was standing in Damien's room.

"So, what's the plan?" he asked, entering the room.

"Same question I have for you," Damien said. "I'm not planning to sit here and do nothing. Napping was just a ruse."

"Yeah, I figured that out. Did you get the impression that

Celine was hedging when she told us she didn't know when the painting would be done?"

"I did. She has to have an idea, even if it's not a specific date. When she said she had no idea, right away I sensed she was hiding the truth."

"Do you suppose that painter leaves his doors unlocked all the time?"

"There's only one way to find out," Damien stated. "Are you thinking what I'm thinking?"

"If you're thinking we should go let ourselves in and check out that painting, then yes."

"All right, let's get moving."

The men made their way out of the house, avoiding any prying eyes by using the back stairs and a little used servant's entrance. Gaining distance from the house, they eased their pace.

"I hope I can remember the path she took," Damien said as they entered a clove of trees.

"Yeah, I don't remember ever being on that path before," Michael agreed.

"Me either. I wonder if this cottage still exists in our time."

"I'm not sure. I don't recall ever seeing it, but that doesn't mean anything."

"At a brief glance the cottage looked nice."

"It did, yeah," Michael agreed.

"I wonder if they'd let you live there, assuming it's still around." Michael glanced at him. "What? It solves a ton of issues. You are on your own, but you're not too far away."

"Good point. Guess we can check on that when we get back."

Damien smiled at him. "Yeah. Having a plan for when we get back makes me feel safer. Like we definitely will get back."

"We'll get back, buddy," Michael said, clapping him on the back, "and we'll have that painting, too." Michael paused, then added, "And more comfortable clothes."

"Okay, I'm with you on the clothes. As fascinating as I find time travel, I do not care for these clothes."

Damien navigated to the correct path as they talked. The house appeared in front of them as the trees opened around it. Damien issued a smirk as he raised his eyebrows at Michael. Michael nodded back, acknowledging Damien's navigational skills.

They approached the house, peering into the front window. No lights shone from within. "We might be in luck," Michael said. "Doesn't seem like anyone is home."

"Let's knock to be sure," Damien ventured, rapping on the door.

There was no answer. He knocked again. Again, there was no answer. They glanced at each other. Damien shrugged and tried the door. It swung open with no resistance.

"Hello?" Michael called in. "Hello!" he shouted again when his first attempt garnered no response. Only silence responded.

"After you, good sir," Damien said, bowing and motioning for Michael to enter the house.

"Why, thank you, kind sir," Michael joked back.

They entered the living room. It was small but well-furnished with classic pieces. Doors led from the room in multiple directions. "You go left, I'll go right," Michael said. "Meet back here in five minutes."

Damien nodded, disappearing through the doorway on the left. He found it led to a bedroom. He took a brief peek around, finding nothing of interest.

Damien returned to the living room. Not finding Michael, he approached the door across the room. He almost ran into Michael as he passed through the doorway. "I was just coming to find you," Michael said. "Painting's here." He motioned to a large canvas which stood on an easel, its rear facing them.

"How finished is it?" Damien asked, circling the easel.

"I don't know much about art, but it looks well over halfway finished to me."

"Oh, yeah. It is," Damien said, studying the painting. "Wow. It really is something."

"Yes, it's captivating. It's like staring into her eyes. It's like the painting is alive."

"I didn't realize when they said the painting contained a piece of her soul it would be so... literal. It IS like the painting is alive," Damien said.

"Yeah. So, he's got to finish the background yet, maybe a few other minor details. How long do you think finishing it will take him?"

Damien shrugged. "That I can't answer. Perhaps we can figure it out by asking when he started painting, then use that information to determine how long it took him to get to this point."

"Good plan. Celine might not be as guarded about the start date as she is about the end date."

"That's my hope," Damien began, "if we can pinpoint..."

An unfamiliar voice interrupted the conversation. "Who the hell are you? And what are you doing in here?"

Both men glanced up. A sandy-haired man stood in the doorway, an irritated look on his face.

"Mr. Abbott, I presume?" Michael said, circling around the painting and extending his hand. "Pleasure to meet you. I'm Michael Carlyle, a distant cousin of your painting's subject. This is my brother, Damien."

Benjamin crossed his arms, refusing to take his hand. "I don't care who are you. You have no business being in here.

And no business viewing an unfinished work of mine without permission."

"Sorry," Damien joined them. "We couldn't wait to see the painting. Mina told us about it. She mentioned it was unfinished, but we wanted to take a quick peek at it. Your work is amazing."

"So, you took it upon yourself to enter my home and wander around?"

"We meant no harm," Michael said. "We knocked, and the door opened. It must not have been latched. As my brother said, the painting is stunning. We couldn't help but peek at it. Your talent is well known, and I can now state your work lives up to the reports."

"An artist's unfinished work should not be viewed," Benjamin said, stalking to the painting and covering it again with a sheet. "Yet I appreciate your sentiments even if I preferred you to view it upon completion, not before."

"Again, our sincerest apologies. We shan't do it again. We'll show ourselves out," Michael said.

Benjamin gave the slightest of smiles. "Since you've inconvenienced me, could I request a favor?"

"At your service," Michael said, turning to face him again.

"Please tell Mrs. Buckley I plan to have her painting completed in the next few days."

Michael and Damien glanced at each other before Michael answered, "We will. The news will delight her."

"Thank you and good day," Benjamin said.

"Good day," Michael and Damien said simultaneously. They turned and exited the house. They made their way along the path leading away from the house. When they had attained some distance from the house, Damien said, "That couldn't have worked out better if I planned it. He will have that painting finished in the next few days!"

"Yeah, we really lucked into that information," Michael said. "We will have to keep an eye on him and that painting."

"Perhaps we should 'forget' to tell Celine about the painting's completion date," Damien suggested.

"I agree and was considering the same. I'm sure she'll find out, but it doesn't have to be from us."

"Good deal. Hey, kudos to you, nice use of the word 'shan't,'" Damien noted.

"Did you like that?" Michael chuckled. "I figured when in Rome and all that."

"Yeah, if you can't use the word 'shan't' in 1791, when can you use it?" Damien laughed. "Well, if we're not telling Celine about the painting, perhaps we should take a brief detour. Check out Alexander's house again."

"Sure, no rush to get back on my part!" Michael agreed. The two continued their walk, branching off on the path that led to Alexander's construction site.

* * *

Gray and Celine entered the sitting room after lunch, having parted ways with Michael and Damien who planned to rest in their rooms. "Brandy, darling?" Gray asked her as he poured one for himself.

"No, thank you," Celine answered, sitting down on the loveseat.

"Something troubling you?" Gray asked, sitting next to her.

"I worry about Michael and Damien with the Duke's impending arrival. I realize you don't trust them, Gray, but if you're wrong, his arrival puts them in grave danger."

"They made no mention that they planned to leave when you toured the grounds this morning?"

"No, none," Celine answered, wringing her hands.

"Darling," Gray said, taking her hands in his, "they are not your responsibility. You've told them the risks, but you cannot force them to go."

"No, I cannot. Even if I tried, I don't think they would go." She sighed. "They seemed intent on protecting that painting."

"Protecting it or taking it?"

"They maintain by taking it they would be protecting it," Celine answered.

"Have they given you any other information about why they want it? More than what they said last night?"

"No, they did not. Other than inquiring if they could view it and when it may be completed, they have been very mum about the entire subject. It almost seems they are avoiding the subject."

"What information did you give them?"

"None. We went to Mr. Abbott's, but he was not home. I informed them he would not wish the painting to be viewed unfinished and he had no estimate on completion."

"Do you believe that wise? Letting them know the location of the painting?"

"That is information they could receive from any member of this household or staff. I gave them no other information."

"I recommend we continue that trend."

"Really? Are you sure we shouldn't question them further on it? Try to determine what they know and why they seem so sure my portrait will not remain in this house? And why they suppose it's the Duke's doing? They must have more information. They must have facts."

"Do you imagine anything they say will be the truth if they offer us any information at all?"

"I am not positive, but it can't hurt to ask, can it? I held off from discussing it at length this morning with them. I would much prefer you listen to their responses also."

"All right. Agreed. We'll ask them about it following dinner."

"It is likely a fool's errand but perhaps we'll glean some detail from their responses that can help in some small way. We need to be as prepared as possible with Marcus arriving soon."

Gray rose from the couch, stalking a few steps away toward the room's massive fireplace. "I hate even hearing that man's name."

"I hate that he's tracked us here, but it was inevitable, I suppose. I'm sorry, Gray."

"Don't apologize. It is not your fault. He's a madman."

"Of course it's my fault. He's obsessed with possessing me. I am the only reason he's traveling here."

Gray shook his head. "It's no one's fault but his." He rejoined her on the couch, taking her hand in his, kissing it. "Let's not speak of him when we don't have to."

She smiled at him. "Agreed."

CHAPTER 22

*M*ichael and Damien met in the hall prior to dinner. They made their way to the sitting room where they were told the family gathered prior to the evening meal. They entered the room finding another family member already waiting inside. Damien smiled at him, recognizing Alexander at once despite the different clothing.

"Hello! You must be Michael and Damien Carlyle, Mina's cousins," Alexander said as they entered the room.

"Yes, that's correct," Michael said, also recognizing him but not giving it away.

Alexander extended his hand toward them. "I'm Alexander Buckley, Grayson's cousin. It's such a pleasure to meet you." They all shook hands, exchanging pleasantries. "May I offer you a drink?" Alexander asked.

"Thank you," Michael said, accepting the offer. Alexander poured drinks for both of them, handing them out. As Michael sat, sipping his drink, the sitting room doors opened. Celine rushed in, followed by Gray.

"Alexander!" she exclaimed, dashing to him and wrapping him in a friendly embrace.

"Mina!" he greeted her with equal enthusiasm. "It's good to be home. Although," he said, standing back from her, "I'm sorry the news is not better."

"Do not trouble yourself about the news. It is not your fault and I thank you for tracking him and reporting to us so we may prepare."

"Cousin," Gray said, shaking Alexander's hand, "yes, I quite agree with Mina. Thank you. Have you met Mina's cousins, Michael and Damien Carlyle?"

"Yes, I have. How delightful to have your family visit. Oh, please, gentlemen, excuse our private moment earlier."

"There is no need to conceal any details, Alexander," Gray replied, closing the doors to the sitting room. "Michael and Damien are well-versed in the troubles of this family."

"Oh?" Alexander asked.

"Yes," Celine responded. "Michael and Damien assisted me the night of the ceremony. The night I became what I am. They are the two who helped me remove the book from Marcus' possession."

"Oh! This is THE Michael and Damien. Well, it is my good fortune to meet such brave men. Celine has told us of your part in that unfortunate night."

"We were happy to help her," Damien said, smiling at Celine.

"It seems they have returned to assist again," Gray said, pouring himself a brandy.

"I wish you both would abandon your scheme of assisting and return to wherever you came from. Marcus is a dangerous man. You cannot risk crossing his path again," Celine said.

"Sorry, Celine, eh Mina," Michael answered, "we can't."

"Then perhaps you can tell us what you know," Gray said.

"We have," Damien said.

"You've told us nothing," Gray pressed. "According to you,

Mina's painting, that is to remain in this house to protect its inhabitants, is stolen by the Duke. We have no clue how you came to this conclusion or any details about the supposed theft."

"The Duke plans to steal Mina's painting? The Abbott painting?" Alexander asked.

"Yes, that's correct. Other than that, we have few details," Michael contended.

"I beg to differ," Gray argued.

"I agree with Gray. Something drew you to this time. What do you know about the painting's disappearance?" Celine added.

Damien covered the question, trying to appease Gray and Celine without giving away any information. "The painting has disappeared…"

"When?" Gray demanded.

"Inconsequential," Damien commented.

"I disagree!" Gray barked.

"I can't tell you…" Damien began.

"Look," Michael interrupted, "do you want to hear what he has to say or not?"

"We do," Celine said. "Please, Gray, let him finish."

Gray sighed but acquiesced. "Please, continue," he said to Damien.

"Thanks. Like I said, the painting disappeared. The Duke is the obvious suspect. The question was when."

"And how," Michael interjected.

"Right. We searched for the painting for months but found no trace of it. I did a tremendous amount of research and couldn't find a reference to your painting anywhere. It was as though the painting vanished before it was ever painted. That's when we put two and two together and came up with the theory that the Duke stole the painting upon its completion."

"Or destroyed the painting before or shortly after it was finished," Michael added. "Although we were assured by... someone very trustworthy that he wouldn't have destroyed it since it held a piece of Celine's soul." Michael was careful not to reveal the person who surmised the last part of his statement was Alexander himself.

"This is all conjecture. You have no proof of anything," Gray accused.

"We have proof that the painting is gone, that is a fact," Michael said.

"Even if this is conjecture, cousin, the threat of the painting being stolen, at any point, is serious enough to garner action," Alexander said. "You commissioned this painting for a reason. It serves as far more than a wedding present."

"I agree, but with no other information it may prove difficult. I prefer not to waste resources protecting a painting when my wife will need our protection. Are you sure you possess no other information?"

Damien shook his head. "Sorry, we don't. We're in the dark too and just trying to prevent this from happening."

"So noted, we will do all we can to prevent it. Thank you," Gray said, dismissing them.

"Gray is right. We thank you for the information. We'll handle things from here," Alexander agreed.

Celine also concurred. "I agree. You should return to your time."

"No," Damien disagreed, shaking his head.

"I'm with Damien on this," Michael said. "There's no way we're leaving until we know that painting is secure."

Gray opened his mouth to answer but the doors swung open to the room before he could. "Good evening, everyone. I am so terribly sorry. I have kept you all waiting," the woman at the door conveyed.

"Good evening, mother," Gray said, approaching the woman and giving her a kiss on the cheek.

"Good evening, Gray. Alexander, welcome home," the woman said.

"Aunt Elizabeth, thank you," Alexander said, also giving the woman a kiss on the cheek. "It's wonderful to be home. Aiden and Leigh send their love. They hope to be home within the month."

"Oh, how lovely that you saw them while in Boston," Elizabeth said. "Good evening, Mina."

"Good evening, Mrs. Buckley," Celine answered, taking her hands as they kissed each other's cheeks.

"Mother, I'd like to introduce you to some of Mina's family," Gray said, leading her to Michael and Damien. "May I present Michael and Damien Carlyle, cousins of Mina's."

Elizabeth extended her hand to them. "Delighted to meet you both," she said.

"Likewise. The pleasure is all ours," Michael said, bowing to her. Damien followed suit, greeting her in a similar manner. "I'd like to extend our gratitude for your hospitality."

"Not at all. We are so pleased to welcome guests in our home. How long will your plans allow you to stay on with us?" she asked.

"We have no firm plans, but we will be careful not to wear out our welcome," Michael said.

"Impossible!" she answered. "How charming your cousins are, Mina. What good fortune for us to welcome them into our home." She gave them all a wide smile. Amos entered the room. Everyone exchanged sentiments before Elizabeth suggested they enter the dining room.

Everyone filed out of the room, Elizabeth and Celine leading the way, followed by Amos, Michael and Damien.

Gray and Alexander brought up the rear, pausing for a moment before following the group out.

"You don't trust them, do you, Gray?" Alexander asked.

"No, I don't. They possess too much information yet no answers to our questions. They are also the two who disappeared with that book and no one has found it since. At least no one we know of. I appreciate why Celine wants to trust them, but I do not."

"I'll keep an eye on them."

"I appreciate that, cousin. Shall we?"

Gray and Alexander followed the group in for dinner. Michael and Damien retired for the evening following dinner, declining nightcaps with the family. Before going to bed, the two compared notes about their discussion before dinner. They determined that any chance they had to retrieve the painting would fall on their shoulders. It didn't appear that anyone, including Celine, would assist them with their plans. They seemed intent on handling the situation on their own. Though Celine seemed more intent on sparing them any confrontation with the Duke rather than refusing their help with the painting.

Without a plan in place, they decided to sleep on the issue and hoped to talk through a plan the following day. The painting was nearing completion according to Benjamin Abbott. They had little time to create a workable plan. Without an idea of when the theft occurred, they were also working in the dark. Still, with the Duke's arrival imminent, they realized time was not on their side. They went to bed frustrated but determined.

* * *

The following morning brought a dreary day to the Buckley estate. Michael and Damien met in Michael's room before breakfast to discuss plans for their day.

"We've got to figure something out fast," Damien said pacing around the room.

"Yeah, but what? Short of waiting around for that Abbott guy to finish the painting then stealing it first, what options do we have?"

"No idea. And what do we do with the painting if we manage to nab it? Celine will not send us back to our time with the painting."

"Hide it?"

"Where?! You saw the size of that canvas. We can't stick it in a closet or hide it under a bed. Besides, that leaves it open to be stolen again. All the Duke needs to do is search the property for it."

"Even if we found a suitable hiding spot, we still need to grab it first."

"There is no guarantee of that. According to Alexander, Abbott got his 'special talent' from the Duke himself. Which means they know each other. What if Abbott is indebted to him? He may give him the painting if asked."

"He didn't the first time around," Michael countered.

"No, but when it first happened, he may not have known to ask for the painting."

"Are we aware of WHEN the painting is stolen? Is it before it's in this house or after?"

"No idea. I found no references to it anywhere. The picture we saw of it, the one that no longer exists, was taken in 1965. So, the painting could be stolen anywhere between now and 1965."

"Well that's just great. Celine will not allow us to take her painting with us and we sure as hell can't stay here to protect it until 1965."

Damien shook his head. "Ugh!" Damien sighed again. "We have so little facts to work with. It's making creating a plan impossible."

"Yes, and making it more and more likely that this trip was for naught and they'll end up with *Ships in the Harbor* instead of the protectress painting."

"Yeah," Damien snorted. "Good old *Ships in the Harbor*. A useless painting compared to Mina's." Damien rolled his eyes, rubbing his chin in thought. His eyes widened and he glanced to Michael. "Unless…"

"Unless what?" Michael asked, scrunching his eyebrows in confusion.

"Unless *Ships in the Harbor* is the answer to our problems!" Damien announced, still parsing through the idea in his head.

"What are you talking about?" Michael questioned, still missing Damien's point.

Damien stood for a moment, still pondering the idea, tying up the loose ends in his head. "Okay, just listen, this idea is rough but…" He paused, still mulling it over. "Even if we steal the painting before the Duke does, like you said, we can't take it with us, and we can't hide it."

"Okay?"

"But what if we can hide it? What if we can hide it in plain sight?"

"What? Hide it in plain sight?"

"Yes! Instead of hiding the painting where someone could discover and steal it or removing the painting from the house it was meant to protect, what if we can hide it right in this house under everyone's noses."

"How?"

"By putting the portrait under another painting."

"Paint over it?"

"Hmm," Damien said, considering his answer. "No. We

have no idea what that might do to any magical properties Mina's painting may possess. No, what I'm suggesting is we wrap the canvas under another painting."

Realization dawned on Michael. "So, when people look at it, they only see…"

"*Ships in the Harbor* instead of *Portrait of Wilhelmina Laurent Buckley*."

"That might actually work, Damien," Michael said, considering the idea. "It wouldn't be obvious where the painting is, so it wouldn't be easy to find. The painting could still hang right in the main hall, protecting the house and its inhabitants."

"Yep. Like I said we may not have the best plan ever…"

"But it's the best plan we've got," Michael said. "It still relies on us stealing the painting first and on our ability to fit another painting over it so we better brainstorm how to make this work."

"Well," Damien began, "the reason this plan sprung to mind was because you mentioned *Ships in the Harbor*. A local painted that painting. It was around this time. If I'm not mistaken, based on conjecture from pictures and information I've found in my research, that painting would fit over Mina's."

"So *Ships in the Harbor* can solve our second issue. For the first issue, I suppose we need to keep an eye on Benjamin Abbott and get our hands on that painting as soon as we can."

"I agree. He said he would finish within the next few days. We will have to keep close tabs on him, so we have the best chance of taking the finished painting."

"Sounds like we have our plan. Start first thing after breakfast?"

"Yes, no reason we can't start on a full stomach!"

CHAPTER 23

With a full stomach, Michael and Damien informed Celine they planned to spend the day exploring the property and the town. Celine offered to accompany them, but they declined, trying their best not to generate any suspicion. They excused themselves from the house, leaving Celine in the foyer.

Celine watched them disappear down the path. Damien pointed toward Alexander's house. His interest in the construction site had been apparent yesterday. Celine imagined he hoped to explore the house again. She smiled as she watched them disappear into the woods. It was good to see them again. Her smile disappeared as she recalled Gray's reaction to them. What if he was correct? What if the gentlemen she trusted, the ones she assumed had helped her all those years ago, were agents of the Duke?

She couldn't believe that, she wouldn't believe that. Even if she didn't, their presence still troubled her. If they were truly who they claimed to be, the Duke's arrival in Bucksville placed them in grave danger. She resolved to convince them to go back to their time.

Celine turned from the window, making her way to the sitting room. She picked up the book she had set out earlier this morning. One chapter into her reading, a cool gust of wind swept through the room accompanied by the sound of a man's shoes on the entryway floor.

"Gray? Is that you?" she called, setting the book down and approaching the foyer.

"No, mon chérie, it is not," a voice answered. Celine froze as the sound resonated in her ears and the man came into her view. "Aren't you going to welcome me, my dear?"

"How dare you come into this house!" Celine snapped.

"Oh, Celine, that's not very welcoming," Marcus chided. "Or shall I say Mina? A less than clever ruse to throw me off the scent."

"What do you want, Marcus?" Celine asked, crossing her arms.

"I should expect that to be rather obvious, Celine. I've come to collect you so we may begin our lives together."

Celine was incredulous. "How many times must you be told? I am a married woman now!"

Marcus rolled his eyes. "This marriage is a farce, Celine. We both realize it, whether you will admit it or not."

"It is not. We are married in every sense of the word by our own free choice."

"It is a mistake, Celine. You'll realize that in time."

"This is becoming tiresome, Marcus."

"As is your stubbornness and unwillingness to admit your mistake," Marcus said, turning more serious.

"It was not a mistake!" Celine shouted at him.

Marcus grabbed her by the shoulders, heat entering his voice. "I have had enough of this, Celine. I have given you ample time to let this ridiculous childishness run its course."

"Take your hands off me, you brute," Celine shouted, wriggling in his grasp.

He released her; she stumbled a few steps backward. He smoothed his cravat and jacket. "If I were you, I would spend the next several hours saying your farewells to your so-called husband and his family. Let's try to make this as painless as possible, shall we?"

"I will do no such thing!" Celine exclaimed.

"I warn you, Celine, I will have you, one way or another. It can be as easy or as difficult as you make it. Remember that, Celine. Anything that should happen as we continue to wage this war is on your hands."

Fury burned in Celine, but guilt accompanied it. Marcus was correct. Any harm that befell Gray's family was brought on by her. Her portrait couldn't be finished soon enough. She hoped it brought some measure of peace to this house.

"Get out of this house, Marcus."

"For now, Celine, I will go. But I shall return and when I do, I expect you to be prepared to leave with me."

"Don't count on it, Marcus."

"We'll see," Marcus said, turning on a heel and leaving the house.

Celine fumed as the door swung shut behind him. She had put years and thousands of miles between her and Marcus Northcott. Yet he continued to create a disturbance in her life and now in the lives of her husband's family. What had she brought to their doorstep? She shook her head as guilt washed over her. Tears formed in her eyes, a few spilling onto her cheeks. She wiped them away as she rushed up the stairs to her boudoir.

* * *

Michael and Damien began down the path from the main house. Damien made a show of pointing toward the construction site where Alexander's home was being built.

They hoped the misdirection covered any suspicion that Celine may have about their intentions for the day.

As the trees closed around them, Damien risked a glance back. "Do you suppose she bought it?"

"I hope so, although I think Celine is the least of our problems. It's Gray who distrusts us the most."

"Yeah, although I can't really blame him. With that madman running around after Celine, I'd be wary of everyone too."

"Agree to disagree. I don't like that guy and I probably never will," Michael said.

"Anyway, let's see what the good Mr. Abbott is up to this dreary fall morning!"

"At least it stopped raining!" Michael said.

They continued down the path, branching off on the path that led to the cottage. As the cottage came into view, they hid themselves behind a thicket of trees. They didn't have long to wait. Within fifteen minutes, Benjamin Abbott exited the cottage, strolling down the path toward the ocean.

"Nobody's home," Michael said, "I'm going in to look at what progress he's made. Cover me."

"Cover you? Wait!" Damien said, springing up to follow Michael as he rushed to the house.

"Keep an eye on the front door, alert me if he or anyone comes."

"Right," Damien agreed, nodding and posting himself in front of the front door as Michael disappeared inside.

Michael snuck through the unlocked front door and turned right toward the studio where they had found the painting yesterday. He circled the easel, pulling the sheet down from the painting. He studied it, trying to memorize the progress and compare it to what they had viewed yesterday. There were minor changes to the scenery surrounding Celine. It appeared nothing else was changed.

Michael covered the painting and hurried out the front door.

"Well?" Damien inquired as they took cover in the woods.

"He modified the scenery a little but nothing else. Nothing major."

"Has he signed it yet?"

Michael pondered for a moment before answering. "No, I didn't see a signature."

"Then he's not done. It's often the last thing the painter does."

"Then we wait. One of us will have to keep watch through lunch, the other through dinner. We can't take a chance on missing anything."

"Oh," Damien said. "Got us covered for lunch." He pulled a napkin from his pocket containing several pastries from breakfast. "I grabbed these at breakfast."

"Nice!" Michael said.

"Dinner we'll need to improvise. It will look strange if we miss it."

"Yeah, we may have to leave him unattended and hope for the best."

The morning hours were uneventful. The artist returned around mid-morning. From their vantage point, they could see the room with the painting. The curtains were open to allow light into the studio. Benjamin Abbott did not visit his studio room before lunch. As the lunch hour drew near, they nibbled on Damien's stash of food to appease their grumbling stomachs.

The afternoon hours proved more entertaining. As clouds cleared, and the sun rose overhead, a visitor approached the cottage. Both Damien and Michael gasped when they recognized the caller. Duke Marcus Northcott strode to the front door, knocked and was admitted entry in short order.

"And there he is," Damien said.

"Making his play for the painting, no doubt," Michael said.

"Yeah, I wonder. I wish we could hear what they are saying."

"Me too, but we dare not get too close. I have zero desire to run into that man again."

"If he comes out with her painting though…"

"We follow him," Michael said.

* * *

Marcus knocked at the cottage door. Within moments, the door opened. Benjamin Abbott stood at the door, shock plain on his face.

"What are you doing here?" he demanded of Marcus.

"Why, Benjamin! Is that any way to greet an old friend?" Marcus queried. "May I come in?"

Benjamin stood aside, allowing Marcus to enter the living room. "You're no friend," he snapped.

"Oh, come now. Let's not entertain such bitterness between us. There is something important we must discuss."

"And what is that?"

"A certain portrait you are working on. A very special painting of a very special lady."

"Mina Buckley's portrait."

"Yes. I'd like to see it."

"It's not finished."

"I don't care."

"No one sees my work unfinished!" Benjamin shouted.

"Surely you can make an exception for an old friend!" Marcus countered.

"I already told you, you aren't my friend."

"Now, Benjamin, must we go through this again?"

"The answer is no."

"Must I be forced to remind you that the only reason your talents are sought after is because of me? You'd still be living in squalor drawing portraits for a penny if it weren't for me. I gave you your talent, Benjamin. And now I've come to collect."

Benjamin sighed. "What's the difference, the other two already saw it."

"What other two?"

"Mina's cousins, the Carlyles," he said.

Marcus' eyebrows raised at the mention of the name. "Michael and Damien Carlyle?"

"Yes, that's them. The pair of them let themselves into the house to gawk at my unfinished work," he grumbled.

"I hadn't realized they were in town. How fortunate that I might have the pleasure of seeing them again. I shouldn't think much of their behavior, Benjamin. They are both impulsive and ill-bred. Now, shall we?"

Benjamin led him to the studio where Mina's painting stood on its easel. Benjamin pulled the sheet draped over the canvas down. Marcus studied the unfinished painting. "Oh, Benjamin. It is exquisite," he said, considering the piece. "You have captured her well."

"You've seen it, is that all?"

"No, not quite."

"What else do you want?"

"The painting when it is complete."

"What? No! Grayson Buckley commissioned this painting! It belongs to him!"

"I don't care if God Himself commissioned it, you will give it to me and no one but me!"

"And how do you propose I explain this to Mr. and Mrs. Buckley?"

"I do not care how you explain it. That is none of my

concern. Now, when can I expect my painting to be complete?"

* * *

Damien and Michael surveyed the house from their hiding spot in the woods. Each pondering what was happening inside the small cottage. The visit lasted less than an hour. Duke Northcott strolled from the cottage into the bright sunshine.

"Well, he doesn't have the painting," Damien said.

"Nope. It's still in there, at least."

"But he's seen it."

"Yep. He's definitely after it. We can't let him get a hold of it."

"Correction," Damien said, "we WON'T let him get a hold of it." Michael nodded his agreement.

As evening approached, they discussed plans for the remaining hours. They determined it would seem too suspicious for them to miss dinner and could also be construed as rude. They reluctantly gave up their stakeout of the artist's cottage and returned to the house to dress for dinner.

After dinner, Michael and Damien attempted to excuse themselves, hoping to make another trip to the artist's cottage without anyone realizing. Their plans were dashed when Alexander and Gray asked them to join them in a game of cards. With Gray already suspicious of them, they found themselves with no other choice but to join. They frittered away the evening hours with small talk and rummy. Unable to separate themselves from the group, they retired for the evening when everyone else did, saying their goodnights outside of their room before Celine and Gray continued down the hall to theirs.

Within seconds of hearing the door down the hall close,

Michael snuck from his room to Damien's. The two discussed an alternative plan since their evening was a bust. They agreed to start fresh again in the morning, opting for some rest before continuing their stakeout. With the painting still unfinished, they determined it a safe bet.

CHAPTER 24

*M*orning dawned with bright fall sunshine. Sunlight streamed through the window of Damien's room, awakening him. He rose from his bed, dressing for the day before making his way to Michael's room. He greeted Michael, finding him almost dressed and ready for breakfast. The two enjoyed breakfast with the family, again excusing themselves afterward to travel to town for business.

They hastened down the path from the house toward town, doubling back when they were out of sight and heading straight toward Benjamin Abbott's cottage. Lights shone from inside the cottage, signaling that someone was home. The two snuck to their hiding spot from yesterday and waited.

"Looks like Mr. Abbott is still home this morning," Michael said.

"Yeah," Damien answered. "I hope he takes a morning walk again and we can check the progress on the painting."

"That's what I'm hoping, too." They waited in silence for a few more moments before Michael spoke again. "You know, this cottage isn't half bad. I kind of like it. It would be nice if it's still there in our time."

"You mean for your move?"

"Yeah. Like you said, it's close but not too close. I'd still get to hang out with you a lot. See the kids, too."

"Kids? Oh, Avery's kids."

"Yeah, Avery's kids."

"They like you," Damien said.

"They like you, too," Michael answered. "And I like them. They're cool kids."

"Yeah, they are." Damien paused. "And you could also see Avery more, too."

"Huh? I mean, I guess I could see everyone more if I stayed on the estate, sure."

Damien smirked at him. "She's kind of pretty."

Michael glanced at him. "I hadn't noticed."

"You hadn't noticed she's pretty? Come on!"

Michael opened his mouth to reply when Benjamin appeared, heading out the door and strolling down the path toward the shore. "Saved by the bell," Damien said. "Come on, let's go do a progress check before he returns."

The two approached the house with Damien taking his post as guard at the front door while Michael let himself in. He darted to his right, entering the studio. Two steps into the room, he ground to a halt. His mouth dropped open, and he closed his eyes for a moment as disbelief washed over him. He raced from the room, returning to the front door.

"Well?" Damien asked.

Michael shook his head. "It's gone."

* * *

Celine walked with Gray and Alexander to the front door. "Going for a morning walk, darling?" Gray asked her.

"Yes. I'd like to enjoy the sunshine," Celine answered. "Are you both going to town?"

"I am," Gray responded. "I believe Alexander may have some other plans to attend to."

"Yes, I'd like to check the progress on the building first. Mina, would you like to join me and walk to the site?"

"I'd be delighted," she answered. "Gray, if you see Michael and Damien in town, could you show them some hospitality? Perhaps take them to lunch?"

"I'd be happy to, darling, but I doubt I'll see them in town."

Celine furrowed her brow. "They said…" she began.

"Yes, they said something similar yesterday, yet they spent the entire day outside of Benjamin Abbott's cottage," Alexander said.

Celine was silent, processing the information. "They are after that painting," Gray said. "The question is why, for whom?"

"I'm not sure but I will do my best to find out," Celine assured him.

"Be careful, Celine, Marcus arrived in town yesterday."

"Yes, I am aware. He visited the house yesterday morning."

"He what?" Gray asked, incredulous.

"I didn't want to upset you," Celine said. "He wasn't here long. He made his usual threats before leaving."

Gray seethed with anger. "How dare he step foot in this house."

"His arrogance knows no bounds," Alexander added.

"Gray," Celine said, taking his hands in hers, "leave it." Gray did not answer. "Gray, please," she continued.

"You'd do well not to confront him as Celine suggests, cousin," Alexander chimed in. "Do not give him the excuse or opportunity to widow her."

Gray sighed. "I detest that man," he said. "But I will not confront him."

"Thank you," Celine said, giving him a kiss.

"I'll see you later for dinner, darling," he said, returning the kiss.

"Shall we?" Alexander said, extending his arm for Celine. She took hold of it after Gray helped her with her cloak. She waved as they parted ways, Gray heading to town on his horse and Alexander and Celine toward the construction site.

They spent the better part of the morning overseeing the details at the site before returning to the main house just before lunch. As they entered the house, Ramsey approached. "Mrs. Buckley," he said, taking her cloak.

"Yes?" Celine answered.

"You have a visitor waiting in the sitting room. A Mrs. VanWoodsen."

Celine closed her eyes for a moment. "Shall I join you, Mina?" Alexander asked.

"No," Celine answered. "Thank you, Ramsey. I shall see her now before lunch."

"Very good, ma'am."

"Good luck," Alexander said, squeezing Celine's hand before she departed for the sitting room.

She pushed open the doors to find her sister waiting inside, seated on the couch.

"Celine!" Celeste said, standing to approach her for a customary greeting of a kiss on the cheeks.

"What are you doing here, Celeste?" Celine asked, crossing her arms.

"I am visiting my sister whom I have not seen in recent months."

"I doubt that. You've traveled here with him, haven't you? And most assuredly you are here to do his bidding."

"Whatever do you mean, sister dear?"

"Stop playing games, Celeste. I've already spoken with Marcus. He's already made his demands. I assume he sent you to reinforce his ultimatum. To provide your sisterly advice to sway me to his side."

"If you plan to dwell on the subject, then I shall discuss it. Consider what he's said, sister," Celeste said.

Celine sighed in disgust. "You really are quite something. To counsel your married sister to accept another man."

"Oh, Celine, your marriage is a charade."

"How dare you, Celeste? My marriage is not a charade. It is real and I am not leaving my husband. Certainly not for the likes of Marcus Northcott."

"The likes of Marcus Northcott? Celine! This is no beggar off the street. You would be a duchess! You could be Queen one day. He is that well-bred!"

"He killed our father, Celeste!"

"Father's unfortunate death is of no consequence in this discussion. The discussion is your future, not the past."

"I am already married."

"Because of a promise you broke to Marcus. You were betrothed to him. With mine and Teddy's approval. You married Grayson Buckley with permission from no one but yourself. The marriage is invalid."

"I promised nothing to him. You may consider my marriage whatever you like, but you'll not question it in my husband's home. Now leave this house and never return!" Celine shouted at her.

"All right, sister dear, I'll go. But I shall return, make no mistake. We are not finished, Celine, not by a long shot." Celeste strode from the room, slamming the front door behind her.

"That did not sound good," Alexander stated, entering the sitting room. "I assume your sister has left?"

"Mrs. VanWoodsen has left. I have no sister," Celine said as she exited the room.

* * *

"Gone?" Damien said, shock ringing in his voice. "What? Seriously?"

"Yes, seriously. It's gone."

Damien stood speechless for a moment. "Oh no. No! Damn it! Now what?"

"No idea," Michael answered, also frustrated.

"All that work! Researching it, convincing everyone, coming back here and it's just gone? We missed it? The Duke stole it right out from under us?"

"It appears so," Michael said.

Damien kicked a stone in frustration, sending it sailing down the path. He placed his hands on his head as he paced around the clearing by the cottage. "No. No. No, no, no, no, no. I'm NOT going to Celine and telling her the painting is gone. I'm not returning to our time without this settled. We have to find it."

"I agree," Michael said. "I don't like to lose either. The Duke couldn't have taken it that long ago. It wasn't even finished yet. Perhaps it still isn't. He can't have gotten far with it."

"Right. Yes," Damien said, calming down. "We have the best chance of finding it here than in our time because the painting's only been missing a few hours."

"Okay, so how do we find it?"

Damien considered the options for a moment. "Start by finding where he's staying? Search the house when he's gone? This painting is not small. It should be easy to find."

"Right. Okay, so where is he staying, do you think?"

"In town? Oh wait, where was he when we first came to Maine? That house by the sea! Perhaps he's there?"

"Only one way to find out," Michael stated.

"Right. Let's go." The two took off down the path, intent on finding Marcus Northcott.

* * *

Celine pulled on her cloak before heading out the front door following lunch. "Going somewhere?" Alexander inquired.

"Yes," Celine answered. "To check on the status of my portrait. It cannot be finished soon enough."

"Allow me to accompany you. You shouldn't go out alone, Celine."

Celine sighed. "Yes, you are correct. I would appreciate your company, Alexander. Thank you."

Alexander donned his cloak and together they traveled across the estate to the cottage. Celine banged on the door when they arrived. There was no answer. Celine pounded on the door again. This time she got results.

"Mrs. Buckley," Benjamin said, pulling the door open. "I didn't expect you."

"Where is the painting? Is it finished?" Celine asked, pushing through the door.

"No, it is not."

"I want to see it," she demanded.

"It's not finished. I am tired of people viewing my unfinished work. I will contact you when I have finished!" Benjamin said.

"I apologize, Mr. Abbott, but I would like to see the canvas itself if not the painting."

"You cannot."

"Why?" Celine questioned.

"It's… It's not here."

243

"Not here? Where is it?" she asked.

"I moved it."

"Why?" Alexander asked.

"Because I'm tired of people bothering me to see it. Mrs. Buckley, your cousins visited me the day before last. They took it upon themselves to let themselves into my cottage and preview the painting."

Alexander knit his brows, processing the information.

"We apologize for their actions," Alexander covered. "They were nothing more than overzealous in their appreciation of your work, Mr. Abbott."

"Take me to it, I want to see it," Celine demanded again.

"No. Mrs. Buckley, I was up late working on the painting. I am tired. I was about to lay down when you barged in. Now, please, dear lady, I request you to leave so I may rest."

Celine opened her mouth to object, but Alexander beat her to it. "Of course, Mr. Abbott. We're sorry to have disturbed you. Our anticipation for the completed portrait is overwhelming. How soon might we expect to receive it?"

"In a few days," Benjamin lied.

"Excellent. Surely, Mina, you can wait a few more days. Now let us leave Mr. Abbott to his rest so there is no delay in his work." He escorted Celine from the house into the bright sunshine. The door slammed behind them seconds after they had cleared it.

Celine was exasperated. "He doesn't have it. He was lying," she said to Alexander when they were alone.

"I am also concerned that may be true. I also find it disquieting that Michael and Damien were here viewing the painting."

"Michael and Damien are not the threat. It's obvious where that painting is."

"Celine, surely you agree this casts an undesirable light on their motivations?" Celine stormed down the path. "Celine? Where are you going?"

"To retrieve my painting," she said, disgusted.

"Let's not do anything rash, Celine. We should return to the house and discuss the situation with Gray."

"I am not waiting for Gray," she said, hastening toward the house where Marcus was staying.

* * *

"There it is," Michael said. "And it appears you were right. There's someone in that house. Do you suppose it's Duke Northcott?"

Damien crouched next to Michael behind the bushes. "Yes. Look!" he said, pointing to a figure on the porch. "Dembe, the servant who traveled with him in Martinique."

"Well, that's one thing solved. Now we need to devise a plan to check the house for the painting."

"We'll have to wait until he's out to do that. And hope Dembe doesn't catch us."

"Do you figure he'd keep it at the house?"

"I'm not sure, but it's the best place to begin our search. Any other ideas on where he might keep it?"

"Nothing concrete, but it might be worth following him. If he's keeping it somewhere else, he'd lead us right to it."

"Good idea. Yeah, we should keep that in mind."

As the lunch hour approached, Damien shared what he stashed away from breakfast with Michael. All remained quiet at the house until the afternoon. Movement along the path to the house drew their attention. As the figures approached, they made out Celine. She marched at a swift pace toward the house. Alexander struggled to keep up with her. He appeared to be pleading with her over something, but they could not overhear their conversation.

"Whoa," Damien said. "She looks super mad!"

"Yeah. If that guy wasn't such a bastard, I'd almost feel bad for him. I've been on the receiving end of that mood more times than I'd have liked."

Celine and Alexander passed their hiding spot, unaware of their presence as they continued their journey to the house. As they passed, Michael and Damien overheard a small snippet of Alexander's conversation. "… a terrible idea. Celine, please, do not continue this madness until we can discuss…"

"Good luck, buddy," Michael said. "There's no talking to her when she's like that."

"Yep, he's fighting a losing battle," Damien agreed.

Celine failed to acquiesce to Alexander's pleadings, thundering her way up the steps onto the porch and flinging the door open to the house. She disappeared inside with Alexander following her, his reluctance obvious.

* * *

"Where is it?" Celine demanded, storming into the sitting room off the main entrance.

"Why, Celine. What a lovely surprise! Am I to understand you've come to your senses and are here to beg my forgiveness?" Marcus asked.

"I will beg for nothing from you. Where is my portrait?" she shouted.

"Portrait? I don't understand what you're talking about," Marcus answered.

"Celine, please, we should not be here," Alexander said.

"Ah, I see you've brought the other Buckley," Marcus commented. "I assume Grayson was too much of a coward to accompany you."

"Do not insult my family, sir," Alexander said, stepping between Celine and Marcus.

Marcus rolled his eyes. "You are well aware of what I'm here for, Marcus," Celine said, pushing ahead of Alexander.

"Celine, I haven't the slightest idea what this bout of hysteria concerns."

"My portrait. The portrait commissioned by my husband from Benjamin Abbott. Where is it?"

Marcus shrugged, feigning ignorance. "I haven't the slightest idea. Perhaps you should check with Mr. Abbott."

"I have. He does not have it," she said.

"And did he tell you it is in my possession?" Marcus inquired.

"No..." she began.

"Yet still you accuse me of such treachery," he interrupted her. "Celine, these accusations are becoming tiresome and my tolerance is reaching its limit. I will not tolerate these accusations in my own home!"

Celine set her jaw in frustration. "This was a mistake, Celine. Come, let us return home," Alexander said.

Celine stood for a moment more, glaring at Marcus. "Buckley is right, Celine. You've made quite a few mistakes of late. I am a patient and forgiving man. Just admit your mistake and all shall be forgiven. We'll end this farce of a marriage. Then we can begin anew," he said, rubbing his finger along her cheek.

Celine flinched. "Take your hands off my cousin's wife, sir!" Alexander shouted, positioning himself between Celine and Marcus again.

"Or what, Buckley?" Marcus growled through clenched teeth.

"Nothing," Celine said, pulling Alexander away. "We are leaving." Celine tugged on his arm again, pulling him toward the doorway.

"Consider what I've said, Celine!" Marcus shouted as they exited. "Come to me when you're ready to remedy your errors in judgement!"

They descended the steps, walking a few steps away before Celine stopped. A tear fell onto her cheek. "I'm sorry, Alex," she cried. "You were right. It was foolish to come here."

"Yes, it was foolish, but not unforgivable. Your quick temper sometimes gets the better of you, yet your courage is one of your most admirable qualities."

Celine smiled at him, wiping the tear away. She threw her arms around his neck. "Ironic. You warned Gray to stay away from Marcus this morning and I end up forcing you to confront him."

Alexander chuckled. "Yes, and Gray will never let us hear the end of it, I'm sure. Come on, let's return home."

* * *

Damien and Michael ducked as Alexander and Celine made their way past their hiding spot. Earlier, Celine and a reluctant Alexander had entered the Duke's abode. Celine had appeared to be perturbed. When they emerged, she still appeared upset. They had spoken a few minutes outside of the mens' earshot, then resumed walking down the path, leaving the house behind.

"What was that about, I wonder?" Michael asked.

"No idea," Damien answered. "Perhaps she learned that the painting is gone."

"I wonder..." Michael began.

Damien shushed him and pulled him down for better cover. Damien motioned toward the front porch. They witnessed the figure of the Duke descend the front steps and stroll down the path past them.

"What should we do?" Damien whispered. "Check the

house or follow him?" Michael considered the question for a moment. "Come on! We're going to lose him!"

"Too much chance of running into his servants. Let's follow him."

Keeping to the woods, the two followed Marcus, trying to maintain a safe distance without losing their subject. His first stop was a house they were familiar with, the home the VanWoodsens used in their time. They surmised he was visiting with Celeste and Teddy. It also added a potential location for the painting's whereabouts along with an added complication. If Teddy and Celeste were here, it was another set of individuals they would need to avoid.

Confirmation that Teddy and Celeste inhabited the house came as the trio made their way out of the home, leaving in a carriage. They deduced the unholy trio was traveling into town.

"Now what?" Damien asked.

"Circle back to the Duke's house? Perhaps Dembe will step out and we'll find a moment while he's out where we can slip in and check his house?"

"Okay, sounds like a plan."

They hurried back toward the Duke's seaside home. Reclaiming their previous hideout, they resumed their stakeout of the house. Their efforts were soon rewarded. As the afternoon waned, Dembe appeared from the rear of the house, trudging down the path.

"Now's our chance!" Michael exclaimed after he was a safe distance away.

Damien nodded, and the two dashed for the house. They let themselves in the front door, checking to be sure no one was home. With the coast clear, they whispered a plan. "I'll start upstairs, you take this floor. We meet back here as fast as possible," Michael said.

"Okay. I'll keep a sharp eye out for anybody returning," Damien agreed.

Michael darted up the stairs to the top floor. Damien glanced around the main level. He began searching the room to his right. It appeared to be the sitting room. He quickly scanned the room. The large painting was not in sight. He opened a few cabinets in a desperate attempt, not believing the painting could fit inside but wanting to be thorough.

He exited the room, continuing down the hall. He found a small study. Entering the room, he glanced around. A cursory scan of the room revealed no painting. He opened cabinets and doors, all locations turning up nothing. He approached the desk and spent a fair amount of time rifling through it. He located nothing of interest and found no references to the painting.

Frustrated, he moved on. Across the hall was a medium-sized dining room. A thorough search of this room yielded no results. The kitchen and the pantry lay at the end of the hall. A methodical search of this area came up blank, too.

He re-entered the hall. There was one doorway left. He was about to open it when Michael rejoined him. "Anything?" he asked.

Michael shook his head. "Nothing. I looked in every corner, closet, and wardrobe up there. Not a trace of it."

"Nothing on my end either. I have one last door to try."

"We'll do it together, it'll be faster. We're already pushing our luck spending this much time here."

"Do you think we should make a run for it? Come back later?" Damien asked.

"No. There's no guarantee we'll have this chance again."

"Okay," Damien agreed, opening the door. He eyed what lay behind the doorway. He glanced to Michael, gulping, as Michael also stared at the stairs leading down. "Why'd it have to be a dark, creepy basement?"

"It's not my idea of a good time either, but it is a great place to hide a stolen painting."

"True. Wait, I saw a lantern in the kitchen." Damien disappeared, returning with a lit lantern.

"That's it?" Michael said, eyeing the lantern's dim light.

"The flashlight isn't invented until 1899. The dry cell battery was invented a few years before it which is what made it possible for…" Damien babbled, nervous energy spilling out.

"Damien!" Michael hissed. "Now's not the best time for a history lesson."

"Sorry," Damien whispered. "Well, I guess this is all we have, no delaying it."

They started down the stairs. Each stair groaned under their weight, setting their nerves further on edge. They reached the bottom. The darkened room opened into a large space. Cobwebs decorated every corner. Various items laid around the room, some draped with sheets.

Damien gulped again. "Looks like something straight out of a horror movie."

"Yeah," Michael agreed.

"Like the kind with a crazed killer."

Michael nodded. "Yeah."

"Where the killer comes home and the innocent people are still in the basement and then he…"

"Will you quit it!" Michael interrupted. "I'm creeped out enough!"

"Sorry."

"Let's search for the painting and get out of this creepy house."

"Sounds good to me. Pick a corner, let's start."

They selected a corner and began their search, finding nothing but dust and cobwebs and a few random items. They worked their way around the room in a systematic manner.

Halfway through their search, a noise sounded overhead. They froze in their tracks, listening hard for the source of the sound.

They soon were able to identify it: footsteps fell on the floorboards above. Damien gaped at Michael, his eyes wide.

"Douse the light," Michael whispered. Damien complied, extinguishing the flame inside the lantern. The room plunged into darkness. The footsteps continued overhead.

"Sounds like they are going to the kitchen," Damien whispered.

"Yeah, probably Dembe," Michael breathed.

"Great! Our way out is in plain view of the kitchen!"

"Yeah, I realize that."

"We're trapped here!" Damien uttered.

"Perhaps he'll leave again," Michael said, hope filling his voice.

A voice sounded overhead. "Dembe, I'll take my dinner in the study. I have some work to complete," said Marcus Northcott.

"Oh, great," Michael groaned.

"Dinner? He's here for the night."

Michael sighed. "Looks like our luck has run out."

"Yeah, we're trapped."

With their eyes adjusting to the darkness and the room cast in the moonlight, Michael made his way to the adjacent wall. He sat down, leaning against it. "Might as well settle in, Damien. We're here for the duration."

CHAPTER 25

*C*eline nursed her sherry following dinner. She sat on the couch next to Gray's mother, Elizabeth. Gray, Alexander and Amos sipped their brandy. "How's the progress on the house coming, Alexander?" Gray's mother asked.

"Very well, Aunt Elizabeth. Mina and I visited the site this morning. I'm pleased with the progress."

"Will it be completed before winter sets in?"

"The exterior should be completed, leaving the interior work which can be done despite the harsh weather."

"And you'll leave us in the spring. What a sad day that will be!"

"Oh, Aunt Elizabeth, I'll only be moments away."

Elizabeth smiled at him before turning her attentions to Celine. "Mina, we missed your cousins this evening. I do hope we haven't put them off!"

"No, Mrs. Buckley, they had some business in town. I'm certain their business ventures exceeded their expectations and they are dining in town."

Elizabeth smiled at Celine before she rubbed her forehead. "Mother? Are you all right?" Gray asked.

"Oh," she said, glancing at him, "yes. Yes, I'm just tired. I think I will retire. Good evening, everyone." She stood before collapsing back to the couch. Amos, Alexander and Gray raced to her side. "Oh, I'm quite all right, quite all right. I merely misjudged my footing. Help me, Gray." Gray offered his hand, steadying her until she was upright.

"Come, Elizabeth, I shall escort you to your room," Amos said, offering his arm.

"Thank you, dear husband," Elizabeth said. Everyone said their goodnights to the couple before they departed the room.

Gray closed the doors behind them. "What do you suppose is the real reason that your so-called cousins were absent from dinner, Celine?"

"I am not sure, although I am growing concerned about them. They left early this morning, and no one has seen them since." She sipped her sherry again.

"It's possible they returned while you were out. You were at the construction site all day."

"No, only the morning," Alexander explained.

"Oh? I returned home for a short while following lunch and found you not here. I assumed you were still going over the building."

"No," Celine said. "Celeste visited before lunch. We had words with each other. After her visit, I wanted to check the progress of the portrait. We went to call on Benjamin Abbott."

"And?" Gray said, swallowing the last of his brandy.

Celine sighed. "He doesn't have the painting."

"What?!" Gray asked, incredulous. "Where is it?"

"He claims he moved it, that it merely wasn't at his cottage," Alexander added.

"That's a lie," Celine said.

"Why would he move it?"

"He maintains he found the Carlyles inside his cottage viewing the painting without his permission, therefore he moved it, so it remains unseen until he finishes it," Alexander answered.

"Michael and Damien?" Gray asked. "That's suspicious."

"I agree," Alexander said.

"And now they have disappeared," Gray added. "I don't like it."

"It's not Michael and Damien," Celine argued. "We both know who has that painting."

"He claims to know nothing about it, Celine," Alexander stated.

"And you believe him?" Celine questioned.

"You spoke with Marcus Northcott about it?" Gray asked.

"We did…" Alexander began.

"Yes. I was furious when we left Benjamin's. Despite Alexander's protestations, I went straight to Marcus and demanded to know where the portrait was."

"Celine, you mustn't do such imprudent things!" Gray admonished her. "At least Alexander was with you. Thank you, cousin." Alexander nodded to him.

Celine sighed. "I realize it was a mistake. Marcus would deny involvement even if he was caught holding the painting."

"And you still are confident that Michael and Damien are not involved? They were caught viewing the painting when Benjamin was out, then spent the day watching his house. Are you sure they are not working with the Duke?"

"I have no reason to suspect they aren't what they say they are," Celine said. "And on that note, I'll reiterate my concern as to their whereabouts."

"They are two grown men, Celine," Gray said. "They can

take care of themselves." Celine paced a few steps away from him, staring out the window. "And if they aren't back by morning, we'll search for them."

"Oh, thank you, Gray!" Celine said, turning to face him.

"Now, shall we retire for the evening?" Gray suggested.

"Yes," Alexander said, finishing his brandy. "Good night."

"Good night, Alexander," Celine said. "And thank you."

* * *

Damien shifted around, trying to get comfortable. Time dragged by; minutes seemed like hours. "Could they have made this floor any harder?" he complained.

"Don't ask. I'm numb from the waist down," Michael answered.

"Is he ever going to bed?"

"Probably not."

"Ugh, are you serious?" Damien moaned.

"They don't have to sleep, right?" Michael inquired.

"Yeah, but they still do! Celine does!"

"Celine's not a power-hungry maniac."

"True." Noise sounded overhead. "Listen, he's moving. Oh, perhaps he's finally going to bed!"

Footsteps moved down the hall toward the front door. The door opened and closed. Voices floated through the floor. Damien stood and staggered over toward the sound to hear the conversation. Michael followed him, after stretching and shaking his leg that had fallen asleep.

"Is that…" Michael asked after joining Damien.

"Yeah, Benjamin Abbott. Oh, perhaps this gamble will pay off."

They strained to hear the conversation overhead.

"Good evening, Mr. Abbott. I had begun to doubt you would come," Marcus said.

"Yes, ah… I just came to tell you I'm not feeling well. I won't be able to work on the painting tonight."

"So, the painting's not finished!" Damien whispered.

"Yeah, that's good news."

"Unable to work? Unacceptable, Mr. Abbott. I want that painting complete, sooner rather than later."

"I cannot work tonight. My hands are, ah, shaky. I'd ruin it rather than finish it."

"Due to your… illness?"

"Yes. I hope to work on it in the next few days, when I've recovered."

"You aren't ill at all, Benjamin, you're drunk!"

"What of it?"

They overheard a scuffle. "I want that painting finished, Abbott. I do not want your excuses."

Another rumbling overhead. "I'll finish it, just not tonight!"

"I expect your work to resume tomorrow."

"Why don't you tell me where it is? Then I can work on it when my hands are steady, and my creativity is at its peak."

"Thank you for the suggestion, Benjamin, but we'll continue as planned. You will report here, and I will take you to the painting."

"Fine," Benjamin grumbled. "Have it your way."

"I usually do," Marcus answered. "Now go home and sleep off your drunkenness. I expect progress to be made tomorrow."

Footsteps fell overhead, making their way to the door. The house fell silent. Within moments, footsteps made their way over the floorboards above. Marcus' voice hollered through the house. "Dembe! I am retiring for the evening. Have my breakfast ready at 6 a.m. sharp!"

An undistinguishable response carried through the air. Footsteps disappeared up the stairs, becoming more and more distant. After thirty minutes, silence fell over the entire house.

"Suppose it's safe yet?" Damien whispered.

"It's been quiet for a while. Give it five more minutes. If there's no noise, we make a run for it."

"Okay," Damien answered. They were silent for a moment. "Probably shouldn't make an actual run though. We should try to be quiet. More like make a slow crawl for it."

"Yeah, yeah, I get it. That's what I meant. I didn't mean like a literal run."

"Well, we could run when we get outside but inside a slow creep is best."

"Okay, yeah, yes! Let's forget waiting and just start our slow creep now."

Damien agreed. They stood, stretched for a moment, trying to loosen their joints. They crept to the stairs, crawling up them one step at a time, wincing at every tiny creak. After what felt like an eternity, they reached the top. Michael reached out and gripped the doorknob, turning it millimeter by millimeter. He eased the door open a crack. Darkness met their eyes as they peered through the opening.

Michael pushed the door open enough to squeeze through the opening. When they both stood in the hall, he eased it shut, releasing the knob as slowly as he opened it. In the dim light, Damien motioned toward the front door then the back door, shrugging his shoulders. Michael motioned toward the kitchen where the back door opened to the rear of the house.

Michael and Damien snuck through the kitchen, escaping through the back door. They skirted around the house, finding the path and racing away from the house. When they reached the cover of the woods, they paused. Damien let out a sigh of relief as his chest heaved from the exertion of running. Michael's breathing was also labored.

He bent over, placing his hands on his knees as he caught his breath.

"Whew," Damien said, still whispering, "oh man, I really thought that was it. We were finished."

"Yeah, me too. And I didn't want to die in 1791."

"Me either." Damien said, taking another few moments to recover. "Well, should we return to the house?"

"Yeah. I cannot wait to crawl into bed."

The two followed the path, returning to the estate's main house. They retired as soon as they dragged themselves to their rooms. Both of them were too exhausted to discuss the day's events or to create a plan for tomorrow. Damien was asleep within minutes despite the evening's excitement. Dreams of being trapped filled his sleep.

Celine, Gray and Alexander left the dining room. They had eaten breakfast alone, Gray's mother remained ill. She took a tray in her room with Amos joining her. Michael and Damien were also absent from the room. Celine worried about them despite Gray's insistence that they were collaborating with the Duke.

Celine planned to check their rooms to determine if they had returned home the night before. She crossed the foyer when the front door opened. Icy wind gusted past her.

"Good morning, mon chérie," Marcus said, entering the foyer.

Celine stopped in her tracks. Gray and Alexander closed the gap between them and Celine. "How dare you come into this house!" Gray shouted at him.

"Grayson, what an unpleasant surprise. I had to come. I wanted to check on Celine. She was so distressed yesterday. Tell me, darling, have you found your portrait?"

"Stealing it wasn't enough, Marcus? You had to come to gloat, too?" Celine asked.

"I'll take that as a 'no.' Such a terrible shame, I had hoped to see it. I imagine it is lovely yet no comparison to your stunning beauty, my dear."

"Get out of this house!" Gray demanded.

"My, my, it seems I've upset you. Oh, I do apologize. I'll take my leave." He turned to exit. Turning back, he said, "Oh, Grayson, how is your dear mother, Elizabeth? I hope she is well." He grinned at them before leaving the house.

Gray slammed the door behind him. Celine glanced to him, shaking her head. "We must find that painting and then leave this house," she said.

"And go where?" Gray asked. "He'll follow us."

"Yes, but somewhere away from the family. Gray, he didn't mention your mother to be kind. Whatever she is suffering from is his doing."

"It's likely she is correct," Alexander said. "But you cannot spend your entire lives on the run."

"He's right," Gray agreed.

"Yes, you both are correct," Celine admitted. "But we should put some distance between us and your family for a short time. Until we can gain a better handle on dealing with him."

"All right," Gray agreed. "But we cannot leave until the painting is in this house. It's too easy for him to stay and draw us back if we leave them with no protection."

"Yes, that is why it is imperative that we locate the painting. On that note, I must determine if Michael and Damien returned to the house last night."

"I hope they have," Gray answered. "I'd like to know where they were and if they possess any information about the missing painting. Although I'm not sure I will believe a word they say."

Celine turned to ascend the staircase as Michael and Damien appeared at the top. "Good morning," she said, glad to see them.

"Good morning, everyone. Very sorry we overslept and missed you at breakfast. Our business took longer than we expected," Michael said.

"I'll bet it did," Gray said, glaring at them as they descended the stairs.

"I hope it proved fruitful," Celine said. "I must admit to being worried when you did not return for dinner."

Damien smiled at her. "Thank you for worrying, but we are just fine."

"What is your business, by the way?" Gray asked.

Michael glanced at Damien. "Ah…"

"Never mind, don't answer. You're not from this time, yet you have some mysterious business in town that takes you until the middle of the night," Gray said.

"We were trying to find the painting," Damien answered.

Celine's brow furrowed. "My painting?"

"Yes," Damien answered.

"That's interesting, considering you'd have no way of knowing it was gone!" Gray said. "Now what is the real story!" he demanded, grabbing Michael by the collar.

"Gray, please!" Celine said, pushing between them.

"That is the real story," Michael maintained, straightening his jacket.

"How did you come to know the painting was missing?" Alexander pressed.

"We've been keeping, ah… tabs on it," Damien answered.

"Oh, I'll bet you have," Gray said, stalking to the other side of the room. "I'm sure it's important to Marcus Northcott to be kept apprised of that painting's whereabouts at all times."

"We are not working for him!" Damien cried.

"I don't believe you," Gray growled, glaring back at him.

Michael glared back at Gray. "You can believe us or not, but that is the truth. Now if you'll excuse us, I'd like to have breakfast before we leave for the day." He pulled his jacket straight one final time before turning on a heel and stalking off. Damien rushed to follow him.

"I do not trust them," Gray said as they left.

"They do behave oddly," Alexander agreed.

"What difference does it make now with the painting gone? What is important is finding it," Celine said.

"I agree. I will visit Benjamin Abbott. Perhaps he'll have more answers today," Gray said.

"I'll go with you," Alexander offered.

"I hope your inquiry provides better results than ours did yesterday. I shall remain here," Celine said. They parted ways, leaving Celine in the foyer as they departed toward the artist's cottage. She stood for another moment as Gray and Alexander disappeared down the walk. She, too, had plans to track down the painting. They did not involve revisiting the artist who lied to them yesterday. Instead, she planned to search a few areas on her own.

First, she checked on Gray's mother. She was doing no worse than she had been earlier but still could not move from bed without bouts of dizziness. Celine left her with Amos and ventured out to begin her search. Her first location was Marcus Northcott's home near the sea. She let herself into the house while Marcus was out for a morning stroll. A quick search of his house turned up nothing. She departed the house dejected despite realizing finding it in his home was a long shot.

Her second stop was her sister's home. She had no desire to speak with her sister, so she waited until the house was empty in the late morning hours before sneaking in. She searched every corner of the top two floors, finding nothing. She crept into the windowless cellar to complete her search.

As she explored the basement, a noise sounded overhead. Hushed voices and gentle footsteps signaled people in the house. She secreted herself away in a dark corner of the basement, waiting.

* * *

Damien trailed behind Michael as he stalked from the foyer to the dining room. When they were out of earshot of the others, Damien stated, "Nice going! That guy really hates us!"

"The feeling is becoming mutual," Michael said. "I'm starving. Missing dinner last night didn't help." They entered the dining room, finding themselves alone to eat.

"No. Today I'm taking enough of those scones to last us in case we get stuck again somewhere."

"I can't believe he thinks we're working for the Duke. We're back here trying to help him, getting stuck in a maniac's basement for hours and he's accusing us of working for the enemy," Michael complained, piling food onto his plate.

"I guess we seem kind of suspicious."

"I guess," Michael agreed after some thought. "What's the plan for today?"

"Well," Damien said, stuffing eggs into his mouth, "we ruled out the Duke's house. Where else might one hide an unfinished painting?"

"Perhaps at the house of his evil comrades?" Michael asked, also diving into his breakfast.

"Right!" Damien said, "Teddy and Celeste are here."

"Perhaps we should try their house?"

"Yeah, that's a perfect place. The Duke has easy access, and it's less conspicuous than his own house. Who better to protect such a precious commodity than your righthand man and his wife?" Damien grinned.

"If all else fails, we can follow the Duke and see where he takes the painter, but that's not my favorite idea."

"Yeah, if he catches us, we're dead meat."

"Oh, good point. I was thinking if we follow him, we can't steal it back then anyway. We'd have to wait until everyone left it alone or hope he doesn't move it before we can get to it. But, yeah, that's another good point. I doubt he'll be thrilled to see us given what happened five years ago."

Damien nodded as he stuffed his pockets with breakfast pastries. "Okay, we're set and I got enough for all day!"

"Let's hope we don't need it."

"Perhaps we should swing past Ben Abbott's place first and see if he's still there, too. He didn't say when he would finish the painting, but we should try to keep tabs on him too."

"Agreed. There isn't enough of us to keep tabs on everyone."

"You're right. And splitting up is NOT an option."

"No way! No splitting up. That's when people get killed in the horror movies, when they split up," Damien said, shaking his head.

"Will you stop talking about us getting killed? It's giving me the creeps!" Michael admonished him.

The two set out through the front door, heading toward Benjamin's cottage. They approached, hiding in their usual spot. Even from this distance they could see Gray, Alexander and Benjamin standing in the living room. They appeared to be having a spirited discussion. They had ascertained Benjamin's location. He was not working on the painting.

They moved on, keeping to the woods until they were clear of the cottage. Their path to the VanWoodsens' home passed Duke Northcott's. As they passed the home, Damien shuddered, reminded of the disturbing night they spent there last night.

They continued on toward the seaside home. They approached it, keeping hidden until they could assess the property. All appeared quiet in the house. Michael motioned to Damien, signaling they should approach the house and determine if anyone was home.

They advanced toward the house, peering in windows. They saw no one. The house looked deserted. After doing their canvassing, they agreed to enter and take a quick look around for the painting.

Michael tried the door, finding it unlocked. They entered the main hallway, this time agreeing that Michael would take the main floor and Damien would take the second floor. They conducted a brief but thorough search but found nothing.

They gathered in the hall after searching their respective floors. "Only one level left," Michael said.

"Yeah, don't remind me," Damien said, realizing he was referring to the basement.

"I hope we have better luck than last night," Michael said.

"Me too. Let's get this over with."

They opened the door to the basement. It was dark despite the sunshine outside. "Must be windowless," Michael said.

"Lucky us," Damien said. He grabbed a candle from the nearby kitchen and lit it. They descended the stairs in the dim light, peering into the darkness.

CHAPTER 26

*C*eline held her breath, pressed into the darkest corner of the basement. With bated breath, she waited as two figures descended the stairs. Squinting into the darkness, she waited to see their faces. As they reached the bottom of the stairs, Celine held in a gasp. Even in the dim candlelight, she recognized Michael and Damien.

Celine took a step toward them, prepared to show herself when noise sounded overhead. Michael swore, extinguishing the flame on the candle. In the darkness, they scurried across the room, out of the staircase's view.

The noise continued overhead. Voices carried through the floor, announcing the VanWoodsens' arrival. Celine overheard Damien whisper, "Are you kidding me?" She smiled to herself at his comment. While the situation was not laughable, his reaction almost made her giggle.

"Seems we have a real knack for getting stuck in basements," Michael whispered back.

Celine considered his statement, determining to follow up on it later. An unintelligible conversation ensued overhead. Celine strained to make words out, but they were too far from her to understand what they were saying.

After a time, the noise quieted. Celine assumed Celeste was resting as was often her routine following lunch. Teddy was likely doing work in his study. Despite the quietness, sneaking out was impossible without the danger of being caught.

They were trapped, waiting until the coast was clear before they could leave the house. A few moments after silence enveloped the house, Celine overheard Damien whispering. "It's quiet. Do you suppose we can make it out of here?"

"I sure hope so, I don't want to be stuck in another basement for hours."

She noted the sound of shuffling feet from across the room. Celine's eyes grew wide. They would be caught. That would spell certain disaster for them if Celeste summoned Marcus to deal with them. She must stop them from making the grave error in judgement.

Celine moved toward them from her corner. They stopped as they heard her feet scuffing against the floor and her dress dragging. "Is someone there?" Damien whispered into the darkness.

"It's me, Celine," Celine answered in a whisper.

"Celine?!" Damien said in an excited whisper.

Celine formed a fireball, leaving it floating above her hand to light the room. "Oh, thank goodness it's you!" Damien said, rushing to her. "What are you doing here?"

"The same thing you two are, I suspect."

"Searching for the painting?"

"Yes. It's imperative that I find it."

"Yes," Michael chimed in, "we know how important the painting is."

"Never more so than now."

"Why?" Michael asked.

"Gray's mother, Elizabeth, is sick."

"Sorry to hear that, but what's that got to do with the painting?" Michael asked.

"She's not sick from any normal illness. She's sick from…" Celine's voice trailed off as she searched for the right words.

"From something the Duke is doing to her." Damien finished for her.

"Yes," Celine answered, surprised he realized the extent of the situation.

"Well," Michael stated, "the painting isn't here. And we need to find it. So, let's get out of here and find it."

"No, no," Celine said, holding out her free hand, "we cannot leave now."

"Why?" Michael asked.

"They're still here. Celeste is laying down after lunch, possibly in the sitting room, and Teddy will be in his study. We will be caught!"

"Ohhhh," Damien said, "good thing you stopped us!"

"Yes. We must wait until they are out of the house," Celine said.

"Great," Michael said, throwing his hands in the air. "Stuck again."

"Again," Celine said. "What do you mean again?"

"We were looking for the painting yesterday. We were stuck last night, it's why we missed dinner. We were there for hours."

"Where?" Celine asked.

"Marcus Northcott's," Michael answered.

Shock shone on Celine's face. "Marcus'? You should never have gone there! If he would have caught you…"

"Yeah, we know," Damien said.

"We have no desire to see him either, which is why we

were stuck in that basement for hours. We waited until he went to sleep."

"You shouldn't have been so reckless," Celine lectured. "You should have informed me of where you were going. At least I could find you or search for you if something were to happen."

"We did find out that the painting isn't complete," Damien said.

"It isn't?" Celine asked.

"No," Michael said, "Abbott visited the Duke last night. Said he was too sick to work."

"He was drunk," Damien added.

"Right. Northcott was not pleased at all. He said he wanted him available to work on it today."

"Benjamin asked him where the painting was so he could work on it anytime, but the Duke wouldn't tell him. He said he'd take him to it to work on it when he was ready," Damien finished.

"I see," Celine said, pacing a few steps away. She returned to them. "This information is very helpful. Thank you. I'll take it from here once we are free."

"No, you will not," Michael said. "We'll work together until that painting is safe and back where it belongs."

"I cannot in good conscience let you become any further involved," Celine argued.

"We cannot in good conscience let you do this alone," Damien said.

"I'm not alone, I have Gray and Alexander."

"Doesn't matter," Michael said, "we're right in this with you until it's settled. And you can't talk us out of it."

"Stubborn," Celine said.

"Same as you," Damien said, grinning.

"Well, no one is going anywhere at the moment," Celine

stated, extinguishing her fireball. "We're stuck here until the house is clear."

"I hope they go out for dinner," Damien said, as they settled against the far wall to wait.

The group waited for over an hour before footsteps sounded overhead. A voice spoke near the front of the house. There was a brief conversation before footsteps led to the front door. The door opened and closed, and silence fell over the house again.

"It sounds as though Teddy may have gone out for a bit before dinner," Celine whispered.

"Yes, but Celeste is still in the house," Damien mentioned.

"Yes, but with Teddy out of his office, you could sneak out through his office window."

"What about you?" Damien asked.

"I'll create a distraction, visit with my sister."

"No way, either we all go or none of us goes," Michael joined.

"No," Celine said. "We do it my way. You two out the window, I visit with Celeste then meet you outside."

"We could wait," Damien pointed out.

"We may be waiting until dinner or later. This is the best plan," Celine argued.

"She has a point," Damien said to Michael. "I don't want to be trapped here for hours. And I only have so many scones!"

"You and your stomach," Michael said, "but you have a point. I'm loathe to be here for hours too. Okay, Celine, I guess we go with your plan."

"Good," Celine said. "Follow me to the top of the stairs. Wait there until you overhear me speaking with Celeste. When you do, hurry across the hall to Teddy's office. Climb out the window and run to the woods. Wait there for me, I'll come to you as soon as I've finished with her."

"Okay," Damien said. They rose to their feet. Celine lit the room with a tiny fireball carried in her hand. They crept up the stairs, pausing at the top.

Celine extinguished the fireball and peeked into the hall. "It's clear," she whispered. "Here I go!"

"Celine," Damien said, grabbing her elbow. "Be careful."

She nodded to him and slipped through the door into the hallway, leaving it ajar a few inches. She snuck down the hall to the front door. When she reached it, she opened and closed it, slamming it for good measure. She stalked down the hall toward the sitting room as though she had just arrived at the house.

"Teddy, is that you?" Celeste's voice called.

"No, it is not," Celine answered, entering the sitting room.

"Now's our chance," Damien whispered to Michael. They pushed the door open further and slipped out and across the hall. They entered Teddy's office, finding it empty. Rushing to the window, they slid it open and climbed out one after the other.

When they were outside, Michael reached up, pulling the window down to leave no trace. Afterwards, they rushed toward the cover of the woods and waited for Celine.

CHAPTER 27

Surprise showed on Celeste's face. "Celine! Oh, sister dear!" Celeste said, crossing the room to embrace her. Celine did not return the hug. "How lovely to see you. I hope you are here to discuss making amends with Marcus, dear. Then we can put all this ugliness behind us and move forward."

Celine sighed. "No, Celeste. I am not here to discuss anything of the sort. I am a married woman with no intentions of leaving my husband for Marcus."

"Oh, Celine. You must stop this foolishness. That marriage is a not real. Now please, let's discuss this as adults."

"I will not discuss this with you, Celeste. I am here for one reason and one reason only."

"Which is?" Celeste asked, frustration building in her voice.

"My portrait."

"Portrait?" Celeste questioned.

"Yes. Benjamin Abbott has been commissioned to paint my portrait."

"What of it?" Celeste asked.

"Don't play coy with me, Celeste. You comprehend what I speak of and why I am here."

"I'm sorry, sister, I do not."

"The portrait has gone missing. Missing just after Marcus arrived in town. He has it. I want to know where it is."

"I've no idea," Celeste said, whirling to face her.

"Really? Don't you? Perhaps Teddy is aware."

"I doubt it."

"I don't. You're thick as thieves…"

"I'll stop you right there, Celine," Celeste said, cutting her off. "I will not be accused of anything in my own home nor my husband's character impugned. If you cannot discuss a reconciliation with Marcus, then I shall ask you to leave."

"Fine, Celeste. I shall leave, having been reminded whose side my sister is undoubtedly on."

Celine turned and exited the room. Celeste called after her. "Your side, Celine. I am on no one's side but yours! That is why you should reconsider!"

Celine walked through the front door, slamming it behind her in answer to Celeste's final statements. She shook her head as she descended the porch steps. Despite being a ruse for her friends to escape, the conversation was still infuriating. She reached the path leading from the house and hurried away from the house and toward the woods.

"Michael! Damien!" she called in a hushed tone as she approached the trees.

"Over here," Damien's voice answered her. She followed the sound, meeting Michael and Damien a few feet away. "Are you all right?"

"Yes, I'm fine," Celine assured him. "I received no information from Celeste regarding the painting. I am not surprised."

"The important thing is you are safe," Damien said.

"We should return to the house. Gray will be concerned as to my whereabouts," Celine said.

"We should split up then. We need to follow Marcus and try to find this painting. We can't miss any chances to find it," Michael said.

"I understand your apprehension, but you need to eat and rest," Celine said. "We can explain the information to Gray and Alexander. Between the five of us we should be able to find the painting."

"I'm not comfortable with this," Michael began.

"Neither am I, but on the other hand, I am starving," Damien admitted.

Celine reached into his jacket pocket and retrieved the scones, tossing them into the open area. "Leave these scones for the birds and come eat a real meal. Afterwards we will discuss a plan for finding the painting. Surely now Gray will believe you are on our side."

"Okay," Michael agreed. "But only because I'm uneasy following the Duke myself."

The trio set off through the woods to the main house. They walked through the main entrance into the foyer. Celine removed her cloak as Gray came down the stairs.

"Celine, where have you been? I was worried," he said.

"Out, searching for my painting," Celine answered. "I assume you learned nothing from Mr. Abbott?"

"No, no, we didn't. He had no answers, kept insisting the painting wasn't finished but was safe. Said he only moved it to keep it from prying eyes."

"My apologies for returning late but we were unexpectedly detained," Celine answered.

"We? You two were with her?" he asked Michael and Damien.

"Yes," Michael answered.

"Yes, they were," Celine added. "They have been searching

for the painting also. That's the reason they were detained last night. They were searching in Marcus' house. They were trapped in the basement for hours when Marcus returned without warning."

Gray shook his head. "I don't care where they were. I don't want to argue. Mother is worse."

"Oh, no!" Celine exclaimed. "Are there new symptoms?"

"Yes. She's having spells of nonsensical talk. She's too unsteady to even stand at this point."

"I'll see her at once," Celine said. "I'll do what I can to calm her."

Alexander entered the house, joining the group. "Good evening, everyone. Gray, how is Aunt Elizabeth?"

"Worse," Gray answered. "Celine is going to her now."

"The news is not much better in town, I'm afraid," Alexander said. "There have been unexplained animal deaths on several of the farms."

"That's only the beginning," Celine said. "Wherever he goes, darkness and chaos follow. Please excuse me while I check on Mrs. Buckley. Michael, Damien, I will meet you outside your room before dinner."

Celine disappeared up the stairs along with Michael and Damien, leaving Gray and Alexander to continue their discussion about the widespread effects of the Duke's presence. Celine parted ways with the men at the top of the stairs, going to Elizabeth's suite.

With a quiet knock, she slid the door open, peeking inside. Amos sat at Elizabeth's bedside, holding her hands. "Excuse me, Mr. Buckley," she said just above a whisper.

"Mina, my dear, come in. Elizabeth is resting," he said.

Celine entered the room, closing the door behind her. Amos stood, allowing Celine to take his seat on the bed next to Elizabeth. As Celine sat, Elizabeth's eyes opened. She smiled at Celine. "Oh, look at me abed while the lady of the house tends to me," she said with a strange accent. "I should be tending to you Duchess Northcott."

"This strange talk started several hours ago. I can't understand anything she is babbling!"

"She must be delirious," Celine said to Amos.

"Have you ever witnessed this before?"

"I have, Mr. Buckley. In Martinique, I have seen fevers of such type which cause confusion. It should pass as soon as the illness wanes."

"Poor woman," Amos said.

"Mr. Buckley," Celine said. "Do you mind fetching a cool cloth for her head? It may help with her symptoms."

"If you suppose it will help, of course."

"Duchess Northcott, I promise I will be right as rain soon," Elizabeth said as Celine turned her attention toward her. "I don't mean to be such a bother."

Celine smiled at her, despite being disturbed by the name Elizabeth used for her. "No bother at all," she said, patting her hands. "I will give you some medicine to help you."

"Oh, how kind, Duchess Northcott. Whatever you feel is right."

Celine touched her cheek, sending her to sleep in seconds. Afterward, she rubbed her temples, whispering a few words in a mix of Latin and French. She finished as Amos entered the room with a cloth and basin in his hands. Gray followed him.

"How is she?" Amos asked.

"Asleep," Celine answered, allowing Gray to take her place. Amos placed the cool cloth on her forehead. "She seemed much more relaxed just before she fell asleep. Perhaps now she can rest."

They stayed at Elizabeth's bedside for a few more moments. "Will you both excuse me? I would like to join my cousins for dinner."

"Of course, Mina," Amos answered. "Please give them our apologies for not attending."

"I will, but I am sure they will understand."

"I'd like to sit with Mother a while longer if you don't mind, Mina."

"Of course not, dear," she said, rubbing his shoulder. "I'll check with you before I retire for the evening."

"Thank you, darling," Gray said, kissing her hand.

Celine left the room, leaning against the door as she closed it. She sighed, thinking of Elizabeth. The poor woman didn't deserve this. She had been so welcoming to Celine when they had arrived. Gray had announced their marriage in a letter. They had traveled on their "honeymoon" for almost one year before they returned to his family home while trying to avoid the Duke. Elizabeth had welcomed her new daughter-in-law with open arms, unaware of the trouble Celine brought with her.

Tears threatened to escape from Celine's eyes. She held them back, setting her jaw. She had work to do. She had to find her painting, had to recapture it from the clutches of the Duke. This house and its occupants desperately needed it. Celine took a deep breath, resolving to continue the search. She would continue her investigation tonight, alone or with Michael and Damien.

But first, she wanted them to eat. They were, after all, human and required sustenance and rest. They could discuss a plan over their meal. She navigated the halls toward their rooms. She found them ready and waiting in the hall as she rounded the corner.

"How is Gray's mom?" Damien asked.

"Not well," Celine answered. "It is imperative that we find that painting."

"I agree," Michael said. "Perhaps we should skip dinner."

"No," Celine insisted with a shake of her head. "You must

eat. Finding it before or after dinner won't a make a bit of difference. It will only jeopardize your own health."

"We'll eat fast," Damien assured her.

"We'll discuss a plan over dinner. Then we will be prepared as soon as we are finished eating."

"Sounds like a plan," Michael said, motioning toward the main hall. "Shall we?"

The trio dined alone. Gray and Amos took trays in Elizabeth's room and Alexander was completing some work, also requesting dinner be sent to his office. It made planning for their evening hunt easier. They agreed that spying on Marcus Northcott was the easiest and fastest way to find the painting. With Celine assisting them, they were comfortable being that close to the Duke.

They finished their meal as quickly as they were able. With no delay, they went to the foyer, donning their cloaks and exiting the house. They began by checking Benjamin Abbott's home, finding it empty. From there, they took the shortest path to the Duke's home, hiding themselves in the woods as close as possible to the home.

They surveyed the house. There appeared to be no one home. Lights lit some of the rooms downstairs, but from their vantage point, they could see no one in the home.

"Great!" Michael groused. "Appears we've missed our chance."

"Yeah, he's gone and so is Benjamin. They have to be with the painting," Damien complained. "Well, that figures! Damn it!"

"I have an idea," Celine said. "Wait here. Do nothing until I'm back."

"Whoa, Celine, wait!" Michael said, grabbing her elbow.

"Yeah, what's the plan?" Damien asked.

"You're right, it appears Marcus is gone. We can't follow

him to the painting unless he's here. So, I'll lure him back here so we can follow him."

"You can't!" Damien exclaimed.

"I'm with Damien on this one," Michael said. "We missed our chance tonight, we won't miss it the next time, even if we have to stay here all night."

"That's ridiculous! There is no reason to wait," Celine argued. "This will work. If I appear on his doorstep, he will return."

"But at what cost?" Michael contended.

"Yeah, you can't sacrifice yourself," Damien said. "You shouldn't go anywhere near that maniac."

"I'm not sacrificing myself! I'm capable of handling a simple conversation with Marcus. I'm in no danger. Once I've returned, we'll wait for him to leave the house again. With any luck, he'll lead us right back to the painting. Now do not go anywhere until I've returned. If he leaves the house before I am back, note where he goes. We'll follow him as soon as we're reunited."

"Celine..." Damien began, stopping short of saying anything further when she began walking away, turning to give him a wink.

"Wish me luck!" she said.

"Wow, she's stubborn," Damien said.

"Yeah. Hasn't changed in two hundred years either," Michael said as Celine increased the distance between them, marching toward Marcus Northcott's house.

Celine strode toward the house. Her purpose was twofold. Not only would she use the ruse to follow Marcus and hopefully find the painting, but she would also use the opportunity to discuss Gray's mother with Marcus. Perhaps appealing to him would help the situation. While she doubted it would, it didn't hurt to try.

Celine approached the house, climbing the stairs to the

porch. She risked one glance back toward the woods where Michael and Damien waited, then knocked at the door. Dembe answered the door.

"Good evening, Dembe," Celine said. "I am here to speak with Duke Northcott."

"Miss Celine," Dembe answered her, "Duke Northcott is not at home."

"Then I shall wait while you fetch him," Celine said, stepping into the entryway.

"Duke Northcott cannot be disturbed," Dembe answered. "If you prefer to wait, you may use the sitting room. I shall make him aware of your presence as soon as he returns." He motioned toward the room off the entryway.

"Dembe, I cannot wait for Duke Northcott to return. My business with him is urgent. It is imperative that I speak with him at once."

"Miss Celine, I do not know his whereabouts," Dembe said.

Celine's eyes narrowed as she tried to determine the truthfulness of his statement.

"I suggest you find him at once!" she exclaimed. "He will, undoubtedly, desire to hear what I have to say."

"Miss Celine, I…" Dembe began.

"Dembe," Celine said, allowing annoyance to creep into her voice, "should Duke Northcott return home to find out I have been here requesting to speak with him and you've done nothing, I can guarantee he will be less than pleased. Now, I shall wait in the sitting room while you fetch him from wherever he is."

"Yes, Miss Celine," Dembe said.

Celine sat on the loveseat near the fireplace, listening as the back door closed as Dembe left the house. Her plan was working. As she suspected, Dembe had at least an inkling of Marcus' whereabouts. While Marcus often kept his plans secret from most people, he also preferred to be prepared for any unexpected occurrences. He had likely left Dembe some way of contacting him.

Celine waited, reflecting on her dealings with Marcus, past and present. She worried for Michael and Damien, waiting for her in their hideaway. Time crept by, marked by the ticking of the mantle clock. After about thirty minutes, footsteps sounded on the porch.

The sound of a man's shoes announced Marcus' arrival in the house. Her heart skipped a beat, and she swallowed hard as she prepared for the confrontation. Within moments, Marcus entered the sitting room.

"Celine, what a pleasant surprise," Marcus greeted her. "I was delighted when I learned you had requested to see me. Am I to assume this urgent late evening call is to announce the end of this mockery of a marriage and your return to your rightful place?" He poured a brandy for himself. "Brandy, my dear?"

"No," Celine said, standing.

"You're right, an occasion such as this calls for champagne!"

"I am not here to reconcile with you, Marcus. I am here to discuss Elizabeth Buckley."

Marcus sighed, sipping his brandy. "How disappointing."

"You must stop your attack on her," Celine said.

"I haven't the faintest notion what you are referring to, Celine," Marcus said.

"She's innocent in this, she doesn't deserve to suffer because of the feud between us. Stop what you are doing to her!"

Marcus chuckled. "Pleading will do you no good, Celine. My sympathy doesn't extend to the Buckley family."

"Marcus, please!"

Marcus was silent for a moment. "All right, Celine. I'll

stop what I'm doing to her." Celine breathed a sigh of relief. "When you leave Grayson Buckley and return to me." Celine's jaw tightened, a scowl settling on her face. "Oh, such a beautiful pout," he said, tracing her jawline with his finger.

"Do not touch me!" she said through clenched teeth, pushing his hand away.

"Do not waste my time," he growled back, grabbing her hand. She pulled her hand from his grasp. "I will not be played a fool, Celine. The next time you summon me it had better be for a better reason than to discuss Grayson Buckley's ailing mother."

"It is an urgent reason, you…" Celine began.

Marcus threw his glass against the fireplace, shattering it into tiny pieces. He grabbed her by the shoulders, pulling a shocked and frightened Celine toward him. "Do not presume, Celine, to ask me for favors. I would have given you everything, anything you asked for. You married that buffoon Buckley. Unless you've come to seek my aid in leaving him, you have lost your privilege to request anything of me." He released her; she stumbled back a few steps before steadying herself. "Now, I have my own urgent business so unless you've reconsidered, we have nothing further to discuss this evening."

Celine composed herself. "Urgent business?" she scoffed. "Do you mean overseeing the completion of the painting you stole?"

"Celine, I would recommend you cease with this childish behavior."

"I'm just curious," Celine pushed.

"My business is none of your concern, my dear. Now run along. I'm sure dear, sick Elizabeth Buckley could use a nursemaid."

Celine glared at him but made no further attempts at conversation. Picking up her skirts, she stormed from the room and the house, down the steps and path. When she was a safe distance from the house, she darted off the path and dashed to the edge of the woods.

She rejoined Michael and Damien. "Everything go okay?" Damien asked as she returned.

"Yes. The plan worked as I expected. Marcus returned home and he said he had urgent business to attend to. I'd stake anything on that business being returning to my painting."

"Right, now we just wait to follow him," Michael said. They waited a few moments, eyes glued to the house.

After a few minutes, Damien inquired, "Where is he? Did he use the back door instead? Did we miss him?"

"Perhaps he's not going back tonight," Michael said.

"He's going. He's scolding Dembe for summoning him away from it at my request. I regret using poor Dembe."

"Hopefully the ends justify the means," Michael said.

Celine nodded her head and returned to surveying the front door. Within another moment, the trio was rewarded. Marcus Northcott emerged from the house, making his way down the path, heading away from them.

"Looks like your plan paid off," Michael said. "Here we go."

"Careful," Celine said, holding him back for a moment, "not too close. He'll sense me."

Michael nodded, waiting a moment before they proceeded. They followed behind Marcus at a safe distance, using the woods for cover when possible. They arrived outside of a rundown barn. Marcus entered the barn after speaking with a man who stood outside the main doors.

"Ah," Celine exhaled."He has Stefano guarding it."

Damien and Michael recognized Stefano. They had seen him in their time. It was the man Celine had almost killed in the alleyway behind the local bar when she learned he had robbed her sister of her life.

It wasn't long before another figure emerged from the barn. "Is that Teddy?" Damien asked, squinting into the darkness.

"Yes, that's him," Celine said. "He's likely the one who knew where Marcus could be found. Marcus wouldn't have trusted Dembe with that information."

"One of us should get closer, try to find out any information about whether or not the painting is complete," Michael said.

"It has to be one of us," Damien said. "He'll sense Celine."

"Rock, paper, scissors for it? Loser has to go to the barn," Michael suggested.

"Ha! Yes!" Damien whispered triumphantly as his rock crushed Michael's scissors.

"Wish me luck!" Michael said, standing from his crouched positions behind the nearby brush.

"Be safe," Celine said, squeezing his hand before he crept toward the side of the barn. Careful to stay out of Stefano's site, he snuck to the side wall, pressing himself against it. A gap between the boards allowed him to spy a small area inside the barn. He peered through the small crack. Inside, the painting stood in the middle of the floor. Benjamin Abbott stood a foot away, speaking with Marcus Northcott.

Michael strained to overhear the heated conversation. By the gesturing, it appeared they were having an argument.

"... tired!" Abbott said. "I cannot work anymore tonight! I'll finish it tomorrow or the next day."

"That is unacceptable, Benjamin. I demand you finish the painting tonight!"

"What put you in such a foul mood? Didn't hear what you wanted from the lady?" Benjamin chuckled.

"That is none of your affair. I have waited long enough for you to complete this painting."

"You've waited two days and inconvenienced me to no end! If the painting hadn't been moved from my studio, I could have finished it! I cannot paint in this light nor at this hour."

"I expect you to finish this tomorrow," Marcus insisted.

"Fine," Abbott said, removing his artist's smock and throwing it down.

"Just a moment, Benjamin," Marcus said. Benjamin paused, sighing. "You'll need this." Marcus brandished a blindfold, slipping it over his eyes. He called for Stefano, instructing him to return the painter to his cottage then return here.

Michael rushed back to Damien and Celine after Stefano left with the artist. "Well?" Damien asked.

Michael gulped some air before launching into his recap. "Your painting's in there," he began. "It's not finished. They were having an argument, Benjamin and the Duke. Benjamin didn't want to finish it; said he was too tired, and the light wasn't good or something."

"Did he say when he'd finish it?" Celine asked.

"Tomorrow. The Duke insisted. He was not happy in the least when Benjamin refused to finish it tonight."

"I can imagine. He is a man used to getting his way," Celine said.

"We will have to keep a constant watch on the building," Michael said.

"Yes, although there should be nothing else done tonight," Celine said. "You both should get some rest."

"No way, we found the painting. We're not leaving it until we have it back," Michael said, shaking his head.

"That's not feasible. As soon as we return to the house, I will send Alexander to monitor the barn for the night."

Michael opened his mouth to object when they saw movement on the path. Stefano was returning. Celine shushed him as they watched him speak with Marcus outside of the barn after announcing himself. After a moment, Marcus strode off toward his home.

"He's going home for the night," Celine said. "We're safe to go home for the night. Mr. Abbott isn't an early riser and certainly not an early worker. We have time for you both to get some rest and breakfast before we return."

"I don't like this, Celine," Michael said, "but I assume you're not taking 'no' for an answer."

"Your assumption is correct," Celine said, standing. "Come, we shall return home for you to rest."

They made their through the woods, away from the barn. They took the path leading to the house. As they entered the house, Celine assured them she would speak with Alexander, demanding Michael and Damien go straight to bed. They agreed to meet early for breakfast and return to the barn as early as possible.

CHAPTER 28

*C*eline paced the floor outside Michael and Damien's room. She was unable to find Alexander when they returned to the house last night. After checking with Gray, she found his mother worse, now feverish. She prepared a concoction of healing aids for Elizabeth, spending the night at her side along with Gray. By morning, Elizabeth was awake but still feverish and still referring to Celine as Duchess Northcott. Celine had left Gray and Amos with her, giving them more of the mixture of herbs she had prepared to keep her fever at bay.

Damien soon joined her and moments after him, Michael. "Good morning," she said to each of them as they entered the hallway.

"Good morning," Damien said. "Let's get some breakfast and relieve Alexander."

Celine sighed. "Yes, I was unable to find Alexander last night when we returned. So, we won't be relieving anyone. But, if I am correct, Benjamin is not even out of bed yet, so it is unlikely he is working on the painting let alone have it finished."

"Let's hope you're right," Michael said. "We'll eat fast."

"How is Elizabeth, by the way?" Damien asked as they descended the stairs to the dining room.

"A bit worse," Celine said. "But awake as of this morning."

Damien shook his head. "Poor Elizabeth," he said as they entered the dining room.

They found themselves alone, given the early hour.

"We must get that painting, sooner than later," Michael said.

They ate in record time. Before they left the dining room, Damien shoved a few extra scones into his pocket. Celine stared at him, an odd expression on her face. Damien glanced up, noting her countenance. "What?" he asked. "We could be there for hours!"

Despite the dire circumstances shrouding the house, Celine giggled, shaking her head at him. "If you're quite finished, we can be on our way," she said, still laughing.

"Yes, I am quite finished, thank you," he said, grinning. He offered his arm, which she accepted, and they followed Michael to the foyer.

When they arrived, Ramsey was closing the sitting room doors. "Mrs. Buckley," he said as she crossed the entryway.

"Yes, Ramsey?"

"Mrs. VanWoodsen is here to see you. She is in the sitting room."

Celine's expression turned to stone. Annoyance was plain on her face. "You two go ahead. I will catch up with you as soon as I've dealt with this issue."

"Good luck," Damien said. "See you soon."

Michael and Damien donned their cloaks, exiting the house. Celine took a deep breath, steadying her nerves before entering the sitting room. She pushed open the doors, entering the room. Celeste waited by the window. She turned to face Celine. "Good morning, sister dear."

Celine closed the doors before speaking. "What do you want, Celeste?"

"To speak with you."

"I'm busy, can it wait?"

"No," Celeste said. "It's urgent."

Celine narrowed her eyes. "Then I suppose you better get on with it. What is it you want to speak to me about?"

"Your visit to Marcus last evening."

Celine rolled her eyes. She stalked across the room, keeping her back to Celeste. "There is nothing to discuss, Celeste."

"Celine, stop acting like a child."

Celine whipped around to face her. "I am not the one acting like a child. I am not the one punishing innocent people because I did not get my way. I tried to reason with him, Celeste. He is impossible."

Celeste approached her from across the room. "Reason with him? He is being reasonable."

"Reasonable? Celeste, Gray's mother is lying upstairs in her bed too sick to move. She is a victim of his wickedness. And for what? Because he cannot accept that I married another man."

"He cannot accept that you broke your promise. You had no business marrying Grayson Buckley while you were engaged to Marcus."

Celine rolled her eyes. "Oh, Celeste, please. My so-called engagement to Marcus was the charade, not my marriage to Gray."

"Yet there you were seeking Marcus' aid last night. You did not cling to your husband, you sought another man to assist you with your problems. Do you think that's fair, Celine?"

Incredulous, Celine cried, "Because the situation is of his creation!"

"The situation is of your doing, Celine! You married Grayson Buckley without the permission or approval of Teddy and I as your guardians nor your fiancé!" Celine shook her head in frustration. "You created this situation, Celine. Then you beg him to take pity on you, to allow you to continue with this folly. To assist you in it even!"

Celine crossed her arms. "This conversation is finished."

The sitting room doors opened as Celine attempted to end the conversation. "Good morning, Celine!" Teddy said. "I trust you are doing well." He entered the room, closing the doors behind him. "By the appearance of my wife's face, the conversation is not progressing as she hoped."

"The conversation is over," Celine said.

"She is no less stubborn now than she was before she married that man," Celeste said, frustration clear in her voice. She turned to face the window, wringing her hands with vexation.

"Celine, as your brother-in-law..." Teddy began.

"You are no brother-in-law to me! I have no sister."

"Now, Celine, I will not tolerate this!" Teddy shouted at her.

"You have no choice. You are no longer my guardian, Teddy. That position belongs to my husband now."

"You don't have a husband, Celine," Teddy countered. "Your marriage is a pretense, a fraud."

"My marriage is anything but fake. Now I will ask you and your wife to leave my home."

Celeste whirled to face Celine. She hastened to her side, taking Celine's hands in hers. "Celine, please. As your sister and someone who only wants the best for you, I beg you to reconsider your actions. Please, Celine, you cannot continue to live like this. The animosity between you and Marcus cannot persist."

Celine pulled her hands away. "You should discuss that with Marcus. The animosity exists on his part."

"Celine, listen to your sister's advice. She is older, wiser and wants the best for you."

Celine made one last appeal to them. "Then you couldn't possibly wish for me a life with Marcus. I love Grayson and he loves me. Please support me in this and be happy for me."

Celeste glanced to Teddy. "Celine," Teddy responded, "We cannot support you in something we deem a mistake."

Celine sighed. "Then again, I must ask that you leave my home."

Celeste opened her mouth to respond, but Teddy stopped her, placing his arms around her shoulders and turning her toward the door. When they reached the doors to the foyer, Teddy paused saying, "Consider what we've said, Celine. I realize you are angry and upset, but please give it serious reflection when your emotions have quelled." They left the room and the house. Celine watched them walk down the path away from the house. Their words rung in her mind. She shook her head, dismissing their comments.

She turned from the window. Many other things crowded her mind. First and foremost was rejoining Michael and Damien and continuing their plan to retrieve the painting. She exited the room, pulling on her cloak and leaving the house behind.

As she crossed the property, her mind could not stop dwelling on her sister's words. Did they really expect her to leave her husband for Marcus? Would her life continue like this forever? A continual struggle, a constant fight for her independence from this man. No, she resolved, this would pass. The sting of her marriage was still fresh for them. It would settle. It would pass.

She pushed the conversation from her mind as she closed the distance to the barn. Within moments, she saw the barn.

She scanned the area, trying to find her friends. They were well hidden. It took her an extra moment to find them. They had shifted hideouts to one that provided a better view of the path leading toward the barn.

She crept behind them, squatting down between them. "Anything?" she whispered.

Damien, who was crouched behind a large bush, fell to his side. Michael jumped, almost revealing himself.

"Geez, Celine," Damien said, regaining his feet and brushing his side off. "I didn't realize silent stalking was one of your skills."

"Sorry," she said. "I didn't mean to startle you, I was trying to be quiet, so we weren't given away."

"You were a little too quiet," Michael admitted. "And, no, nothing, no movement. That Stefano guy came in and out once, but nothing else, no visitors. I snuck up and peeked inside and no one is in there."

"So, we wait," Celine said, settling in.

"Yeah. How was your conversation with Celeste?" Damien asked.

"Useless," Celine said.

"I assume she's still on the Duke's side in this whole thing?" Damien inquired.

"Yes, she is and so is Teddy."

"I cannot understand how she is so delusional," Damien said. "You're her sister! How can she want you to marry that guy?"

"She is blinded by the power he offers her," Celine explained. "And she finds it easier."

"Easier?"

"Yes," Celine said. "This struggle, the constant battle between us. She imagines it would be easier if I succumbed to his wishes."

"I've heard of jealous ex-boyfriends before, but this guy takes the cake," Michael chimed in.

"Ex-boyfriends?" Celine asked.

"Yeah, like your previous boyfriend. The man you dated before you married Gray." Confusion crossed Celine's face.

"Your sweetheart," Damien said, using vernacular of the times.

"Oh!" Celine said, catching on. "Yes, well anyway I suppose Celeste has a point about my, what is it you said?"

"Ex-boyfriend?" Michael said.

"Yes, my ex-boyfriend."

"What do you mean she has a point?" Damien asked.

"I assume much of the trouble that has surrounded everyone near to me since my marriage to Gray would no longer be an issue."

"But at what cost, Celine?" Damien posed.

Celine shook her head, staring at the ground. "What is it costing everyone already?"

"Celine, no!" Damien said, grabbing her by the shoulders and shaking her. "You've got to remain strong. You cannot give in to him!"

"Yeah, I agree. He's a maniac. And besides, you love Gray and Gray loves you. You've done nothing wrong," Michael added.

Celine nodded, giving them a tight-lipped smile. She grabbed each of their hands. "Thank you, both of you. I needed to hear that."

Damien put his arm around her, giving her a half-hug. They settled into seated positions on the ground. There was no movement at the barn for several hours. After a while, Damien offered everyone some of the scones he had pocketed earlier after telling Celine that he was right to bring them. She giggled at him, though turned them down. She had less need to eat than they had, one benefit of being the way she was. She allowed them to keep them in case the hours wore on toward evening and they had to snack on them later.

The noon hour came and went and, after their meager lunch, they made quiet conversation, trying to make the passage of time as pleasant as possible. Afternoon wore on. They ran out of small talk, reverting to silent watching. Damien yawned as late afternoon approached. Celine worried he hadn't gotten enough rest, though he assured her he was fine, merely bored.

A few moments later, their patient waiting was rewarded. Movement in the distance caught Celine's eye. "There!" she whispered, pointing down the path.

The men squinted into the distance. Three figures were making their way down the path. As the party approached, they could make out the forms of Marcus Northcott, Theodore VanWoodsen and a blindfolded Benjamin Abbott.

They led the artist inside the barn without removing the blindfold. Michael stood. "I'll go take a peek at what's going on," he whispered.

Celine grabbed him, pulling him back down. "Stop!" she hissed, motioning toward the barn. Marcus Northcott emerged from the doors and strolled down the path away from their hideout.

"Close call!" Damien said.

"Yeah, thanks for the save," Michael said.

"It appears Marcus has more important things to do than wait for Mr. Abbott to finish the painting."

"Wow, I expected him to want to be here the moment it was finished," Michael said.

"Oh, I imagine he will be," Celine said. "I'm sure one of his minions will fetch him so he can be here for the momentous occasion."

"The question is, how long will that take?" Damien pondered, posing a rhetorical question.

"Yes," Celine said. "Did you catch a glimpse of the painting last night?" she asked Michael.

"Yeah, I could see it. But I'm not sure how long his final touches will take him. Perhaps a few hours? That's just a guess though," he said, shrugging.

"Well, I suppose it takes as long as it takes. You've got enough scones to hold out for hours."

"Very funny, Celine," Damien said, shaking his head at her. They settled in for another wait. After an hour passed, Michael snuck toward the barn to peek at the progress. He returned within a few minutes, reporting that Benjamin was working on the background of the painting. By Michael's amateur estimate, he thought they were in for a few more hours. Damien offered him another scone to nibble on while they waited.

As the sun lowered toward the horizon and mid-afternoon turned to late afternoon, Stefano left the barn, hurrying down the path away from them. Within thirty minutes, he returned with Marcus.

"He must be close to finishing!" Celine exclaimed in a whisper.

"Yes, then we'll have to grab it once they've all left," Michael stated. "I'm going to check it out." He stood and crept toward the barn, stationing himself outside of the gap in the boards.

He peered through the gap, shifting around to position himself for the best view. Benjamin Abbott stood in front of the painting, putting a few finishing touches on it.

"Impeccable," Marcus said, admiring the painting over Benjamin's shoulder.

Teddy and Stefano stood a few feet away. Benjamin

smiled at Marcus, dropping his arm to his side. "I'm pleased with the result, yes."

"It is stunning. A piece of Celine's soul alive inside this beautiful painting. All that's needed now is your signature."

"Yes," Benjamin said. He picked up a small brush, dipping it into black paint. He signed the portrait at the bottom. "Finished!" he exclaimed, tossing the brush into a can.

"Yes, you are," Marcus noted.

"Well, Duke Northcott, I suppose I'll be on my way. I assume there's no further need for the blindfold?"

"Just a moment, Benjamin, we've not yet completed our business."

"Excuse me?" Benjamin queried. "You wanted the painting of Celine, you have it! My work is done here!"

"Yes, I have my... special painting of Celine. However, I want to be sure I have the sole painting of this kind of my sweet Celine." Benjamin's brow furrowed. Marcus continued, "I do not want a duplicate created."

"All right. I won't paint another," Abbott agreed.

"I'm afraid a simple assurance won't be enough," Marcus said. Teddy and Stefano each grabbed a hold of Benjamin. He struggled against them as Marcus approached him. "I cannot take the chance that Grayson Buckley or Celine will make a strong appeal and you create a second painting out of pity for them."

"I... I won't. Duke Northcott, my loyalties lie with you," Benjamin pleaded. "I swear, I won't paint another for them. I... I'll leave town, yes. I'll leave town tonight, disappear, they'll never find me."

Marcus smirked at him. "An admirable attempt, Benjamin, but I prefer a sure bet." He stalked closer to him. Benjamin strained against the two men holding him, but to no avail. Unable to escape, he made one last attempt to reason with Marcus.

"Please, please. I've done what you asked, I've always been loyal to you. You created me, gave me my talents. I'm forever grateful. I would never betray you. You have my word."

"Yes, and now I will have my own assurance," Marcus said, grasping Benjamin's hand. Benjamin cried out in pain, dropping to his knees. Marcus twisted the hand, crumbling it as though it were only a sheet of paper. Benjamin howled in agony.

Shocked, Michael backed away a few steps, his eyes wide after what he witnessed. Gulping down his fear, he approached the gap. Marcus strode away from him, back toward the painting. "Now you may go, Benjamin. Return him to his cottage."

"Should we blindfold him?" Stefano asked.

"It's unnecessary," Marcus answered.

Benjamin writhed on the floor in agony, his hand twisted into a grotesque shape. "My hand," he cried, "my hand! You've broken my hand!"

"Yes, I'd venture to say you'll never paint again. Such a terrible shame," Marcus said, "you did such exquisite work!"

"You bastard!" Benjamin screamed as Stefano pulled him off the floor.

"Good evening, Benjamin," Marcus said. "Oh, and no rush for you to leave town. Take your time."

Stefano pulled him out of the barn. "Well, Marcus," Teddy said, "you have your painting. Shall we go? We can stop at my home for nightcaps to celebrate if you'd like."

"No, Teddy. We have business to attend to. The painting must be moved tonight."

"Tonight?"

"Yes," Marcus answered.

"Surely, Marcus…"

"I said tonight! I want it in my home tonight."

"Of course. Stefano and I will move it at once."

"Good." The two men turned their attention to the painting, commenting on various aspects. Michael backed away, returning to his hiding spot.

* * *

Celine and Damien waited in the shadows, the setting sun behind them. Celine gripped Damien's hand. She focused her attention on Michael, pressed against the side wall of the barn and peeking through the gap in the boards.

After a few moments, Michael went stiff, backing away a few steps. A shriek tore through the air. Celine's mouth dropped open. "What happened?" Celine asked.

"I'm not sure, but whatever it is, it doesn't sound good," Damien answered. Celine gripped his hand tighter. Within moments, the barn door opened. Stefano emerged, dragging Benjamin Abbott with him. He held his right arm at the wrist. Damien gasped. He glanced to Celine, disgust on his face.

"My God!" Celine exclaimed, matching his expression. "He's broken his hand!"

Damien was speechless. They returned their gaze to the barn. Michael stood watching for a few more moments before backing away and returning to them.

Celine welcomed him back with a hug. "I assume the painting is complete?" she asked.

"Yeah," he said in a shaky voice. "Yeah, it's done. And so are Benjamin Abbott's painting days." He raked his trembling hand through his sandy blonde hair.

"Yes, that much was apparent when he emerged from the barn with Stefano," Celine said, putting her hand on his shoulder.

He shook his head, trying to dismiss the memory. "Anyway, we have other problems."

"Oh, are you kidding? What else?" Damien asked.

"They're moving the painting to Northcott's tonight."

"What?" Damien asked, incredulous.

"Yeah. He insisted."

"How the hell are we going to get it now?" Damien exclaimed in frustration.

"We snuck in once before, we'll have to do it again," Michael said.

"Yeah and we got stuck there for hours. On top of that, how do you expect us to sneak back out with a giant painting?"

"I don't know, I don't know," Michael answered, collapsing back onto the ground.

CHAPTER 29

"Calm down," Celine advised. "Both of you have just sustained a great trauma witnessing Marcus' misdeeds. We shall see where they take the painting and we shall make a plan to recover it then." Michael nodded, as did Damien. She took both their hands in hers. "We'll solve this, together."

They waited as the sun lowered in the sky. Darkness was already creeping over the area when Stefano returned. They spent a few moments inside the barn before the barn doors opened again. Stefano pushed them back, opening them to their maximum. A moment later he and Teddy emerged, carrying the painting. The Duke followed behind them. They were careful with the large portrait, ensuring they did not damage it.

"It's a beautiful portrait, Celine," Damien said, smiling at her.

"Thank you, although I can take no credit for it. You should compliment the unfortunate Mr. Abbott," Celine answered. "Let's follow them."

They allowed the trio to get far enough ahead that they

could follow at a safe distance unseen. As Michael stated earlier, they took the painting to Marcus' home. Michael, Damien and Celine watched from their hideaway as Stefano and Teddy carried the portrait up the stairs, placing it in one of the bedrooms.

Stefano retrieved brandies for each of them from the sitting room. The three men appeared to toast the painting before sharing a drink. After finishing the drinks, Teddy and Stefano left Marcus to enjoy his new acquisition alone.

Marcus spent several more minutes admiring the painting. As they watched, Damien said, "Is he... is he talking to it?"

"Yes, I'm pretty sure he is," Michael answered.

Soon after, Dembe appeared, relieving Marcus of his glass and helping him undress for the evening. "Well," Celine said, "he's retiring for the evening. There will be no retrieving the painting tonight."

"Yeah, looks like he's going to sleep with the portrait," Damien said. "I mean in that room."

"We won't be getting that painting tonight," Michael admitted.

"It's an appropriate time to return to the house, regroup, discuss a plan and rest," Celine said.

"I guess," Damien said. They followed the path back to the house. With the household upset from Mrs. Buckley's illness, formal dinner had been canceled. Celine offered to have trays delivered to them since they had missed dinner. She disappeared into a hallway while Michael and Damien went to the sitting room to wait. They were both in desperate need of a drink to calm their frayed nerves and soothe their disappointment.

They found Alexander and Gray already inside, conversing over a brandy. "Where have you two been and have you seen Celine?" Gray demanded.

"We were with Celine, searching for her painting," Michael answered, pouring both himself and Damien a drink.

"You were with Celine? Then where is she?" Gray questioned.

"She's getting us something to eat. We missed lunch and dinner," Michael answered.

"How terrible. My condolences," Gray grumbled.

"Wasn't asking for your sympathy," Michael muttered.

"Any news on the painting?" Alexander asked.

Michael began to answer but Celine's entrance into the room interrupted him. "Sandwiches are being sent up... Gray, Alexander, I didn't realize you were both here. How is Elizabeth?"

"Not well. I was just speaking with Alexander about making the arrangements for us to travel. Celine, we must draw the Duke away from here so Mother can recover," Gray said.

"Yes, I agree, Gray."

"Alexander will stay here until things improve," Gray informed her.

"I'm very sorry about all of this," Celine said.

"It's not your fault, Celine," Gray said. He poured her a brandy, guiding her to the fireplace to sit. "Have a brandy for your nerves and the chill you've been in. I understand from Michael and Damien you've been searching for the portrait."

"Yes, we have," Celine said, sipping the brandy.

"Have you found anything?" Alexander asked again.

"Yes," Celine said, sighing. "The news is not good." She paused for a moment. "Marcus has the painting."

"You're sure?" Gray said.

"Positive," Michael chimed in. "He has it."

"Where?" Gray asked.

"In his bedroom," Damien said. "Creepy right!" Gray

made a face at him. Damien swallowed some of his brandy, staring at the floor.

"Is it finished?" Alexander asked.

"Yes, it is," Celine answered. "Benjamin finished it earlier today." Celine's expression clouded.

"What is it, Celine? What's wrong?" Gray asked. "If it's the painting, don't fret, darling. We'll get it back or we'll have Benjamin paint a new one."

"That will prove difficult, Gray," Celine said, her voice breaking. "I doubt Benjamin will ever paint again."

"Why, Celine?" Alexander asked.

"The Duke broke his hand," Michael said.

"Irreparably, too, I might add," Damien said.

"You saw this happen?" Gray questioned.

"I did," Michael said.

"Damien and I only witnessed the aftermath. It was obvious even without witnessing the actual event that…" Her voice trailed off.

Gray put his arm around her. "Don't remind yourself of it, darling."

"We'll find a way to get it back," Michael promised.

"While I'd prefer the painting be in this house before we leave, that may not be an option," Gray said. "I'm not sure how much longer Mother can hold out. We must prepare to leave within the next few days."

Celine nodded. The painting was important, but not more important than the health of the house's inhabitants. It was useless to retrieve the painting if there were no family members left alive for the painting to protect.

A maid arrived with a tray of sandwiches for Michael and Damien. "You should eat, too, Celine," Gray told her.

"Yes, I second that," Damien said, biting off a piece of sandwich. "You missed lunch, too."

"You must take better care of yourself, darling," Gray said, retrieving a sandwich from the tray and delivering it to her.

"She didn't want to eat any of the scones I pocketed at breakfast this morning," Damien said. "I think they're still tasty even after a few hours in my pocket!"

Gray gave him a sideways glance. Celine held back a laugh.

"Cook's scones are delicious, I quite agree, Damien," Alexander added.

They finished eating their small meal. "You should try to rest," Gray suggested to Celine.

"As should you two," Celine said, nodding to Michael and Damien.

"I'll be up in a short while," Gray said.

Celine smiled at him. "Good night, Alexander," Celine said. Everyone articulated their good nights to each other, and Celine, Michael and Damien left the room. They walked upstairs together, stopping outside of Michael's door.

"It sounds like you have many things to attend to, Celine," Michael said. "Let us worry about the painting."

"Nonsense," Celine said. "Despite Gray's hurry to leave, I have every intention of reclaiming the painting. I propose we meet early for breakfast to discuss a plan. Are we agreed?"

"Agreed," Damien said.

"Sure," Michael said.

"Good night, then," Celine said. They both wished her a good night. Celine strode down the hall to her suite.

Michael grabbed Damien's elbow before he entered his room. "Let's talk," he said.

"Sure," Damien said. They entered Michael's room, shutting out the rest of the world.

Michael slipped off his jacket and loosened his collar. "This trip has gone from bad to worse," he said, tossing his jacket down in frustration.

"You aren't kidding," Damien agreed. He shook his head. "We need a plan to retrieve that painting!"

"It's a tall order but, yeah, we do. It sounds like our time is running out."

"We've got to make a move tomorrow," Damien said.

"Yeah, but how?"

"Knock on the door and politely request the painting back from him?" Damien suggested. Michael shot him a glance. He held his hands up. "I'm just kidding!"

"It's not the worst idea, and right now it's our only idea."

"It's not our only idea, it's just the only idea I wanted to express out loud. Neither of us want to say the truth here," Damien admitted.

"That our only option is to sneak into the Duke's house and steal the painting right out from under him?"

"Yep," Damien concurred. "And then get that painting hidden inside another painting, put that painting in the house AND return to our own time!"

"And all before Gray takes Celine wherever they're going to get away from the Duke." Michael closed his eyes, shaking his head.

"As much as I hate to say this, we might have to involve Celine in our wonderful plan."

"Plan? I wouldn't call what we have a plan. It's more like a wish and a prayer," Michael said.

"Still, I can't figure out how to get everyone out of the house so we can steal that painting. Celine will need to distract somebody somewhere along the line."

"She can't distract everyone at once. There's the Duke, Stefano, Dembe. Plus, I doubt he will leave that painting unattended for any period of time. He didn't steal it and break Benjamin Abbott's hand just so one of the Buckleys could waltz in and take it right back while he's out having tea with Celeste and Teddy."

Damien threw his hands in the air. "This is impossible."

"We'll do whatever we have to do, perhaps some sleep will help."

"Yeah. We can't solve anything tonight, anyway. The creep is sleeping with the painting in his room. There is no way I'm sneaking around with him that close."

"Agree. Let's sleep on it and see what we come up with."

"Okay, see you in the morning. Hope you sleep."

"You too," Michael said. He squeezed Damien's shoulder. "We'll figure it out, man. Try not to worry." They parted ways, each climbing into bed, preparing for a night of tossing and turning.

* * *

Celine paced the floor of her bedroom in her dressing gown. The news was not good. Gray's family was paying the price for her choices, as were people in the nearby town. She had brought all of this onto them. She fought for her independence, not wanting to be shackled to a life with Marcus Northcott. Was she selfish? Should she have accepted her fate, married him and bent to his will? No, she reflected. Michael and Damien were right, she had done nothing wrong.

They would leave, Marcus would follow. The family would be safe then. After a while, tensions would ease, tempers would cool, and Marcus would give up the chase. They could then return to their home and live out their lives in peace.

Before she left, she would prefer the painting sheltered inside these walls. Gray had commissioned it for a reason. It was designed to protect the inhabitants of this home, capturing a piece of her soul to forever guard them. Now that piece of her soul was trapped in Marcus' clutches.

A knock at the door interrupted her rambling mind. She hurried to the door, pulling it open.

"Celine," Alexander puffed, "you must come quickly."

"What is it?" Celine exclaimed.

"It's Aunt Elizabeth," he said, steadying his breath, "she's taken a turn for the worst."

Celine and Alexander raced down the hall to Elizabeth's room. They burst through the doors. Gray sat at Elizabeth's bedside along with Amos.

"Mina, thank God you're here," Gray said. "One minute she was talking, the next she had collapsed. Her breathing is shallow, and her fever seems worse."

Celine pushed past him, laying her hand on Elizabeth's forehead and cheek. She pressed her head against Elizabeth's chest, listening to her struggling breaths.

"Well?" Gray asked as she stood.

"Her fever has risen, and she's struggling to breathe."

"Can you help her?" Gray inquired.

"I can try," Celine said. "But I must gather some ingredients."

"I'll accompany you," Alexander said.

Celine nodded to him. "Give me a moment to dress," she said. Turning to Gray, she said, "Stay with her. Shift her onto her left side, keep a cold cloth on her face, as cold as you can but keep her chest warm to help her respiration."

Gray nodded. "Please be careful."

Celine squeezed his hand. She dashed from the room, racing back to her suite. She tore off her nightclothes and donned a dress, hastening to fasten it. She met Alexander in the foyer. He helped her don her cloak before they entered the chilly night air.

Celine informed Alexander of the ingredients she sought and together they hunted for them. After gathering them, they returned to the house where Celine prepared two mixtures to help Elizabeth.

"How is she?" Celine inquired, hurrying into the room.

"Her breathing is worse," Gray said, fear entering his voice.

"My poor Elizabeth," Amos said. He turned to Gray and Alexander. "Prepare yourselves, gentlemen, I imagine she is taking her last breaths."

"Not if I can help it," Celine said.

"What do you want us to do, Mina?" Gray asked.

"Move her onto her back and tip her head back. We must get her to drink this," Celine said, holding the first concoction she had prepared. "This should reduce the fever." Alexander and Gray positioned Elizabeth to allow Celine to pour the mixture into her mouth. "This one," Celine said, rubbing it onto her throat and chest, "should help with her breathing."

They waited a few moments. Elizabeth moaned. "What's happening?" Gray asked. Her breathing became more labored, she panted as if struggling to catch her breath. "It's not working, she's getting worse. Is there something else you can try?"

"Give it another minute, this should work," Celine insisted.

Elizabeth gasped, then exhaled a long breath. "She's not breathing!" Alexander exclaimed.

Gray reached for her, but Celine stopped him. "Wait," she cautioned.

A moment passed and Elizabeth appeared lifeless. They waited with bated breath. Elizabeth's body shuddered as though a shock-wave passed through it. An unearthly groan escaped her lips. Then her breathing resumed.

"She's breathing again," Alexander said, sighing with relief.

"Her breathing appears normal again," Amos said.

Celine breathed her own sigh of relief. "She isn't cured," she said to Gray, "but this should keep the more dangerous symptoms at bay until we can depart."

Gray nodded to her. "Can we step outside for a moment?" He led her from the room, closing the doors behind them. "Celine, we need to leave tonight, now."

Celine shook her head. "Gray, we can't. I understand your concern for your mother, but I cannot leave until I return Michael and Damien to… wherever they're from."

"Wake them, send them back now, we cannot delay this."

"We won't delay it, but we've no arrangements. We'll leave tomorrow, I promise. But you must give me time to finish my own preparations."

"Fine," Gray said, nodding. "We'll leave tomorrow evening. I'll make the arrangements in the morning."

Celine agreed. "Tomorrow evening, yes. Now, go spend time with your mother and father. I'll be in our room if you need me." She turned to leave.

"Celine," he said, pulling her back into his arms. "I love you."

She smiled at him. "I love you, too, Gray."

"Get some rest, darling."

"I'll check with you in the morning before you leave to make the arrangements to travel." They kissed goodnight. Celine returned to her room to pace the floor for the remaining hours of darkness.

As the sun rose, Celine checked in again with Gray. Elizabeth was still asleep, but her fever had lessened, and her breathing remained steady throughout the night. Celine dispensed more of her medication to Elizabeth before leaving to meet Damien and Michael for breakfast.

She paced the floors outside of their rooms until they

emerged. "Good morning," Damien said as he entered the hall.

"Good morning," she answered. "Come, we mustn't waste any time. We have precious little time left."

"Has something happened?" Michael asked.

"Elizabeth nearly did not make it through the night," Celine admitted. "Gray and I will depart tonight from Bucksville. I must send you back to your time at once."

"But we have to get the painting!" Damien exclaimed.

"I'm not sure there is time. I must open a time portal for you and send you back. I won't take that chance that you are trapped here!"

"You're not leaving until this evening. We have the whole day to retrieve the painting. You can send us back later before you leave, painting or not," Michael said.

Celine shook her head but acquiesced. "Agreed. Only because I would feel much more comfortable leaving Bucksville with the painting in this house."

"Then we'll need a plan and fast," Damien said. They walked together to the dining room. "Here's our plan so far: we steal the painting from the Duke when no one is in the house."

Celine gaped at him. "How do you propose we clear the house?"

"No idea. I hoped a good night's sleep would give me the answers, but so far I haven't been enlightened."

"Do you think you can lure the Duke out of the house, Celine?" Michael asked.

"No way!" Damien said. "That's way too dangerous."

Celine ignored him, considering it. "Yes," she answered after a moment. "Yes, I probably could, but it will take some effort. But that doesn't help us, you'd still have Stefano and Dembe in the house."

"Do you think you could get ALL of them out of the house at once, Celine?" Michael joked.

"The unfortunate thing is even if I am able to summon Marcus away, he will not take Stefano and Dembe with him. I'd be able to lure away either Marcus or the other two, but not all three," she conceded.

"Yeah, too bad being in two places at once isn't one of your powers," Damien joked. Celine stopped what she was doing, staring at him. "Sorry, just a joke," he said, confused by her reaction.

"Your joke has given me an idea. I'm not sure it will work but…" She paused, staring sideways. Her gaze refocused on Michael and Damien. "Suppose I could lure both Marcus and Dembe and Stefano out of the house. Could you enter the house, retrieve the painting and get it away in, say, fifteen minutes?"

"Assuming we were hiding in our normal spot, yes, I'd say we could," Michael said.

Damien nodded in agreement. "But, Celine, that's impossible. I mean you can't do both, so this plan isn't going to work."

"You said it's too bad I couldn't be in two places at once," Celine said. "But what if I could be?"

"Huh?" Damien exclaimed.

"Come with me," Celine said. She led them upstairs to her bedroom suite. "I'm not sure this will work. I've only witnessed Marcus do it once before. But I'm a quick learner. If I pull it off the effects will be temporary, but they should last long enough for us to execute our plan."

Celine stood in front of a full-length mirror that stood in a corner of the room. Holding out her hand in front of her, she knit her brow in concentration. She uttered a few words in Latin before closing her eyes in deep concentration. Opening her eyes, she uttered a final few words in an unintelligible language. The scene unfolding mesmerized Michael and Damien, though they did not understand what she was attempting to achieve.

When Celine finished speaking, she reached her hand into the mirror. Damien turned to Michael to ask him if his eyes were deceiving him or if Celine's hand had disappeared into the mirror, but he found himself unable to speak. After a moment, Celine pulled her arm back. Her hand, which had disappeared into the mirror, held another hand. She tugged the hand toward her. Michael and Damien were further stunned into silence as a figure emerged from the mirror. Celine pulled the woman closer to her, a smile crossing her face.

"Hello, Celine," she said.

"Hello, Celine," the figured answered.

She turned to Michael and Damien, a triumphant look on her face. "Now I can be in two places at once," she exclaimed, clapping her hands.

CHAPTER 30

*D*amien blinked his eyes a few times, staring at the scene in front of him. "I... I... I... what is that thing?"

"She's me!" Celine said. "She's a doppelganger, a mirror image of me."

"Is it real?" Michael asked.

"Yes, she's as real as I am. Although only temporary. She'll only exist for a few hours before she dissolves back into the mirror world. Until then, though, she can walk, talk and act as I do. She can distract Stefano and Dembe while you steal the painting back!"

"Wait, wait, wait. If she's the copy, send her to deal with the Duke," Michael said.

Celine shook her head. "No, he'd realize, he'd sense it wasn't me. The dance would be over before the music even began."

"I still hate the part of the plan where you have to deal with him," Damien said.

"I won't be alone."

"What do you mean? Who will be with you?" Damien asked.

"In order for this to work, it must appear legitimate that I want to speak with Marcus. After the last incident, he'll be wary of indulging me with another spontaneous meeting. I'll go to my sister, cry on her shoulder. If she and Teddy request his presence, he'll come. Then my doppelganger," she said, motioning to the second Celine, "will create a distraction to remove Stefano and Dembe from the house. Then you will retrieve the painting."

"Uh, okay," Michael said. "When should we start?"

"Now," Celine said. "We have little time. Come. Let us go to Marcus' home first and check a few details."

They followed the two Celines outside. Celine was careful to hide her doppelganger under a hooded cloak as they left the house. Michael and Damien trailed behind the two women as they made their way to Marcus' house.

"I can't believe she pulled a second Celine out of a mirror," Damien marveled.

"I'm not sure anything surprises me anymore," Michael responded. "We're in 1791 retrieving a painting from a time traveling Duke after I was bitten by a vampire. A faux-Celine seems reasonable in the grand scheme of things."

"Good point," Damien admitted.

They arrived at the Duke's house, taking their usual hide-out. Damien stared at the two Celines, still finding it over-whelming to see the twins. "The painting is in the same spot," Celine said, calling their attention to the upstairs window.

"And Marcus is there, having his breakfast," the second Celine whispered, pointing toward the dining-room window.

"This is weird," Damien said.

"Pay attention," both Celines stated simultaneously.

Damien's eyes went wide, and he swallowed hard. "Sorry."

"Well," Celine said, "let's begin our plan. I shall go to my sister's. Once they call for Marcus, you, Celine, will retrieve Stefano and Dembe. Once the house is empty, Michael and Damien, waste no time in retrieving that painting. We'll meet at the house later."

"We got it, Celine... s... Celines, both of you, all of us," Damien stuttered, adding an "s" to Celine's name. "Okay!" he settled on.

"Don't worry, we'll have that painting," Michael said. "Be careful, though, Celine."

Celine nodded her head. "Oh, is there anything we need to do with, ah, her when we're finished?" Michael asked, nodding his head toward the twin Celine.

"No, she understands what to do once her job is done," Celine assured him.

Michael nodded. She smiled at them before heading off on the path toward her sister's home.

"Here goes nothing," Michael said to Damien.

Celine approached her sister's home. She took a deep breath, smoothing her dress before she climbed the steps. She disliked lying to her sister, but she reminded herself of her sister's role in her current situation. It had to be done, she assured herself.

She lifted her trembling hand to knock at the door. Teddy opened the door. "Celine!" he said, surprise in his voice. "Come in, my dear, come in." He ushered her into the entryway.

"Thank you, Teddy. I hope I'm not interrupting you, but I need to speak with you. Both you and Celeste."

"Not at all, Celine. Please sit down, let me fetch Celeste."

After a few moments, Teddy returned with Celeste.

"Now, Celine, what is it you'd like to speak with us about?" Teddy asked.

Celine paused a moment, her heart pounding in her chest. She summoned everything she could for the performance, there was no room for error, she could not fail. "Elizabeth Buckley nearly died last night," she said, genuine upset entering her voice.

"I'm very sorry to hear that, Celine, but I fail to understand how this concerns us," Teddy said.

Celine sighed, swallowing hard. She hesitated as though searching for the right words. "I... I..." she stammered.

"Oh, out with it, Celine," Celeste said, exasperated.

"Let the girl speak, Celeste," Teddy counseled.

"I'm wondering if I've made a grave error in judgement," Celine lied, pouting for dramatic effect.

Shock and relief showed on Celeste's face. She rushed to her sister's side, sitting next to her. "Oh, darling," she said, stroking her hair.

"Do you mean by carrying on with Grayson Buckley, Celine?" Teddy questioned.

Celine nodded. "I don't know what to do," Celine cried, squeezing a few tears from her eyes.

"There, there, darling," Celeste consoled, "you've come to the right place."

"Indeed, Celine," Teddy said, "you are taking the right steps to correct the situation."

"I fear there may be no correcting it!" Celine wailed, throwing herself across the arm of the loveseat she shared with Celeste.

"Celine, there is no need for hysterics. Nothing is unfixable," Teddy assured her.

Celine sat up, shaking her head. "But how?" she croaked.

"Just leave it to us, Celine. We shall help you correct this error in judgement, darling," Celeste said.

"Your sister is correct. We are your family. We shall guide you in this delicate matter," Teddy agreed, offering his hand-kerchief.

Celine nodded her head, drying her tears with Teddy's handkerchief. "That's it, darling, dry your tears. From this moment forward, you will have no more tears, only joy," Celeste promised.

"What must I do?" Celine posed.

"You must speak with Marcus at once," Celeste answered.

Celine feigned shock. "Oh, surely not, Celeste," she said, standing and stalking a few steps away. She made a show of wringing her hands.

"Well, of course, darling. Oh, I understand how hard it will be, but once it's over, you can both put it behind you and move forward."

"I cannot," Celine stalled.

"Why not, Celine?" Teddy asked.

Celine shook her head. "How angry he must be with me. How can I face him?"

"Oh, sister dear, it won't be easy. You must admit you were wrong, apologize and earn back his trust. I shall counsel you in what to say. Listen to me and it will all be over soon with the outcome you desire."

"Indeed, I'm certain your sister's advice will soothe the raw feelings between the two of you. And, of course, we shall speak on your behalf."

"Oh, yes, and Marcus values Teddy's input. I'm sure it will help in correcting this situation."

Celine nodded. "When do you propose I speak with him?" Celine asked.

"Right away," Teddy suggested. "I shall appeal to Marcus at once. Celeste will ready you here to speak with him. I shall return with him as soon as I can."

Celine swallowed hard, nodding. "You'll feel better once

it's over, darling," Celeste said. Teddy pulled on his overcoat and exited the house. Celine watched from the window as he made his way down the path.

"Now, darling," Celeste said, guiding her to the loveseat, "everything will be just fine. Follow what I tell you and all will be forgiven. You'll be back in Marcus' arms by evening, I promise."

Celine wanted to shudder at the idea, but instead she smiled and nodded at Celeste.

* * *

Michael, Damien and Celine's double stared at the house. Minutes seemed like hours as they waited for action. Damien spent much of his time studying the clone as discreetly as he could.

"There!" the clone Celine said, pointing down the path leading to Marcus' house. They followed the line of her finger. Coming down the path toward the house was Theodore VanWoodsen.

"Damn, she's good," Michael said, shaking his head.

Teddy approached the house, knocking at the door. Dembe greeted him and he entered the house. The trio spied him speaking with the Duke in his sitting room. After a few moments of conversation, Marcus pulled on his coat, exiting the house with Teddy. The pair strolled down the path, returning in the direction Teddy approached from.

They kept watch on the time, waiting until Marcus and Teddy should arrive at Teddy's house before Celine said, "My turn!" She stood, smoothing her dress. She was so like Celine, Damien mused.

"Good luck, ah, other Celine," Damien said.

She winked at him and climbed from their hiding spot. She stalked down the path, pausing for a moment. Then she charged onto the porch, banging on the door. Dembe opened it. "Dembe!" she shouted, "you must come with me. It's Marcus. He's… please, you must help!" Celine's voice was shrill. Her ravings were so loud, Michael and Damien could overhear her without trouble from their hideaway.

Dembe answered her, though they could not hear him. He started out the door, but she stopped him. She shouted again at him and he nodded. They overheard her call Stefano's name. He raced into the hallway and she retold her story, gesturing wildly, near hysterical.

Together, they raced from the house. The fake Celine took them in a different direction than Teddy had gone with Marcus. As they disappeared from sight, Michael said, "Now or never."

"Let's do this," Damien said. They stood and raced toward the house, finding the door unlocked and ajar. In the confusion, Dembe had not bothered to latch it. The two sprinted up the steps, taking them in twos. They burst into the bedroom containing the portrait.

"There it is," Damien said.

"Yeah, let's not waste time admiring it. Grab that side, I'll get this one. And let's get the hell out of here," Michael declared.

Damien grabbed a sheet from nearby and tossed it over the painting. "To protect it since we're going through the woods."

"Good idea," Michael said, pulling it over to his side.

They hefted the painting up, turning it on its side to make carrying it easier. Michael backed out the door. Carefully, they turned the corner and began down the staircase.

"Almost there!" Damien announced a few steps from the bottom.

"Don't jinx us," Michael said, already at the bottom of the staircase.

"And straight out the door," Damien said, reaching the bottom stair.

They cleared the doorway and descended the few steps to the path. With no obstacles, they each turned so they could walk facing forward. "Are you able to go faster?"

"Sure," Damien said, picking up the pace to a jog. "And into the woods for the win!" he said as the trees closed around them.

Sweat beaded on both their foreheads as they continued their journey toward town. "Whew, man, walking was a terrible, terrible idea," Damien said.

"Yeah, we should have driven," Michael answered.

"Hilarious, Michael," Damien said. "I meant we should have asked Celine for a carriage."

"Oh, yeah, good idea," Michael paused. "Do you think…"

"We can't ask now; I'm not explaining this painting to anyone or taking the chance that we're caught."

"Right. Okay, we stick to the plan. You hide with the painting in the alley near the painter's house and I'll buy the other painting from him with the money from Celine."

* * *

Celine waited with Celeste. She paced the floor, stopping a few times to stare out the window. "Relax, Celine," Celeste said. "He'll be here soon enough."

Celine was uninterested in the whereabouts of Marcus. Concern filled her over Michael and Damien's end of the plan. Had they retrieved the painting? Were they safe?

"Celine, please," Celeste beseeched her. "You'll wear the floor out with your pacing. Sit down. Darling, please, everything will be fine! Remember what I told you."

Celine nodded, although she had no intention of begging forgiveness while batting her eyelashes at Marcus. She wasn't sure what she planned to say, but it would be none of the things her sister advised.

If she was correct, Michael and Damien should have absconded with the painting before her conversation with Marcus began.

"Stop scowling, Celine, it is most unattractive! Please try to appear pleasant, agreeable. You're a pretty girl, Celine, you must use it to your advantage now more than ever."

Celine found herself wishing Marcus would arrive soon, bored with her sister's lecturing. Within moments, her wish was granted. "Here they come. You'll wait in here. I'll speak with Marcus when he arrives, then we'll send him in to speak with you. Oh, Celine," she said, wrapping her sister in an embrace, "I am thrilled for you. I'm so pleased you've come to your senses."

The door opened. Celeste gave her one last tight embrace before disappearing through the doors, closing them behind her. Celine sighed. She hated lying to her sister, but the situation gave her little choice.

She overheard voices conversing in the hallway. Her stomach clenched into a knot. She swallowed hard, readying for her performance. She stared out the window, wondering if she could climb through it and flee to freedom. Her decision was made for her when the door opened behind her. She closed her eyes, steadying herself.

"Hello, Celine," Marcus said, closing the doors behind him. His voice pierced her like a knife.

She turned to face him. "Hello, Marcus."

"I understand you felt an overwhelming need to speak with me right away."

"Yes, I did," she admitted.

"And what does this urgent matter concern?" Marcus asked.

"This battle cannot continue between us," Celine began.

"I agree," Marcus answered. "I would have much preferred it never to have started."

"You must end your attack on the Buckley family."

Marcus stalked to the drink tray, pouring himself a brandy. "Celine, you are aware of what terms I require for it to cease."

"I am aware of what you stated the last time we spoke. I'm afraid the price is too steep."

Marcus cocked his head. "It was my understanding you felt the price was acceptable, hence your insistence on speaking with me."

"I may have miscommunicated my intentions, my apologies."

Marcus narrowed his eyes. "Am I to understand that you are not, in fact, leaving Grayson Buckley?"

Celine deliberated a moment about her response. "That is correct," she said, staring straight into his eyes, "I do not intend to leave my husband."

Annoyance covered Marcus' face. "How dare you waste my time, Celine. This is not a game!" he shouted.

"No, it is not!" Celine shouted back. "You are the one who treats it as such. You play with lives as though they are pieces on a game board. You must stop! I have made my choice, it was not you, you must accept that."

"I will never accept that, Celine," he growled at her.

She approached him. "You must. I will never choose you, never."

She turned to walk from the room, but Marcus grabbed her arm, pulling her back. "Then you shall never know peace, Celine. Not until you are mine."

She pulled her arm from his grip, narrowing her eyes. "I will never be yours."

"I wouldn't be so sure, Celine," he called after her as she left the room.

Celine entered the entryway where Teddy and Celeste waited. She walked past them without a word. "Celine?" Celeste questioned.

"I'm sorry, Celeste, I've made a mistake."

"Mistake? Celine, explain yourself," Celeste demanded.

Celine pulled the door open, turning before stepping out. "I love Gray, Celeste, try to accept that." She pulled the door shut as she stepped onto the porch. She hurried away from the house without a glance behind her.

* * *

Celine's replica led Stefano and Dembe down the path toward the beach. "This way," she said. They came to the cave that led downward to the beach. "Through here," she said, entering the cave.

"Celine, what's happened? Can you explain?" Stefano asked as darkness surrounded them.

"Please hurry," she said, continuing on.

As they emerged from the cave, Stefano grabbed Celine's arm. "Before we go any further, I need you to explain what happened."

Celine's lip trembled. She glanced to Stefano. "My sister and Teddy betrayed Marcus. They attacked him. Please, we mustn't waste time."

"Wait," Stefano said, unwilling to move. "Why would you care, Celine? You wouldn't shed a tear if he died. You'd be free."

Celine shook her head. "I realize it would be easier, but it would also be wrong. I cannot do nothing. Now, please!"

Stefano considered her answer. "All right, take us."

"Come, we must row to the island, it's just there," she said pointing into the sea. A boat was nearby on the beach. They climbed in. Dembe pushed it into the water before climbing in. Each grabbed an oar and began to row. "Straight ahead, keep rowing."

They rowed until the beach was a speck on the horizon. "Celine, where is the island?" Stefano asked, glancing around.

Celine stared at him without answering. She stood, peering over the side of the boat. No reflection stared back at her. She was the reflection. It was her time to return to the mirror world. Her job was complete. She pitched headfirst into the icy waters.

"Celine!" Stefano shouted. He lunged after her, unable to grab hold of her. She sank into the waters below the boat, disappearing from view. Stefano stood, removing his jacket. "I'm going after her."

Dembe grabbed him. "No."

"She'll drown! Duke Northcott will kill me if I let her die!"

"No, no. Something is off. We should return to the house."

Stefano sat down. "Yes, we must return to the house straight away."

* * *

Damien sat on the pier, hidden by stacks of crates and barrels, his arm around the painting that stood next to him, still covered by a sheet. Michael had disappeared down the alley toward the local painter's house. With any luck, he'd be back soon, and they could take the next step in protecting the painting and Celine and her family by extension.

Nervous butterflies filled his stomach. Every sound made him jump a mile, every shadow alarmed him. They were so close. They couldn't fail now. Questions crowded his mind. Would the artist have the painting finished? He recalled the date of completion to be in the spring of this year. Did he have the date correct? Would it fit over Celine's painting?

What if it didn't? What would they do then? How was Celine? Her part of the plan forced her to speak with the dreadful Duke. If he harmed her, it was their fault.

Worry consumed him. So much so that he failed to hear Michael approaching.

"Hey, buddy, check it out!" Michael said as he approached.

Damien almost slipped off his perch, scrambling to his feet. "Oh, whew, it's you. Sorry, I was distracted." Michael carried a large package. "Is that it?"

Michael pulled the wrapping aside. "Behold! *Ships in the Harbor*! He had it framed already, too!"

"Aha! There it is! That stupid painting we assumed was so useless here to save the day!"

"Let's hope it fits," Michael said.

"Yeah, cross your fingers, toes, anything. Let's try it," Damien said.

They glanced around the alley, making sure they were alone. Satisfied they were and hidden by the crates and barrels, Michael unwrapped his painting while Damien pulled the sheet off the portrait. Michael turned his painting backwards. Damien lined up Celine's portrait.

"Here goes nothing," Damien said. Taking a deep breath, he slid the painting into the open space behind the canvas of *Ships in the Harbor*. "It's tight," he said, grimacing,

"Will it fit?" Michael asked. Damien grunted a bit, adjusting the portrait, pushing again. "Careful not to damage it."

"I know, I know," he said. "Just another inch… almost got it… there!" He exhaled, throwing his arms in the air in triumph. "How's it look from the front?"

"Good! Can't even tell it's under there. This painting is vibrant, it covers it well." Damien moved around the painting, inspecting it from the front. "How's it look in the back?"

"Upon a close inspection, you may realize there's another painting stuffed in there, but at a quick glance, I doubt anyone would know."

Michael switched positions with Damien, viewing the back of the painting. "It's good," he agreed. "Almost looks like one canvas, not two separate paintings. The frame hides it well."

"Here's to hoping it works. Come on, let's rewrap this painting and deliver it to the house."

* * *

Celeste burst through the sitting-room door. "What's happened?" she asked.

Marcus finished his brandy before answering. "Your sister has made another grave error in judgement."

"What?" Celeste was incredulous, not understanding. "There must be some misunderstanding!"

"If there was a misunderstanding, it was yours, Celeste. Your sister made it very clear she had no intention of leaving that swine she's married."

"Marcus," Teddy interjected, "there was no misunderstanding on our part. She said she made a mistake, I asked her if it concerned her relationship with Grayson Buckley and she said yes! The girl was in hysterics, sobbing."

"Yes, that's right," Celeste agreed, "and the solution we offered was clear."

"We advised her to reconcile with you at once," Teddy added. "Celeste counseled her, advising her she first needed to admit to her wrongdoing and apologize."

"I do not care what she told you. She had no interest in reconciling with me when I spoke with her."

"I'm afraid I don't understand," Teddy said. "She couldn't have changed her mind that quickly!"

"No! She didn't express any reservations to me even at the moment you arrived!" Celeste insisted.

"It matters not. The outcome is infuriating."

"Perhaps I should speak with her..." Celeste began.

"No. She must learn through painful experience," Marcus said.

Celeste nodded her head in agreement, stalking across the room, upset.

"Please let me apologize on both my and Celeste's behalf, had we known..." Teddy began.

"I do not care to hear your apologies, Teddy. What I desire now is your allegiance again."

"You have it, Marcus. Anything."

"Good. Together we will crush our opposition. Celine will have no choice but to return to me. Now," he said. "I shall return home. I expect not to be disturbed by any more erroneous summons."

"Yes, Marcus. Shall I walk with you?"

"No!" he exclaimed, storming out of the house. He strode down the path toward his home. As he approached the house, Stefano and Dembe raced up the path from the opposite side.

"Duke Northcott!" Stefano yelled. "Are you all right?"

"Yes, why wouldn't I be? Where have you been?"

"With Celine! She told us she needed us to help you. She lured us into a boat. We rowed her into the middle of the ocean, and she threw herself overboard. I fear she may be dead, Duke."

"With Celine? Impossible! Where have you really been?"

"It's true, Duke Northcott," Dembe confirmed. "Miss Celine came to the house, hysterical, begging us to help."

"No, she couldn't have. She was with me." Realization dawned on him. "How long has the house been unattended?"

"I'm not sure," Stefano said, "one half of an hour?"

Marcus closed his eyes for a moment, sighing. He hurried to the house, racing up the steps to his bedroom. He burst through the door, his focus on the easel where Celine's painting had rested. The easel stood empty. "CELINE!" he roared with anger.

CHAPTER 31

"Careful, careful now," Damien said, backing through the door of the house. "Don't want to damage it now!"

"Got it? I'm almost through," Michael said as he cleared the door.

"Yep, set it down here," Damien answered, nodding his head toward the large table in the center of the entryway. He wiped his brow. "Whew, what a trip!"

"Yeah, tell me about it," Michael said. They leaned against the table on either side of the large painting.

Amos made his way down the stairs. "Well, good afternoon, gentlemen!"

"Good afternoon, sir!" Michael said, standing straighter. Damien jumped to attention as well. "How is your wife?"

"Oh, Elizabeth is holding her own. She's improved a bit with Celine's medicine. Just a few moments ago she awoke and asked for toast."

"It's a good sign that she has an appetite!" Damien said.

"I quite agree!" Amos said, rounding the table. "Well, what

have we here? Appreciation of local art? Souvenir of your time here?"

"Ah." Michael stumbled. "It's, well, we... that is, sir, we will be leaving today and as a show of our appreciation for your gracious hospitality we hoped you would accept this painting."

"Oh? Leaving so soon, what a shame! We have enjoyed having you and I'm certain Mina has enjoyed your company. I regret we weren't able to spend more time together, but with Elizabeth's sudden illness, I was plainly distracted."

"Oh, we completely understand, sir. As we said, we were so grateful for your generosity that we wanted to impart this small token of our appreciation. It's not much, just a local artist's painting, but we hope you will enjoy it in your home for years to come."

"What a lovely sentiment. Shall I open it now?"

"Please feel free, sir, it's all yours. Oh, there is one provision you must promise."

"Provision, Mr. Carlyle?"

"Yes. It may sound strange, but we'd like you to agree not to get rid of it. Even if you don't display it in the house."

"You have my word, gentlemen! Well, what have we under the wrapping?" Amos said, opening the wrap to unveil the painting. "Hmm."

"It's titled *Ships in the Harbor*, sir," Michael told him.

"It's very well done. It reminds me of our fleet. What a nice choice, Mr. Carlyle! I'm sure it will provide much enjoyment for us to gaze upon it. It's quite a large painting, it might do nicely in this very room. Yes, yes, I imagine so. I shall have it hung at once!"

"We're so pleased you like it," Michael said. "We shan't keep you any longer. If we do not meet again, we wish you the very best."

"Thank you and same to you! Safe travels, gentleman, and I hope you will return to visit us soon."

With that, Amos left them standing in the entryway. "I guess that's that," Damien said.

"Guess so," Michael agreed.

"Well, I guess we better change back to our original clothes and meet Celine. Time to go back to our time."

"Not a moment too soon," Michael said. "Let's go." They ascended to the second floor, navigating to their bedrooms and changing clothes. Celine had left a note in Damien's bedroom, giving them instructions on meeting her later to return to their time.

Damien entered Michael's room, waving the note. "Got a note from Celine. She says to meet her on the cliff near the cave leading to the ocean at five. She'll send us home then. She apologized for not being here to help us with the painting, but she is making arrangements to travel."

Michael checked the clock in the room. "That's a few hours from now," he noted. "Want to grab something to eat before we leave?"

"Sure. I hate to say it, but we could walk into town and eat at the pub."

"I had the same idea," Michael said, laughing. "Just what we need, another walk to town, but hey, it's our last few hours in 1791, let's live it up!"

"But I still don't understand," Stefano stated as they walked through the woods. "How could Celine be in two places at once?"

"She created a mimic, a mirror image of herself. Then the real Celine was free to distract me while her doppelganger distracted you and Dembe leaving the painting unguarded for someone to steal. Most likely her husband or his cousin."

"Do you imagine we'll be able to get it back?"

"No, Stefano, I do not. I'm sure that portrait is under lock and key."

"Then where are we going? Why did you want to find Celine?"

Marcus stopped walking. "It is imperative that she realize there will be consequences to this betrayal."

They resumed walking. When the house came into view, they spotted a figure walking down the path toward them. Her blonde hair peeked from under the hood of her cloak. "Ah, Celine," Marcus said, approaching her.

"Yes, good evening, Celine," Stefano added, "I presume it is the real you we're speaking with since your mimic threw herself into the ocean earlier."

"What is it you want, Marcus?" Celine said.

"To congratulate you! You must be thrilled with your latest achievement."

"Achievement? I don't understand what you're talking about," Celine said, attempting to step around him.

"Oh, you mustn't be so modest, Celine. Your theatrics at your sister's coupled with your doppelganger's hysteria to draw Stefano and Dembe from the house all designed to reacquire your painting. Are you satisfied now that you have your precious portrait?"

"Portrait? Why would I need to draw anyone away from your home to acquire my portrait? You claimed not to have it. How could I have taken what you never possessed?"

"Touché, my dear." Celine again stepped to the side. "Celine, you've accomplished little with your stunt..."

Celine interrupted him. "As much as I would enjoy continuing this... discussion, Marcus, I am busy. Many things require my attention before tonight."

"Tonight?" he inquired.

"Yes. My husband and I are leaving town tonight," Celine said, turning to depart. She turned back toward him. "You'd do well to follow suit, Marcus. You have no further business here." She turned away from him, striding down the path away from them.

Marcus fumed as she marched away. "Leaving town?" Stefano questioned.

"Of course she is. She's gotten what she wants. The painting is in her possession, likely protecting the inhabitants of that bloody house."

"Why not stay, Duke Northcott? Continue the pressure on her new family? Surely the painting cannot protect them against your power!"

"While the Buckleys are important to her, it would do no good to continue my attack on them now. She would still have her precious Grayson. No, we must keep the pressure on Celine herself. She musn't be allowed to slip away. She must be made to feel overwhelmed, alone, to see that Grayson Buckley cannot help her."

"So, what shall we do?" Stefano asked.

"Prepare to travel tonight. We will follow her to the ends of the earth if the need arises. Return now to the house, inform Dembe. I shall return soon. I have a few matters I must attend to."

"Yes, Duke," Stefano said, bowing to him. He trotted off down the path toward the house, his duties clear. Marcus turned on his heel, moving down the path toward town.

* * *

Michael and Damien strolled up the path, both howling with laughter. "Okay, okay, but the food was good!" Damien said.

"Yes, but the clientele was scary!" Michael joked.

"I admit, some of them were intimidating…"

"Intimidating? Man, I am glad the standards of hygiene have risen astronomically by our time!"

Damien laughed again. "Yeah, I agree one hundred percent. Well, it was still nice to experience a real 1791 restaurant."

"It'll be good to experience our normal time. Hey, let's hit the café in town when we get back."

"Oh, that sounds great, yes! I am dying for those fries again!"

The two continued along the path, discussing their plans once they returned to their time. They approached the woods, entering the tree line. The trees hid the other individual coming down the path toward them. The two parties almost collided before noticing each other's presence.

"Whoa, sorry, we didn't…" Damien's voice trailed off as his eyes went wide with shock.

"Well, if it isn't the Carlyles, Celine's two troublesome, meddling little friends," Marcus said, his lips curling into a smile. "How fortuitous for me to run into you like this. I don't suppose you have my book with you?"

"No, we gave your book to…" Damien began, ferocity entering his voice, when Michael interrupted him.

"We don't. Now, if you'll excuse us…"

"Perhaps you'd like to share the location of the painting you stole from me?" Marcus paused, waiting for a response. He received none. "Nothing to say? Well, no matter, I'm sure I can elicit a response. I can be very persuasive." He lifted his hand in front of him, preparing to strike Michael and Damien.

Damien cringed, tensing his muscles, preparing for the blow. Michael shut his eyes, sure this was the end for them. A fireball whizzed past them, striking not them but Marcus' arm, knocking his aim away from them. Damien stared in the direction the missile came from, trying to discern the source. Celine raced toward them. She positioned herself between them and Marcus.

Marcus closed his eyes for a moment in annoyance. "Celine, stand aside, I have unfinished business with the Carlyles."

"I will not. You have no business with them. I will not allow you to harm them."

"Celine, I am growing weary of your games today. Stand aside, I do not want to harm you."

Celine responded by stamping her foot on the ground and curling her fists into balls, her jaw set in determination. The ground shook, and the skies darkened. Thunder boomed overhead and lightning danced in the sky.

"Oh, how adorable! But I regret to inform you I am unfazed by your show of force. It's rather like watching a child have a tantrum. Now stand aside, Celine, this is your last warning!"

"Michael, Damien," she shouted, "RUN!" Michael and Damien sprinted down the path, heading toward the cliff. Damien risked a glance over his shoulder. Celine and Marcus were locked in a lightening battle, each of them hurling a continual assault against the other.

Celine shrieked, breaking off the attack and deflecting his to a nearby tree. It smoked and singed from the blast it received. Celine launched another attack. Marcus fired back, deflecting it. The battle lasted a few more rounds before it ended.

"Stop, Celine," Marcus said. "You'll only hurt yourself."

Celine narrowed her eyes at him. "I doubt that, Marcus."

"You can't win!"

"Neither can you," Celine told him. Their powers were too evenly matched for one of them to win a battle of this nature outright.

"Don't be so sure, my dear."

"Leave my friends and family alone, Marcus."

"I will do what I must, I will possess what is mine."

Celine glared at him. "I am not yours," she spat at him before turning and storming off.

Celine hurried through the woods toward the cliffs. She hoped Michael and Damien were waiting in the meeting spot she set forth in her note. They could waste no time in returning them to the future.

Celine emerged from the woods, hastening toward the cliff. "Michael! Damien!" she called.

The men emerged from the cave leading to the beach. "Here!" Damien called. "Celine, are you all right?"

"Yes, I'm fine. Are you both all right? Are you hurt?"

"We're fine. Thanks for the save!" Michael said.

She nodded. "We must return you to your time. We mustn't delay. Come," she said, leading them a safe distance from the cliffs.

"Will you be all right, Celine?"

"I will, we leave tonight."

"Where will you go?

"My husband has made arrangements for us to stay with his friends in Scotland, a small town called Dunhaven."

"Good luck, Celine. I hope you are safe there."

"I assume the painting is safe?" she asked as they positioned themselves.

"It is, it's safe. It's hidden, but in the house," Damien said.

"That's enough for me. Thank you. I'll never forget what you've done to help us. Now you must go. Are you ready?"

Both men nodded. Celine returned the gesture, placing her arms in front of her and squeezing her eyes shut. Within moments, the winds picked up, and a twinkling began in front of them. Seconds later, the portal was open. Michael and Damien raced through.

They stumbled a few moments in complete darkness before their eyes adjusted. They gaped around, unsure of their location. They stood nearby on the cliffs. Damien glanced in the direction of the house. He smacked Michael in the chest, pointing ahead. "Look!" he exclaimed. "Car lights on the road!"

"Yeah!" Michael said. "We're back! Haha! We're back!" Michael clapped him on the back.

"Come on! Let's go tell everyone we were successful in retrieving the painting!"

"Yeah and get into some normal clothes!" Michael said.

"Race you?"

"You're on!" Michael said.

The two men raced to the house, Michael beat Damien, reaching the house first. Out of breath, they plowed through the door, excited to see everyone. The house was quiet.

"Celine? Gray?" Damien shouted.

"Hello?" Michael yelled.

"HELLO?" Damien tried again. "Where is everyone?"

"No idea. Celine? Anyone?" Michael tried again.

"It's not that late, they can't be in bed."

"Guess we better have a look around. Maybe we can change clothes, too. I'm excited to share the good news with everyone, but first I want out of these clothes."

"Agreed. We can check Celine and Gray's suite as soon as we've changed."

They wandered through the house, not finding anyone. They changed clothes, meeting back in the hallway outside their rooms. Damien knocked at the door leading to Celine and Gray's suite. There was no answer.

"Where could they be?" Damien said, scratching his head in confusion.

"No idea, but I'm getting creeped out by this."

"Me too. Perhaps we should try Alexander's?"

"Good idea," Michael agreed.

They made their way downstairs to the foyer. As they reached the entryway, Gray and Alexander came through the door.

"Oh, wow, whew!" Damien said, relief obvious in his voice. "Man, are we glad to see you! We've been searching the house."

"Michael, Damien, you're back," Gray said.

"Yes, we are," Michael said.

"Did you recover the painting?"

"We did!" Damien beamed.

"Well, where is it?" Gray asked.

Damien motioned for them to follow. He led them to an unused wing of the house, grabbing a pair of flashlights from a nearby cupboard. After a few minutes of navigating the dark halls, they arrived outside of a room, now being used for storage.

Entering the room, Damien lead them straight to the far wall. He focused his light on a painting.

"What the hell is that?" Gray asked. "That's not Celine's painting!"

"No, it's *Ships in the Harbor*," Michael said as Damien began pulling the painting from the wall. "I remembered seeing it here when we were exploring the house with the kids."

"*Ships in the Harbor*? The painting that hung in the entryway instead of Celine's?" Alexander asked.

"Not instead of, in addition to," Damien revealed. He swung the painting around with Michael's help. Together, the two of them pulled the second painting free from the first.

As the second canvas came free, they turned it around.

"And there she is!" Damien announced.

"Celine's portrait, it's been here the entire time!" Alexander declared.

Damien grinned at him. "Yep. At least... it is now. Or was it always here? I'm not totally sure how this time travel stuff works." Damien scratched his head, pondering his own questions.

Gray sighed with relief. "Well, one thing solved. At least we have a piece of Celine back," he said, stalking away from them.

"Yep, she's back!" Damien exclaimed. "By the way, where's the real deal? I can't wait to see the expression on her face when she sees her painting!"

Gray said nothing. Alexander stared at the ground.

"Ah, guys? Celine? Where is she? I'm sure she's dying to hear the news," Damien said. Gray glanced to Alexander.

"Does someone want to clue us in? What's with the secret glances?" Michael asked.

"I'm afraid we have some rather bad news," Alexander said.

"Bad news?" Michael asked, growing concerned.

"There's no easy way to say this," Alexander said, trying to temper the news.

"Where is Celine?" Damien insisted.

"She's gone," Gray said.

"What? Gone? Gone where? For how long?" Damien rapidly fired questions at them.

"No one knows the answers to those questions," Alexander said.

"What do you mean? What are you saying?" Damien questioned.

Gray answered, "I'm saying no one has seen or heard from her in almost a week. She hasn't called, she hasn't texted, she hasn't come home. No one can find her, it's like she's disappeared. She's gone."

EPILOGUE

$\mathcal{C}$eline opened her eyes, stretching and breathing a deep inhale. Despite it being morning, the stars still lit the sky, twinkling far above her.

"Good morning, Celine," Marcus voiced through the small grating in the door. Celine sighed, not answering. "I assume you are aware your painting is back in the Buckleys' possession?"

Celine pondered for a moment. Yes, that was what had awoken her. A flood of new memories rushed into her brain. She recalled Michael and Damien helping her retrieve the painting from Marcus, their daring plan, creating her mimic, her performance at her sister's, a standoff between her and Marcus, and the subsequent fallout as she and Gray left Bucksville to travel abroad. Mixed in with those memories was a brief conversation before she had opened a time portal for her two friends in which they told her the painting was secure. She didn't have all the details, but they had assured her this was the case.

Celine smiled to herself. "I wouldn't be too euphoric,

darling. They have your portrait, but I possess the real thing. Tell me," he continued, "what made you send them back to 1791? How did you determine that was when I stole it?"

Celine stood, brushing herself off and approached the door. "Damien tracked it down. So he was right, huh?"

"Ah, yes, dear Damien. That boy is a bit too clever for his own good," Marcus mused aloud.

Celine grew serious. "You stay away from Damien," she threatened.

"Or what, my dear?" he said, staring at her. She glared at him. "Oh, don't worry your pretty little head, I won't lay a finger on your precious Damien. You know, my dear, I think you may be more protective of him than you are of your beloved Grayson."

"I'm protective of all my family."

"A fact I am well aware of."

"How did you manage to go back to a time you already existed in?"

"Let's not discuss the details, my dear, we must keep some secrets between us."

Celine sighed. "I suppose it doesn't matter, does it? You only altered history for a brief time. It's corrected now."

"Gloat all you want, Celine, as I said before, they may have retrieved the painting, but I have the real thing."

The End

Stay up to date with all my news! Be the first to find out

about new releases first, sales and get free offers! Join the Nellie H. Steele's Mystery Readers' Group on Facebook! Or sign up for my newsletter at www.anovelideapublishing.com!

Her painting is back, but Celine is gone! Curious to know what will become of Celine? Find out now in Book 3, *Gone*!

Like cozy mysteries? Check out the Cate Kensie Mystery series. Misty Scottish moors and a quirky castle. Read Cate's first adventure, *The Secret of Dunhaven Castle*! You can also read Jack's version of the story!

If you love cozies, you can also check out my newest series, Lily & Cassie by the Sea. Grab book one, *Ghosts, Lore & a House by the Shore* now!

Love immersing yourself in the past? Lenora Fletcher can communicate with the dead! Can she use her unique skill to solve a mystery? Find out in *Death of a Duchess*, Book 1 in the Duchess of Blackmoore Mysteries.

Ready for adventure? Travel the globe with Maggie Edwards in search of her kidnapped uncle and Cleopatra's Tomb.

Book one, *Cleopatra's Tomb*, in the Maggie Edwards Adventure series is available now!

If you prefer adventures set in the past, try my newest pirate adventure series. Book 1, *Rise of a Pirate*, is available for purchase now!

Made in the USA
Middletown, DE
14 February 2022